J.M. Benjamin Presents...

HAVE YOU EVER...?

A NOVEL BY FIFI CURETON

HAVE YOU EVER...?
FIFI CURETON

Cover designed by Ultimate Media. TV
Cover Model Shavon Desire
Edited by Danielle E. Miller
Interior design by Pisces

A New Quality Publishing L.L.C. trade paperback printing 2009

For more information about the author or to purchase copies, visit or email correspondence to:
A New Quality Publishing
P. O. Box 589
Plainfield, New Jersey 07061
anewqualitypublishing.com
anewqualitypublishing@yahoo.com

ISBN: 09817756-3-2
ISBN-13: 978-0-9817756-3-0
10 9 8 7 6 5 4 3 2

First Paperback Edition
Printed in Canada

HAVE YOU EVER…?
FIFI CURETON

Acknowledgments

FIRST, I WOULD LIKE TO THANK MY GOD FOR GIVING ME THE STRENGTH TO BE
THE PERSON THAT I AM. I HAVE WEATHERED THE STORM WITH MY HEAD UP
HIGH AND MY GOD ON MY SIDE, HE TOLD ME THAT ALL THINGS WERE POSSIBLE
WITH HIM BESIDE ME AND I HAVE NEVER DOUBTED HIS WORDS!!

I WOULD LIKE TO THANK MY FAMILY; ESPECIALLY MY MOM FOR JUST BEING WHO
SHE IS AND MY DAD FOR TEACHING ME THAT SPEAKING YOUR MIND WOULD
SAVE YOU FROM ULCERS!
TO MY SIBLINGS; HARVEY, SABRINA, FELITA, RICKY AND WILLIE. MY NEICES AND
NEPHEWS; CHANTE', DEE- DEE, BIG DADDY, KHIRY, STANK AND EMIR, SEAN,
TAMIR , TIFFANY AND IYANA. YASMINDA, KIA, HARVEY, DONDRE' AND MIESHA.
LOVE ALL Y'ALL! DASHOUN I AM SO PROUND OF YOU, KEEP GOING, THE SKIES
THE LIMIT!!! DAVION, SHA-SHA. LOVE Y'ALL TOO. TO MY GREAT NIECE
ZYBRIAYYAH (BRIAH) LITTLE BREONYCE', AND MY GREAT NEPHEWS, MANNY,
JOZIAH AND QUADIE. Y'ALL ARE THE BEST!!!

MY BABIES, TANIYA AND JA'MEEK… BE ON THE LOOK OUT FOR TANIYA HER
BOOKS ARE COMING SOON, JA'MEEK I CAN SEE BIG THINGS FOR YOU, AND I
HOPE YOU SEE IT TOO, NEVER LET ANYONE TELL YOU WHAT YOU CAN OR CAN
NOT DO, BECAUSE YOU CAN DO ANYTHING YOU PUT YOUR MIND TOO!!!

ROSLYN, MY SISTER WE'VE HAD SOME FUN, AND WE'VE HAD SOME ARGUMENTS,
BUT IN THE END WE ALWAYS REALIZE THAT, THIS IS WHAT REAL, TRUE FRIENDS
DO. LOVE YOU. TASHA, MY OTHER SISTER. YOU ALREADY KNOW!!! MONIQUE,
DOING BIG THINGS IN ROCHESTER, NY, NAKIA MY BFF FROM THE BRONX!!!
TO TABITHA, YOUR WORDS ARE INSPIRING, TONISHA, TONISHA, TONISHA… JUST
KIDDING, ALWAYS BELIEVE AND ALWAYS KEEP THE FAITH.

ALICIA, AMIRA, SHANELL, ANGEL, NAKIA, YOLANDA, GWEN, AUNT BRENDA…. HEY
LADIES STAY SEXY. SHOUT OUT TO EVERYBODY FROM HAWTHORNE AVE,
TILLINGHAST, WEST RUNYON, AND CLINTON PLACE…. HEY Y'ALL. YOU KNOW
WHO YOU ARE. TO ALL THE BARBERS IN CUT CREATORS YOU ARE A BUNCH OF
SEXY ASS MEN!!! TO THE LADIES AND FELLA'S IN RUN TELL THAT HAIR SALON.
TO THE LADIES IN HAIR CHALET, Y'ALL KEEP, KEEPING THE PEOPLE IN THE HOOD
HAIR TIGHT!! TO NAHJEE AND ALL HIS PEOPLES, YOU KNOW WHO YOU ARE!!!
POP (JAMES WESTLEY) MARK, WAYNE, RIQ, DALE, T, BORN, O, LIL' SAMMY, SAL,
ALL YOU NIG***'S THAT WORK WITH HIM ON HIS TRUCK!!! ALI, ANGRY MAN C, HAK,
GRUNDY, ART…ETC. TO ALL THE CITY OF NEWARK SANITATION WORKERS!!!!
KEEPING OUR STREETS CLEAN! TO THE PEOPLE IN MARLO'S, BROKERS, FOX
TRAP (AKA FOXES) TO EVERYBODY, EVERYWHERE. DEXTER, URBAN
KNOWLEDGE BOOK, NARIBU STORE AND EVERY OTHER NJ SPOT THAT
SUPPORTS ME, WHA'UP!!!

3

HAVE YOU EVER…?
FIFI CURETON

ALL MY FAMILY IN NEW JERSEY, NORTH CAROLINA, SOUTH CAROLINA, CALIFORNIA… YOU KNOW WHO YOU ARE, LOVE Y'ALL WE NEED TO SEE MORE OF EACH OTHER!! LOVE Y'ALL. TO ALL MY BUS BUDDIES, WHEN I WAS CATCHING THE BUS; THE 71, 29, 94… TO THE N.J. TRANSIT DRIVERS FOR SUPPORTING ME, AND THE PASSENGERS. MUCH LOVE AND THANKS FOR THE SUPPORT. YOU GUYS KEPT ME GOING, THANKS FOR THE MANY GOOD ADVICE!

TO MR. J.M. BENJAMIN, IT IS NOT A MISTAKE THAT WE MET… THIS IS WHAT GOD WANTED, THIS WAS IN HIS PLAN, HE KNEW THAT YOU WOULD COME HOME AND MAKE SOME BIG CHANGES. THEY SAY THAT THE SIZE OF YOUR ISSUES DETERMINES THE SIZE OF YOUR BLESSINGS! SO HE ISN'T EVEN FINISH BLESSING YOU… YOU ASKED ME, WAS I READY, BUT THE REAL QUESTION IS; ARE YOU READY? I THANK YOU SO MUCH FOR GIVING ME BACK MY DESIRE, MY DREAM! MUCH LOVE AND MANY BLESSINGS TO YOU. AND TO MY ANEW QUALITY FAMILY, NYEMA (BACK STABBERS), J-ROD NIDER (DIAMONDS ARE FOREVER), T. COLON, THIS IS OUR SUMMER!!!

I JUST WANT TO SAY THANKS FOR THE LOVE AND SUPPORT AND MAY GOD CONTINUE TO BLESS EVERYBODY.

I HAVE NO REGRETS!!!

I ESPECIALLY WANT TO THANK THE MEN WHO INSPIRED ME TO WRITE HAVE YOU EVER…?/SPRUNG. YOU GUYS HAVE TAUGHT ME SO MUCH, YOU HAVE HELP ME GROW INTO A STRONGER MORE MATURE WOMAN, YOU HAVE LEFT ME WITH A BROKEN HEART, WONDERING WHAT THE HELL DID I DO WRONG, YOU HAVE WENT DAYS WITHOUT SPEAKING TO ME AND NOT LETTING ME KNOW THAT YOU WERE MAD, OR IF WE WERE BROKEN UP. YOU LIKED THE FACT THAT I WAS BREAKING MY NECK TO STAY WITH YOU, YOU HAVE SPOKEN TO ME IN WAYS THAT I THOUGHT I WOULD NEVER GET SPOKEN TO, YOU HAVE EMBARASSED ME IN FRONT OF YOUR FAMILY MEMBERS AND FREINDS, YOU TRIED TO ENCOUARAGE ME TO **NOT** WANT ANYTHING, YOU ALMOST TOOK MY SELF-ESTEEM AWAY, ALL THE WHILE I WAS LOVING YOU, WANTING YOU TO SEE THAT IF WE WORK TOGETHER THE SKIES THE LIMIT, I WANTED TO SHOW YOU THAT NO MATTER WHAT I WAS GOING TO LOVE YOU AND STAND BY YOUR SIDE WITH ALL YOUR FLAWS, BECAUSE I'M WOMAN ENOUGH TO KNOW THAT YOU ARE HUMAN AND THAT YOU ARE NOT PERFECT, BUT I JUST WANTED TO SAY AND WITH ALL MY HEART….. **YOUR LOST!!**
2K10 IS MY YEAR, THE YEAR OF THE 1ST BLACK PRESIDENT, THE YEAR FOR ALL AFRICAN AMERICANS!!!

-*DEDICATION*-

*TO MY DAD **R.I.P. LOVE YOU MISS YOU!***

CLEMENT R. CURETON LEFT US ON 10/5/2009 @ 10:59AM…

If Your Heart Isn't In It!!

When I think of Love, I think about pain.

Why, you asked?

Well, every time I fall in Love with someone I end up in a lot of pain.

I don't know why so many people say Love is a wonderful thing.

How?

Not the Love I've been through and seen.

All you get out of Love is pain.

Do we as women misconstrue the word "LOVE?"

Are we that blind, if it hurts, it must be Love, cause to me, Love hurts.

I'd rather not fall in Love, if I have to cry damn near every night, fight and beg for attention and pray to god he's not cheating on me, and all that other shit we encounter. Then I don't want LOVE!

FUCK THAT!!!!!!!

~Prologue~

"Stop ringing my muthafuckin' phone!" I said yelling through the phone lines. "I do not want to talk to your fuckin' ass right now!" There's nothing to talk about Raquan! Do you understand the words comin' out of my mouth! Ok, well understand this (click).

Ooh. I am telling you god must be by the man side tonight! If I had a gun, it would be raining blood tonight!

Tossing and turning in my bed for the most of the night, as tears made it impossible for me to focus, images of how much damage could be done to him flashed through my mind. Only God can keep my weary body plastered to the bed.

How could he hurt me? I can't believe I let this man hurt me again. Why the fuck can't I just walk away. Sleep couldn't erase the pain that slashed across my heart like a surgeon's knife, leaving a visible mark. That is it, I'm never gonna hand my heart over to another man again! And to think I thought Raquan was different, he swore up and down he wasn't like the other clown ass nigga I dealt with. Humph, our relationship was going to the next level so I thought, marriage, maybe more kids, even buying a home together. Granted, he isn't the affectionate type but he was trying to be, at least with the trips, the sneaking to my house in the middle of the night just to cuddle, the just because kisses, I mean that's what it seem to me anyway.

Just when I thought this is the one, he turns out not being the one. Not saying that he can't be the one, but how I'm feeling right now he ain't the one! I mean I might say fuck'em, but knowing me I'ma end up back fucking him.

Placing a medium size feather filled pillow over my face, trying to suffocate those toxic thoughts. Damn, even the pillow carried his scent, causing anger to resurface yet again, so I sent the pillow flying across the dark filled room, knocking down the unlit candles on top of the dresser. Sleep is clearly staying away from me tonight Home Safe Securities is expecting me to be in at eight

7

o'clock, hah! If sleep doesn't come soon-anger would take over again, leaving no room for common sense. Then my job would have one less employee to worry about.

Slowly turning over in the bed, a cool breeze from the crisp fall air flowed through, caressing my smooth, thick, mocha tan skin, leaving a sudden calm in its wake. That calm was short lived. I was ready to brave the New Jersey chill to take care of business, to show that muthafucka who not to fuck with!

"God, please help me fall asleep, and free my mind of these thought." I whispered, as I looked up at the ceiling with a tear resting on the corner of my eye. Thoughts of how I let this man come into my life and destroy my self-esteem.

Damn! Fell from my lips echoing in my bedroom like a rooster hollering in a tunnel. What the fuck happen? What had I done? Then just as sudden as the thoughts swept in, reason followed: Why do we as women blame ourselves, it not us, it's them! How come it just can't be the man's fault and not ours? Why do we sit back and ask why he does me like that? Why? Because we let them, that's why.

I swear somebody put a curse on my ass, and it is all because of my past. Back then, I must admit I've done some fucked up shit to niggas. I would cheat, have at least two of them helping out with my kids birthday party, and inviting both of them, I've token them for their money, made them buy my friends shit and even made them leave there wives or girlfriend and have them stay out all night with me, fucking, eating and mo' fuckin' me. I would never commit to them and wouldn't allow them to say I love you. It they did they would never hear from me again. Now, at age 31, maturity has finally kicked in changing a wild, spontaneous, don't-give-a-fuck girl into a responsible, caring, stay at home woman.

Now that I'm trying to change and become serious about falling in love and settling down with one man, look what happens. He treats me like I'm a hood rat disturbing his peace. Getting the hang of this falling in love and getting him to

8

fall in love with me shit is damn near impossible, I'm convinced loves means pain.

Shit, the next time a man tells me he loves me, I wouldn't give a fuck how fine he is, how professional and paid he is, I wouldn't give a fuck how big his dick is, I'ma run as fast as I can, like one Crypt member running from a gang of Bloods, fuck that! Love to me sounds more like: I'll rip your fuckin' heart out and stomp on it! I'll crush your self-esteem! I'll cheat, and most importantly, I'll make you pray to god every night that you wished you'd never met me! It is not love anymore when I'm left feeling empty, and killing is the first and last thing on my mind. Suddenly I sat up slipped into my Baby Phat black sweats pants, black hoodie, and black Timbs, having lost the battle with sanity, I grabbed a large wad of cash from my safe deposit box that is safely hidden in my closet, I prepared to face the cold, buy a gun from Monta from the Trap and take back my heart the only way I knew how. But reality kicked in when I heard my son Ja'Mil voice "Where you going, ma," he said rubbing his eye. That nigga ain't worth it, I thought.

~Chapter One~

The phone startled me out of a deep sleep. My eyes bucked open as one thing crossed my mind, who the fuck is calling me so early in the damn morning? A quick peek out the window showed me that the morning sun hadn't touched the clear blue sky. This better be important.

"Snatching the cordless from the nightstand, I said, "hello"

"What's up?" a deep male voice on the other end of the phone said with a light chuckle.

"Not me," I snapped at my brother, recognizing his voice, its fucking six o'clock in the morning, and I don't get out or answer my phone this early on a Saturday!"

"Then why'd you pick up," he snapped back

Without thinking I replied, "Because I'm horny! And I was hoping it was Raquan wanting some early morning sex." My pussy had been marinating overnight too. Just the thought of an ancient Chinese tongue massage was enough to get me wet. Reality kicked in as I said to Will, "But it's only you. So, what do you want?" I sounded every bit of pissed off. Whenever my brother feels like talking, regardless of the time, he'll ring your ass.

"Ilk! Don't talk to me like that," he shot back. "I wanted to know if your stanking ass wanted to go to New York to go shopping, and Kim wanted you to come with her on Broadway to get some shoes.

"Oh y'all treating?" I asked lifting my head off my pillow awaiting an answer.

"I know you have money, but I got you."

Grimacing at the thought of missing out on a free pair of shoes, I balled up my pillow, clutching it tighter to my chest. "No thanks, I'm staying in bed today" it hurts for me to say that.Really it did.

"A'ight. But if you change your mind, call me before eight 'cause I'm pulling out early."

"Aight, bye."

Will knew damn well his slow ass girl wasn't going to be ready by eight. Hell, they wouldn't be leaving until after ten. And if the weather held true to its possible thunderstorm, shopping would be more thought than action. They could have it. All week, after work, kids, and cooking my plan was to catch up on all the sleep I'd missed.

Wrapping an olive green, goose down Nautica comforter over my thick form, sleep claimed me in a matter of seconds...Ahhhhhh.

About thirty minutes later, just as I was dreaming of me being butt as naked on a beach, lying on the sand and being massage by two gorgeous men, both of them had very long straight black hair, with deep dimples, for some reason they were identical but weren't related, just as they were about to massage between my legs...I was disturbed by that ringing as phone again... "I should've unplugged this shit!" I groaned before reaching for the cordless, bang my elbow against the nightstand, "Ouch" and let the person on the other end feel my wrath, "What!!"

Did I bother you? The husky, deep voice replied, sending an instant tingle to my wet spot, and making all anger disappear faster than it came. Clearing my throat I managed to say, "No."

Are you still in the bed? He asked. His voice thick with lust, in that moment I pictured his big dick in his massive hands, stroking and massaging himself.

"Yesssss" I whispered as I started to play with myself, imaging Raquan inside of me, parting my pussy lips with trembling hands and a finger gyrating over my clit. Closing my eyes, seeing the two men from my dream along with Raquan gave me a sensation that made my pussy feel like it had its on heart, and his voice only helped matters as he said, "I was coming over...but not to sleep."

"You don't always have to sleep when you're in bed, ya know." A smile instantly appeared as my finger worked in and out of Lolita," there are other things you can do."

Raquan favored that response with a throaty chuckle. "Like what?"

"Like reading"

His laughter deepens. "Whatever. I'm on my way so make sure the book is," he said then inhaled sharply. "Ready to be read."

11

"It's ready," I said, as moisture pooled between my thighs and my nipples stood at church-like attention. "All you need to do is…cum."

As the first orgasm slowing slid down my finger, the phone dropped to the bed, moaning loud enough for Raquan to hear me before hanging up the phone.

Raquan…what can I say about this emotionless as brotha? I love him, but I'm tired of his ass not expressing himself. Just once hearing him say, "I love you" or "you look sexy today," would bring a glow to my color and a smile so big you'd be able to see my momma teeth. The man has never said those words to me. Just once I would love for him to say, 'take this ride with me' or 'let's chill, or even the level of this damn relationship! Shit I can't read his mind; I ain't a damn psychic.

Some men think as long as they are there then that's enough, they don't need to express themselves. Those men are stupid and wrong; eventually they end up old and alone. Men if you are listening never stop telling your girl or wife that you love her or how sexy she looks. It is very important; you would be amazed how healthy your relationship would be.

Other than being impassive and emotionless, he's a good man-doesn't drink, do drugs, or go out clubbing. He has custody of his thirteen-year old twin boys, Tahjee and Tahir, whom I have grown to love. But mostly, he's all about work, and spends seven days a week on the job. He works full time for a computer company as a network engineer in Long Island and part time for the local cable company on the weekends. Making money is always good, but Raquan tends to forget about my other needs, and it is not always sex.

Sometimes I want to hang out with him and just chill but he always tell me 'not today' or I have some running around to do.' Complaining only makes, him upset and then he calls me selfish. So I just sit back and wait for him to have time. Sometimes he'll only make an "appearance" one day out of a whole month, like today. It wasn't like that in the beginning of our relationship. After about six month into the relationship, he changed, but he tells me I changed. And look at me, still here and dealing with it; Dumb as hell.

He told me one day that since he had me, he didn't need to do all the things he did in the beginning of the relationship. My mouth dropped, because he was serious. But I told him to keep me; you need to stay the same way he was when he met me. He just sucked his teeth and left. We met almost two years ago at his company picnic, he was there with his kids and I came with a friend. Larry, he didn't want to go alone so I being the friend that I am, and had nothing else to do with myself that day went with him. The picnic was at a park called Frogbridge Park, about an hour away from Newark.

As I was talking to other people, I knew from the job and scanning the food area my eyes stopped on a tall, slim, brotha, with braids neatly going to the back. Although he was a slim guy, his arms were perfect he looked like he can pick my ass up. Yanking on Larry's extra long white Galaxy Tee, I asked, "Who's that guy over there? Since it was his company's picnic, he should know everybody.

I don't know that nigga! He replied, shrugging his shoulders, as he snatched a plate from the buffet, preparing himself some grub.

"Damn, why you say it like that?"

Larry glared at me and stormed off to eat his BBQ ribs he had on his plate along with the burgers and fries he had on top. Hell, he wasn't my man or nothing— we'd been friends for a while now. No way did he think he was getting some pussy. We had never been down like that, and would never be down like that. The smell of the ribs, burgers and even the hot dogs change my train of thoughts. I had to snatch me up some of those ribs, and the extra large cocktail shrimps looked good too, had to get some of that too, got me a Pepsi and I was good to go. I scanned the area again, until I saw my future man. God said claim it and you should have it. I saw him still sitting at the wooded table alone, so I licked my lips, fix my clothes, and walked straight to his table, feeling confident and looking confident. The space next to him was empty, so I stood next to him.

"Hello." I said slowing sitting in the empty seat.

He turned, his dark brown eyes examining over my breast, thighs and my

13

backside before he answered, "Hello," with a deep, sexy voice that matched his slim build and gorgeous dark eyes.

"The name's Stormie," I said with a small smile and what I hope was my sexiest voice. He didn't take his eyes off me and since the halter-top was very low showing just a taste of my breast, and my Capri Jeans clung to my curves like a leech, he couldn't take his eyes off me, hell he was mesmerize.

"My name's Raquan," he replied, displaying a straight set of pearly whites within a sexy smile

We sat quietly for a moment, as I looked around the picnic, I notice a big, black chick exposing her skin to the people at the picnic, she was not ashamed of her dimples and cellulite I thought what self-esteem she has, then I notice the India lady laughing at whatever the young man said to her and I'm thinking she got to be hot, it felt like a thousand degrees today although the weather man said a high of 95 degrees, hot and humid, and looking at her just made me hotter, with her oversize chenille sweater. The yelling and screaming from the kids in the pool showed they were really enjoying themselves, I should've brought my kids, I thought. I turned to him.

"So, do you work for this company?"

Yeah, and you?" this time his gaze landed on my face

"No, I just came for the food."

A tiny laugh joined his hearty laughter as he nodded toward my full plate and his Actually, I'm an accountant for a small security company." I said eating my shrimp. "I was a temp working at your company, and then I change jobs and was lucky enough to find a job working with people who didn't mind teaching me the ropes for an accounting." I felt he needed to know this and I wanted to keep his attention

"That's Whassup."

"I started out filing, making copies, answering the phones and making a little bit of money, but my office manager saw my gift within and decided to teach me everything she knew, plus paid for some night classes, well the company paid for it anyway I said while throwing shrimps in my mouth.

"How long has you worked for this company?"

"Two years, and I have my own office, my own desk, and a paycheck I oh so love, not that I'm bragging, it's just for a person with a GED, people tend to think that it is not possible unless your college educated, but me I believe all things are possible. Like I said I was lucky, cause now and days it just ain't possible unless you own your own your own shit or a rapper."

"He looked at me then laughed, well that is a fairytale come true."

"Indeed it is, God is good." I said staring at my shrimp. "Oh did I tell I was the only African American there." I said proudly.

"Oh now that's really what's up." He said handing me his hand to shake.

I didn't shake his hand because it was full of barbeque sauce. So I just smiled and continued peeling my shrimps. He then looked at his hands and realized he had sauce on them, then moved his hand back to his rib

I took a peek at his plate and thought this man can eat, he had a hot dog, two burgers and some bake beans and beef ribs.., and two large cups of juice. The DJ announce the next event which was a pie eating contest the cheers from the kids made us look, the kids couldn't wait to sit at the table and eat all the chocolate filled cake they wanted, as they prepare themselves I said "they are going to be shitting for days"

"For real," Raquan replied with a smile.

As I looked around the park I noticed that it was a lot of white kids there, it was a few Puerto Rican and African Americans there, the ones that were there, didn't act black at all. And I ain't mad at them. I notice another nice looking brother watching me from the bar set-up, he nodded for me to come to him, but I just gave him a nice fuck off smile along with a soft nod. I don't really care for a guy to do that, he doesn't know if I'm sitting next to my man or not. I didn't bother to look back in his direction, I was killing the BBQ ribs, trying not to drip sauce on my breast, so I was peeled the ribs off of the bones. I wanted to pick the whole rib up and take a big ass bite out of it, then lick my fingers, but that was not a good look. So I took my time and ate like a "lady" suppose to in public.

I gave this man opportunity to talk to me and he still hasn't, so I must continue this conversation. Checking him out thoroughly and liking the view, my body shifted a little closer to what I hoped would become Mr. Right. "Are you here with someone?" I asked placing my hands under my chin waiting for a sign to warn me that he was lying, but nothing happen.

"Just me and my kids. And you?"

"A friend. You might know him. He's right over there," I said with a nod in Larry's direction.

"Nah, I don't know him," he said looking at Larry with a raised eyebrow. "That's your man or something?"

I almost sputtered out a mouthful of shrimps. My man? Larry dog ass? Please. "He didn't want to take this long ass ride by himself, so he asked me to come with him."

"Oh. Okay. So why do they call you Stormie?" his gaze, intense and stern followed the form of my breast before looking into my eyes. "Is that your real name?"

"Yeah, although people often ask am I a stripper because of my name."

"Are you?" he asked curious pausing for a second before taking another bite of his sandwich.

"At times, I do private shows," I said with a straight face, seriously, I said finishing my soda, "My mother gave me that name because I was born in the parking lot of Elizabeth General Hospital during the worst storm of 1971." Actually, the truth to that question was if someone pissed me off, I could and would bring the muthafuckin storm, but Raquan didn't need to know that yet.

"So, you have kids?" he asked looking around the park this time as if he was looking for someone.

"Yes, I have two kids; Tania, who's 11, and Ja'Mil, who's 8. My daughter's a little mini me and my son whew, words can't describe him." Ja'Mil, my spoiled, lazy ass son is a handful. When he knows he's about to get his ass whipped, he suddenly has an asthma attack, he spent more time in Beth Israel Hospital to avoid ass whipping than actual emergencies. And as soon as he felt better, be it a day or so, I still whip that ass.

"That bad huh?" he chuckled. "One father?"

"Nah, I have two baby daddies, so you can imagine the arguments they have sometimes."

"Wow."

Something about Raquan drew me, his eyes, his smooth brown skin, clear not a bump in sight, his neatly trimmed goatee, but mostly the innocence that surface around the stronger lines of his face—almost like he wouldn't know how to hurt anyone, but could take care of business if he had to.

As he stood stretching I admired his body, although he was a Slim Jim, his arms were nice, his shoulders showed strength, and I'm imagining my legs around his neck, with his arms holding me up, Whoa! He is tall, about 6'4 and just under 200 pounds, the total opposite of what I normally dated. Usually the men I chose had to be at least 6'5 or taller, weighing 300 pounds or be damn near obese. I once believed that since a big man loved to eat, he could eat the pussy longer and better. Time and a few big niggas that wasn't hungry enough told the truth: just because a man could clean a plate with his beard and chin, didn't mean he could find a clit without a microscope.

He had long fingers and, oh yeah, big ass feet, and you know what they say about a man with big feet, "The bigger the feet, the fatter the meat, or something like that."

Raquan extended his hand, and slowly I placed mine in his. "You wanna play some ping pong?"

"That's the green table, the paddle and the little white ball right?" I said wiping my hand on a napkin.

He winked, sending a sudden shiver up my spine. "Somethin' like that."

"Are you gonna teach me how to play, because I am no Forrest Gump."

His eyes lit up, then chuckled devilishly. "There's a lot I'd like to teach you."

"I'm sure there is."

We played ping-pong, miniature golf, basketball (of course I watched), and even got on a water ride together. I really enjoyed the water ride because I got to sit between his legs, let me tell you, as we were going down that steep hill, I scream and held him tight, as I did this I felt his manhood greet my back side. My thongs were wet and not from the water either. We both knew what the outcome of this friendship would be.

After the ride we sat down and ate some desert, I had strawberries and whip cream, and he ate ice cream. He said he came with his kids, but the little time I spent with him I seen no kids, but just thought they are somewhere having fun. I also found out then that he was a few years younger than me, but that was okay. We talked about everything under the sun. By the end of the picnic, it felt like we've known each other for a long time.

"Well Ms. Stormie, I enjoyed your company today."

"Like wise."

"Can I call you later?"

"Sure, you have a pen or something?" I asked smiling on the inside.

"Call my cell, when I get to my car I'll save it and call you as soon as I get in the house."

"Okay."

"I have to find my boys, talk to you soon," he said walking toward the rides.

I couldn't wait to leave Frogbridge and get back to Newark; I had to find Larry so we can bounce. Walking back over to the bar, then the basketball court, then to the pool, Larry was nowhere in sight. Where the fuck is he? He seemed angry earlier, but deep down I knew he didn't care. With me out of the way, he could get his flirt on with the half-dressed females littered around the park like packs of bitches. And Larry would be the "perfect pet" for them—he was a dog—all he is about is fuckin'em and leavin'em.

We became friends when I was a temp at his company. Initially, when I first saw him I was attracted to him. He is a big man 6'3" about 300 pounds or better,

18

light skin with braids. He dressed very nice and always smelled good. Then he opened his mouth. Attraction ran in the opposite direction. Don't get me wrong, his mouth wasn't raggedy, the conversation was. But, in spite of that, we became friends and we've been cool ever since.

Larry slowly walked up to me smirking like a thief, "So, did you get his number?"

"You know I did. And he single too." Humph "I just hope he's sincere and not like your ass."

Larry looked me up and down. "Wha'chu mean by that?"

"You know exactly what the fuck I mean." A slow grin spread across my lips. "How many numbers did you get?"

"None, I was chillin', try'na stay focus, na'mean," he said, trying to sound innocent-and failing miserably.

"Whatever," I said, but didn't miss him stuffing a wad of papers into his wallet. Lyin' ass bastard.

As promised, Raquan called that night, asking whether I wanted to go to the movies, I accepted and from that day until recently, we became inseparable. Every weekend we either hit the movies, plays, dinner or going to a comedy club. Wherever I wanted to go, we went, and whatever I wanted to do, we did. During those first six months, I would look in the mirror at some new outfit that I'd put on, saying, "I've never had a man like this before. I could get used to this." The fact that other men were trying to get at me only proved the point— when a woman has a man everyone wants her, when a bitch is single a man would walk pass her like she is see-through, can't land a man even if she had free pussy written all over her ass.

Raquan made me a man magnet, even on my worse days they were coming at me. But he had my heart and mind. About two or three weeks after we met he brought his sons over to my house, I was a little nervous at first; they were tall and slim like their father very handsome boys. They were identical, they both wore their hair braided like Raquan, one twin Tahir had a chip tooth and Tahjee

19

had a dimple a little over his left cheek, so I had something to go one to separate them. They were a shade or two lighter than Raquan so I assumed the mother was a red-bone. Raquan wanted me to meet his boys, and he wanted his boys to meet me. My kids couldn't believe how much his twins looked alike, and kept getting them mixed up; Ja'Mil asked if they could be his big brothers since they were thirteen. I told him sure as long as they helped out with his homework and did the things big brothers do. That was all Ja'Mil wanted somebody to play basketball and video games with because Tania couldn't play.

Of course, after we ate, talked and I bust they ass in Street Fighter a video game for Ja'Mil Playstation 2 I passed "the test"—the, 'what do you think test?" which I knew I was going to, I had no worries there.

Sometimes he would come to my home late at night, and slept on the floor. But, what's fucking with, the nigga didn't mind sleeping on the floor. Next to my bed! I would try to make him get in the bed with me, but he wouldn't, he would just roll over and say, "I'm a'ight." I would be pissed and lay there tossing and turning and my bed wondering what the fuck! Knowing he was coming over, I'd be looking all sexy-n-shit in my see-through Victoria Secret's nightie. And this muthafucka wanted to sleep on the floor! I should've known then he was strange one! But, hell I figure I was tired of being single, and he was giving me all the attention I needed and wanted, and the fact that he was so sweet, kept me from kicking his ass out for sleeping on the damn floor, he could've stayed his ass home for that. Boy, I would give my left tit to have him touch me. He would place a kiss on my lips before leaving then say, "I'll call you later".

Oh, something is definitely wrong with this nigga. I would tell Isis, he was a little too damn respectful for me; I wanted him to touch me. Though only a month had passed, we had spent a lot of time together; we were damn near a couple but he never came on to me. Sometimes I would purposely bend over and put my ass all up in his face, but he'd be on some ole', *move your ass out of my face type shit*. I wanted to pick my oversize Coach bag and smack him right in the face with it. Then because he didn't try to kiss me, touch me or fuck me, I started to think something was wrong with me. But one day as I was passing my full length mirror in my bed room, I took a long look at myself and said 'hell no' that couldn't be the case, I was getting numbers from niggas left and right, all day long, so it wasn't me. And I was told by many of men that I looked good, damn good to be exact!

My hair is shoulder-length draped to my shoulders (but I hardly wear it out since some-smartass person invented quick weaves). I've been told by plenty of people that I favor Toni Braxton when she rocked the "short cut"." I am 5'9, with a dark tan complexion and thick in all the right places. My stomach is flat, hips are shapely and yes, I do have a phat ass. I'm not one of those skinny, hungry looking bitches and I definitely don't look like I can't push away from the dinner table, either. He could take me out in public, I was/am eye candy…so what was his problem? I was hot!

The nigga made me second-guess my decision about being with him at times.

He made me wonder about his sexuality and if pussy was even his game

~Chapter Two~

Saturday night and I was home, the rain whipping around my house. Lighting snapped and thunder growled. The weather was just downright nasty. The kids were at my mothers and going out was not in my plans.

Raquan showed up at my door dressed in a pair of Omavi Jeans, and a Sean John pullover beige shirt, with his timbs unlaced. How about we make it a blockbuster night?" I suggested.

His smile wavered a little. "That's cool, whatever you want," he replied, giving me a hug and kissing my neck. The smell of his Insurrection Cologne was very intriguing; it sent my imagination straight to my bedroom visualizing us in the nude. Pressing my body against his allowing the moisture of his body to consume me, I said, "I'll cook dinner while you go and get the movies."

"Can you cook?" he asked, twisting up his nose.

"No, but I'm a fast learner." I said, laughing. "Now go and get the movies,"

He turned to walk away, but then paused, saying over his shoulder, "What type of movies do you want me to get?"

"Something scary." Pretending to be scared would give me a reason to jump on his lap and hold him close.

He gazed at me for a moment before he said, "Man, I'm not about to sit and watch some stupid ass scary movie. Never mind, I'll pick out something,"

My kitchen was a mess. Telling Tania to clean it before she left to go with my Mother went right over her head. The stainless steel stove had pots piled up, the matching refrigerator could use a good wiping off. The island, shaped in a half moon curve, separated the eating area from the cooking area had empty plates and half empty cups. The mahogany wood cupboards--which Home Depot lifted quite a bit of my stash to install, doors, were open displaying a box of pop-tarts. My marble floors and countertop were stained and the matching marble tabletop kitchen set was sticky from syrup. I took a deep breath when I walked in my kitchen because I really wanted to run the other way. We rarely ate in the kitchen (and I rarely cooked), so I don't know why it stayed so dirty. I proceeded to clean the kitchen; there was no way I was going to cook with my kitchen like that.

Once I polished off the dishes, swept and wiped everything down, the plan was to cook something simple; fried chicken, yellow rice and some canned sweet peas. I would cook some cornbread and collard greens, but that takes too long. Besides, I need to see his skills in the bedroom first before I show my skills in the kitchen. Collard greens, cornbread, barbecue turkey wings and a box of Goya Spanish rice were my specialties too… Nah, he ain't ready.

While the rice and the chicken simmered on the stove, I picked up the phone to call Isis. Talk about a bitch, she gives the word a whole new meaning. She wasn't always that way--especially when I met her, she was quiet and shy. Then one day she woke up and turned into 'The Incredible Bitch,' and she's been that way ever since. Of course she's been through some shit with the men in her life but damn!

"What's up stank mouth?" I asked as soon as she answered

"Whatever bitch. " Isis replied

I'll hold on while you go and brush your teeth. I can smell you all the way over here." I said laughing holding my noise

"If you smell anything, it would be your man's stinking ass," she snapped, her high pitched voice and country accent. "Where's his broke ass anyway? I'm surprised he ain't there. Oh, I forgot, if he was I wouldn't be talking to you right now, would I?" she said, sarcastically. "You know you don't know a bitch when he's there."

"Whatever", Isis was right, when Raquan was in view, nothing else mattered. Lifting the lid on the stainless steel pot, I stirred the rice a little. "We decided to have a blockbuster night."

"How cute, Makes me want to throw up, ugh" she makes the sound then laughs a little showing her jealousy as usual

"Girl, you really need to get rid of the hate in your heart. If you'd take it down a notch and come up off that high ass horse of yours, maybe you'd meet somebody and be able to ride their big ass horse." She inhaled, but I didn't give her a chance to speak. "I'll call you back."

Replacing the phone on the headset, I sighed. If the conversation kept going, it would to turn into something ugly. She hated when I told her the truth about herself. And I hated that she couldn't accept Raquan. She enjoyed me being single and miserable like her, and she feels Raquan took me away from her, well my time anyway.

Isis had the worst luck in finding a man. She always blamed the men, but it was her funky ass attitude. She went to college, got her BA (in 'in being a bitch' as I call it), has her own business, and belongs to some academic sorority group, and thinks she's the shit. Leave it up to her, a man should be lucky to even be in her presence. Well, the ones that stayed away were even luckier. Isis's okay looking she's cute; brown skin 5'8", thick, with no ass at all, and long black hair, but what men notice first are those big ass triple D's. That and the hair is really the one thing she has going for herself.

Raquan walked in carrying Bad Boys II, Five Fingers of Death and a Jet Li movie, The One. After we ate dinner we laid on my sofa. I fell asleep while he was still watching the rest of the karate flick. Next time I'll tell him to bring anything but Bruce Lee. Ass kicking was a part of everyday life--give me a Jason or a Denzel any day.

"Hey," he whispered, softly against my ear. My pussy lips answered first, and my sexual thrived perked up. I didn't want to answer 'cause I had no inkling what my breath smelled like. A risqué' gaze accompanied the smile I gave him. Hoping that finally after five long weeks some dick was going to be my desert.

"I'm out, go get in the bed," he said standing up, and then stretching his long arms and legs.

Grabbing hold of his hand, I pulled him toward me. "You don't have to go."

"It's late," he replied, yanking his hand away. "It's like three in the morning."

The dead silence between us lasted maybe two seconds, but felt like two hours. My mind raced, trying to think of ways to get him into bed. "What are you scared of? I won't touch you…" I was lying my ass off, cause as soon as he touched my bed that was it, he was mine. Sex had been absent in my life for months and the pussy was throbbing. Hell, my pussy was saying its own prayer that the dick stayed the night.

"I'm not worried about you touching me," he said softly, but I could detect the irritation underneath. "And I'm not scared either, Stormie."

I loved it when he said my name. The way it rolled off his tongue, Stormie…

This time, I crossed the distance between us. "What is it then? Why don't you come on to me?" Rubbing up against his chest, I tried to get him to relax. "I understand you're trying to be a gentleman, but damn, I need you and I want to know that you need me, too. It's okay."

He brushed past me, walked over to the window, gazing out at the fog the rain left behind. "I don't want this relationship to be based only on sex. I want more from you, Stormie."

I turned off the television, hit the light switch and started walking toward the stairs, I growled, "Fine, I'll see you later. Let yourself out." My anger pushed me forward, but my pussy screamed, 'What the hell are you doing! Minutes later I heard footsteps and keys coming up the stairs.

Inwardly, I smiled before saying, "I thought you were leaving?"

"It's too late and I'm too tired to drive." He stripped off his clothes, piece by piece. The shape of his arms and the muscle that expanded in his stomach made my pussy snap. I was hoping tonight be the night he didn't sleep on the fuckin' floor. If he did, he was going to have to go; I wouldn't care how horny I was. But he didn't he got in the bed.

"Are you happy now?" I whispered to my now throbbing pussy.

Raquan paused. "What?"

"Nothing, uh, I was--um--thinking out loud." Smiling from ear to ear, thinking of all the nasty things I was going to do to his bony ass. He made me wait almost a little over two months too. My plan was to take him on the most audacious roller bitch ride he could ever imagine; breaking this nigga down until he screamed for mercy. I tried to take my time, but a bitch was horny and the last thing on my mind was taking it easy, so I wore his ass out. He didn't have to do anything but lie there. I made him whine a few times, made his toes curl up and for sure I made sure he went straight to sleep after that.

The sound of Raquan keys interrupted my thoughts.

Yes, he has keys to my house. I must be whipped, huh? But that's okay, because right now, I'm in love and he could have anything that belonged to me.

"You ready?" Raquan asked, ripping his clothes off like a lunatic.

"Yes, I am," was the only thing said out loud, but I finished the rest in silence-- I'm ready to be licked, flipped and fucked but, most importantly, licked.

He climbed in the bed bare as a baby's ass. His manhood was pointing at me, letting me know how happy he was to see me. I always slept in the nude, so I didn't need to strip. We started out kissing and play fighting under the covers, then started touching areas of the body that needed and wanted to be touched.

He slowly slid to the edge of the bed and started teasing and caressing 'Lolita' (that's my nickname for my pussy), and that's when all the playing stopped. I take eating pussy serious. If a man can't eat it right, then what's the use of having him around? I loved when Raquan licked 'Lolita' because he knew exactly where and how to lick it. He did it slow, no rush job there. Oooh, my body couldn't take it anymore, I was about to explode. I felt my knees tremble. My head went back and my eyes rolled to the back of my head, and then I came. My bed, Raquan's face and my sheets were soaked.

After eating my pussy, he slowly entered me, guiding his penis into the center of my being. We were moving in motion, looking into each other's eyes. His sweat dripped onto my face and our bodies locked with pleasure. We began to moan aloud, I think my neighbors heard us but I didn't care. With every movement and kiss, I was falling deeper and deeper in love with him, and by the way, his body was hitting mine, I knew he was falling in love with me also. The more we moved our bodies together, the stronger he pumped. He began to kiss my neck, lips and nose; the sweat was causing our bodies to stick together.

'I'm cumming,' I whispered.

He felt it on his dick and pumped harder, shutting his eyes. "Uggghhh!" he yelled, shooting his seed inside of me, not pulling out until every drop of semen was inside of me.

I love this man, I thought.

To me, the sex was different this time. I mean the way he looked at me while we were making love, the way he kissed and caressed my body. Every movement, every kiss was telling me something. He brought me to a peak I didn't know existed. This was definitely the type of sex that had side effects: May cause pussy to throb when thinking about it later in the day, drowsiness, aches to your body, and may cause you to fall in love for all the wrong reasons. It may also cause you to become stupid or do stupid things.

I had at least ten orgasms, (maybe not, but it felt that way), broke two nails, and lost the scarf that had been wrapped around my head. Okay, maybe I didn't break two nails, but I broke my man's back in for sure. After sex he held me close to him until he fell asleep. I couldn't sleep because my mind was racing.

~Chapter Three~

"I know your ass is there, answer the damn phone, bitch! Your broke ass man must be there, and ya know what that means, you can't talk!" Isis screamed into my answering machine.

Moments later the phone rang again.

This time Raquan answered the phone with, "What?" upset because the ring woke him up from his sleep.

"Oh, is that how ghetto folks answer the phone?" she asked, in a tone cold enough to freeze hell.

"Stormie, it's your ignorant ass, lonely friend 'Coldness'" Raquan said. Coldness is what he called Isis.

Raquan held out the phone, his face twisted with anger, at being interrupted from his sleep.

"Why are you calling me like you're crazy?" I said with my head still lying on my pillow.

"I thought we were going shopping today," she said in a sudden rush of words. "You said to wait until you got paid, and duh, you did get paid yesterday, right?"

All the anger I felt eased away as I looked up at Raquan. "I really don't feel like going anywhere right now."

"Please, every time that big head boyfriend of yours comes around, you get all discombobulated on a sistah."

"Nah, it ain't even like that, I'm tired. We went out last night and didn't get in until this morning."

"Okay what does that have to do with shopping?" she asked, knowing that at one time I could work seven days a week, party and drink four of them days and still find a way to go shopping. Nothing came between me and a good sale.

"You know what, Isis? You're a trip. I told you I'm tired and don't feel like--"

"Fuck that, Storm," she yelled. "You always do this to me. Every time he's there, you can't leave. But once his ass leaves, then you want to go somewhere."

Raquan stared openly at me, waiting. The covers draped around his waist

I turned my back to him faced the bathroom door, giving Isis a chance to speak her mind. "You know as soon as he gets up, he's going to put his clothes on and leave you in the bed saying, 'I'll be back, I've got some running around to do.' You know how he do. The muthafucka never spends a whole day with your dumb ass anyway, so you might as well get up and leave him in the bed for a change."

She was right on both accounts. Might as well beat him to the punch this time.

"What time are you coming to pick me up, 'cause I ain't driving." I said trying to sound upset.

Raquan's hot glaze almost put a hole my back. I didn't dare turn around.

"I'll be there around twelve. Have your ass ready, please," she said in a huff. "Don't make me wait an extra five minutes while you tell your man where you're going. Do all that shit before I get there."

Dragging myself out of bed, only a few steps landed me in front of the closet.

"Where you going?" Raquan asked, sitting up in the bed.

"To the mall with Isis."

"Don't go spending your little bit of money on shit you don't need."

Frowning at him, I said, "What? I need everything that I buy,"

"Okay, smart-ass. Don't come back crying broke to me."

The Dolce & Gabbana baby tee landed on the chair next to the burgundy Ralph Lauren bra and panty set. "I never do and never will."

The Moschino jeans landed right next to the baby tee. I wanted to be comfortable walking around the mall.

"Okay, just remember what I said," he said, rolling over on his stomach, shutting his eyes. Turning to him, while trying to keep my anger in check, I replied, "I don't need you to lecture me on how to spend my own fuckin' money. You act like I'm spending your fuckin' money, what is this some new shit you monitoring my money now, tell me how I can and can't spend my shit! Huh?

This time he stayed quiet. Fine with me." he muttered. Truthfully, I didn't need anything, but now that he'd pissed me off, I would find something to buy. The

September chill blew through the house, so I took an extra hot shower, letting the water run down my body. After throwing on my clothes and putting on some eye shadow and lip-gloss, I went downstairs' to my kitchen and made me some hot chocolate and a bagel and waited for Isis to come.

Raquan's voice carried through the house, "Remember what I said!"

I didn't bother to reply. He was pissed and has been acting all anal for a while now, complaining about everything I do. I was this way when he met me and Im'a be this way when he leaves. Plus, I make damn good money and I'm going to spend some of it on me, not only on my bills.

"Don't come crying broke to him," I can't believe he even fixed his lips to say some dumb shit like that. Bitch, I ain't never broke! I thought. I just tell your ass that when I don't feel like spending my money…

Ms. Isis, the disdained sistah. I met her at a hair salon about three in a half maybe four years ago; I was on my cell cussing out some joker I was dealing with at the time. His fuckin' wife had called me the night before to tell me that he was married. Now he wanted to call to talk. But in the background when his wife was asking, "Whose Stormie?" he was like, "I don't know no Stormie."

My eyes damn near bulged out of their sockets. "So, you don't know any Stormie? Then why the fuck are you ringing my phone now, huh! You never told me you were married and have been for two fuckin' years!" Home girl broke out laughing.

I turned to the big boob, brown skin woman, ready to cuss her ass out. My facial expression alone should've knocked her out. "Uh, do you see something funny?"

"I don't mean to be all up in your business, but you're loud as hell," she said in a ridiculously country accent. Then I laughed, 'cause the hair dryer was going full blast, so I probably was louder than normal. From that day on Isis always seemed to be at the hair salon on the same day I had an appointment, waiting on the same slow ass chick to do our hair. So we just started having conversations about some of the chicks that were getting their dos done.

"Whatever happened to that guy you were on the phone cussing out?" Isis asked me one day when we were at the salon.

I shifted in my seat, while trying not to scratch my head—especially since Kia was gonna put in a relaxer and I didn't want it to burn. "I gave him his walking papers. He told me that he wasn't married, and that he lived with his sick aunt who didn't like company. So, me being a naïve woman, believed his lie." Then I thought for a moment. "Or maybe I didn't, maybe I just wanted to be with someone, I don't know. But then his wife called-," Anger welled up inside me and with three long breaths it helped to ease it away. "Anyway, he's out of my life."

Back then, almost every man I met had someone, but at that time, I wasn't really looking for a commitment so it didn't matter. I was "doing me" –clubbing, going out on dates with men who only wanted one thing. Some got what they wanted, while others got dismissed big time. The ones I "dissed" were probably good men, but I always fell for the 'thug niggas with the I don't give a fuck attitude, SUV driving, big platinum chain wearing, getting high and drinking all day, and more than one baby momma type. Yes, I was stuck on them niggas, but back then I was having the worse luck with men and I soon found out that Isis was too.

She met her boyfriend at that time over the Internet, fell in love and moved to New Jersey from Texas to be with him. I thought that was a crazy and desperate move. She'd been in Newark for about eight months. We develop a friendship from the salon. You can tell she was desperately seeking a friend, and I always have room for meeting new people. One day I asked while we were hanging out after getting out hair done." What type of work do you do?"

"I work as a customer service rep at a company in Parsippany"

"Why do you work as a customer service rep, you seem to have so much more going for yourself." From the way she spoke and carried herself, you would've thought she was some type of Administrator working for some high-class

business or something. Although she had a country accent, she spoke in a very professional and proper manner, not like the other chicks from around the way. Isis took a long and deep huff. "Because my man wanted me to find something quick so I could help with the bills. He knew someone at L'Oreal and they got me this job. But I'm still looking because I can't see myself doing this for the rest of my life. What type of work do you do?"

"I work for a temp agency." I said blowing air from my noise, almost ashamed. "So far they've been getting me bullshit ass jobs, but I have two kids an eight year old and a five year old and they've got to eat. We live with my mom, so I don't have rent to worry about. So I have to take whatever they give me until something permanent comes through. Hopefully, that'll be soon."

Every time we met up, we would talk about everything happening in our lives. She didn't want to end up like her Mom and neither did I. Don't get me wrong, our Moms aren't bad people, we just don't want to put up with the bullshit they put up with from their men. We wanted so much more, we actually had goals of having our own shit and running our own shit. We didn't want a man to make decisions for us. Isis's mother Sandra and mine had no goals and no intentions on having any. Both were married and living the life their husbands wanted them to live.

"My Mom's never gonna leave Texas," Isis said, staring straight ahead looking at the passerby on the opposite side of the beauty salon window. Isis had long beautiful black straight hair; you could tell that she has Indian in her. As she stared and twirled her hair, she blurted out. "Fuck that, I had the opportunity to leave so I hauled ass. My mother was a little upset that I left college and came to New Jersey, but she got over it, she really had no choice. Now I'm free from all the bullshit going on in Texas."

Though curious, I never asked her what type of "bullshit" she meant. I wanted to, but I wanted her to tell me when she felt comfortable. I just sat there looking through Hair Magazine, hoping she would tell but she didn't. We exchanged numbers and began to hang out. We weren't making a lot of money but we went shopping every weekend anyway. We stayed in stores like Marshalls, TJ Maxx and Burlington because we couldn't afford to pay full price for name brand shit at the regular stores, like Macy's and Lord & Taylors'. We even hit Canal Street a couple of times, where you can buy all the fugazy shit you wanted. The fake name brand clothing you want is in the garment district on 27th Street. We called it the black bag spot 'cause everybody came out of that tall, brick face, dingy place with a shiny black bag.

Every now and then, Isis would mention Fred. She'll say things like "Boy if Fred can see me now, he would be hatin' on me," or "I want to see Fred, he need to see me doing good and looking good". "I would always tell her to Fuck that Nigga! If you saw him your dumbass might take him back, so be happy you don't see him."

Fred wasn't feeling me and the feeling was mutual. He didn't like the fact that I was showing her things besides working and paying all the bills. He would tell her that I was a bad influence and would demand she ignore my phone calls, and when she wouldn't, he would get angry and stay out late, making Isis worry and stay up all-night paging him, and crying and begging him for forgiveness. Isis didn't go out to any clubs; the only time she was out was when she went to work or at the Hair Salon.

I had to make her go shopping. But once she got started, it was over and Fred hated that. One night when he didn't come home, she called and I told her to come go out and have a drink, not to sit around waiting on him because that was what he wanted her to do. He enjoyed seeing her miserable, and he wanted to stay out anyway he just needed and excuse. Isis became my little sister. She needed protection, since she wasn't from my neck of the hood. The men in Texas didn't have shit on the men up here. Isis was fresh meat and not from these streets. I would tease her by saying Texas men are slow in the game; up here everything and everybody is fast, so be careful.

We were getting dressed so we could go to this club in East Orange called 'Brokers.'

"How do I look, Storm?" Isis asked, as she spun around and tried to see what her backside looked like. She wore gray dress pants, and a very low-cut V-Neck shirt. "Is this too stank…? Is there too much of my breasts hanging out?" She said placing her hands over her breast.

"No, your breasts are supposed to hang out. Trust me, you couldn't hide them big ass knockers if you wore a turtleneck," I said, laughing.

"That's not right, Storm," Isis said, checking herself out in my mirror, as she contemplating on changing in throwing on a small black mini skirt. She checked herself out a few more times than mumbled, I'm fine, and I look good.

"You look good, girl. Hell, we both look good tonight." I said looking at myself in the mirror, I was wearing a pair of black Laundry dress pants which hugged my hips perfectly and they had my ass looking right and round, a baby white tee, with my pointy toe Kenneth Cole shoes, all which I purchased from Marshalls. My hair was pulled up into a Jennie Ponytail, damn near touching my ass, as we stood there admiring ourselves I said, "Let's go meet some men," as I grabbed the keys to my hooptie.

At the time, I had a raggedy baby blue Plymouth Acclaim. The paint was chipped, the inside lining in the ceiling was falling and I only had a tape cassette, but I got around in that $500 car. I wasn't beat.

By the time we got to the club, the music was jumping and the club was packed full of nuts; I mean the men were in the house tonight. We had the thugs, the professional, and the dread heads. I was more enthralled with the thugs of course. DJ Qua was doing the damn thing, playing nothing but old school club music and I was loving it. I walked in the door dancing, and Isis, who wasn't used to this kind of music just followed, watching me shake my ass. We made our way over to the bar and ordered some drinks, a Tangaray and cranberry juice for me and a Southern Comfort for Isis.

"I'll be back I said to Isis, I am going to the dance floor unless you want to come."

"Nah, I am alright. Go on girl and enjoy yourself." She said sipping on her drink. I went on to the dance floor and Isis stayed at the bar.

A tall, brown-skinned nice looking man was watching us as we stood at the bar. He wore a Sean John tan blazer, a tan and white button up shirt and some jeans. He was a cutie; tall and slim with braids, but with small beady eyes and a sloped forehead, he looked sneaky as hell—one of them thug niggas. I could warn my girl, but Isis didn't look interested anyway.

He walked up to Isis, bent down to her, leaned over, and asked, "Can I buy you a drink?"

Isis clutched her purse, signaling to the world that she was from out of town. "I'm okay."

The stranger leaned up against the wall staring at Isis' breasts. "Well then, can I dance with you?"

"No, I don't dance," she answered, staring straight ahead and holding her purse even tighter.

He noticed her clenching her purse and he just smiled and said, "Okay, Then can I help you hold up the bar?"

"No I got it," she said not registering the question. "Wait, "What did you just ask me?" Isis said, looking at him for the first time.

The outward appearance from his face went blank of all facial expression I said, "Can I help you hold up the bar?"

"Oh. If you want to, but I got it, I have a strong back," she said, laughing. Taking a sip of her drink and watching me on the dance floor with a tall, dark skinned brotha dancing.

"Let me buy you a drink. I won't bite, I promise."

I have a drink already she said, waving her drink in the air smiling.

That's okay; I'll buy you another one. "What's your name?" he asked, as he turned to face the bartender to place their order.

"Isis. And yours?"

"Jared. Can I hang out with you for the rest of the night?"

"I'm here with my friend. Isis said, pointing to me.

Jared gave Isis a half smile then replied. "And what does that have to do with me?"

"Nothing. Look, thanks for the drink, but I have a man," she said, this time sounding agitated.

"Whoa, I'm not asking to be your man," he said over the loud music. "I'm just trying to hang out with you tonight." as I made my way back to the bar I gave a hand gesture for us to walk around the club to see what was happening on the upper level of the club. Before we left, dude leaned over and whispered something in Isis' ear. She just smiled and put her hand out; I waited a few seconds then left her ass right there. As I walked up the stairs the mixture of female perfumes, men cologne and the funk within gave me a headache. I just placed my hand over my nose and tried not to be obvious that I was trying to cover my nose from the smell. Drunk folks can't smell and obviously everybody upstairs was drunk. I saw a familiar face staring at me from across the room. Oh boy, I mumble beneath my phony smile. It was a male friend I used to fuck around with. He now works at Brokers doing security. He is a big nigga to, 6'5, 280 lbs. and can dress his ass off. Every time I see this nigga he looks good. He came walking towards me almost knocking people down. I pretend I didn't see him coming so I made my way to the back of the club where the mirrors are all over, so I can see myself dance. He walked up and started dancing with me even though they are not allowed to dance during work hours. They needed to stay focus. We talked briefly until Isis came over, looking as if she was having a terrible time. She tried calling Fred a few times, but to no avail. The club song "Flowers" came on and I tried to make her dance by pulling her onto the dance floor, but that didn't work. She found a table in the corner and sat there playing with her cell until the club closed. I knew she wanted to leave, but I refused to take her back to that house to wait on Fred. He needed to wait on her for a change. I purposely stayed on the dance floor and at the bar just for that reason.

"So, did you get his number?" I asked wiping the sweat from my forehead, once I got off the dance floor and getting ready to leave the club. She checked her cell phone again and then answered, "Who?"

"The guy you were talking to."

She shrugged. "Yes I did, and no I'm not."

"No you're not what?" I asked taking my keys out of my purse

"Going to call him," she said, flicking her phone open then closed.

"I didn't ask" I said, leaving the club walking towards my car.

"But you were."

"No I wasn't," I shot back, unlocking the doors. "Anyway, it seemed like all the ugly men with red pimp daddy suits were trying to get at me."

"Bitch, you must be drunk," Isis said, laughing and looking at me as if I had lost my mind.

"Why do you say that?" I said pulling away from the curb.

She took a moment to collect herself. "Because all night the same man kept trying to talk to you and was buying you drink's."

"Shiiit, I must be drunk," I said, laughing with her.

As we drove past the Caribbean Club, and a few other spots we were recalling the details of the evening, we laughed all the way to her house. We had a good time that night even though I didn't meet anybody. I walked Isis inside of her home, just to make sure he didn't fuck her up, but her man wasn't home and it was after 4:30 in the morning. She was mad as hell; she started dialing his number, pressing the numbers on the phone hard and cussing him out on his answering machine. She left a message saying if he didn't call her right back, his shit would be out the door. She slammed the phone down and went into their bedroom. She grabbed all his shit starting from the dresser drawers to the closet and threw it all in the living room. Since his ass wants to keep staying out, I'ma put him out.

"Isis, you should calm down and wait to talk to him tomorrow." I was hoping to calm her down. She stopped throwing his shit out and began to cry. I stayed for five extra minutes but I was fucked up and needed to get home to my bed.

A couple days later, she called me waking me out of a sound sleep. The sobs on the other end as she squeaked out my name made me sit up. "Isis, what's the matter? Why are you crying? Did that muthafucka jump on you?"

"Storm," Isis said, crying into the phone.

"What's going on?"

"Why he gon' leave me here with nothing? I left everything to come up here with him and he just up and left me like this," she said, crying even harder.

My heart sank as I realized that Isis did everything, lied, fought with her mom and left college so she could move from Texas to be with him and then he leaves. Pulling the cover around my waist, I strolled to the kitchen for a cup of juice realizing this was going to be a long talk. "What happened? I mean, what did he say?" I still wasn't sure, why she was crying, as much shit she had to say about him, she should've been glad he was gone.

"Nothing, he just packed up his shit and left. I tried to make him talk to me, but he wouldn't. He just ignored me and wouldn't answer any of my questions." Isis said continued crying.

I make $11.00 an hour; I can't afford this place on my own. He left me with nothing but shut off notices for the lights, phone, cable, everything! What am I gonna do? I have no money in the bank."

At that moment, if I could get my hands on Fred, I would choke the snots outta him, the fag ass nigga.

"When I got paid Thursday, he took my check after I cashed it, saying he was going to pay some bills! He didn't even pay the fuckin' rent for this month! I can't believe he'd do this to me!" I could hear her footsteps pacing the floor, contemplating her next move.

I didn't know what to say to her, I had no place for her to go. Hell, I was living at home with my mother in the basement. So my situation wasn't any better. I told her I would talk to my mom and see if she could help her. My mother lived on the first floor; I went to her bedroom and watched her for a few seconds. "Mom" I said, standing in front of her door.

"What?" My mother answered, looking at me as if she was waiting for me to say something bad. I explained Isis's situation and asked her if she had any more rooms for rent. My mom she had a room in the attic part of the house, and that Isis was welcome to stay there if she wanted. Isis came to meet my mother and to see the room. The room was big enough; it had a walk in closet, which she really liked. She just had to share the bathroom and the kitchen with the tenants on the second floor. Isis didn't care; as soon as she was able to get help, she moved all that she could and left the rest for the landlord to toss. She didn't care; hell the lease was in Fred's name. Mommy took Isis in and pretty much adopted her. Isis became part of our family.

The following year Isis started designing web pages for a couple of small businesses in New York, plus she kept her customer service job. I got a job with a security company doing entry-level work, getting paid $13.00 an hour. Shit, I thought I was making good money compared to what my last job paid. We worked and made plans to be on our own by the following year. Of course, we still had our men problem. I kept meeting men with women, and Isis had more one-night stands than comedians did, but we stayed focus. And now, three years later, her business is doing well. She bought a house and I followed a few months after my job had given me a promotion and my pay went from thirty thousand a year to well over fifty thousand a year, and we are enjoying every bit of our success.

"Did you hear me?" Raquan yelled through the house, as the sound of the doorbell broke my thoughts. Raquan opened the door, glaring at Isis before saying, "Coldness is here!"

"A'ight, I came out of the kitchen, then ran upstairs to grab a jacket. "I'll be right back." I said running up the stairs. Shit, I still wasn't ready.

Raquan walked into the living room, picked up the remote to his PS2 and switched on the game. Isis walked in behind him, frowning trying to think of something evil to say.

"So, is this what ghetto folks do on a Saturday? No work today? I'm surprised, I thought working was all you enjoyed doing."

Raquan just looked at her and shook his head. He usually didn't feed into Isis' bullshit comments. He thought she was crazy and lonely, and didn't think too much of her. But this time he grinned. "Did you find a man yet?" He asked, never taking his eyes off his game. "Do they ever stay after the sex, I heard they haul ass after the sex."

"Fuck you!" She snapped rolling her eyes.

"Not even with Stormie's fake dick she's got hidden in her closet under all those bags," he laughed. Isis laughed too.

"What's so damn funny?" I asked almost laughing with them.

"Nothing," Raquan said, still playing his PS2.

Isis stood up, gathered her things, then looked down at Raquan while he was sitting on the floor and said, "I can't stand a man who sits around and gets enjoyment out of playing video games. You really need to grow up," Isis said, with her nose turned up.

"And I can't stand a bitch who always wants my girl to hang out with her lonely ass because she can't find a man to spend time with her," Raquan shot back, looking at Isis with his nose turned up, mocking her. Then he smiled, ignoring her middle finger pointing at him, Then he said, "While you're at the mall, why don't you see if they have men on sale, you lonely hoe!"

Irritated by his bitter tone, I turned to him. "What's your problem?"

"Nothing. Go ahead so you can hurry up back, Storm."

"Why did you—"

"Don't start asking me shit about your bitch ass friend," he then ended the conversation with "Just hurry the fuck back." Still concentrating on the game he was playing.

Isis walking slowly grabbed her bag and walked out the door. I stood there for a minute not wanting to make a scene in front of her. I just turned and left. When I got into Isis' SUV, I was too embarrassed to look at her. I just pretended like I was looking for something in my bag. Isis and I had the same Cadillac truck, only hers was white with black leather interior, and mine was black with tan leather interior. Both were fully loaded with chrome rims. When I purchased my truck, Raquan was so pissed he wouldn't even look at it. He would walk past it like it was invisible. But even that didn't compare to the hatred he felt about my best friend.

"What the fuck was that all about, girl?" Isis asked, as we drove off. "He was in there acting like some kind of wife beater. Let me find out."

"Please, he knows better. I don't know what's wrong with him. Lately he's been acting all moody and shit. Everything I say and do irks the hell out of him." I sat in her truck staring out the window, thinking what has gotten into that man.

Isis suddenly turned the corner, the wrong corner. "What the hell are you doing?"

"I've got to run back to my house,"

"Why?" I asked. But I knew why, she had forgotten something—again and I said it out loud at the same time she did, "I forgot something".

This woman had the nerve to be gated living in the hood. She lived in the Weequahic section in Newark—a nice area, but being gated is just ridiculous. You gotta get buzzed in when you come to her house and, get this; she's even got a remote control to open her gate. She is stupid!

To top it all off, the bitch lives in the white house. All of her rooms have white furniture; the bedroom, living room, all the way into the dining room. She has white plush carpet throughout and even a white wood bedroom set (not that cheap shit, either) I know 'cause I was at The Furniture Gallery trying to talk her out of it. She also has a white, 100% goose down queen size comforter.

Guests damn near have to strip just to walk in. My kids hate going over to her house: "We can't do nothing over there!" they always say.

"Isis, tell me again why everything is all white?" I asked, entering the split-level house, slipping my shoes off in the foyer. "Damn, I'm scared to walk when I come into your house! What the fuck, you wanted to be in the white house that bad!"

"I don't like dark shit," she answered nonchalantly, taking off her shoes.

"Besides, white tends to make a house look cleaner and bigger. Any more questions?"

She walked over to the dining room table, picked up her cell, checking to see if anyone had called her. Her house phone rang.

"I'll be right back," she said, as she ran up the stairs to answer her phone in her bedroom. She only has a phone upstairs, because the phone jack in the kitchen doesn't work. "Hello," she said, out of breath.

"What's up Ice?" a man's voice asked.

"What?" The facial expression on Isis face suggested that she did not like the person on the other end.

"Yo, why do you always talk to me in that tone, girl!"

"And I'll say it again, what!" She said walking back down the stairs.

"You know what? Fuck you, that's what! You ain't even all that and you acting like you the shit. I'm doing your muthafuckin' ass a favor by trying to be your friend."

"Do me a favor little dick, don't ring my fuckin' phone again!" Isis replied. "Like I told your ass before, if you don't see my number on your caller ID, then I didn't call you. If you don't get a message saying to call me, then don't call me. Now, do you see my number on your caller ID, no!" she answered for him, then kindly hung up on his ass.

"What was that all about?" I asked, as she walked towards me and placed the phone on her table.

"Nothing. That was Kenny, the guy I met at the Chinese Store on Clinton Ave. Remember the guy with the gold teeth, I was a little iffy about his ass, but gave him a try anyway. Do you know this nigga came up in here, laid in my bed and did what he might've thought was making love to me, and girl, I didn't even cum."

I bust out laughing hitting the table.

"No, fa'real, I didn't know the nigga was in me. He was huffing and puffing," Isis said, blowing out breath like a mad bull.

42

I continued to laugh, not saying word, just remembering some pass experience I had encountered a time or two.

"Saying who's you're daddy and shit, like he was really laying down the pipe. I stopped him in the middle of that what he called sex and told him you got to go. I told him he didn't know my daddy and to get the fuck up off me and get the fuck out!" Isis said pointing her fingers towards the door with a serious look on her face. I couldn't stop laughing; the tears were sliding down the side of my face. I could barely talk.

"Girl I know damn well you didn't put him out."

Stretching her eyes and smacking her teeth, Isis replied with "oh yes the fuck I did. "I put that no-dick-having-ass-man out!" she re-enacting that night. "I told dummy man, don't call me, I'll call you. And what does the stupid ass do?"

"What? Call you." I said, trying to control my laughter and getting up from the table.

"That's right he calls me!" In the middle of all her venting, her phone rang again.

"Hello," Isis said, changing the tone in her voice instantly trying to sound sexy.

"Hey, baby," the voice, said.

"Heyyyyyy." Isis smiled.

"What are you doing?"

"I'm about to go to this cheap ass Jersey Garden Mall with my sister. Why, what's up?"

"I wanted to see you later, maybe go out to eat," the man said.

"What time later?" She was smiling from ear to ear, twirling her long black straight hair.

"Around 8 o'clock," the deep sexy, slightly accented voice said. "A'ight?"

"Alright, I'll see you then," Isis said, still smiling.

"Who was that?" I said, after she hung up. I knew who it was but I asked anyway.

"Jared."

"Oh," I said before muttering, "That nonsensical ass nigga."

"He wants to take me out later," she said, oblivious to my tone.

"Where?" I asked

"An expensive restaurant in New York. I forgot the name just that quick. Anyway, let me check my answering machine before we leave," she mumbled as she walked backup stairs to put her phone back on the charger. I followed behind her so she wouldn't fuck around and start doing something else. I was ready to go shopping.

The message, in a heavy Spanish accent said, "Hey, Senora Isis. I no com'a today. Okay, bye."

"No this bitch didn't say I no com'a today," Isis snapped, eyes flashing with anger. "I needed her to go to Pathmark and pick up some things for me, wash my clothes and mop the floors in the kitchen and laundry room," she said, whining like a thirteen year old.

"Damn, bitch, you're sickening," I said, shaking my head at her. "How long have you had maid service?"

"Not long. This house is too big for me to keep clean by myself."

"You can't even go to the fuckin' store for yourself. You're wasting money. Pay me, I'll go and get your fuckin' groceries," I said, laughing. "Girl, let's go to the mall and spend your money on more tangible things."

Isis whimpered, "I need the help, and why shouldn't I do it when I can afford it?"

"Girl, bring your ass on."

Once we got to the mall, all my problems melted away. The aroma of CinnaBun made want to buy the place; those damn buns smell good as hell, but they are too sweet for me. Jersey Garden Mall wasn't as crowded today and I was glad, because it gave me a chance to look at what I wanted to buy. The mall is big as hell; it takes at least two days to walk around the entire place. As soon as you walk in the food court is on our left hand side, but I didn't want to eat just yet, I had to shop a little first. I love to shop and swear to God I had an orgasm when we stood in front of the display in the Steve Madden window. I turned into Homer Simpson, 'Um shoes, must buy shoes,'

My happiness was broken by a familiar ring on my phone. All the important people in my life had their own "ring tone." This one particular ring belonged to my niece. She could wait.

Isis stood next to me, eyeing the silver stiletto high heel boots, and I had my eyes on the brown and tan cowboy boots. Our noses pressed up to the glass like two pigs in a blanket. The phone rang again.

"What, Dee Dee?" I asked, still trying to keep contact with a cute little pair of strappy sandals.

"Nothing," Dee Dee said.

"Then--why--are--you--calling--me?" I asked very slowly.

"Why are you talking to me like I'm retarded?" She said laughing a little.

"I figure if you called me for nothing, then you must be on the dumb side today. "Where you at?"

I had to count to five before answering, "The mall, why?"

"Oh man, that's where I wanted to go but Bianca started buggin' about this stupid house and--"

My niece whimpers when she talks, the patience it takes to listen to her whine is almost painful.

"Okay, why are you calling me?"

"Can I stay at your house tonight? I have things to do tomorrow and I need to be down in your area." Now she was speaking so fast all of her words were coming together signaling that she was asking me on the sly.

Picking up the cowboy boots and a pair of black, low heel riding boots and holding it up for Isis, I said, "Nah, you'll be a'ight."

"But, why?" she whined, "I hate living all the way up here, there's nothing to do. Can I stay at your house tonight, huh? Pleeeeease."

"Listen, let me finish shopping, I'll call you back."

She hesitated and I could hear her take in a long breath before finally realizing that arguing with me would get her nowhere. "Okay."

If I know my niece, she's trying to get out of doing something and I ain't getting involved in that. I had some sales racks to hit and some money to spend; I had no time for Dee- Dee's dramatic ass today.

Dee Dee is my sister Bianca youngest daughter. Dee Dee and Bianca fight all the time because Dee- Dee don't want to listen and forever scheming. I love my niece, but I do not come between my sister decisions when it comes to her kids.

"Who drank my soda?" Bianca yelled after closing her refrigerator door. "Chantell, Dee Dee, Ahmir, and Malcolm! Bring y'alls asses here right now!"

As each one of her children gathered into the kitchen, Bianca stood there with her arm folded over her chest. Chantell' is the oldest she's nineteen, and a freshman at Seton Hall University. She's 5'4 with a very dark beautiful complexion; her hair is long and straight and her skin is flawless. Dee- Dee's seventeen, she's 5'7 with dreads and a dimple so deep it looks like it hurts. She's a cocoa brown complexion with a smile that would fool you into thinking she's a sweetheart Ahmir he's fifteen he's short for his age and skinny as hell, but he's always flashing his chest like he's a big boy. He too has dimples that are deep as hell. The youngest is Malcolm, thirteen who is a splitting image of his dad. The way he talk out the side of his mouth like his father is almost scary. He have big dark eyes, a little 'fro and a beautiful complexion. And all he does is play basketball. As she unfolded her arms and began to fuss again, she pointed at each one of her kid, and working her neck, saying.

"I'm getting tired of y'all fuckin' with my soda," she said opening the refrigerator door again, making her soda was not there. "I tell ya'll time and time again not to touch my Pepsi but y'all do anyway." She faced the row of squirming children. "Now who drank my damn Pepsi?"

"Not me," all of them said at once.

Malcolm's dark brown eyes lowered as he said, "All I know is--"

"All I know is somebody better go get me another soda," she said walking past her kids, almost knocking Ahmir down.

My sister has four kids and three baby daddies. Chantell and Dee Dee have the same father, and the two youngest boys have different fathers. I can't speak about their fathers 'cause her business is her business, but I do know that they don't pay child support. Trifling muthafucka. Bianca is 5'10 dark brown complexion, with deep dimples on both sides of her cheeks; even when she is not talking, her dimples are always showing. Her butt is so big you can place can soda on it. People tend to think we are twins, especially when we go to the clubs together. You would never catch Bianca without a wig on, but if she didn't tell you, you wouldn't know. She has hair, she just like having a different look whenever she wants. Bianca had a pair of stretch shorts and a wife-beater. She wasn't going anywhere; therefore, she had no needs to get dress.

She finally lucked up with a man that owned two Bails Bond agencies one in Newark and one in East Orange. They've been married for a few years now. Keith has no kids, but he loves my sister's kids like they were his own. He gives her any and everything she wants, so she doesn't have to work. Once in a while she "helps out at the office," which means she spends all day on the phone. He bought a home in Short Hills and she's been there ever since. Bianca only comes to Newark occasionally. I don't blame her cause ain't nothing here but thugs, drugs and stolen cars. She won't let her kids come down to Newark either, but if they had it their way, they'd be down there every day, especially Dee Dee with her fast ass. She needs to stay her ass right where she's at. By any means necessary, my niece would try to get from up there. She said it is too boring, but the real reason is because ain't no boys around for her to hang under. Dee Dee only calls you when she needs you and wants to get out of doing something.

"Keith!" Bianca called out, coming into the bedroom.

"What?" Keith said, sitting up in the bed with a glass of dark liquid in his hand.

Bianca glared at him. "Did you drink my Pepsi?"

He glanced quickly at his glance then back at her. "Yeah I did. Why?"

"Cause I'm thirsty and I wanted my Pepsi."

His big brown eyes flashed with worry. "What, I wasn't supposed to drink that soda?"

"Yeah, you could drink the soda, Keith, but if you look and don't see any more than you should take your lazy ass to the store and buy some more."

Keith laid back on the bed and shut his eyes. His dark brown skin, short fro, neatly trim goatee and, straight white teeth combined for a handsome man. A handsome man that was close to getting his butt kicked if that Pepsi didn't appear out of thin air.

"Do you know I blamed my kids?" she said, standing in front of the television. She then snatched the pillow and popped him upside the head. "Get up and go get me another soda, Keith."

"I'm not going anywhere right now," he said dodging the blows. "I'll get it later. Go drink some Kool-aid or something."

"Kool-Aid, I don't drink fucking Kool-Aid!" She snapped." Get the fuck up!"

"Why do you make such a big deal about that damn Pepsi, there's other drinks in there, and you complaining about a fuckin' Pepsi."

"So what! Just get the fuck up!" she lifted another pillow to hit him with. Ahmir and Malcolm stood by listening to Bianca fuss about her soda. As they giggled, she looked at them and yelled for them to shut up and to go back to their rooms. As soon as they were away from room, she started again.

"You know what?" She said to Keith, pointing her finger and shaking her head as if she was going to get his ass back, but before she could get everything out Keith said, "Move, I'll be back," Keith said, getting out of the bed and stretching his 6'2 frame. He knew that if he didn't get another Pepsi, there would be no piece in the house.

"Where the fuck are you going?" Bianca said stepping aside.

"To get you a fuckin' Pepsi, because if I don't, you're not gonna give me one minute of peace."

"I thought so," she said, satisfied that she had gotten her way once again.

Bianca was spoiled. All she had to do was look at him a certain way and Keith would jump, (okay, maybe he wasn't that stupid, but he wasn't far from it). But he was a good man and women would give everything just to have one like him.

"Hello," Bianca said, answering her cell. Looking behind her to make sure Keith was gone. "Hey Hasson."

"What's good? Your man there?"

"No, he's not here. He went to go get me a soda."

"So what you doing later?" he asked

"I don't know what I'm doing later. Hopefully I'll be letting you lick my wet spot." She heard foot step so she began to whisper, No, I'll call you back, bye." As soon as she hung up with him, she called me on my cell phone.

"What you doing?" she asked, after I said hello.

"Shopping, why, what's up?" I asked, looking at a very low-cut shirt in H&M.

"Nothing," she said, humming a song. "Listen, I'm going out with Hasson later so don't call here, okay. I'm using you to get out the house." She said whispering.

"Girl, you lucked up and found a good man and you gon' fuck around on him?

"Oh, please. You think that muthafucka ain't cheating on me?" Bianca retorted, making hand movement and ugly facial expression. "Anyway, you heard what I said." She paused for a second then said. "I just called your house."

"And?" I said nonchalantly.

"What's wrong with Raquan crazy ass?"

"I don't know."

"He sounded all indignant on the phone when I called your house." She said as she was walking towards her closet.

"Well, since I'm not there with him, I don't know what's wrong with him."

"I just asked, not that I give a fuck anyway," she said, then hung up. I can't stand her sometimes," Bianca mumbled.

"Who can't you stand sometimes?" Keith asked, startling her as he walked up behind her.

"Stormie, she can be a bitch at times," she said, placing the clothes she was going to where on the bed.

"Where are you going?" Keith asked, looking at the clothes she was laying out.

"Out."

"Out," he mocked her, while kissing her on the back of her neck.

"Move, Keith, I'm going over to Stormie's house, okay. I need to get out of this house sometimes," she said, sounding annoyed.

"So get out then. I don't make you stay in the house. But before you leave can we have sex?"

"Please," she said, pushing him to the side, I'm about to get in the shower."

"Okay, but I'm getting in with you," he said, following her into the bathroom. She pushed him away. "No you're not."

A few seconds passed before he said, "Who you fuckin'?"

"What?" She said in a high pitch voice, trying not to look guilty. She returned the question, "Who you fuckin', nigga?"

"I ain't fuckin' nobody, not even my darling wife." He said with sad puppy dog eyes. He then turned and walked out of the bedroom and into the kitchen to make a sandwich.

Bianca didn't care how hurt he looked, she had a date with Hasson, and she wasn't breaking that for no one, not even her husband.

~Chapter Four~

The familiar number flashed on my cell. Raquan. "Talk to my voice mail muthafucka" I chanted.

I know she hears her fuckin' phone ringing, Raquan said to himself. He dialed my number again and the voice mail came on. He said, "It's me, call home!" *It's fuckin' 5 o'clock, she's been at the mall all day. I know she ain't buying that much shit!* He said to himself, pacing the kitchen floor. The phone rang as soon as he hung up.

"Hello," he answered, hoping it was me. "Oh, Mrs. Luv, she's not here. She went to the mall early this morning."

"Spending all her money, huh?" My mom said.

"I know, come next week she'll be crying broke. She knows she can't hang with Isis."

My mom just laughed, then said, "Okay, tell her to call me," ending the conversation.

"Okay, I'll tell her. Bye," Raquan said, hanging up. Man, bump this. I'm gonna try Stormie one more time then I'm leaving. I'm not waiting around here for her.

Who's calling me from a private number? I thought, looking at my ringing cell phone.

"Hello," I answered puzzled after the phone rung two more times.

"Yo, I thought I told you to hurry the fuck back," he yelled. "Its 5:30 and you've been gone all day. I'm hungry and I want to go out to eat, so hurry the fuck home!" The next thing I heard was a click.

"No he didn't just hang up on me, talking, and cussing at me like I'm one of his fucking kids," I said with the cell phone still placed on my ear. "Yup, this damn man done lost his damn mind. Isis, take me home, please." All of sudden he wants to go out. He only wants to take me out 'cause I'm with Isis, stupid muthafucka, I thought.

"Isis didn't do it, your man did. Don't get an attitude with me," she said bopping to a beat that was playing in her head. "As soon as I pay for my shit we can

51

split."

"You stupid," I said trying to give her a half smile. "I don't know what's gotten into him, or what he's gotten into. Lately, he has nothing but attitude. One minute he's okay, the next he's not speaking to me for days over some dumb shit. He's starting to talk to me like I'm nothing. I know one thing, when I get home he's gonna let me know what the fuck the problem is."

"Do what you gotta do, Storm," Isis said. "All I know is I got a date tonight."

Man, we spent so much money in the mall today. We had hit damn near all the stores in the mall; and the side stores; Purfumia, Icing, and some others I don't remember the names of. And I bought something out of each store. Although I may have a lot of shit, trust and believe, everything has been marked down. Marked down clothes were just as good as full price.

A lot of people front like they don't shop out of the outlet malls, but I saw some of their asses today shopping and paying for shit like they were paying full price. Not that I can't afford it, but why front like I don't like shit on sale. Where do you think them rich ass white and Korean people shop, they don't always pay full price. They shop for the bargains just like I do. They'd rather spend more money on their homes and school then clothes.

"Girl, look at all the bags we got. This is sickening," I said, laughing and putting my bags from Saks, Nieman Marcus, Daffy's, Victoria Secret's, Burlington, Steve Madden, Against All Odds, and H&M in the back of Isis' truck.

"It's a good thing I drive a truck or we'd have to leave something behind."

"Not my things!" I replied.

"Mine either," said Isis, separating her bags from mine. Then she looked at me and noticed the blank look on my face.

"Girl is you alright?"

"Yeah, I'm alright." Knowing I wasn't alright. I just wanted to know what made this brother tick. The ride from the mall was quiet, I was to busy thinking.

Isis pulled into my driveway singing along with Ashanti's 'Unfoolish' in a really loud voice and very much off-key. I just stared at my home, noticing how beautiful my home is. I can't believe I own this house. With the help of my brother, I was able to buy this house at a low cost. I was able to pay off my debt and up my score and I started to save. And with the pay increase and the power of prayer, here I am. My older brother has a real estate business and he found this house for me on a, nice quiet block. Not too many folks know about this block; it's a down low street in Newark. It isn't as big as Isis' or Bianca's, but it's mine.

On the first floor, there is a bedroom, bath, living room, dining room, and kitchen. The second floor has three bedrooms and a bathroom that is next to the stairs leading to the two rooms in the attic--one an office, the other my bedroom, bathroom and walk-in closet. Dark burgundy carpet matches the mahogany king-size bedroom set and the Zenith 42-inch plasma television hanging on the wall and I'm still not finished decorating. As I was thinking about my home Isis interrupted.

"Hey, are you alright?" Isis asked.

"Yeah, let me go and put up my things. I'll call you later," I said grabbing my bags. "Are you gonna help me? Damn!"

"Okay," she said as she dropped the bags by the door, then ran to her truck, yelling, if you need me holla, but ya better holla before eight cause ya know I got a date."

"Bye, Isis," I said, as I carried my bags in the house.

As I turned my key to go into the house, I heard Raquan say, "Hold on she just walked in the door." He handed me the phone and stormed away.

"Hello" I said standing in my doorway.

"Where have you been all day?" a female voice asked

The voice didn't even sound familiar. "Who's this?" I asked puzzled

"Rhonda! Are you busy?"

"Nah. I thought you were out of town, I haven't heard from you in a minute." Raquan watched me as he leaned on my kitchen island.

"I'm back now."

"Give me your number and I'll call you back when I get settled."

"It's 973-555-1212."

"Okay, I'ma call you back." I hung up the phone and scaled the stairs two at a time, bags in hand.

"Damn girl, it took you all day to shop?"

"Yup," I answered and kept walking.

"Hey, Storm?" Raquan yelled up at me.

"What?" I yelled, from my bedroom door.

"Do you want to go out for dinner or what?"

You know you are one sick son- of-a-bitch, I mumbled before answering, "Can you wait until I come downstairs? I can't stand all this yelling."

When I got downstairs, he was eating on some fruit. "Raquan, why are you acting like you didn't do anything wrong today?" I asked, standing with my arms folded, leaning in the kitchen doorway.

He stared at me for a moment with his dark brown eyes. "I didn't, what did I do wrong?" he asked with fruit in his mouth.

"Please, you embarrassed me in front of Isis. You were being very disrespectful toward her and--"

"Oh please, Storm," he snapped. "I'm sick of that girl thinking she can talk to me any kind of way, like I'm her friend 'n' shit. Remind her she ain't my friend, she's yours. I don't have to respect her, you do," he said placing a grape in her mouth. "You don't try to stop her when she speaks to me like I'm a nobody to you, or when she calls me big head, you just laugh like its okay. If she can dish it out then she should be able to take it. Ole dyke looking bitch. I really wish--"

"You really wish what?"

"Nothing," he said, picking up the bowl of fruit. "Are we going out or what? Better yet, why don't you cook something?" he said, taking the bowl of fruit upstairs with him and leaving me hanging.

"No, tell me, don't just stop in mid- sentence," I said grabbing his arms.

"Get off me. I said nothing, right?" He snatched his arm away and walked up the stairs toward my room.

He always does that just when he knows I'm about to tell him the truth about his ass; he always has to have the last word. I wish I would cook something for his ass. He didn't want to go out in the first place, that was just an excuse for me to rush home. The phone rang, causing me to jump.

"Hello," I said, answering the phone, wondering what else could happen.

"Ma?"

"Yes, Tania," I answered, happy to hear my daughter's voice.

"What are you doing?"

"Nothing, what are you doing?" I said, picking up the dishcloth and wiping down my refrigerator.

"Nothing."

We were quiet for a minute, then I glanced at the pile of dishes in my sink and remembering the state of my kitchen. "Thought I told y'all to clean up before y'all left," I said, walking toward the sink.

"We did," she said breathing heavy in my ear, not having anything to talk about.

"No you didn't. Y'all's rooms are a mess, and I told you to clean the kitchen."

"Oops, I forgot, my bad," she giggled a little.

Standing by the sink, preparing to clean the kitchen, I asked, "Where's Ja'Mil?"

"Downstairs in the basement playing with his cars. Are you coming to get us?"

"Are you ready now?"

Tania hesitated a moment, and I knew what would come next. "No, I want to stay the night."

"Then I'm coming in the morning."

"Okay, I'll see you then. Love ya, Ma."

"Love ya too, baby."

As I was walking up the stairs, I heard Raquan talking, but who the fuck was he talking to I thought. So I tipped -up the stairs to the bedroom as Raquan's voice echoed into the hallway. "Yeah, a'ight," he said, to the voice on the other end. "I'll be over later, I'm about to eat right now."

He was so into his conversation he didn't notice me standing at the door. The volume on his phone was up loud enough for me to hear a female's voice on the other end of the phone. After listening a few seconds, I said, "Who the fuck is that?"

He jumped, turned, and looked at me with angry eyes. "Let me call you back," he said before placing the phone on the cradle. "Yo, why are you yelling at me like you're crazy?"

"Who was that on the phone?" I said lowering my voice, wanting to snatch the phone from him and call the bitch back.

"Since when do I have to tell you who I'm talking too?" he said, placing the bowl of fruit down on the nightstand. "I'm a grown ass man and I don't answer to nobody. I don't ask you about your friends," he said walking toward me with his fist balled and a smirk. "Shit, I really don't give a fuck. I got too much on my mind to be worried about who the fuck you're talking to."

"Okay, I see," I said balling my fist too, ready to knock the snot outta that nigga. I thought about picking up the bowl of fruit and tossing the grapes in his face." What the fuck is your problem, Raquan! Why are you doing this?"

"Doing what? What am I doing?" he said, walking around the room.

"Treating me like shit; talking to me any kind of way, like you really don't want to be here. I'm not stupid; I see the change in you. I know what the fuck you're doing," I said, fighting back the tears. He snatched up his things. "I'm out cause you're about to start some shit." Within seconds later, he was in the hallway. "Oh, okay, it's like that; you don't want to tell me? Well bye, and lock the door behind you, please," I yelled. I really wanted to throw a pair of my pointy ass shoes at him, but I didn't.

"Motherfucker!" all kinds of crazy thoughts were flowing through my mind. He had no clue as to how evil I could be or what type of bitch I could become. I've been good to this nigga, and I never cheated on him, either. Ooh, I should fuck up that raggedy ass Lexus, but that's okay. And the nigga wearing the outfit I brought! "Ooh, this nigga was gonna get it."

~Chapter Five~

Where the fuck is this Jamaican ass blood clot! Isis said, looking at the clock again. It's after 8 o'clock and this nigga ain't here yet! "Here I am looking all good. I hope he doesn't stand me up again," she said, pacing the floor peeking out the window from time to time.

Isis was standing in front of her mirror checking herself out. She had on a Donna Karen spaghetti string dress, which was cut so low in the back the crack of her ass greeted everyone with a smile. {Damn, the way the dress hugged my hips and grabbed my breasts would make any nigga drop to his knees and beg to stand near me. Jared should be lucky I'm even fuckin' around with him.} I'm sick of his lying ass anyway. I really need to leave him alone," Isis said, while pacing the floor. She finally picked up the phone. "Where the fuck are you!" Isis yelled, as soon as he answered.

"Yo, don't call me yelling in my ear," Jared shot back. "What the hell is your problem? I'm outside your fuckin' house, buzz the gate."

Isis punched the little white button next to the alarm box on the wall; smiling from ear to ear as her heart did a little leap.

Jared was born in America, but his parents are from Jamaica, so that would make him Jamaican, right? He don't think so, this nigga is confused, and a convict. The accent came through when he was upset, but looking at him no one would know he was Jamaican. All he did was smoke weed and sell drugs all day long.

Jared is 6'3, about 190 pounds and a very nice looking guy, but his appearance says I'm sneaky as hell. His eyes say, I'm keeping secrets'; his whole persona is fucked up, but hey, never judge a book by its cover, they always say.

When Isis finally got over that sorry ass man she had been living with, Fred, and got herself together, she decided to give Jared a call. He remembered who she was and was happy to hear from her. He was good to her in the beginning, as all men are. They would go out for drinks; he would take her out to dinner and movies and would spend almost every night at her house. Isis thought it was a relationship; she was ready for him to move in. Then three months into their relationship he changed, he didn't want to commit which made her think he was probably married. He never invited her to his house, she didn't have his house number or address, and holidays he was like a ghost. I would always say, "Please wake up, the man is married or he's definitely hiding something. But Isis loved him anyway and she had no intentions on letting go."

When Jared was locked down for a year for violating his parole, she put money in his account, sent him food, but she was never allowed to visit. He would say to her, "I don't want you to see me like this." Bullshit! I told her that that muthafucka was getting visits from somebody. Come on, every brother on lock down wants somebody to come see their sorry ass. But love can makes a woman blind. Love is a muthafucka!

When he came home, he made a baby on her. He told her he was drunk and that the girl meant nothing to him, blah, blah, blah. That's all he's about, but again that's love for ya and she's still there supporting him. I tried to tell her to move on, but you know we have to learn from our own experience. Now he only comes around maybe once or twice a month, if that. He hits her off with sex, tells her things are going to change for them, that he's just going through something and then he leaves. She walks around for a couple of days on cloud nine before it hits her that he had; once again, told her another lie. It seems like we always fall for the one man who don't give one flying fuck about us. Soon you'll find a good man I would tell her, someone that will satisfy your mind, body, and soul. Hell, I need to be telling myself that.

Isis stood in her doorway, dressed and ready to go out, happy that Jared had followed through with the plan.

"Why you all dressed the fuck up?" Jared asked Isis when he came through the door, and looked at her from head to toe. His eyes were red as the devil and he smelled like he had just had a weed bath. "I thought you said we were going out?" Isis said turning so Jared could see the back of the dress.

"Man, I don't feel like going anywhere. I feel like chillin' here tonight with you, a'ight." Jared said, walking up the stairs toward the bedroom. "Now go in the kitchen and try to cook us a meal,"

"Hold the fuck up!" Isis yelled, throwing up her hands. "I just paid $252.39 cents for this dress and you talkin' 'bout you don't feel like going nowhere? You must've bumped your fuckin' head!" Isis said, pulling at her dress and walking in a circle and waving her hands, more irate than ever. "No, you gotta go, Jared, get out of my house! I can't go on like this anymore. You keep coming up in here with your lies 'n' shit whenever you want! I'm playing myself out fuckin' with you!" Isis said as she pointed toward the door for Jared to exit. Jared stared at her for a long while, and then slowly began walking back down the stairs. Once he reached her, he gave her a hug. "Dang, Ma, you look sexy as hell, especially with that dress on." He gave her a kiss on the lower back. That shut her right the fuck up. A bitch was frozen for a minute. Usually that would be enough to make you say I'm sorry to them.

"No," she whispered, with her eyes shut, enjoying the moisture from his lips, "Not this time. I'm not falling for your bullshit again." But that didn't stop Jared from kissing her bare back, trailing his long pink tongue all the way to the crack of her ass. "I know what you're trying to do, but it's not working... She was falling, hell she had already hit rock bottom.

Jared never said a word, he just kept nibbling, dropping to his knees and kissing her inner thighs. From there he went up under her dress, and Isis opened her legs wide enough so his face could fit between her thighs. He started kissing on her lips, then slowly began nibbling on them, before sliding his tongue up and down and inside her sex. He was moaning while holding onto the wall for security before she came in his mouth. Jared was nasty like that; he loved swallowing her sweetness. He stood, dropped his pants, and released his rigid dick, which was long and hard.

"Wait, we can't do this here," Isis said.

"Why not?" he asked, holding her hand.

"Cause I don't want stains on my carpet," Isis said, pulling her dress off then walking up the stairs towards her bedroom. "Besides, all of my toys are in the bedroom." You know I'm a freak, we can use them in any fashion desirable," She said with her eyes seducing Jared.

Jared ran up the stairs behind her, trying to make her stop so he could insert his penis in her right there on the stairs.

"I want to sex you right here on the stairs." he said breathing heavily. In a very deep, Jamaican voice, "Turn around so I can get it from the back," he said, while inserting a finger into her pussy.

Isis turned around and Jared slowly slid his dick inside of her. Their bodies were moving in motion; she was holding onto the wall and banister. As he started moving faster and faster in and out, Isis moaned, biting her bottom lip. Thoughts of how much she loved this man were flowing through her mind while he was sexing her. Faster and faster, his hips were moving, slapping against her ass. He was screaming and moaning and so was she and together they came.

He held her for a minute, then grabbed her hand, looked her in the eyes and said, "Now go cook us something to eat. I'm hungrier than a muthafucka." He smacked her on her ass before yanking up his pants and strolling to her bedroom.

Isis forgot that she had told him to leave. She took her just been fucked ass downstairs to cook. As she opened the refrigerator and contemplated on what to cook, she picked up the phone. "Stormie, what are you doing?" Isis asked, as soon as I answered my phone.

"Lying down, trying to go to sleep." I said with one arm over my eyes, lying on top of my comforter.

"Guess what I'm doing?"

"What, cooking?" I heard the grease popping in the background.

"Yup, I'm cooking dinner," she said, laughing.

"I thought y'all were going out?"

"We decided to eat at home, cuddle and watch some movies and maybe fuck all night."

HAVE YOU EVER…?
FIFI CURETON

"Way too much info, Isis," I said, moving my arms and laughing a little. "So is he staying all night this time?"

Isis hesitated a brief moment. "I guess he is. He's in the bed waiting for me to finish cooking. He ain't going nowhere tonight. I tried to make him leave, but he dropped to his knees, damn near in tears and started eating me out."

Cringing at the mental picture I said, "Girl, I don't care to know all that! Damn. Anyway, at least you enjoyed yourself."

"For real. Where's that big head boyfriend of yours.

"Right here sleep. I'll talk to you tomorrow about this nigga."

"What?" she whispered, as if he could hear us.

"Tomorrow, Isis damn!" I said, trying not to get into it. He just might be pretending to be sleep anyway.

"Girl bye."

"Bye," Isis said, hanging up the phone.

~Chapter Six~

After Bianca got dressed, she left her kids and husband to hang out with Hasson. She called Hasson and told him to meet her at Mommy house, like always, and they could go from there. Knowing Mommy did not agree to with that.

"Ma!" Bianca yelled out as she came through the door.

"What?" Mommy yelled up from the laundry room.

"Where you at?"

"In the basement washing clothes, why?"

"Did Hasson come by?" she asked poking her head down in the basement, sounding crazy for asking that question.

"Why would he come by here?" she asked, watching Bianca come down the stairs in her short skirt and long leather boots

"I don't know, Ma," she said, turning around to go back upstairs. Mommy followed.

"I don't know why you don't leave that nigga alone. He is married and so are you! I just don't get you, Bianca. Do you have a heart? 'cause I think God forgot to give you one. How can you be so cold? The one person that deserves the cold treatment is treated like a king. You give him your body like it's his." Mommy could for days. She talks even when we stop listening. Bianca kept it moving, walked outside of the house to sit on the porch, and waited for Hasson, not listening to a single word.

"You got a lot of nerve meeting him here at my house." Mommy stood in the doorway with her hands on her hips. "He can't come in here! And when he pulls up, I'm gonna ask him how the hell can he mess around with a woman who's happily married,"

Bianca not listening asked. "Anyway, where's your husband?"

"I know what you're trying to do, Bianca." Mommy said with a smirk on her face. "But it's your life and your business," mommy said walking back inside of the house, slamming the door behind her.

As Bianca set on the porch waiting for Hasson, she wondered if she could let him go. Her mind said yes, but her body said no.

They had dated years ago when she was a teenager. He moved away before her nineteenth birthday. He was more of a friend than a boyfriend. He would come over and sit on the porch with her, and from time to time, they had sex. Hasson was just another one of Bianca's playmates, as she would call them. Then he told her he was moving to North Carolina and she hadn't seen him since. Then one day while she was out shopping a man's voice yelled her name across the parking lot in Pathmark.

"Bianca!"

She turned, just in time to see this light skinned, medium built brother with dreads walking up to her. At first, she didn't recognize him, back then he was too skinny to shit now he was a'ight. Although he had a little gut from drinking beer obviously, he was still looking good. "Hasson! Oh shit, where the hell have you been?" Bianca asked giving him a hug, and loving the masculine scent of his cologne.

"I was living in North Carolina for a minute, and then I moved to Florida about ten years ago… I had to change my life." he said, admiring Bianca body noticing how well she bloomed from when she was nineteen, hell Bianca was skinny too, but she always had a big ass. "I had to get away from all the bullshit that was going on around me. I got married, had a couple kids," he said smiling. "So, what's up with you?" he asked, licking his lips and touching her elbow.

"I've been married going on two years now and I have four kids," she said, waving her big ass diamond in his face.

"Must be nice."

"It is. I live in Short Hills on a cul-de-sac."

He laughed a little a sound she remembered so clearly. "What the fuck is a cul-de-sac?"

"It's where I live. Maybe I'll tell you another time what a cul-de-sac is," she said, laughing at him, hoping he was joking about not knowing what it was.

"Here, take my number," he said, thrusting a paper with his number in it into her hand. "Give me a call, I'm curious as hell to know what a… cul-de-sac is. Let me walk you to your car."

"My truck," she corrected him, pointing to two cars down from where they were standing. "I'm parked right there, it's the red Escalade."

"Must be real nice," Hasson repeated, with an upside down frown.

"It is," she said smiling, admiring her truck. "I'll call you."

And from that day on, they'd been creeping around and meeting at Mommy's house, keeping their little get together a secret from their partners.

When the blue Neon pulled in front of Mommy's house, Bianca stared for a minute, trying to get a handle on who it could be. Hasson lowered the window so she could see his face. She jumped up before her Mommy could realize he had arrived, and hopped her happy ass to the small car.

Hasson was all smiles, happy to see Bianca. He wore a pair of Sean Jean jeans, a white tee, and a Starter Jacket. He stared at her, loving her in that short skirt, waiting on a kiss, like she normally did.

"Whose car is this?" she asked, closing the door and signaling for him to pull off. Mommy stood in the doorway--lips moving and finger wagging. Too late! Bianca thought.

"Why?" he asked, vexed.

"Cause I want to know, that's why!" she snapped. "Don't have me riding around in some other bitch car. I only ride in your car or your wife's shit!"

He stared at her like he wanted to knock the shit out of her, then replied,

"Yo, why do you say stupid shit like that?"

"Why do you do stupid shit?" she snapped back still looking around the car.

He stopped the car, staring at Bianca. "What the fuck are you looking for?"

"I'm not looking for shit, I'm just looking." She continued to look around the car from back seat to the front seat. "What, your ass paranoid or something? Look, baby, you know I don't give a fuck as long as you respect me." She said moving her head to the music coming from the radio. Her favorite words are, "I don't give a fuck!" Bianca knew she did give a fuck, but she didn't express her feelings to nobody, not even her husband.

Once they had started seeing each other, Hasson rented a one-bedroom apartment so whenever they got together they could bypass the hotels. The apartment was situated on a quiet street in Maplewood, New Jersey and had just enough furniture to look occupied. They met up about once or twice a month, but who knew how many times he went there without her.

When they first walked into the apartment, Bianca looked around, fell to the floor, and said to Hasson, "Come on."

"Come on what?" he asked, glaring at her like she lost her mind.

"I want you to take me right here on the carpet," she said, spreading out on the plush carpet caressing it with her hands.

Hasson stood there with a smile, turned on by the movements of Bianca, "I don't think so. I'm not getting any rug burns. That shit takes too long to heal and it hurts like hell."

"Okay, but if we go in the bedroom you're gonna have to do whatever I want you to do."

"Okay," he said grinning, picking her up and stumbling a bit as he tried to make it to the bedroom.

Bianca danced around the room taking off her clothes slowly, piece by piece and throwing them at him. Hasson sat on the foot of the bed smiling, loving every twist and turn Bianca's body made. He tried to touch her, but she pushed him away.

"I'm not ready," she whispered. "I need for you to get on your knees and do that thing you do with your tongue," she said in a very low voice.

Hasson stood and she slowly unbuckled his pants, pulling at his growing penis. He was enjoying the feel of Bianca hands on his dick. They hadn't been together in awhile, so he was ready. Bianca looked at Hasson and thought "What the FUCK! All of a sudden, Bianca stopped dancing, pushed him back on the bed, and sat down beside him.

He jerked backward, resting on his elbows while looking at her as though this was part of her sexual game.

"Hasson, I can't do this anymore. Please take me back to my Mom's house," Bianca said, softly.

"What?" Hasson yelled, with his erect dick pointing at the light fixtures. "Yo, you playing, right?" he said, calmly, reaching for her, placing his hand on her shoulder.

"No, I'm not playing," she said, moving his hand off her shoulder. "I can't do this shit anymore! Now, take me back to my truck," she said, putting her clothes back on.

"A'ight," he said pulling his pants up, trying to fit his hard dick in his pants. "Let's go!"

"Don't be mad, be glad," Bianca said, trying not to laugh at the print in his pants. "Listen, I need time to sort through some things in my life."

"No problem, Bianca." he said snatching the keys from the nightstand, showing his anger. They drove back to mommy's house without saying one word.

When he pulled up to the house, Hasson looked at Bianca and said, "Call me when you get your shit right." He turned to look out the window.

I should knock this muthafucka in the back of his head. She thought, she decided he wasn't worth it.

"Then I guess I'll never call your ass again," she said, getting out of the car and slamming the door.

"Ma!" Bianca yelled out, as she entered the house.

"Yeah!"

"Where are you?"

"I'm in the basement," she yelled. "So, are you finished fuckin' that man?"

Bianca just shook her head as if Mommy should be ashamed of herself. "Whatever ma. What did you cook?" she said walking towards the kitchen smelling the cornbread.

Laughter trickled from the basement. "You mean to tell me that man couldn't feed you after you gave him all of your husband's loving."

HAVE YOU EVER...?
FIFI CURETON

"Ma?" Bianca asked, walking back toward the basement door.

"What?" she said, coming up the stairs, prepared for an argument.

"Are we beefing?" Bianca wanted to tell her that she had broken it off with Hasson, but she didn't.

Mommy stared at her for a quick second, and then answered. "No, but you need to be asking your husband that damn question not me. You're the one out here fuck—"

"Okay, Ma, let me go before I say something to hurt your feelings."

Mommy is a good person but sometimes she can provoke a person into saying things that shouldn't be said. She won't stop until someone hurts her feelings.

"You already hurt my feelings when I saw you leave with that married man. Hell, you hurt me even more when you had the nigga pick you up from my house," she said, following her to the door.

Bianca got in her truck, never looking back. She had other things on her mind and would deal with mommy later, when she was calm.

As she drove up South Orange Avenue, she dialed her house.

Keith answered with a groggy voice. "Hello, hello."

"Hey, baby. Are you sleeping?"

"Yeah, but I'll wake up if you promise to make love to me when you get home."

She smacked her teeth, then smiled "Go back to sleep, Keith. I'll wake you up when I get there."

"And just how are you gonna wake me up?"

"Go back to sleep so you can find out how, and no cheating."

"Okay, bye," he said, rushing off the phone.

"Bye," she said, laughing. She hung up and dialed my number.

"Wha'chu doing?"

"Sitting here pissed the fuck off at Raquan," I said, with a serious attitude.

"What happened?"

"Girl, I didn't know. This nigga has been blackin' on me for a minute now."

"Why?" she asked, turning her radio down so she could hear every word I said.

"I think he's found himself a little friend to fuck around with. I heard him on the phone with some bitch and when I asked him about it he snapped and was like, "I'm a grown ass man and don't have to answer to no one.' Stupid muthafucka."

"No he didn't!" Bianca yelled "Leave his ass, then he'll see how grown he is without you."

"I'm not going to go that far. I haven't caught his ass doing anything yet," I whispered. "I need more tangible evidence. Bianca, I've got to go, I hear him coming upstairs."

Once Bianca got home, she walked into her bedroom to find her husband awake and ready to make love to her. He had candles lit and the remote to the CD within reach. An old school slow jam played on the stereo.

Bianca stood at the door smiling, but didn't move.

"It's been a month, Bianca. Let me make you fall in love with me again . . . tonight," Keith said, reaching out for her hand, kissing up toward the mid of her elbows then trailing to her upper arm. He put her favorite Blue Magic song on and was singing to her while slowly kissing her all over her body. Bianca was glad she had saved her lovin' for her husband. She allowed him to do what he wanted to her. He walked her into the bath where he had a tub full of water with rose pellets and bubbles inside the round shape Jacuzzi tub, and a bottle of champagne rested on top of the tub. Keith had beautiful red candles on each step of the Jacuzzi, which made the mood just right. Bianca didn't drink, but she planned to have a drink tonight. Keith whispered in her ear, that he needed her, and wanted her to feel his love tonight. "I think we lost it, but tonight I promise we will find it." He then slowly peeled her clothes off piece by piece. Bianca more excited than she could ever remember couldn't wait to feel her husband's manhood inside of her. He was already naked, all he had to do was drop his green, Ralph Lauren robe on the floor and Poke'em Peter was waiting. As they sat in the tub together, he sang and massaged her body. She drank the champagne and was floating on cloud nine. Bianca started kissing and massaging Keith's back, she joking said "If I could hold my breath I would go under water and taste you." Keith laughed he knew even if she could hold her breath she was going to, that was just something Bianca was not into. Instead, she sat on his lap and rode his dick until he exploded inside of her. Keith closed his eyes and whispered, "I love you, Bianca."

Bianca kissed him again and returned the words. Bianca looked at him, thinking, I have a fine ass husband. Stormie and Mommy were right; I don't need Hasson in my life.

She would put her efforts into her marriage and though she had kicked Hasson to the curb, he was known for bouncing back when he wasn't wanted. Hopefully, he was pissed off enough to stay away--for good.

~Chapter Seven~

"How can you talk to me that way, Raquan?" jumping out of the bed, ready to knock the shit out of him "If you want to break up, then do it. There's no need for you to be somewhere that you don't want to be," I said, walking around the room.

"I never said I didn't want to be with you," he said nonchalantly.

"Where did you go, Raquan?" I asked arms folded across my chest.

"Home, now don't ask me no more questions please."

Ignoring him, I asked, "Who was the bitch on the phone?"

"A friend. Are you happy now?"

"Does she know about me?" I asked looking him in his eyes.

"Please, what the fuck, should she know about you? What... You my best kept secret." He said with a slight laugh.

I was furious, I felt the blood racing through every vein in my body, I saw blood, but I kept my composure, I had to really ignore his last comment "There's no way I can keep accepting your bullshit and your female friends. Especially those type of female friends—friends today, fuck buddies tomorrow. I should be the only friend you need, Raquan!"

He listened for a minute then walked downstairs to the kitchen. I followed because the conversation was far from being over. "Man I can have friends if I want to. I never told you not to have male friends. My female friends were here before you and they'll be here when you're gone. You knew I had a lot of friends in the beginning, now you have a problem with it, you need to get over it 'cause they ain't going anywhere." he said calmly as if he didn't care that it bothered me.

A sick feeling came over my stomach and I was ready to break. "Is that right? When do you plan on letting me go?" I asked, shocked at the words flowing from his mouth, leaning on the Island on the kitchen.

"Stupid questions cause unnecessary arguments," he said, while looking in the refrigerator for something to eat. "You didn't cook?"

"No." All kinds of evil thoughts raced through my mind.

"Why not?"

"I went out to dinner with a friend." With that, I stormed toward the door.

"Who? What friend?" he said with a dumb look on his face. Then muttered, "Yeah right."

"I'm a grown ass woman." with a raised eyebrow, continued. "Who I chose to go out to dinner with is my business. I didn't know I had to tell you," I said with a smirk lifting the corners of my lips before I turned and walked out the kitchen. "Good night, Raquan. Lock the door behind you, please."

Minutes later, he eased his way in the bed, trying not to touch me. When I woke up the next morning he was already gone.

"Tania, Ja'Mil, get up! Come on, your school bus will be here in a minute!" I yelled down from my bedroom. "Ja'Mil, please brush your teeth today,"

Lawd knows my son barely washes his ass or brushes his teeth. I have to stay on his ass because he'll run around here for days without washing his ass. I tore his ass up for that one day. I was searching around the house trying to find out what that smell was. Come to find out it was his little ass smelling like fried garbage.

"I brushed my teeth," Ja'Mil said, coming into my room showing me his teeth.

Tania came upstairs fully dressed in Baby Phat jeans with the shirt to match and her boxing shoes. Ja'Mil threw on his Sean John jeans, a white tee, and his blue Timbs. My son liked looking thugged out, although he looked rather handsome. My kids are spitting imagine of me, especially my daughter; my son has big dark eyes, like his grandmother on his father side, and my daughter is skinny as hell, like her father side. Other than that, I couldn't deny them kids if I tried.

"Y'all ready?" I asked, still trying to get myself together. "Go get your book bags and jackets and wait on the porch for the school bus."

"Can we get a pop tart?" Ja'Mil asked.

"Go ahead. I'll see y'all later. "Love ya. Now go and wait for the bus." I said placing a kiss on each of their foreheads.

I looked through my closet, grabbed my black A.B.S. dress pants, a pastel yellow button-up shirt and black Gucci shoes with a Gucci bag to match. Thank God for quick weaves. I took a shower, got dress and left for work.

I hadn't heard from Raquan since Saturday. I'd call him when I get to the office, I thought, as I was driving to work. He leaves pretty early in the morning since he works on Long Island. He owns a couple of houses; a three family home in Newark on Tillinghast Street, and a two family on N.19th Street and one in Hillside NJ. He lives in the house in Hillside; it's a one family brick face home two-car garage and a backyard big enough for his dog Killer. He is not into shopping so his home is pretty plain. He said as long as he had a roof over his head, that's all he needs. He has a living room set, but no dining room set because he made the dining room his computer room. His bedroom only has a bed and a dresser. After the first time I went to his house, I did not intend to ever spend the night. Clothes were everywhere in his bedroom, the sheets looked liked they hadn't been changed since I don't know when. You could tell by the white limp balls on the sheets that he had the lowest thread count, in other words they were cheap. The kitchen had dishes stacked up damn near to the ceiling, and they smelled like everything, like Chinese chicken and Haitian food mixed; the smell burned my nose. The living room set was so raggedy that I was afraid to sit.

My first thought? What the hell am I dating? By the time I saw what he was really like it was too late; I was already in love with his nasty ass. I figured the only way for me to continue this relationship was to never go to his house again. I didn't want to hurt his feelings, so for a while, I'd tell him that I didn't have a babysitter, forcing him to stay at my house.

At first, my kids hated going over there, but it's much better now. I figured he just needed someone around to get it in order. It took me a minute to get his house clean; I had the boys scrub and dust, tossing out dishes and sheets that were no good, clothes that they couldn't fit. Raquan room and the kitchen look a lot better now; I don't mind staying the night. I had to buy him some 400 thread count sheets before I laid down on that bed, and the comforter had to go to. I went to Wal-Mart and racked on some lined and things for him with my money, because he wouldn't buy them. Raquan's boys shared a room, which basically had a bunk bed, dresser and a mirror. The dresser was used and worn down, the drawers didn't fit anymore. The moment I walked the door, the dresser went out. Raquan was mad but he got over it. I think he appreciated the help, he just didn't say it. I had to make him buy his boys some new dressers, 'cause he made them keep their shit in bags and told them 'y'all had no business throwing out y'all shit!" he was very strict with his boys and didn't allow them to do anything. The way he leaves his house is the same when he comes back.

Raquan was different from any guy I had ever dated. He wasn't materialistic at all. I used to spend so much money on clothes trying to keep up with the other jokers I dated. But with Raquan, he didn't notice whether my clothes were name brand or not. To him, clothes were clothes and Raquan wasn't picky; he liked whatever I bought him as long as he looked good in it. His boys would always tell me that I was spoiling their father and that I bought him too much stuff.

They would say, 'you should've bought that for us.' I wanted to take them shopping a few times, but Raquan would get mad and tell me that they didn't need anything. Those were his boys so I didn't argue with him. He has had custody of them since they were six; their mother is out of the picture. Raquan doesn't talk about her and I don't ask. I love and treat those boys as if they were mine when he lets me.

Lately, he has been coming over to the house without his boys, and when I ask where they are, he just shrugs his shoulders and says, 'I don't know.' But I know he knows. He's just don't want me to know. His attitude has changed toward me drastically. It's almost like he thinks he's too good for me, like I'm no longer worthy. He looks at me now like I'm dirt and that hurts. His eyes use to light when he saw me; now he looks pass me. I don't think he realizes how much it hurts me to see him looking at me like that, or if he even cares how I feel. I practice sometimes in the mirror what I'm going to say to him, about the way he looks at me, but by the time I talk to him the coldness in his voice makes me change my mind. I try very hard to keep the relationship going, but deep down I know this is not where he wants to be. Everything that I do for him and his kids, are because I want to, not because I can't. I didn't know by doing those things, I was turning him away.

My mother always tells me if you find a man certain ways you had better keep him that way. I see what she means now. As I walked into the job, I spoke to my co-workers. "Good morning."

"How was your weekend?" one of my co-workers asked.

"Not long enough," I said, pointing over her shoulder to the young woman, trying to ease pass her and sneak into my office. She is known around the office as the "whining bitch." My lips twitched as I tried to smile. "Hey." I said, unlocking my office door. She caught me, here she comes...

"Girl, I'm so tired," Aretha said, beginning with the same three words she always says.

Sometimes I close my office door when I see her wide ass coming. Damn, I wasn't quick enough today.

"Why are you tired?" I knew the answer, but I asked anyway, as I placed my pocket book and coat on the chair next to my desk.

"Tom came home at two in the morning, wanting me to cook for his drunken ass again."

"Hmm, I guess you got up and cooked then." I said turning on my computer never giving her eye contact and hoping she got the picture.

She folded her arms and looked down at my carpet, "Yeah, but I told him don't ask me again."

This conversation needed to end before it got started. Aretha doesn't know how or when to leave I pulled out my folders and place them on my desk then looked at her and said, "Well, I have a lot of work to do get done. So, can you please close my door on your way out? I started moving my mouse around pretending like I was looking up something.

She stood up straight, unfolded her arm and reached for the door saying I guess I should leave, huh?"

"Please, and close the door behind you," I repeated. I looked at a picture of a woman with a big Afro. Half of her fro covered one eye and the other eye is Green. The name of that picture is called "Green Eye." The picture hangs right next to my door so when I look up, I look right at her. A coat rack in a sofa that is filled with boxes of paper that were printed out is adjacent to the door. Once I close my door I am secluded from all things. I have a window behind my desks, but not a beautiful view at all. I get to see the trees and dumpster and shit. As soon as she left I called Raquan.

"What?" he answered dryly.

"What are you doing?"

"Storm, what you think I'm doing?"

"I guess we're still beefing, huh?" I asked, turning his picture around on my desk so it would face the wall. "Well, I guess you still beefin'."

"I'm going to call you later," he said, hanging up the phone.

The dial tone followed. I sat straight up, with the phone still planted on my ear. I called him right back.

"Did you just hang up on me?" I said with my elbows on my desk and my hand out like I was waiting on change or something.

"No, I said I would call you later," he snapped. "Any more questions, Ms. Luv?"

"Why didn't you call me Sunday?"

"I had things to do, I was busy."

"The whole day?"

"Yup. Any more questions?"

"Can I see you later," I asked, biting my bottom lip hoping his bi-polar wasn't acting up, cause I swear the man is Bi-Polar. Up today and down the next.

"Doubt it."

"Why?"

"C'mon, no more questions, I'm working. I'll call you later."

Dial tone again.

"I'm so stupid," I said, putting his picture in my bottom drawer.

The whole day at work, I thought about Raquan the man in my life. How he goes for days at a time not talking to me, not seeing me and not missing me. But yet, he don't want to break up with me. After work I wanted to call him, while waiting in traffic but didn't. I knew if I'd call him, he wouldn't answer the phone.

"Tania, Ja'Mil, come eat!" I said, putting the chicken and macaroni cheese on their plates. "Did y'all do your homework?"

"I need help," Ja'Mil whined.

"I tried to help him but he told me to get out of his room," Tania said, with a hand on her little hip.

I didn't feed into Tania's comment. "Go get your homework, boy! If you bring another F in this house, your little ass will be on a punishment 'til you're eighteen. Raquan calls me a house gangsta, because I'm always making threats to my kids and never following through with them. I don't agree with beating my kids for everything they do. If I did, they'd get their asses whipped every day all day. And who has time for that?

After dinner, I helped Ja'Mil with his homework and made both of them get ready for bed. The phone rang and I picked it up, hoping it was Raquan so I could cuss his ass out, hanging up on me two times in one day would not be tolerated.

"Hello," I snapped.

"What are you doing?" Isis asked.

"Sitting here doing nothing," I said, with a small sigh, walking into my living room and dropping down on my sofa.

"Girl, you sound half dead, you alright?"

"Yeah, and stop asking me." I said closing my eyes and stretching out.

"Isis didn't do it," she sang. "You need to cheat on that big head, bum ass man of yours, ol' dirty bastard! You need to find some outside dick; maybe you'll feel good about yourself. You don't need him anyway. Why the fuck is he mad at you this time?"

"I don't know," I said, rubbing my forehead, trying to make a monstrous headache go away.

"Oh, bitch, you know. Since when did we start keeping secrets from each other? You don't need to be in distress, Storm."

"Isis?" I said sitting up ready to cuss her out, ready to take the anger out on her.

"What?"

"Could you please shut the fuck up for a minute?" Damn! "I'm not worrying myself over him. Whatever and whoever he wants to do is his business," I said, trying to believe it myself. "Besides, two can play that game. If he thinks having female friends is all right, then he shouldn't mind me having male friends. Hell, he said he didn't give a fuck anyway." Shit, nigga don't get it fucked up, I may be a good woman now, but I am capable of being bad. Shit still in me."

"I just don't get it, men say they want a good woman, but when they get one, what do they do?" I asked, confused, with my eyes shut.

"They fuck up big time. A man likes a woman that doesn't give a fuck; he likes a bitch that keeps drama. Raquan ain't used to a woman like you; he probably dated projected bitches or hood rats!" Isis said in a rant.

I laughed a little, because Isis was angrier than I was. But I see that being faithful can get a woman hurt. I thought I was dealing with a man, but how does a woman tell when she's dealing with a nigga or a man? "Raquan tricked the shit out of me. I really thought he was different."

"Shit, in a way he is different, weird muthafucka! Girl, I gotta go," Isis said, getting ready to hang up the phone. "Get yourself some sleep, and stop waiting on that man to do right, 'cause he ain't."

"Aight," I put the phone on the floor and thought, I don't feel like playing a game; that is not why I entered this relationship, but since he wants to play, I guess I'll show him what a bitch is made of!

~Chapter Eight~

"When I tell you to do something, do it!" Isis yelled over the phone to one of her employees.

She has four people working for her and she thinks she's top shit of the year. But she'd better stop yelling at those geeky ass white boys. They're the ones bringing in the cheddar.

The high pitch secretary's voice came through the intercom. "Isis?"

"What!" she answered rudely.

"There's a young man out front who says he has an appointment with you today."

"An appointment?" she repeated, checking her calendar

"Yes."

Isis got up from behind her desk, only to walk out front only to pause at the wonderful addition to the scenery: 'Well, hello, Mr. Fine Ass Chocolate Brother,' she mumbled. He hadn't said a word to her yet, but her smile was in place anyway.

He extended his hand. "Ms--,"

"My name is Isis," she said, shaking his warm hand while trying to sound proper and sexy at the same time. "How can I help you? I don't remember setting up an appointment with you." Her smile widened. "I know I would've remembered you."

"Well, actually you didn't. I figured if I said that we had an appointment you'd see me," he said, with a flirtatious smile of his own.

Isis was melting. This brother was fine and he had the look of confidence. She looked him up and down, checking out his assets as well as his gear--a pair of True Religion jeans, a button up shirt with a white tee underneath, and a pair of tan and white Prada shoes... She inhaled sharply. Damn, the nigga smells and looks good. He must be wearing Jean Paul Gaultier. I wonder if he fucks good too?

"So, again, how can I help you today? She asked, losing the smile and

78

straightening her shoulders, trying instantly to look like a professional businesswoman instead of a groupie. "Know what, how about we step into my office and talk," she said, wishing she could fuck him on the chaise in her office. "Have a seat," she said, pointing at the chair in front of her desk once they had entered her office.

"So, I see you really like yourself," he said, looking around the office at all the pictures--which, of course, were of her. "By the way, the name's Tony," he said, before she could answer.

"Well, Tony, look through this portfolio so you can get an idea of what you want your web page to look like. I'll be right back."

Isis walked away thinking of a way to snag him for lunch. Maybe they would discuss business. Then our eyes met as soon as I walked into Isis' office. Who is this fine ass chocolate brother up in here? I know Isis ain't keeping secrets, let me find out. If you close your eyes and picture Morris Chestnut from the movie, Two Can Play That Game, that's who this brother looked like, --a thuggish Morris. He was taller, about 6'4 or 6'5, but with the same body build and haircut.

"Hello, I'm Stormie," I said, greeting him with my ring-less hand.

"Tony," he replied, standing slowly, looking me from head to toe, breast to ass. Not all men could do that without getting cussed the fuck out, but I promise he wasn't gonna get cussed out. I was looking right today. I had on my very low, very sexy Seven jeans, with just a touch of my thong peeking out, and a white Juicy Couture baby tee and my half cut jean jacket and a strip colored thin scarf wrapped around my neck.

"Where's Isis?" I asked, ending a very intense stare between us.

"She in the ladies room"

I felt a little nervous with him staring at me, so I said, "What?" cause I didn't know what else to say.

"Nothing, I just think you're a very sexy lady."

"Well, you're not so bad yourself," I said, blushing.

I hadn't had a compliment like that in so long that I almost forgotten I was sexy.

While Isis was in the ladies' room scheming on how to get Tony, little did she know he was already being got.

"Storm, what are you doing here?" Isis said with attitude, as soon as she entered her office.

"Surprise, I didn't feel like working today," I said, smiling as I swung around in her chair.

"Well, as you can see I'm very busy, so can you please wait out front," she said pushing me up out of the chair and pointing for me to exit the room.

"Oh, it's like that? Since when do I have to sit out front? Normally it would be okay, but not today, huh," I said, knowing exactly what that bitch was doing.

"No problem, Isis," I said, standing up preparing to leave her office.

"Isis, it's okay. Actually, I was getting ready to show Stormie the designs that I chose. I'd really like her opinion." Tony smiled as he looked directly into my eyes.

"Stormie? Oh, you two know each other?" Isis rolled her eyes so long; I thought the bitch was asleep

She walked over to her desk, sat down and began to talk to Tony, ignoring the hell out of me. It was as if I was transparent. I would make a suggestion and she would keep on like I wasn't there. But I didn't give a fuck, I was representing.

"I'm hungry," I said, looking at Isis.

"Why are you telling me," she said, with a 'who gives a fuck' look on her face.

"Well, I was hoping we could do lunch," I replied, with a mischievous grin.

"I'm busy right now, Storm. You go ahead; I'll talk to you later."

"If you don't mind waiting, I'll go with you," Tony suggested, touching my knee and looking into my eyes.

"I don't mind waiting. Isis, are you coming too?"

"I'm a busy woman and I have a lot to do, Storm. Unlike you, I have a business to run," she said, with daggers in her eyes.

"Tony, do you mind waiting out front for me, I need to talk to my sister," I said to him, holding my hands together as if I was about to pray."

"Sure, I don't mind. Are we finished here, Isis?" Do I need anything else? He asked, standing up.

"Yes, we're finished and you have everything. Thank you for your business," she said extending her hand to shake his hand with a small smile.

As soon as Tony closed the door behind him, I snapped on Isis. "What the fuck is your problem?"

"You! Popping your happy ass up in here, all unannounced and shit!" she slammed her portfolio down on her desk.

"It's because of that nigga, ain't it? I said, pointing towards her door. Please, girl, I'm too hungry to get upset over a man. Anyway you snooze you lose... now c'mon, let's go eat and please leave that hate behind," I said, pulling her up out of her chair.

She made a vomiting sound, laughed and said. "Nah, bitch, I had my eyes on him first. He's fine as hell," she said, biting her bottom lip, thinking of ways she could fuck him.

"Girrrl, fine is beneath that man! I could fuck him, Isis" I said, looking at the door as if he was still standing there. "I really could."

"I could too. Hell, I was in the bathroom planning to fuck him later, anyway. Come on, let's go eat, girl."

"You're treating, right?" I asked, walking out her office.

"Please, you better make Mr. Fine Ass Chocolate pay for lunch," she whispered, then laughed.

We went to eat lunch at a Chinese Buffet across from Madison Square Garden.

We enjoyed lunch, but, as usual, Isis brought hate. Tony and I exchanged numbers and I promised to call him later that night. He was really nice and could hold a conversation about anything. We talked about books, traveling, and most importantly, shopping which is an A+ in my book. Yeah, Tony would definitely do, he made me smile and feel good about myself.

During lunch, I wanted to call Raquan at work since I hadn't heard from him, but I said 'fuck it.' I was always calling him first, apologizing for something he did or didn't do. Once Tony walked me to my truck and I closed the door, my mind went to thinking about Raquan. I wondered what he saw when he looked at me; did he see an ugly woman with no goals, a needy woman. Was I too ugly for him? What the fuck did he see? Tony saw a very sexy lady, but I'm curious to know what my man saw. I would tell Raquan all the time how good he looked, but he never returned the compliment. I could have on the baddest shit and he'd walk away, never looking at me, or he'd get an instant attitude and not speak to me. If we went to dinner and my breast showed just a little, the whole night he would look past me. After he finished eating he'd be ready to go, and the son- of-a- bitch would walk fast, to the point I had to damn near run just to keep up. I would say to him 'we gonna get a cramp in our sides for walking this fast, hell we just finished eating.' he wouldn't respond, he'd just walk faster. Sometime I'd let him go; I got tired of trying to keep up. Sometimes, I wish he would just say, 'Ma, you look good as shit in that outfit.' I wish he would tell me how he felt about me.

When I would ask, "Do you love me?" he would just stare at me and never answer. One day, he told me to stop asking him, and I was like, maybe if you told me I wouldn't have to ask. Anyway, the more I think about shit, the more I realize how stupid I am for putting up with his ass. It becomes my fault if I let a man continue to hurt me, not his. He is doing exactly what I am allowing.

For the past month or so, he's been getting upset for stupid reasons. Once he got upset with me for asking him about his next-door neighbor. I simply asked why she was at his house all the time. Every time I came over, she was either there, getting ready to leave, or she was coming through the door. Once I popped up at his house because wanted to see him. I'd been calling and paging him and he wouldn't answer my calls or return them, so I went by his house and walked in because the door was unlocked. He was sitting between her legs smiling and joking while she was taking his braids out. When I saw him all smiles, I grab his hands and told him to follow me to his bedroom so we could talk. "What the fuck is this about? Hell, you could've called me to take your braids out. Are you fucking her! He didn't give me an answer and he didn't speak to me for a few days after that. He wouldn't even answer my calls. When he finally did call, he acted like he hadn't stopped speaking to me for a few days, as he always does. I didn't even bother bringing up that incident; I just left it alone.

One other incident happened when I came by the hair salon where he was at getting his hair braided. I came by to see if he wanted to get something to eat after he was finished getting his hair braided. It was a Friday and I hadn't seen him for over two weeks and barely talked to him on the phone- 'cause of course, he wouldn't answer. He looked at me and told me to go home; he didn't need me there watching him. I was waiting for him because the girl was almost done. Instead of going home, I went to his house to wait for him and, when he got there, he wasn't happy to see me. That muthafucka told me to go home! I didn't leave because it was late, so he left and didn't come back 'til four o'clock in the morning. I guess he figured he'd "punished me" by not talking to me for three days. Of course I called him, but I knew he wasn't going to answer when he saw my number on his caller ID. Finally, I left a message on his machine, "When you decide to talk to me again, you really need to let me know when we're having problems, because it isn't fair for only you to know." When he decided to talk to me, he told me he was mad because, I didn't speak to the beautician. I cussed his ass out that time; I told him, "I don't have to speak to a muthafucka if I didn't want to! I spoke to the bitch; if she didn't hear me that's her problem!" He then told me that she told him that I didn't speak and that was the reason he was not talking to me. He told me that I was to jealous. I have no choice but to be jealous; I'm dealing with a man who enjoys spending time away from me. Fuck that! I'm not apologizing this time. This stranger made me feel good about myself today. This is the reason why so many people cheat on their mate. This is the reason; I'm going to cheat on my mate. I never been the type of woman who gave a fuck whether or not a man saw me, spoke to me, or acknowledge me. I don't know when I turned into this type of woman, but I hope it goes away quickly because it is killing.

The cell phone rang, startling me, interrupting my thoughts. "Hello," I said.

"What's up?" Raquan asked.

"You tell me," I said, nonchalantly.

"Why you're not at work?"

"I had things to take care of." I said smacking my teeth.

"Like what?"

"What's with all the questions, Raquan?" You have a lot of fuckin' nerve calling and talking to me like we've been speaking all along!"

"You needed a break. Besides, I had a lot of running around to do. Listen, I'm coming over tonight. Where are you now?

"I needed a break? Or did you need a break? Which one?"

"Yeah, I needed a break, I needed time to think."

"Think about what, Raquan? Tell me what you had to think about for four fuckin' days!" I yelled into the phone.

"Things… Where are you at, Storm?" he said never raising his voice, not caring about how hurt I sounded.

"New York," I said, while thinking about ending this over the phone.

"Why are you in New York?"

"Having lunch."

"With who?"

"Listen, I'll talk to you later," I said, hanging up. "Yup… I'm going to cheat on this muthafucka, I mumbled after hanging up. I can't trust a man that needs more than me for a friend. It may start out innocent but it damn sure don't end that way. Hell, I use to be friends with men who had girlfriends, some even had wives, and believe me we did more than just talk on the phone. Do you think a bitch gives a fuck if a man has a woman? NO! And I don't need a man that cannot express their feelings. Fuck that!

~Chapter Nine~

"Hello," Bianca said, answering her phone. She sat in her kitchen watching her thirteen inch television that hung on the wall.

"What's up, Sis?" I asked, stuck in traffic, trying to get out of New York.

"Girl, you know I broke it off with Hasson."

"That's good! You should've done that shit a long time ago."

"I know, but he looked so hurt and upset when I told him I couldn't see him anymore," I realize that I do have a good as husband, and I prayed a long time for God to send me a man like Keith. Now Hassan's been calling my cell phone like crazy leaving me a lot of threatening messages."

"Like what? And what are you going to do about the threats?" I asked concern.

"I want to tell Keith, but how? Who knew Hasson would be buggin' like this, Storm."

"Bianca, just be careful." If that crazy fuck comes after my sister, Lord knows he'll get fucked up. My family may not be as close as some, but in times like this, we come together like Kool-Aid and sugar.

"I'm not worried about him causing harm to me. I'll cut the shit outta that muthafucka! But I can't keep my phone on cause dummy man keeps calling me back to back. Monday Keith answered my phone and Hasson hung up. Keith just looked at me then walked out the bedroom. Later that night he asked who that was that keeps calling. I told him that lately I've been getting a lot of prank calls. I'm gonna call him and tell his ass to stop doing that dumb shit.

"You should call his wife,"

"Then he'd call Keith," she said, sarcastically. "Don't help me Storm, let me call you back. I'm going to call Hasson right now." As soon as Bianca hung up the phone she called Hasson from her cell.

"Has why the fuck are you blowing up my cell? Are you fuckin' stupid?" She screamed into the receiver as soon as he picked up his phone.

"Why haven't you called me back?" he retorted.

"Maybe because I'm not fuckin' with you like that anymore!"

"How can you just up and leave me like this, Bianca? How can you break my heart? Girl, I love you. How can you fuck around with me for this long and not have feelings for me?"

"Please, Hasson, stop with the gay shit!"

"Nah, it ain't over, you don't even love that joker, you're only there for the money, the house, and the other bullshit. And I can give you that!"

"You can't give me shit, you broke bastard! How the fuck you gonna make me stay with you? How? You're not that good and neither is the dick! And for your information, I do love my husband and only my husband! You're what I call 'in the meantime.' That's all you were to me. And by that, I mean, in the mean while my husband was at one of his businesses, I'd let you eat my pussy, you stupid muthafucka. Now stop calling me!"

"Watch what I told you!" Hasson said before hanging up on her.

Bianca was upset… Hasson had made one too many threats and she wasn't about to let some man come between her and her family. Bianca called me back to tell me about their phone conversation. I told her to just be careful because she had a nut on her hands.

The ride from New York gave me enough time to think rather or not I wanted to stay in my unhealthy relationship. Now that I've met Tony we'll see what happens. Isis called me as soon as she got in from work. Of course, she wanted to know if I had called Tony.

"Not yet, but soon. Isis, I'm not in a rush. I may seem desperate but I'm not, bitch."

"Well, I guess I'll go to Pathmark then. I'll call you later," Isis said, before hanging up.

"I hate coming to this damn store. I'm going to fire that Mexican bitch or whatever her ass is,' Isis mumbled. "Excuse me, but can I use this cart?" she asked one of the workers. "I needed to get a bunch of shit" Isis continued to mumble.

"Are you talking to me or yourself?" a man's voice asked from behind. Isis gave him that 'nigga please' look and kept moving. He'd better go and get a job, looking like he was ready to rob the joint. 'I really hate this place,' she kept repeating in her mind.

"Excuse me, but you look confused. Like you don't know what to get," the stranger said to Isis.

"Can you please leave me alone and stop following me?" she said, pointing her finger in his face. "Let me find out your ass is a stalker."

"I'm not following you. It's just a coincidence that we keep ending up in the same aisle. Can I cook you dinner?" the stranger said, smiling at her, placing his hand on her shopping cart.

"No, but can you get your weird ass away from me before I scream," she said, noticing that he was kinda cute.

"Why would you scream, I haven't touched you… Yet," he said still smiling, and hoping for a smile from her in return.

"Okay, I'll have dinner with you only if you pay for my groceries," Isis said, finally giving him a smile.

"I'll pay for your groceries only when I know you're really going to let me cook for you," he said, picking up a loaf of bread before stepping off.

Damn, he was cute, Isis thought as she finished her shopping.

When she got to her truck, she noticed a business card on her windshield. The front of the card read: DJ'S STUDIO: We rent studio time, produce and make music for up and coming singers/rappers. She turned it over to read the back. "Call me when you're ready to have dinner."

Isis looked around to see if he was still in the area, and wondered how the hell he knew what she was driving. He really is a stalker, she thought. As soon as she got in her truck, she dialed the cell phone number on the front of the card.

"How did you know what I was driving?" she asked as soon as she heard his voice.

"Hello to you too," he said, laughing.

"Whatever?" she shot back. Are you a stalker?"

"Not at all."

"What's your name?"

"Damien. And yours?" he asked.

"Isis."

"Isis, huh? Are you cold or something?"

"Or something sounds about right," she replied.

"Wow," Damien said after a few seconds of being quiet. "So describe or something."

"I can't right now, but I'll warn you if I feel like a situation is going to bring on the or something, okay? Oh yeah, do you always follow women into grocery stores?"

"Not always, only sometimes. I figure if a woman shops for food then she can probably cook. I've been wrong a lot of times," he said, with a hearty laugh. "But I feel lucky this time." he said jokingly.

"Was that a joke? 'Cause it wasn't funny."

"I'm only playing. You're the first, and hopefully you'll be the last, woman I follow into a grocery store."

"Whatever," she said; as I asked you before, how did you know what I was driving?"

"I was parked next to you. My man was in the pharmacy picking up his prescription while I was waiting in the car. When you walked past me, I followed you in the store only to meet you, and then I realized I needed some bread."

"That's that bullshit, but I'll take it this time. What are you driving?" Isis asked, changing the subject.

"Does it matter?"

"No, but I want to know," Isis said, hastily. "You know what, it doesn't matter. I'll call you later; I need to get my groceries in the house. And by the way, I can cook." With that, she hung up. When Isis got in the house, she immediately checked her caller ID. Jared hadn't called her since his last visit. "I'm tired of this shit," she mumbled, "I'm so tired of his ass. All he ever does is lie, and my dumb ass keeps falling for his shit. I'm not waiting for him anymore; it's time for me to move on. " She prayed to God to give her the strength to move on.

Isis decided to cook herself a steak with fries for dinner, turn her ringer off, and cuddle up in her bed. She took about three tablespoons of Nyquil so she could go to sleep. She needed to get her thoughts clear.

You can be the baddest bitch, have the longest hair and the biggest income, it still doesn't save you from getting your heart ripped out and stomped on. What Isis' biggest problem was, she thinks because she's successful and has her own money, that a man will never hurt her, but she's sadly mistaken. I told her once before that it's because she is independent, successful and has her own shit, is the reason that men hurt her.

I tried calling Isis several times, but kept getting her answering machine. After not being able to reach her, I decided to give Tony a call. Yes, that fine ass chocolate brother from New York.

Clearing my throat before he answered, "Hello, may I speak with Tony?"

"This is Tony. You don't have to ask to speak to me I'm the only one answering this phone," he said recognizing my voice.

"Okay," I said, feeling like a teenager again "Are you busy? 'Cause I can call you back later?"

"No, I'm not busy. I didn't think you'd call," then he paused before saying, "And can I say again—I think you're one sexy sistah."

"Thank you again." I said blushing; I didn't know what to say after that. So I asked. "So, what do you do for a living?" we didn't discuss our careers at lunch.

"I'm a photographer. I have my very own legit studio and modeling agency in Manhattan."

"Why did you say it like that?" I asked curious.

"Because there's a lot of fake modeling agencies in New York, and they make it hard for real businessmen. I deal with only professional models and people that are serious about the industry."

89

"How did you hear about Isis?"

"Word of mouth. People are always talking about her style, saying some good things about her. Anyway, do you have a man?"

"Nope, but I have two kids though. And you?"

"No woman in my life, except my daughter. She's five and lives in Ft. Lauderdale with her Mom and Grandmother."

"How old are you?" I was hoping he wasn't younger than me 'cause Raquan is younger than me and I think that has a lot to do with his relationship issues.

"I'm thirty-three. Is that a problem?"

Good! I thought. "No, it's not a problem. I was just asking that's all." He sure didn't look his age. We talked on the phone for hours, up until I heard Raquan walking up the stairs. When he strolled into the bedroom, my whole attitude changed. I didn't end the call right away, and Raquan didn't say one word to me while I was on the phone. Eventually he told Tony that I'd call him back.

Raquan sat on the edge of my bed, took off his boots, switched on the television and picked up his bowl of spaghetti that he placed on the nightstand when he entered the room. He didn't say a word to me as if me being on the phone didn't bother him.

I placed the phone on the cradle and turned to him. I must be stupid for letting this nigga get this comfortable in my home. I said staring at him thinking and wishing the stares could set his ass on fire.

"Who was that?" Raquan asked, shoveling another forkful into his mouth.

"Please, I wish I would answer that question." I got up from the bed and strolled toward the door.

"I guess you went out and found yourself a friend, huh?" he asked, grabbing my arm and stopping me in my path.

"Raquan, get the fuck off me!" I said, snatching my arm away. "This is how you wanted it, right? Besides, why do you care? You said you didn't give a fuck about my friends or me," I said, shrugging my shoulders pacing the floor. "You walk around here like I should be lucky to have your black ass in my life," pointing to myself. "Shit, your fuckin' ass should be thanking God everyday for sending me into your life. I'm good as hell to you and your kids, and how do you show your appreciation? By treating me like shit!" I looked at him and waited for an answer. He sat at the edge of the bed, not really listening just looking at me like I had just lost my mind, as he ate his spaghetti.

"So you're not gonna answer me?

"You know what I'm sick and tired of you coming and going at your leisure and talking to me when you feel like it. I'm not sure if I even want to be in this unhealthy ass relationship anymore, if this even is a relationship. I think somewhere during the relationship you broke up with me, you just forgot to tell me! "

"Please, that's just dumb," he mumbled shaking his head.

"That's dumb, huh? You have me confused and not sure of myself Raquan," I said looking at all my perfume bottles. "I don't want to end it, but I'm afraid if I stay you might hurt me more than you already have, and I'm tired of getting hurt," I said with tears stuck in my throat, waiting for him to console me. "I've been hurt too many times by too many men, and my heart can't take it anymore. I'm no longer happy in this relationship," I said, turning around to face him again. And I really wasn't happy, I was just afraid of being alone.

"Oh, you're not happy, huh? You want to break up?" he asked, looking me in the face for the first time in a long time.

Normally, he would look around me. If he did look at me, it would be for a hot second. I would tell him that he was afraid to look at me, cause if he did, he just might realize that he do love me.

"Raquan, I don't know what happened in your life, but whatever it was, it handicapped you from expressing your feeling. I can't deal with this shit anymore. I need a man who doesn't mind acknowledging me, loving me, holding me, and talking to me," waving my hand, I said I need space to think.

"It's over then? You want it to be over?" He asked again, holding my hands, while looking into my eyes. That's all it takes? Threaten to break up and he "sees" me.

"I don't know what I want anymore, I'm so confused. How can you get mad and not speak to me for days? I don't understand how you can do that." I dropped my head trying to hide the tears." Do you realize how much pain you put on me? Do you realize how much I'm in love with you, and how much it hurt knowing you don't feel the same? It hurt when you stop speaking to me," I said letting the tears flow freely.

"That's just how I deal with things, Ma," he said touching my face and wiping a traveling tear. "When I'm upset, I like to keep to myself. Sometimes you do things I don't like."

"Like what? "Half the time I don't know why you're mad at me! I think you just wake up and say to yourself, 'I'ma be mad at Storm today.'"

"Please," Raquan mumbled. "You want to break up?"

"No," I whispered, stating the wrong answer, but that's how I felt. Like Jahiem said, 'Love is not a game that we play to win or lose.' He continued to wipe the tears from my face, then kissed me on my forehead, my nose, and then my lips. Once I closed my eyes, I let him take my body and my heart once again. He slowly took my clothes and placed his manhood in the palm of my hand and began to massage it. The whole time we were making love, I was thinking about Tony and our conversation on the phone earlier; especially the part when he kept saying how sexy and beautiful, and how he would love to be with me. After the sex I put my arm around him and kissed him on the shoulder, then asked "Do you love me?"

He sat up, looked in my eyes, gave me a kiss, and then said "Go to sleep."

The way he paused, I thought he was about to finally say yeah, but he didn't. He turned his back to me and threw the cover over his shoulder, closed his eyes and went to sleep. I know he's cheating on me, I feel it in my guts. A woman knows when her man is cheating, I don't need to see it, but I won't try to stop him that's for sure. Some women think by fighting or fuckin' up their man's car, clothes or whatever, it will make them stop cheating. It doesn't, it just pushes the man further and further away. What I'm gonna do, is me! Or Tony! I closed my eyes, turned my back to him and contemplating on cheating.

He shook me out of a sound sleep. Waking me three in the morning. "Was that a guy you were talking to on the phone earlier?"

It took a minute for that to sink in. "What? Raquan, I know you're not waking me up with that shit!" I sat up, staring at him.

"Well, was it?" he asked again, not acknowledging my anger.

"Listen, if you want to leave then leave, you don't have to start a fight!" I said, pulling the covers over my head.

Raquan leaned over, draping his heavy body all over me. "I'm not tryin' to start a fight and I'm not leaving, I just wanted to know"

"No, that wasn't a guy on the phone, it was Rhonda. Now can I please go back to sleep?" I said, lying.

"That didn't sound like Rhonda on the phone."

"Then why don't you tell me who I was talking to?" I said moving the covers from my head. "Why didn't you ask me this earlier?"

"I did, but you never answered me," he said, giving me a blank look.

"Did you have a nightmare or something? Is that why you're awake at 3 o'clock in the morning asking me dumb ass questions?" I said sitting up again. "Fuck, you wouldn't let me ask you questions at this time of the morning. You'd put my ass out if I did some shit like that. Anyway, we have to get up in a couple of hours, let's talk about this in the morning, okay." I gave him a kiss on the cheek and turned over.

"Oh, I see. You're trying to play me the fuck out, right," he said, grabbing the back of my neck. "Let me find out you're cheating on me, Storm. I will beat the shit out of you."

I hope this nigga doesn't think I'm scared of him, 'cause I'll fight him the same way I would fight a bitch, just harder. "Raquan, if you ever grab my neck again, I'll cook your bony ass for dinner!"

The next morning Raquan got up, kissed me and apologized. "Would you really cook me, Storm?" he asked, as he was getting dressed for work.

"Like you were a boneless chicken," I said, in the coldest tone possible. "I don't play the abusive relationship shit. I saw my Mother go through that shit and I refuse to ever let a man beat me like I'm one of his kids. I had to calm my nerves for a minute; I had to count to ten. As I lay under the covers thinking about Tony; his smile, his body, his scent I started smiling. I imagined him touching me, and with that thought I decided that I would call him when I got to work. My thoughts were suddenly interrupted by Raquan's voice.

"Call me when you get to work," Raquan said, before leaving out.

"Yeah, alright," I mumbled, pulling myself out of bed.

What Raquan doesn't know is that he changed me. All those days apart from him left me time to think about all the things that I didn't want in a man, and everything about Raquan was exactly what I didn't want. I had to put my thoughts about Raquan away for right now and get the kids together.

"Another day another dollar," I said to my co-worker Doris, as I walked by her to get to my office. Of course she followed me into my office. "You know they got rid of Aretha," she said, with smirk on her face, standing in my doorway.

"Yeah," I said absently. Aretha was the least of my worries.

"Well, you know she never did anything anyway. She just walked around here complaining about everything." Doris said in her Italian accent. Doris was a short, stocky lady with short red hair, and she did not like Aretha. She probably got her ass fired.

"Well, she had it coming then," Anyway, Doris, let me get myself situated and I'll come talk to you later. Right now I have a lot of shit on my desk that I need to take care of." I said, turning on my computer and looking at all the paperwork piled up on my desk.

"Of course," she said, then turned and walked out of my office.

I wasn't shocked that Aretha was gone. That girl was a pain in the left titty. Before I jumped into work, I picked up the phone and dialed Isis.

HAVE YOU EVER...?
FIFI CURETON

She answered on the first ring and I said, "Girl, where the fuck have you been? I was ringing your ass all night,"

"Good morning to you too," Isis shot back.

"Where you at?"

"Where did you call, stupid," Isis said, laughing.

I had to laugh myself. "Did you have company last night?"

"No, last night I didn't feel like talking to nobody, so I turned off my phone. I just felt like thinking," she said, in a depressed tone that gave me the impression that she was upset about Jared.

"So, what did you think about?"

"Everything, every fuckin' thing that's happening in my life," she vented. "I wish I was somebody else, and that my life was different. I pray to God every day to just be normal, Storm. I've been running from something all my life and I'm tired of running. I've always been told to be the best, don't settle for less, never want for nothing, take care of yourself, and don't trust anyone. Whatever happened to being taught how to love others or myself? I was never taught that. That's why I can't find love or, as soon as I find it, I lose it. There was a quick a silence before she said, "Storm, what's wrong with me?" then broke down in tears.

Shit! What a way to start the morning. "Don't cry, Isis." I can't stand to see or hear somebody cry, Hell, I might start crying and then I won't get nothing done. "Listen, how about we have dinner tonight and talk about something more positive?"

Sniffles echoed through the phone as she tried to get herself together. "Sure, I'll come by your house once I get off," she said, before hanging up.

I never heard Isis talk or sound like that before. I sent her an e-mail telling her that whatever the reason she was buggin', she would overcome it, and that if the reason was Jared, she needed to get over it quick and not let that man bring her to her knees.

But I knew Jared had her buggin'. She hadn't heard from him since his last visit a couple of weeks ago. He did that to her every time, he would come around then disappear for weeks. And she thinks she's in love with that joker, but I don't think it's being in love, it's just being in stupid. We don't like to admit when we're being in stupid; we deny that shit to the fullest extent. But I knew Isis would be alright, she was just going through some changes right now.

~Chapter Ten~

I spoke to Tony after dealing with Isis, and as soon as he said hello, I nearly came all over myself. I swear I need to wear a panty liner when I speak to that man. We decided to meet at Madison Square Garden on Saturday, and I was going to be there by any means necessary. Raquan works all day Saturday, so he'll never know I'm gone. Besides, he said he doesn't mind me having friends. One thing about me is I don't forget shit. His exact words were, 'I don't give a fuck if you have friends,' so I think Tony will become a good friend. While thinking about my upcoming outing with Tony, my phone rang.

"This is Stormie."

Raquan's voice blasted into the phone, "Yo, why haven't I heard from you all day?"

"I'm working, that's why." I said, frowning.

"Are you busy?"

"Kinda, sorta," I said, enjoying the fact that he was pissed off.

"I can hear you typing," Raquan said in a low tone.

"What do you really want, Raquan?" I said rolling my eyes gazing at the photo on my wall. "Listen, I'm going to New York Saturday with Rhonda," I said, before he could answer, knowing that he wouldn't call to check on me.

"Since when did you start hanging out with her?"

"I've always hung out with her, you were just too busy running around to notice," I said, sarcastically. "Listen, let me go. I've got to finish my work before four-thirty. I'll call you when I get home."

"Well, make sure you find a babysitter for tonight."

"Why?"

"Because we're going out."

"Where?" I asked, curiously, I had to look at the caller ID to make sure I was talking to Raquan.

"I don't know yet. Let me surprise you."

"Whatever. Bye, Raquan," I said hanging up.

Now he wants to surprise me. Well, I got a surprise for his ass too, I also wanted to get to know Tony and surprise him too. The phone once again broke into my thoughts.

"Hello, this is Stormie." I said with a huff.

"Stormie, you have to come over here right now!" Mommy yelled into the phone.

"Whoa, Ma, slow down. What happened?" I said sitting back in my chair so I could listen better.

"Hasson followed Bianca to Chantell's school and jumped on her. Chantell and Dee Dee were there and they jumped in it!"

"What!" I said damn near falling from my chair.

"Dee Dee picked up a brick and busted Hasson upside the head and knocked his ass out. Somebody called the ambulance."

"Is he dead?"

"No, but he was unconscious for a few minutes. They said his shit is all swollen," Mommy said with a bitter laugh as she paced the floor. I knew she was pacing because I heard her slippers every time she made a step.

"Hold on, Ma. I got another call. I checked my caller ID it was Bianca. "What happened, girl?" I asked as soon as I switched lines

"Girl, Hasson followed me from Mom house up to Chantell's school and busted my damn nose. I think its broken." she said touching her nose softly. "Girl, I tried to slice that bitch. When my girls saw the blood gushing from my face, they lost it. They jumped on Hasson like he was some bitch on the street. Dee Dee busted his head open."

"Mommy told me, have you called Keith yet?"

"No, I haven't thought of a lie to tell him yet. Chantell and Dee Dee were asking me who he was and why he hit me. I told them not to say anything to Keith. I thought the cops were going to take Dee Dee away.

"Why she was defending you"

"I know, but they put her in the car and questioned her. But some witnesses who saw what happened told them that Hasson jumped on me first and she reacted, so they let her go." Bianca was rambling.

"I told your ass to be careful."

"I know, but it's a little too late now, isn't it."

"I'm coming over after work."

I'll see you later; I've got to call Keith."

Damn, I forgot to click back over to my mother. She hung up anyway.

Once Keith picked up the phone, Bianca burst into tears. "Keith."

"What? What's the matter, Bianca?"

Bianca fearing the worse couldn't get the words to come out.

"Why are you crying, Bianca? What happened?" Keith asked again now fearing that something terrible had happened.

"Somebody tried to steal my truck! When I caught the guy messing with my truck, he busted me in the nose with something, and I think it's broken!" Bianca said, crying harder. The lie almost sounded believable to her.

"I'm on my way home right now!" he said, hanging up.

Bianca, wiped her eyes, gathered her thoughts, then turned to her girls and said, "When Keith comes homes, y'all tell him that we caught somebody trying to break into the truck, okay?"

Chantell and Dee Dee looked at their mom like 'What the fuck' but they didn't respond, they continued to listen.

"Then tell him that the guy hauled off and hit me with something in the nose then took off running. We don't know what the guy looked like either. Don't worry, I'm gonna get that bitch set the fuck up." she mumbled walking toward her bedroom to get ready for Keith.

She had a small cut on her nose, and her eyes were starting to turn black and blue. What if he had cut her throat or did serious damage? What if he had hurt her girls? She was scared and really needed to tell her husband the truth, but how?

Keith came through the door with five other guys who all look like they did security for somebody. All of them were well over 6 feet; three were big and black, with big ass stomach, and the other two, were brown skin with their stomachs sticking out as well. They work for Keith and they looked like they were ready to fuck a nigga up.

"Where was you at when this shit happened?" Was the first thing he asked when he walked in the room. He was quiet but, don't let that fool you, he would knock a nigga out if they fucked with his family.

As soon as Bianca saw Keith, she cried even harder. Not because she was in pain, but because she had gotten herself in some deep shit.

"Where were you parked at when this shit happened?" Keith asked, again mystified.

"Chancellor Street," she said, not expecting him to ask that question first.

Keith turned to one of his boys. "Yo, take her truck and ride around Chancellor and ask any and everybody if they know something. If they so much as look at a nigga, hold that muthafucka till I get over there!"

"A'ight bet," one of the guys said before leaving and waving for the others to come. Keith went into the bathroom, got a wet washcloth and washed Bianca's face off and told her that her nose wasn't broken.

"The next time somebody tries to take that truck let them, don't try to be wonder fuckin' woman." he said continuing wiping her face. "Shit, I'll buy you another one, don't fight over no truck; it's only material. I can replace that, I can't replace you, Bianca," he said, kissing her nose.

Bianca felt so guilty because she knew she had a good man. He didn't mind breaking down and letting her know how he felt about her.

"Let me ask you something?" he said, picking up her cell phone and scrolling through her incoming calls.

"What?" She said frowning looking at her phones in his hand, hiding her fear.

"Does this have anything to do with those phone calls you've been getting lately?" He stood over her, checking her phone, waiting for a reaction from Bianca.

"No. I don't know. Why would anybody want to hurt me? I think that guy followed me from Chantell's school." He had never checked her phone before, and it was a lucky thing Bianca had deleted all incoming and outgoing phone calls. She had put Hasson under a female name.

"He followed you all the way from Seton Hall?" He was still searching her phone for clues.

"What are you looking for, Keith!" She yelled, exposing her veins in her neck, getting up from the bed. "My fuckin' nose is cracked open and all you can do is search my fuckin' phone!" She walked over to him and snatched it from him. "I don't know who the fuck that guy was! We went to get something to eat out of that little restaurant on Meeker Street and I parked the truck on Chancellor 'cause there was no parking spaces on Meeker." Damn! She said turning off the phone and put it away.

The house phone rang in the middle of Bianca's lie. Keith answered it. "Hey, Mrs. Luv, he said, looking at Bianca. "She's all right." He paused. "The girls must be in their rooms, I haven't seen them yet."

Bianca, becoming more nervous walking around in circles while looking at Keith, and biting her bottom lip, she was afraid her Mom would let something slip without realizing it. In other words, she talks too much.

"Give me the phone, Keith," Bianca she said, holding out her hand.

Keith didn't say a word, and he didn't give up the phone either. He watched Bianca as he listened.

What is she saying, Bianca was trying not to look nervous. Keith began to walk out of the room, still listening to mommy

"Give me the phone, Keith!" Bianca said trying to snatch the phone. "Did she call to speak to you?"

"Why are you attacking me for the phone?" Keith asked, looking at Bianca like she had lost her damn mind. "Well, Mrs. Luv, here's your crazy daughter," he finally said, handing the phone to Bianca. "I hope you feel better." he said, checking his pager. "I'll be back. I'm going down to Chancellor. My boy just two-wayed me. I hope he found somebody, 'cause I wanna do this muthafucka in. Stay in the house until I come back, okay?" he said, kissing her on the nose again.

"Okay," she said, wishing he would hurry up and leave so she could question mommy.

Keith hadn't made it all the way out the door before Bianca asked, "Ma, what were you saying to Keith?" she said in a whisper, peeking out the door again.

She paused for a long time before replying, "Nothing. I was just telling him about my doctor's visit and all the medicine the doctor gave me, why? You thought I was talking about your little adventure today?"

"Please don't tell him about Hasson," she said, looking at her nose in the mirror "I told him somebody tried to steal my truck while I was on Chancellor. So him and his friends are out looking for the guy now." She giggled a little, though inside she feared that the truth just might come out.

"That's not funny. You need to stop your mess, Bianca."

"I'm trying, but I don't need any lectures right now. Ma, hold on, my phone's beeping," Bianca said, before clicking over.

"Hello."

"I heard you got your wig pushed back," Isis said, laughing.

"Fuck you, bitch! Hold on for a minute, Mom's on the other line," she clicked back over and said, "Ma, I'll call you back." She switched to Isis. "Damn, news travels fast."

"Stormie e-mailed me and told me what happened. How's Dee Dee?"

Bianca got up from her chaise lounge, walked out of room, and down the stairs toward the kitchen, while talking to Isis. "She's alright, just a little shaken up. Shit, she thought she killed the man. I was kinda hoping the muthafucka was dead, so he would be off my back."

"You wasn't wishing that shit before, and you damn sure enjoyed him on your back. Honestly, Bianca did you really think it was gonna be that simple to walk away? Obviously the man cared about you and you hurt him. Now he wants to hurt you back and try to destroy your happy home. How can you be so naïve, Bianca?"

"What don't tell me you feel sorry for Hasson?" Bianca asked walking around her home, realizing that despite the lies and cheating she was very fortunate to have Keith in her life.

"No, I don't feel sorry for him, but I don't want you to be oblivious to the obvious either. I don't want to lecture you, but you really need to have an honest talk with your husband. Listen, I gotta go, but we're coming over after I get off work."

"We who?"

"Me, Storm and her kids. I'll see you later."

"Do you think we should tell Keith what really happened?" Dee Dee asked Chantell as they sat on the bright blue sofa in the center of the basement room.

"No, Bianca said not to tell him."

"What if that man tries to hurt her again? What, we just keep lying for her? I don't care, I'm going to sneak and tell Keith." Dee Dee was almost in tears, scared of the thought of that man coming back to hurt their Mother again. "What if we weren't there with her? She couldn't see when he hit her because blood was everywhere. I was scared, wasn't you?"

Chantell is the type of person that doesn't show too much emotion. "Yeah, I was scared." She laughed a little. "Shit, I didn't know who the fuck that was hitting Bianca. All I know is when I saw blood I tried to kill that muthafucka. I don't think he knew we were with her cause he jumped when we ran up on his ass. Where did you find that brick?"

"I don't know. I don't even remember picking that bitch up. All I know is he was laying flat on his face and I thought I had killed him. I was ready to run when he didn't move. Bianca is so lucky we were there to save her ass."

"Who called the ambulance?" asked Chantell.

"One of the bystanders, I guess."

~Chapter Eleven~

I went to my mom's house after work so we could talk about Bianca and her situation.

"You know, I don't know what's wrong with my child," Mom said, shaking her head. "I didn't raise y'all to be like that."

"I'm not like that," I quickly interjected. Mommy would get mad at the whole family if one of us did something wrong.

"Please, you messed around with married men yourself. I don't know why my girls would degrade themselves like that," she said, still shaking her head.

"Mom, don't start on me because Bianca got you all upset," I said walking toward the front door, looking for my kids so we could leave. I knew exactly where this was going. As soon as we make a comment about the other sibling, she throws shit in the game. "Remember, we were talking about Bianca, not Stormie. I know I made some bad decisions in my life, but I dealt with them and now I've moved on, damn!" I mumbled, grabbing the keys to my truck. "I'm on my way to Bianca's house; I'll talk to you later."

"I'm going with you," she said, going into her room to put on some clothes. I really didn't want her to ride with me because she was gonna start talking crazy and shit, plus she already pissed me off. My cell phone rang and I answered with, "What?"

"I'm on my way to Bianca's house, meet me there," Isis said, then hung up.

I called Bianca to let her know that we were on our way over. She was bitching about us coming over.

"I don't need y'all to come over, I'm all right," she said.

"I know you're all right. I'm really coming over so I can see how much damage he caused to your nose," I said, jokingly "And to make sure Dee Dee's all right." Then I mumbled, "And to bring Mommy."

"What, Don't bring mommy! I don't want to hear her shit right now. I'm not gonna open my fuckin' door," she yelled. "Mommy didn't know how to talk to a people. She was forever disparaging somebody and I'm not in the mood for her criticism."

"I know you don't, but she wants to come. I'm not staying long anyway so don't worry," I added,

"I'm ready," Mommy said, waiting for me at the door. "I'll be back," she yelled out to my father, who didn't take his eyes off the television, hell he probably didn't hear her, since he had the volume turned up to the max. That's why he never knows what's going on, he's always watching television.

"Hello," Isis said, answering her cell phone.

"What's up, Ma?" Damien asked.

"Nothing," she replied, "Actually I'm on my way to Short Hills."

"You're going shopping?"

"No, I'm going to my sister's house." Listen, I hate driving and talking on the phone, so let me call you back,"

"Alright, you do that," he said in a hushed tone. "Wait, listen! I really want to get to know you and not just physically."

"Whatever, we'll see," she said, before hanging up. 'I don't trust men anymore,' she whispered. 'I doubt if I'll ever open up to another man the way that I opened up to Jared and Fred.'

Fred was the cat she was living with when she first moved to Newark. He used to beat on her and spend all of her money on himself, and made her pay all the damn bills. He helped out around the house when he was in a good mood, but she did the majority of the housework.

Isis was so blinded by love that she didn't realize how much Fred had dogged her out until after he had left. Later she found out that he had gotten married to some chick from his job he had been dealing with for a while. Now, she had Jared to deal with, which personally I think he's involved with someone, if not married.

Isis pulled up in front of Bianca's house and shook her head. This bitch was living the life. Living in a goddamn mansion yet fucking with some nigga living in a tenement. Now that was asinine. 'She needed her nose busted the fuck open,' Isis mumbled taking off her seatbelt and grabbing her bag. As she walked through the door, she said, "Girl, look at your face." She slowly walked around Bianca, examining her face. "Your eyes are going to get black, blue and purple before it's all over with. They're already swollen. Where's Keith?"

"Out looking for the joker that did this to me," Bianca said, letting out a nervous laugh, trying to hide the fact that she was embarrassed. "Stop looking at me like I'm some kind of sideshow freak," she said, walking toward the mirror in the hallway so she could see her face.

"You are a sideshow freak. When are you gonna accept it," Isis said trying to sound like she was joking, but she was dead serious. "Bianca, from the look of this house one would assume that Keith loves and wants to spoil you. But from the look of your face, you don't appreciate it. How do you thank him? Oh," she said, putting one hand over her mouth, pointing a finger at Bianca. "I know, by fuckin' around on the man. I wish I could meet a man like Keith; I would love him forever. Since I've known you, I've never heard you complain about him. Did he do anything to annoy you, what caused you to cheat?"

"Shut the fuck up, bitch! You watch way too many soap operas, I am hurt." Bianca admitted, and I do love my home. Every day I thank God for Keith." Bianca took another look around her home. "I don't know what the fuck I was thinking. I was just doing something to pass the time, ya know." She said walking into her living room.

"No, I don't know," Isis replied. "Do you love Keith?"

"Bitch what'chu think" She said looking at Isis with her nose turned up. "It's just sometimes he can be so . . . boring. We don't do anything together, if I go to the mall it's with you, Stormie or my kids. I go to dinner with my kids... I do everything without him. So I went looking for some fun, which I regret now." Bianca noticed my truck pulling up the driveway, and walked towards the window and pulled back the curtain. "Oh boy, here comes my mother and Stormie." Her attitude changed, because she knew mommy was gonna say some dumb shit, and she had to prepare herself for it.

106

HAVE YOU EVER…?
FIFI CURETON

"Damn!" I screeched as soon as I saw Bianca's face. "What did he hit you with?"

"See, Bianca," mommy whined, ready to cry after seeing her baby's face. "I told you to leave that man alone, didn't I?"

"Ma," Bianca said, trying to walk past her to go into the kitchen, "can we not talk about the 'I told you so's please? Not now, I'm not in the mood."

"Okay, I won't tell you anything anymore, I mean it. Whenever I try to help my kids, y'all get all upset at me. I didn't do it. Hell, I was trying to teach you some prevention methods, Anyway, let me go check on Dee Dee," she said, walking toward the basement stairs.

Bianca had the basement done up for her girls. They had their own room, they had a phone, television with cable and computers they only had to come upstairs to eat or cook. Sometimes they would chat with each other online just because they could.

"Guess what?" Isis said smiling, twirling her hair.

"What?" I asked, eating some of the food Bianca cooked.

"I met this guy at Pathmark yesterday and he left this on my windshield," she said, handing me his business card.

"He needs me to hook him up with a better business card," Bianca suggested, reading the card over my shoulder,

"I know that's right," I said, laughing at how plain and ugly the card had been designed.

"Doesn't he know his business card says a lot for him when he's not around?" Bianca added.

"I want to do his website for him, but I'll discuss that later with him," Isis said softly. "Right now he wants to get to know me. I ain't gonna lie, I'm scared to get close to another brotha because I always end up hurt," Isis said, eating and looking at her food like she was talking to the food. "I might just wait until Saturday to call him."

"Why Saturday?" I asked, perplexed.

"I don't know, just because it's Saturday," she responded, sarcastically. We stayed for about three hours, laughing about how Dee Dee had busted Hasson in the head. It's funny now, but it wasn't funny earlier. My brothers heard about the incident and was ready to kill Hasson, but Mom told them to mind their own business. She didn't tell them the real reason why Hasson had did it and how they knew each other because she was afraid that one of them might tell Keith.

"Hand me my phone, Tania. Hurry up, it's ringing! I yelled pointing towards my cell phone. "Hello,"

"Where you at?" Raquan asked as soon as I answered.

"At Bianca's house," I said to Raquan… "Okay, I'll meet you at the house," I hung up the phone and turned to Bianca and Isis. "What the fuck is y'all looking at?" They were looking all crazy-eyed.

"Girl, your man, your business," Isis said, throwing her hands up as if she were giving up on me.

"I take it he's not mad at you anymore?" Bianca threw in, looking like our mother.

"Hey, I'm human you know. I can't just walk away like that, I do love the man," I said, gathering my things so I could meet Raquan at my house. "C'mon, Ma, Tania and Ja'Mil," I said, walking toward the front door. I saw how everybody was looking at me and I knew exactly what they were thinking--that, I was stupid for talking to him. But hey, it's my life and nobody's perfect.

"One day you gonna realize that you deserve better." Isis said.

"Yeah, and one day you will realize the same." I threw back at her.

"Whatever" she mumbled then turned to Bianca. "Listen, be careful and take care of yourself," Isis said to Bianca as she gathered her things, too. "And the next time he runs up on you be ready to end his life because it ain't over. He's gonna keep hounding you until you're seriously hurt or dead." The way Isis was talking was like she had experienced with this type of relationship. She made me wonder why she really left Texas. The truth will come to light, that's for sure.

'Before I go home, I'm gonna call Tony,' I said to myself, as we were walking towards my truck.

"What's up, Tony?" I asked, as soon as he said answered.

"Just sitting here thinking about your smile," he said.

Now I felt like a damn teenager, again. "Why didn't you call me? I was waiting for your phone call,"

"I didn't know if you were busy. Besides, I can wait for your call. I'm a very patient man," he said, sounding sexy as hell.

I swear his voice makes my pussy thump and get all wet. I'm so ready to sleep with him even though I just met him. I have such a strong attraction toward him that I can't fight the feeling.

"Listen, about Saturday, what are we doing after lunch?" I asked, hoping we could have some hot sweaty, no holds barred sex.

"Whatever you want," he said, seducing my earlobes.

"Bet. I'll be seeing you then," I said, before hanging up. I felt my Mom staring and my face started getting hot. "What Ma?" I said, not bothering to look at her.

"I don't have anything to say." She turned and looked out the window, never saying another word.

By the time I got home, Raquan was already cooking. "Y'all go shower and get ready for bed." I told my kids. "Hey, baby," I said to him, giving him a big hug,

"What's up?" he said dryly, not returning the hug. He stood there waiting for me to let go of him.

"Why can't you hug me back?" I asked frustrated, thinking this was the reason why I needed someone else in my life.

"C'mon, Ma," he snapped. "I'm not into all of that."

"Well, you need to get into it. Little things like hugs is what makes me happy," I said, walking upstairs to my room to take a shower and get ready for bed.

He really thinks that acting so hard is going to keep me around. I show him in more ways than one how I feel about him, and he can't show me shit. We don't make love the way we used to, and if his lovemaking determines how he feels, then he certainly doesn't care. Sometimes I fantasize about love and how I want a man to love me. How my man would come up behind me, hold me and kiss my neck. Then he would whisper softly and seductively in my ear, 'I love you.' The thought of a man doing that to me brings tears to my eyes. I swear if I had a man like Keith I'd never cheat on him. I wouldn't even entertain the thought. I should whip Bianca's ass on general principle. When I look at Raquan, I don't know what I feel anymore. It's almost like I'm making myself be in love with him. The weird thing is I feel in my gut that this is not the man for me, but I can't get the strength to leave even though he gives me absolutely nothing but headaches and hard aches. Keith surprised Bianca with gifts and trips on a consistent basis. One day she walked into her garage and in there was a big ass gift, wrapped in gold paper with a big red bow. The note that was attached read: "To my beloved wife. Please unwrap carefully. It took me all night to wrap this gift, but for you it was worth it! Love your husband for life." He wasn't a poet, but he knew how to make her feel good. Why was it so hard for Raquan?

She slowly started to un-wrap her gift. She needed a ladder to reach the top. By the time she was finished, she was tired. The gift Keith brought her was a fully loaded Escalade SUV.

I was full of jealousy and, of course, he didn't want to hear about the gift. He hung up on me when I tried to tell him. When I tried to call the nigga back, the call went to voice mail. He's stupid like that. He never likes to hear about Keith and Bianca.

I don't understand why Bianca cheated on Keith. I used to wish I met him first because she didn't know how to treat that man. I don't feel sorry for Bianca, I feel sorry for Keith because, when he finds out the truth, he's gonna flip on out her ass. I wouldn't be mad at him if he busted her ass, which I doubt, cause she'd murder his ass.

Tonight, I'll be sleeping in a very long maxi-pad. And no, my period wasn't on, I just don't want him touching me. I'm saving myself for Tony. I need to have sex with someone other than Raquan, maybe then it would be easier for me to get away from him. It's not like he's having sex with me only anyway.

110

Suddenly, my phone started to ring. "Hello," I said, answering my phone.

"Girl, Keith is buggin'. He took my fuckin' truck from me," Bianca said, crying on the other end.

"Why?" I said, sitting straight up in the bed, thinking he had found out the truth.

"He said it's too dangerous to drive," she said, between sniffles. "He wants to go look at a new car tomorrow, but I'm not going outside with my face like this."

"And why are you crying again? I don't get it." Finally she was feeling guilty.

"I don't know why I'm crying. I'm not sleeping in the same room with him, I need space." She paused for a few seconds. "My boys are ready to kill the nigga who did this to my face. I can't even get them to go to bed; they're walking back and forth, taking turns checking up on me."

Before I could listen to Bianca carry on any further like a fuckin' victim, I had to let her know that she needed to get to know herself a little better. It's hard trying to give advice to a person that knows it all because they don't hear you. But I'm taking a chance tonight while the ball is in my corner.

"It would be a lot easier to deal with this whole situation if you start being honest with yourself," I said, wondering what makes Bianca do the shit she does. "Sleep in the room by yourself, but while you're there don't just sleep, do some thinking about you, your husband, your kids and, most importantly, your life. I've got to go, it's late. I have three more day of work and I want to hurry up and get that over with. Goodnight, I'll talk to you tomorrow" I said to Bianca, before hanging up. I couldn't take being on the phone with her for another minutes

Raquan came upstairs, full and ready for sex. He was stopped by the long maxi-pad that ran from my stomach all the way up my back. 'Not tonight,' I sang to myself, pretending to be asleep.

Bianca told Keith she wanted to sleep in the guest room by herself. "I need time to think," she told him. "I'm still in shock and I don't want you looking at my face like this."

"I don't mind looking at your face you're still beautiful to me. A little swollen, but still beautiful," Keith said, kissing her face.

Bianca couldn't stop crying as she said, "I just want to be by myself tonight, Keith. Did you find out anything while you were out?"

"Not one thing and that seems strange to me. I'm gonna buy you a little simple car tomorrow. Get you an Intrepid or something," he said, hugging her, but pulling away when she winced.

"I don't need a car, I could drive my truck," she said, pulling away from Keith. Next time I'll be better prepared. As a matter of fact, there won't be a next time," she added, hoping he would let things go.

"I know, because I'm taking the truck and buying you a car tomorrow," he said, walking out the room to go Chantell and Dee Dee's room. "What up" he asked walking down the stairs. By now he was standing in their living room waiting for them to come out of their rooms.

They walked out and said, "Huh?" at the same time.

"How y'all doing?" he asked, hugging them both. "Alright?" he added.

"Yeah, we're doing okay," they said in chorus.

"That's good," he said. "I guess y'all were scared, huh? Why didn't y'all help?" he asked, before they could answer the first question.

Dee Dee looked at Chantell, waiting for her to say something, but she didn't. "It happened so fast, we didn't have time to help," Dee Dee finally said, walking toward the sofa "We couldn't do anything but stand there, we couldn't move."

"I was scared," Chantell mumbled. She hated to lie, she rather not talk if she had to tell a lie, but Dee Dee she was good... "When she fell, we ran over to Bianca to help her up and that's when he ran to a car parked around the corner," Dee Dee said.

"Wait a minute, your mother fell?" Keith asked, surprised. "I didn't know she fell, he must've hit her pretty hard, huh? Did you see what kind of car he was driving?"

"No, I was too busy trying to pick my Mother up," Dee Dee answered cautiously.

"What about you, Chantell?"

"Nope. Well, I gotta go finish my report." She then turned and walked back into her room.

"Dee Dee, why did you get suspended from school?"

Smacking her teeth, she said "Cause the stupid teacher put her hands on me and I pushed her down," she said, talking fast and moving her neck.

"Oh, so you wanna be a gangsta, is that what it's all about?" Keith asked, pissed off.

"This has nothing to do with me being a gangsta, it's a matter of respect. I told her not to touch me, but she did," Dee Dee said, moving her hands in motion and shrugging her shoulders.

"I pay a lot of money to keep you in that school. If you want out let me know, don't have me wasting money. Money doesn't come easy."

"I want to stay in that school, I just..."

"Then act like you do Ms. Dee Dee," Keith said, cutting her sentence short.

He turned and walked back upstairs. When he got in the room, Bianca was asleep on top of the covers. He gently removed her clothes and put her to bed. He then gave her a kiss and whispered goodnight in her ear. Keith sat on the edge of the bed for a minute looking at the television, but not really paying attention to what was on. 'What is going on,' he said to himself. He knew the girls were lying about something, he just didn't know what. Keith stood up and walked out of the room and slept in the guest room.

Bianca woke up in the middle of the night only to find her husband not there. She walked to the guest room where he was sleeping. She climbed into bed with him and whispered, "I love you too," in his ear and fell back to sleep holding him tight.

"Are ya'll ready?" Keith asked Chantell and Dee Dee.

"For what?" Chantell asked, slowly and circumspectly.

"I'm taking y'all to school today," he said, walking out the kitchen.

"Well, I don't need a ride cause I don't have class today," Chantell said.

"That's okay, you can ride with me to get Dee Dee back in school!" he yelled into the kitchen.

"Why does he want me to go?" Chantell asked Dee Dee.

"Because I bet he suspects something. I think he knows that we're lying." she tried to whisper holding one hand up to the side of her mouth.

"You real silly Dee Dee."

"Why I gotta be silly," she said, walking upstairs to Bianca. "How's your face today?" she asked, entering Bianca's room with a smirk on her face and laughing a little.

"Don't fuckin' play with me, Dee Dee. It's too early in the morning for your jokes. I suggest you go and get yourself ready for school," she said, walking into the bathroom to look at her face.

She was black around her left eye. It wasn't completely shut, but it wasn't completely open either. She stood there staring at her reflection, shaking her head. Keith walked in behind her, pretending like he wasn't looking at her, but he was. He stood there for a minute then walked out the room.

"Let's go, Dee Dee," he said, snatching up the keys to the truck. "Bianca, be ready when I come back. Find some makeup or something to cover that bruise around your eye."

"What bruise?" Dee Dee said. "That's not a bruise, that's a black eye that's swollen. You can't cover that with makeup," she said, sarcastically.

"Go get your sister and meet me in the truck," Keith said, ignoring Dee Dee's comment. He didn't talk to them the whole time they were in the truck. Keith was mad but didn't know why, he just had a feeling they were keeping secrets from him. Keith and Chantell dropped Dee Dee off, and as soon as they left the school, Keith drove down to Newark to the restaurant that Bianca claimed they were at yesterday.

"C'mon, let's get some breakfast," Keith said to Chantell.

She got out of the truck and walked into the restaurant, not looking at Keith. She was mad, but didn't show it. He kept his eyes on Chantell, hoping she would notice somebody from yesterday's attack. He ordered breakfast to go and called Bianca to see if she wanted something. He didn't tell her where he was at because he didn't want to hear her mouth.

"Did you see the nigga that hit your Mom?" Keith finally asked, as they were walking back to the truck.

No, because it didn't happen around here you dick, Chantell thought to herself, but she finally said, "No."

"I'm taking your Mom to buy a new car today. She won't be driving this shit, not until I find out what really happened and who tried to steal it. If he tried once and didn't succeed, then he'll most definitely try again."

Hasson's angry voice blared from Bianca's voicemail. "Yeah, bitch, you think it's over, you stupid bitch! It ain't over! I'm gonna rape the little bitch who hit me with that brick. That's right, I'm gonna take her virginity, me and my boys, and turn her into a little slut just like her momma! So you better keep a good eye on her skinny ass!" Hasson sounded like a deranged lunatic on her voice mail.

If this muthafucka so much as go near my child, I'll personally pull the trigger myself, Bianca thought. She was scared, even though she didn't want to show or admit it. She called me at work and told me about the message. I told her to tell Keith, our crazy ass brothers, our father, and everybody in our surrounding area, because it was obvious this nigga was crazy.

"Chantell, come here," Bianca said, as soon as she walked through the door.

Chantell walking slowly up the stairs to Bianca room. "Huh?"

"Go get dressed so you can come with us," she said, nervously walking around her room looking for makeup.

"I'm already dressed."

"Bianca, what are you looking for?" Keith said walking into the room, watching her pace the floor.

"Makeup."

"For what?" he asked.

"You're the one who told me to cover my bruise," she answered.

"Oh, I forgot."

"It not that serious, plus you don't own any makeup," Chantell intervened. "You don't wear makeup remember," she said, snickering.

"I got some makeup around here somewhere. Help me look in these pocketbooks, Chantell."

"Why don't you just put on shades?" Keith suggested

She turned to Keith. "Are you going to work today?"

"Nah, I think I'm going to take some time off. I feel the need to protect my family from someone," he said, looking from Bianca to Chantell. "I feel like y'all forgot to tell me something about yesterday, I mean, me and my boys rode up and down Chancellor and nothing looked out of the ordinary. We stopped and asked a few people and nobody knew or even heard about some shit like that, and news travels fast in the hood, that's for damn sure. You sure it was on Chancellor?" Keith asked Bianca, looking into her eyes in hopes that she would tell him the truth. He felt in his guts she was lying. He took a bite out of his bacon, eggs and cheese sandwich and waited for an answer from Bianca. "Bianca, were you fucking around on me? Is this the work of some jealous muthafucka acting crazy? He paused, "You'd better come clean with me, 'cause I don't believe shit you said yesterday." Keith kept his composure while he was talking to Bianca, but he was full of vehemence.

Chantell stepped out of the room while he was talking; she didn't want to get caught up in some more bullshit.

"Believe whatever you want, Keith, I don't care," Bianca said, turning and walking out of the kitchen She was looking for make-up in the kitchen. "I'm going back to bed; I don't have time for this shit!"

Keith sat at the table alone, noticing how they had both stepped out when he stated his opinion about yesterday. He got up, went into the bedroom and said, "I guess you don't want to go and get your car today, huh?"

"No I don't. But since you want the car, you can go pick it out yourself. You don't need me there," Bianca snapped. "Listen; can you please just go somewhere? Anywhere, just leave me alone for a couple of hours. As a matter of fact, stay gone for the rest of the day," she said, pulling the covers over her head.

"Just don't forget to pick up Dee Dee from school,"

She wanted to tell Keith but didn't know how. The words wouldn't come out, and now with his sarcastic remarks, they might come out the wrong way and she didn't want that to happen. She also had to worry about Hasson finding out what school Dee Dee went to. What if he grabbed Chantell? He knew she went to Seton Hall and he didn't know who hit him with the brick. Tears starting flowing down her face as she thought about the 'what if's.'

Keith stood over her and replied, "I'm not going anywhere, I'm staying home today. When I move to go out the door so will you." He pulled the covers from his wife's face, seeing the tears stains on her face. He wanted to comfort her, but his anger kept him from it. He just said, "Let's go find you a car with tinted windows."

"Fuck you," she said, sluggishly pulling herself out of bed. "I don't feel like going anywhere."

"Here," Chantell said, handing her some makeup.

"Where did you get this from?" Bianca asked, taking the make-up and only applying it around the bruise eye.

"In Dee Dee's room," she said, laughing.

Chantell wouldn't tell you if you looked a mess, she'd just laugh at you, and that's exactly what she did to Bianca.

"What's so funny?" Bianca asked one side of her face lighter than the other.

"What about the other side?" Keith asked, as he tried to blend the makeup.

"The other side is alright. I only need to cover the side where the bruise is besides, I'm wearing shades."

"Okay," he said and walked out of the room.

"Aight'," Chantell said, laughing and following Keith. "Your wife looks a hot mess," she said to him.

"I know," Keith agreed. I'm just not gonna look at her while she's got that makeup on, he thought. Every time Chantell looked at Bianca she laughed; she laughed so hard tears came to her eyes, but Bianca didn't care, she was wearing makeup. At the dealership, Chantell chose to stay in the truck.

"C'mon Chantell," Keith said, getting out the truck.

"Nah, I'm good, she ain't embarrassing me. I'll just stay in the truck."

The salesman took a double-take when he saw Bianca's face. Keith just laughed under his breath. "Bianca, go wash that shit off your face. It looks too obvious," Keith whispered to her, as the salesman walked away. "These people are going to think I'm buying you a car because I beat your ass or something. The purpose of makeup is to hide the flaws not make them more visible. You got the shit on half your face looking like you just got beat the fuck up."

"Please!" she yelled, and I did just get beat the fuck up, remember? She said, pointing to her face, noticing an old white man looking at her. She stared back at him, rolled her eyes, and walked towards a car she liked.

"You know what, come get me when you're ready," he said waving his hand and then walking back to the truck with Chantell to wait.

"Your mother is a trip," he said to Chantell as he got in the truck.

When Bianca finished picking out the car she wanted, she gestured for Keith to come and do the paperwork. Everything was in Keith's name, since he has the business and excellent credit.

"Yo, why would you pick this shit?" he asked, walking toward the black GS300 Lexus with tinted windows she had picked out before going inside the dealership. "You're just itching for attention, ain't cha?" he said looking back at the newer model Lexus with tinted windows.

"I told you I didn't want a car, but you were the one that was adamant that I get a car," Bianca said, grinning. "So this is the car I want. Shit, what did you thought, I was going to pick out a brand new Intrepid?" "Please," she said following behind him.

Chantell, liked her Mom's new ride and whispered, "At least you got a Lexus out of the deal, huh?"

Bianca just stared at the back of her head, not finding that comment funny at all.

~Chapter Twelve~

"Did you see Bianca's new Lexus?" I asked Isis, sounding jealous. It was Saturday and Isis came over early to my house. She was meeting her new friend at the House of Pancakes on Bergen Street for breakfast.

"What?" Isis was flabbergasted. "That bitch is pushing a Lexus now!"

"Black with tinted windows and fully loaded," I added. "She has no clue how fuckin' lucky she is. I hate that bitch sometimes," I said, in some ways happy for my sister, but wishing I had the same kind of man.

"Why tinted windows?" Isis asked, pouring herself some orange juice.

"So that crazy muthafuckin' ex of hers won't know who's driving. Keith suggested the tinted windows," I said fixing some sausages and pancake for my kids and me.

"Keith knows; he's not stupid, not by a long shot," Isis said. "What type of pussy does that bitch have?"

"I don't know, but I sure wasn't blessed with it." We both laughed.

"You know Hasson has threatened to rape 'the little bitch' that hit him with that brick," I said, making me a sandwich out of my sausages.

"What?" Isis yelled, almost choking on her juice. "Oh, my God, she'd better tell Keith cause. This is not a game, this shit is real; believe me, I know. Hasson is not gonna stop until someone gets hurt. Maybe we should tell Keith."

"No, we shouldn't, it's not our place."

"But what if your nieces get hurt? She asked cutting me off. You know what? I'd rather you not tell me anything else about that stupid sister of yours. I gotta go, I've gotta meet Damien," Isis said grabbing her jacket and pocketbook. She left upset.

She'll be alright, I thought. Isis didn't talk much about her new friend, so it must be serious. Anyway, let me get dressed take my kids to my mother's while I shoot over to New York. I guess tonight is the night that Tony makes me feel like a woman. But before I go, let me call Raquan and hit him with some bullshit.

"Hey, Raquan," I said, as soon as he answered his phone. I'm surprised he answered. Normally, he'd see my number and send it straight to voice mail.

"What's up?" he said.

"Nothing. Listen, I just wanted to tell you I was going to New York with Rhonda today?"

Seconds later he said, "Y'all going to New York?"

"Yeah," I said signaling my kids to go eat.

"For what?"

"I don't know yet. Anyway, I'm driving so you know I won't be gone long. So, I guess I'll see you later."

"What time are you coming back?"

"I don't know. I'll call you when I get in okay? Bye," I said, hanging up before he could ask another question.

I got my shaving kit and started shaving every part of my body I felt needed to be shaved, took a long, hot shower and contemplated on what was going to happen today in New York. After my shower, I put on my matching Dereon bra and thong set. The thongs strings went around the waist and the back were made of diamonds. I wanted to choose a pair of jeans that were very low and very seductive, so Tony would be able to get a sneak a peek at my thong.

I stood in the mirror and thought about sleeping with Tony, pretended he was in front of me. I started to make what I thought were very sexy and seductive facial expressions, then laughed at the pretend jokes he would make. It was a beautiful thought, and I couldn't wait to make it happen.

'What am I going to wear today?' It was kind of cold outside, so I put on a pair of low rider jeans and my A/X sweater that stopped just at my waist. I called Tony to make sure our plans for the day were still on.

"May I speak with Tony?" I asked, looking at myself in the mirror, fixing my hair.

"What did I tell you, you don't have to say that when you call my house. I'm the only one answering my phone," he said, laughing.

"I'm sorry; I was just calling to let you know that I'm getting ready to leave."

His voice made me horny as hell. My panties became soaked when I hear his voice again; I can imagine what will happen when he touches me.

"I'll be outside waiting for you," he said. "Just call me when you get about five minutes away,"

"Okay, I'll see you then."

Grabbing my short burgundy leather jacket and things, I yelled to my kids. "Let's go!"

When I got to Madison Square Garden, Tony was standing out front looking good as hell. He wore a black leather jacket, a pair of black Rocawear jeans and some Black Gucci Boots and a fitted Gucci Scully. I caught a chill that made my whole body shake when I saw him. He was standing there, looking thugged the fuck out. I gotta thing for them thugs, well the thug look anyway. I'm not into men who wear suits-n-suits. As I approached him, he smiled

"What's up?" I asked, getting out of my truck to give him a hug.

"You," he said, looking me up and down. "No doubt...you look good."

"Why thank you." A grin parted my lips. "So, do you want to eat? I'm not really hungry, I had a big breakfast," I said looking him straight in the eyes, hoping he could read my mind.

"Not really, it's whatever you want, Ma," he said hugging me, pressing his penis up against my legs, letting me feel how happy he was to see me.

My pussy was thumping, begging me to let him inside. "How about we go back to your house... so I can know how to get there the next time I come over."

"Okay, maybe I'll cook you some lunch."

Or maybe you'll just fuck me for lunch, I thought, before saying, "Okay, I'm going to park in the lot and I'll ride you, I mean I'll ride with you."

"Yeah, okay," he said, blushing.

As soon as we got to his condo, I felt right at home. "Nice place," I said looking around, noticing how clean it was an admiring the very expensive furniture and the black art that hung on his wall.

His home was very bachelor like; a black leather living room set, a silver 52 inch plasma television, and an Ericsson surround sound system. As I looked around his home he walked up behind me and started kissing me on my neck. Instantly, I became wet. I was a little tense at first, but I closed my eyes and relaxed.

I turned around and started tongue kissing him while lifting off his shirt. I didn't have time to waste; I had to be back in Newark before Raquan got off from work.

We were kissing and caressing each other, acting like two wild animals in heat. When I felt his dick against my leg, I stepped back to get a look at the print in his pants and was very impressed. I started unbuckling his pants so the vision could be clearer.

Once I pulled his dick out of its hiding place, I saw that it was perfect; not crooked or anything and it was all the same color. His long, hard penis was ready to enter my world, and my world spread open and welcomed him with everything I had. He started peeling off my clothes piece by piece, kissing me everywhere (thank God I shaved). He wasn't shy like Raquan; he was a freak!

Wait a minute, why am I thinking about this nigga? I'm about to get soo-ooo-ooo satisfied, I don't have room in my mind to be thinking about that nigga. Tony took my hand and guided me into his bedroom. He laid me down on his king size bed, and started kissing and licking my body. I kept my eyes on him while he was licking me; he is so sexy, I thought. He took his dick and started playing around my pussy, teasing me, making me crazy, acting like he was going to enter me, but didn't. I wanted him bad. With or without a condom, I was ready. I started begging him to just give me a little.

He shoved his penis in me and it felt sooo good. I screamed, not from pain, but from the feeling that he put on me. He did it again but quickly pulled his penis out." You are so wet," he whispered, kissing my stomach. My pussy was beating like my heart was down there. He stopped, went to his dresser and put on a condom. Then he was ready and so was I.

He stood in front of me, allowing me to get a good look at his dick. If he was my man, I would've sucked the skin off of it. That's how beautiful it was and that's how nasty he made me feel. I wanted to do things with him I only dreamed of doing with Raquan.

As soon as Tony entered me, I exploded. He was gentle and knew exactly how to make love to me. Our bodies were in tune with each other; every time I was ready to cum, he would slow down so I could feel myself cum on his dick. I screamed a little, putting an arch in my back so he could go deeper inside of me. I felt like a contortionist, with the way he had my legs positioned. We made love for a long time; he knew how to control his erection and he made sure I was completely satisfied before he came. And when he came, we came together. He gave me a kiss and a smile, and then we laid there quietly until we fell asleep. I slept for a good hour and a half, I eased out of the bed, got my things together and went inside his bathroom to wash and get dress. As I was fixing my hair because it was a mess, and was getting ready to leave, Tony still naked came up from behind and held me.

"I've got to go," I said closing my eyes, still mesmerized.

"Why? Let me make love to you again, and again and again," he whispered.

"Stay with me," he said, gently kissing my neck.

I thought for a minute. "I can't; I've got to go get my kids. And I don't feel like hearing my mom's mouth," I said, looking at his face through the mirror. I thought, the next time Raquan is mad at me for two or three days, I'll hang out over here. In the mean time I gotta go, besides Raquan is getting off of work in about an hour and I supposed to meet him at my house. As I was thinking Tony started kissing me and I felt his erection on my butt. I turned around, and that only made matters worse because then I felt his dick on my pussy. I became weak. Fuck it, I thought. We made love over and over again. Before I knew it, it was after 7 o'clock in the evening. My body was aching, but it was a good ache.

'Damn, I could easily love a brother like this. Maybe I should walk away from Raquan and see what life would be like with him,' I stared at Tony's fine chocolate ass. He looked so much like Morris Chestnut. I felt lucky to be here with him, I'm sure he could've had any woman he wanted here tonight.

"I really got to go, Tony," I said, putting on my clothes. "I had left my cell phone in the truck and know my kids are calling me like crazy."

"All right," he said, slipping on some gray Sean John sweat pants. "If you want to come back give me a call. If I'm not at home, call my cell." He grabbed his car keys and opened the door for me to exit out his condo.

He drove me back to the parking lot, where I had left my truck and we kissed for so long that I got horny all over again. There wasn't anybody in the parking lot, so I suggested we get one off for the road.

"I didn't bring a condom," he said, laughing, rubbing my leg.

"Bam!" I reached in my bag and snatched one out. We got out of his car and walked to the side of my truck so we couldn't be seen. I turned around and held on to the iron rail so he could get it from the back. He pulled my pants down to my ankles and did the same with his. I moaned so loud that my voice echoed. He made my night, and I was going to sleep with no worries. Tony didn't cum fast, so we ended up getting a blanket from my truck and finishing up with me on top. I rode his dick like it belonged to me. I had never made love in a parking lot before; it was gratifying. After we came, we laid there naked like we were at home or something. We were cold, but we said fuck'it!

I kissed him softly, saying, "Now, I've really got to go."

"I feel used," he said jokingly, pulling up his sweats.

"I'll be back," I said, getting into my truck and blowing him a kiss.

"Call me when you get home," he said, as I drove off.

On my way home, I cut my cell phone back on and saw that he had called a million times. I knew he was mad, but he'll be a'ight; that's what he always tells me. I then called Mommy and asked her if my kids could stay there for the night. Even though she wasn't too happy about it, she agreed. I turned on my Alicia Keys CD and started singing along. I played the CD until I reached my home. When I pulled up to my house it was damn near 10 o'clock, and he was still there. I decided to take the battery out of my cell and pretend that I had lost it, and tell him that's why I didn't call him back.

I walked through the door and all the lights were out.

"Raquan!" I yelled out, peeking around reaching, for the hall light switch.

"What?" he answered. He was sprawled out on the living room floor on his back.

"I'm sorry," I said, whining, falling down next to him on the floor. I didn't want to get too close because he might smell the sex I had just finished having.

"Why didn't you call?"

"I dropped my cell phone and lost my battery, and Rhonda doesn't have a cell phone," I said, getting up off the floor before he took a big sniff.

"You couldn't use a pay phone?"

"No, I couldn't," I said, walking upstairs to take a shower.

"You didn't buy anything?"

"I didn't see anything I liked." Damn he fucked me up with that question; he usually never notices shit anyway. I smelled like sex. I hadn't put my thongs back on because they were too wet, so I stuffed them in my purse. I locked the bathroom door behind me and started stripping; smelling my clothes as I took them off. I threw them off in the hamper and hid my thong all the way on the bottom, just in case.

He came upstairs behind me and turned the bathroom door. "Yo, why is the fuckin' door locked?" he asked, rattling the door.

"I want to douche in private, but you can come in if you want." I unlocked the door and sat back on the toilet so he could see me insert the douche inside of me.

"I don't want to see that nasty shit. Is your period off?"

"Yes, and I'm ready for some sex. "So be ready when I come out the bathroom."

"I thought it just came on? You went off already?"

"I don't bleed long; two days is the norm for me. Anyway, why are you clocking my shit?"

He stood there for a second then closed the door. I took a long shower, put the massager on the shower so it could hit my back real hard, 'cause it was sore. I thought about Tony while standing under the water, then smiled. When I was finished and came out the bathroom, Raquan was lying on top of the covers naked. I was not turned on at all, but I had to pretend. So I laid on top of him and started to gently kiss his chest. I even moaned a little, just to make him think I was turned on. I gently massage his dick, and tease him with my pussy, trying to get it wet. My body was in pain, and I couldn't show it. I tried to imagine Tony's face, but couldn't. Once Raquan was ready, he flipped me over on the bed and did about ten humps, and a few huffs and we were done. It was so quick and dry I don't even know if I had an orgasm. I moaned and pretended to enjoy it. Once he came, he rolled over like he had just worn my ass out. I gave him a kiss good night, then turned over and thought about Tony. Talk about a sore pussy, I developed DRI (Dick Related Injuries). My shit was finished for a minute. I told Tony that I was coming back tonight, but I'ma have to see him some other time.

"Raquan, do you have to work tomorrow?" I asked, hoping he did

"Yup."

Good, you keep right on working, and not spending time with me,' I thought before going to sleep. For some reason I didn't feel guilty; I actually enjoyed fuckin' Tony. Raquan had it in his mind that I would never cheat on him, regardless of how he treated me. Boy was he so wrong!

A couple of weeks had passed, and the nights Raquan didn't come over to my house, I went to New York late and left early in the morning, hanging out with Tony and having plenty of sex. The more I spent time with him, the less time I wanted to spend with Raquan. Hell, I didn't even care or ask to spend time with him since Tony came along.

My conversations with Raquan had become limited. I wanted my keys back but, of course, I didn't know how to ask for them. I pretended like I had lost my keys so I could get them back from him, but that didn't work. Instead of giving me my keys back, he went and had another set made.

I tried making him mad at me, but nothing made him upset these days. What the fuck was going on? I wondered if he felt that bubbly feeling in his stomach that a woman feels when her man is cheating.

~Chapter Thirteen~

Isis was itching to tell me about Damien, but before she started bragging on him, she wanted to make sure he would be around after the sex. It had been well over a month and he was still there and coming back for more. At first, she ignored the hell out of him, not answering his phone calls but he was tenacious, he didn't stop until Isis gave in.

Damien invited her to his home. He lived in the Forest Hill section of Newark in a very big, one family home. He cooked her a scrumptious dinner of lobster tails in butter sauce, baked potatoes and a Caesar's salad. He also had a chilled bottle of white wine. She was flattered and, from there, they went to New York and took a carriage ride around Central Park. It was cold, but she enjoyed cuddling up under her soon to be man. Damien brought a smile to her face, not too many men could do that. Isis was turned on by his charm.

Damien is a 6'5, 210 pounds dark skinned brother with Iverson braids. He's very clean cut, well-groomed. He owns recording studios in Newark and in L.A., and he's all about making music and money. He told Isis he had no room in his heart for games, and that if she wasn't serious about a relationship, to let him know so he could go. He was ready to settle down with a strong woman, and he wanted that woman to be her.

Isis was still unsure about Damien, and didn't give in too easily. Although he was showing her that it could be all about her, she was still unsure. She could go to his house anytime of the day and Damien would be there playing music. If he wasn't there, he was at his studio. He was always happy to see her.

"This is my home away from my other homes, "Damien told Isis as she entered his place. "I only invite family and important friends to this house. So you know you must be somebody important in my life because I've never brought another female over here before."

"Whatever," she said, digging his home. He had a lovely home but he needed a woman's touch. "Why don't you have any pictures around? You don't like pictures?"

"I'm not into all of that shit pictures of what anyway? Myself?" he asked, walking over to give Isis a hug. "I'm really feeling you, Ma. I don't know why either, 'cause you have the worst attitude in the whole wide world! This is definitely going to be a challenge for me. What you really need to do is loosen up a little bit and let me in, 'cause I plan on being here for the long haul, baby," he said, slapping her on the ass.

"Now I really want to throw up," Isis said blushing, knowing deep inside she was feeling him too.

"Let me make love to you, let me show you how I feel," Damien started singing to Isis. The brother could sing; he actually had a nice voice.

While Damien was singing, he was kissing Isis slowly. They went into one of the guest rooms on the lower level of his home and made love until the next day. They only stopped for food, water and air. Isis had finally found the man she deserved.

It was Saturday and Isis called me and told me to meet her at Damien's house. I wanted to see who or what had her smiling from ear to ear these days, anyway. "I'm glad to see that you keep a smile on her face even when you're not around," I said to Damien, after being introduced to him.

"Please, don't let this bitch soup up your head, sweetie," Isis said to Damien, walking toward the kitchen. "Anybody want some grub? I'm about to cook."

"Nah, I'm alright. Besides, I'm going out to eat with Raquan later," I said following behind her. I really don't want to go."

"Then don't go!" Isis said

"We haven't been out on a date in a while; I guess I have to go," I said, pulling out a chair from the table.

"Is this your man you're talking about or just a friend?" Damien asked, surprised.

"He's supposed to be my man, but lately I don't know what to call him," I answered.

"Fuck that big head ass boyfriend of yours, continue doing you, Stormie. For real…you're too good for him. He treats you like shit and you deserve so much more," Isis said, still looking for something to cook quickly.

"I know God will soon send me somebody because I'm not looking for Mr. Right. You have a beautiful home, Damien. Did you decorate it yourself or did you hire someone to help you?" I said, changing the subject before Isis said something to piss me off. I got up from the table and looked around his home.

"Man, I did this shit myself," he said following me. "I took my time with this house, but my other house where I take people I don't trust looks like shit. Everything in that house came from thrift shops and garage sales."

"Well, just don't let Isis decorate your shit, because everything will be fucking white!" I said yelling, so she could hear me.

"I heard that! Fuck you, Stormie!" Isis yelled from the kitchen.

"I'm out. It was a pleasure meeting you, Damien," I said grabbing my things getting ready to leave.

"Likewise, hey, stay sweet. You seem to be a good person and I know some guy would love to make you their wife," Damien said, walking me to the door.

I thought about what Damien, Isis and everybody else has been saying to me about Raquan. It's true, he wasn't ever gonna change. He'll never love and care for me the way that I want a man to.

I put Jahiem's CD, 'Still Ghetto,' in the player. He's got a song on that CD named, 'Put That Woman First,' which I absolutely love. As I was driving along, I played it over and over again 'cause the words were serious.

Lately, I've been thinking about my relationship with Raquan a lot. I think it's over, but it's hard to say right now. I've also been thinking about Tony too. I want to be with him but I'm too scared to take that chance. I love being with him 'cause he makes me smile and he's always complimenting me, no matter what I'm wearing. What was I gonna do about this threesome love affair? Somebody had to go. Before making any decisions, I decided to see how this date with him ends up first. I was going to put on the baddest dress I could find in my closet. If he doesn't say, 'Ma, that dress looks good on you,' I'm going to have to let him go and stick with the man that makes me smile, even if it's only temporary. Why can't that man make me smile? It's not that he can't, he just won't, and I hate that about him.

"Hello," I said, answering my phone.

"Where are you?" Raquan asked.

"In my truck, why?"

"I just wanted to know. What time are you going to be ready to go out?"

"Um, around 7 o'clock. I'll be home waiting for you," I said, hanging up. My cell phone rang again. "Hello."

"Yo, why did you hang up, I wasn't finished talking to you!" he yelled pissed off that I had hung up on him.

"My bad, humph, I thought you were done talking to me. Shit, you never have much to say anyway!"

"Well, I'm coming to your house to get dressed. I wanted to know if I had any clothes over there."

"Yeah, what are you looking for?"

"My tan Omavi button up shirt and my Omavi jeans, I can't find them at my house, I've looked everywhere."

"I'll look when I get home."

"Where you at?" he asked again.

"I just told you, in my truck," I answered, sarcastically.

"Headed where?"

"What's up with all the questions, you don't trust me or something?"

"Hell no, I don't trust you. Lately, you've been going on your little excursions, not telling me where you're going or when you're coming back-n-shit!

"Well, you do it all the time. You leave out, don't call me and then you get mad at me over bullshit. So, I figured this was how you wanted it to be. I'm only following your lead." I know damn well this nigga doesn't care.

"Whatever, Storm. I work you know that."

"Please," I said, cutting him off. "You don't work all the time, Raquan. We'll talk about this later. But you don't have to worry about my excursions when I'm out; it's a good thing. I'll call you when I get home."

"I'm on my way to your house now. Meet me there."

"Alright. Now this muthafucka wants to talk. 'God, please give me the strength to walk away, today!" I yelled. I shouldn't go home, I should call Tony and go to his house. As a matter of fact, that's exactly what I'm gonna do.

"Hey, Tony," I said, once he picked up the phone.

"What's up, baby?" Tony said in a deep, seductive voice.

Damn, I think I came on myself again, I thought. "Can I see you tonight?"

"Sure, what time?"

"How about now. I was in my truck headed to nowhere land and I started thinking about you and ya know."

"Come over. I'm here trying to develop these pictures I took earlier this week. By the time you get here I should be almost finished."

"I'm on my way," I said, hanging up. Then I called Bianca.

"Bianca, can Tania and Ja'Mil stay at your house tonight?" I said, once she picked up the phone.

"Why? Where are you going?"

"Out with Tony, and I doubt if I'll want to drive back to Newark tonight."

"Where's Raquan?"

"On his way to my house to wait for me to meet him there. But I'm not going home. I don't want to hear the bullshit."

"I know that's right," Bianca mumbled, as she sat at her computer desk, looking at pictures of her wedding. "Well, you've got to do what you got to do, Storm. It's not like he goes out of his way to make you happy, so you've got to make yourself happy. It took me a long time to find a good man, now look at the stupid shit I've gotten, myself into. Sometimes people do things to hurt the only person that really loves them, not realizing at the time that they have it made. I realize it now and I hope it ain't too late. Raquan wants to talk now because he probably knows that he's on the verge of losing you completely."

"All of sudden he wants to know where I'm at, where I'm going, and what time I'll be back. When I'm with Tony I feel so at ease, Bianca, you just don't know. Since Raquan pretty much demanded I meet him at my house, I decided to go to Tony's house instead. Let him sit there and wait for me, the same way I used to sit and wait on him. I'm going to give you Tony's phone number just in case you need me, cause I'm turning off my cell for the rest of the evening."

"Well, enjoy," Bianca said, laughing before hanging up.

"Yo, call me!" Raquan screamed into my voice mail. "I've been waiting at your house since 5:30, and it's now after 8 o'clock. What's up? If you didn't want to go out you should've said so! You know what this means, right? I now know your fuckin' ass is cheating on me. If you found another man just let me know…fuck, let me go!" he said slamming the phone down on the kitchen table.

After hanging up, Raquan called my Mother. "How you doing, Mrs. Luv? Have you seen or heard from Stormie?"

"No, I haven't. Why?"

"We were supposed to go out to dinner tonight. I spoke to her around 4:30 and she said she was on her way home. I told her I would meet her there but she never showed up."

"Well, is everything alright between y'all?"

"Yeah, as far as I know. We haven't had any arguments lately," Raquan said walking towards the front to look out the window.

"I don't know where she's at, but if I hear anything, I'll call you. Are you at Stormie's house?"

"Yeah, I'm going to stay here tonight, maybe she'll call."

"Did you call her cell phone?"

"Yeah, and her voice mail comes on. She must have her phone turned off. Anyway if you talk to her, let her know I'm looking for her and to call home."

"Okay."

I got to Tony's house around 6:30, but before I went I decided to go to the grocery store to pick up something to cook so he could see some of my other skills. I picked up four T-Bone steaks, yellow rice and a can of sweet peas. For desert, I got a bottle of Whip Cream, for him of course. I also called Isis to let her know where I was at, just in case you know who called her. I doubt he would call her cause he knew she wouldn't tell him shit.

By the time I finished cooking and talking on the phone, Tony was finished developing his pictures. We ate and talked a little. I wanted to tell him about Raquan and the whole situation, but I couldn't fix my lips to say the words.

"So, when are you going to invite me to your house?" Tony asked, pushing his plate the side, putting his elbows on the table.

"Whenever you want to come over. I just didn't think you wanted to come to Newark since you always want me to come over here," I said, knowing I couldn't invite him over to my house right now.

"I felt you couldn't invite me. I don't even have your home phone number," he looked at me like he knew I wanted to tell him something, but couldn't or didn't know how. "If you need to talk to me about anything Storm, you can. You don't have to be afraid." He reached his hand out to touch mine.

"I'm not afraid. I just don't want to talk about what's going on in my life right now," I said, not looking in his eyes, but down at the table. "I come over here to get away from things, and bringing you to my house right now isn't a good idea." I paused for a second, and then looked into his eyes. "I need to get rid of all the things I don't need in my life and in my home. I enjoy your company more than you know, and I wish to God I could just walk away from what's keeping me from giving all of myself to you." I got up from the table and went in the living room. "Never mind that, I didn't come over here to talk about things that keep me despondent," I said, wanting to end this conversation.

"You don't have to talk about it now, maybe some other time. Okay?" Tony said, following me into the living room and hugging me from behind. "You're a very beautiful person, Ms. Luv, and you deserve the best of everything. If you give me a chance, I can give you that and more. I understand you have to rid the bad out of your heart, but I'm not going anywhere," Tony said, as he slowly kissed and caressed my body.

I love how he takes his time and makes love to me. He makes sure he caresses every inch of my body. We made love at least four times throughout the night, and the lovemaking tonight was definitely talking to the both of us.

After we had finished making love, I laid there thinking about my relationship with Raquan. I know he's not going to speak to me for at least two weeks now. I need that break any way to get my head on straight and to give me more time with Tony to see if this is where I want to be.

"I stayed at your house and I've been calling your cell all night!" Raquan shouted at my voicemail. "You didn't even try to reach out to me. I guess this is your way of telling me it's over, huh? I wanted to go out to talk, but you never came home. I will not forgive you for this Stormie...ever? There will be no, 'let's talk about it,' no explanation, no nothing. I don't want to hear it!" Raquan yelled, into my voice mail at 7 o'clock in the morning.

"Bianca, wake up. We need to talk," Keith said, sitting on the edge of the bed.

"What's so important that it can't wait until I get up?" Bianca asked eyes still shut.

"Get up! I want to know the truth about the fuckin' truck incident. I've been asking questions like crazy and nobody knows what the fuck I'm talking about!"

"No you didn't wake me up with this bullshit. Whatever you think happened, happened. Shit, I don't give a fuck anymore. I'm tired of you always questioning me!"

"It's not going to work this time, Bianca. Your ass is wrong. You can't put this shit on me, not this time. You were fuckin' around on me, and the crazy muthafucka you were fuckin' with flipped out on you." Keith said, getting out of the bed. "What happened? Did you break up with him? Is that what happened? That's what happened, right," Keith asked again. Bianca didn't say a word.

'I can't believe this bitch,' Keith mumbled under his breath, but Bianca heard him.

"Oh, now I'm a bitch! Don't act like you never cheated on me!"

"I haven't! There's not another woman out there I want! Sure I could've fucked plenty of bitches, but I chose not to because I thought I had a good wife at home. I thought you'd be the woman who would love and treat me with respect, the same respect that I give you. How the fuck could you go out there and fuck around on me?" Keith was so mad his voice was beginning to break. "I don't believe this fuckin' shit! I'm so good to you, Bianca. I tried to give you the world and show you the love that you said you never had before. How the fuck could you do this?" he said, pacing the floor, fist balled, ready to hit something.

"It just happened, I don't know why. I know I shouldn't been cheating, that's why I broke it off with this guy." Bianca said sitting on the edge of the bed.

"What the fuck you mean, 'it just happened?' What, you just fell in the bed with him by mistake? It didn't just happen, Bianca, you made it happen. How long have you been cheating on me?" he asked, pacing the bedroom floor.

"For a couple of months. I knew it was wrong, but."

"Oh, cut the bullshit!" he said, cutting her off. "This ain't a scene from the movies or some fucking soap opera. You're a heartless ass sistah. I don't know what's going to happen, but whatever happens; just know you caused it to happen." Keith was so mad his eyes turned red, the veins in his arms were popping out, and he hit the bedroom wall and put a hole in it. He then put on his clothes and left without telling Bianca where he was going.

It was 5:30 in the morning and Bianca got up out of bed, went into the kitchen and took food out to cook breakfast, acting as if nothing had just happened between them. She walked over to the window to see if he was sitting outside, but he wasn't. She walked to the garage and saw that he had taken her Lexus and the keys to the Escalade. "Damn!" Bianca said out loud. She was stuck in the house today. She went into the living room and laid across the sofa, wishing this was all a dream. Unfortunately it wasn't.

"What's the matter, Mom?" Ahmir asked, sitting on the edge of the chair.

"Nothing."

"Where's Keith?" he asked.

"I don't know. He left sometime this morning."

"Is he coming back? I thought I heard y'all arguing." Ahmir was fifteen and he knew what time it was. He had heard the whole argument, so he wanted to make sure his Mom was all right.

"I don't know, Ahmir. Listen, I need time to myself. Wake up Malcolm, Chantell and Dee Dee and y'all catch the bus to Grandma's house. And take Tania and Ja'Mil too."

"Aight', but if you need to talk, holla at me," Ahmir said, walking out the living room and closing the doors behind him.

Since Ahmir was the oldest son, he thought he was the father to his siblings. Before going to their Grandma's house, he wouldn't let any of them go into the living room because he knew his Mom was stressing and needed time to think. He even had to knock Malcolm upside the head for trying to sneak in the room.

Once the kids were gone, Bianca got up and took a long, hot bubble bath. She sat in the tub and thought about all that she had before chaos came to town. Damn, if only she would've walked away or thrown Hasson's number away. Keith didn't bother to call or come home. She had known this day was coming, she just didn't know how soon. She wanted so badly to call him first, but pride prevented her from doing so.

Bianca ate and went into her bedroom to check the caller ID. She was only checking for Keith's number, and he hadn't called. "Oh well," she said out loud, "I'm not gonna run behind this nigga. I'ma pack my shit and leave. I've got money saved anyway."

She went back into the living room, curled up on her chaise, and put her goose down comforter over her body before finally falling asleep. When she woke up, her kids were cooking and getting ready for bed. She heard Chantell tell the boys to shower then come to the table and eat. She continued to lie on the chaise before she finally picked up the cordless phone to call her husband. Her heart was racing, not knowing if he was going to answer or if he would just hang up on her. After the third ring, Keith finally answered.

"Can we talk?" Bianca said very low, almost in tears. But Bianca wouldn't break, not yet anyway.

I left Tony's house around 10 o'clock in the morning. Before I left, he made pancakes, sausages, grits and eggs for breakfast. I didn't eat the eggs because they didn't look done, but everything else was good. We talked a little about the conversation we'd had last night. I told him a little more about Raquan but not too much, and the reason why I loved being around him. Tony told me whenever I needed to get away I was always welcomed at his house. I gave him a kiss good-bye and told him I'd call as soon as I stepped in the door of my house.

Tony showed me the attention Raquan didn't. I fell in love with Raquan because, at the time, I thought he cared simply by the way he used to look at me and make love to me. I thought that was a sign of love, now I know it wasn't. Raquan never promised to make me happy, he never promised to take care of me, he never promised me anything. So, why was I mad at him? I should be mad at myself for accepting the bullshit from the door.

When I got in my truck, the first thing I did was check my voice mail. Goddamn, Raquan had left me a trillion and one messages. How could he get mad at me for acting exactly the way he acts? I called Bianca but she didn't answer her phone. I called her cell and got her voice mail. I called Keith to see if they were together. He didn't answer his cell phone either. I then decided to call Mommy.

"Ma, have you heard from Bianca?"

"She's home. The kids said she was in her living room lying across the sofa. She told them to catch the bus to my house and to bring your kids with them."

"What happened?"

"I don't know. Raquan called here looking for you last night. I asked him were y'all fighting."

"No, we haven't been fighting. I just didn't want to be with him last night. Mom, I'm tired of Raquan. I feel like I'm wasting my time being in this relationship with him."

"Well, if you know like I know you'll leave before it's too late. If not, you'll end up just like me; with a man you never really loved and not sure if he ever loved you. I wish you could really see my life and how it turned out. Do you know that we've never told each other 'I love you'? Do you want that, Stormie? Step back and take a good look at my life because you're headed in the same direction if you stay with Raquan," Mommy said, lecturing me. "I like Raquan. He can be a good man if he took the time to get his priorities straight. What you need is a man that's going to let you know that you're the most important thing in his life beside his kids. You understand, Stormie? I didn't raise a dummy, and I'm sure you see that man for what he really is."

"I do, but it's hard to just walk away. It's like I can see him being a good man, giving and showing me the love he knows I desire. He just needs to be taught."

"You keep trying to train a dead horse, and you're wasting your time. Let it go. You'll hurt, but you're strong and will get over it. I bet you Raquan has issues from his past that has him acting the way he does."

"He's never told me about his past, his mom, or anyone in his family. I didn't think he had family."

"That's why he's the way he is, he needs some serious help. Where did you go last night, are you just getting in?" Mommy asked.

"Yeah, I'm just getting in. I'll tell you all about where I was later."

"Well, you did the right thing. Don't feel bad about the move you chose to make. You can't go back and change it cause it's a done deal. I wish I had the strength to leave and find me a good man, or damn, just leave," Mommy said, timidly.

After I hung up with Mommy, I started crying. I don't know why, the tears just started flowing. I really love Raquan and I don't think anybody understands the pain that's flowing through my heart. Even though I enjoy my time with Tony, I still wish it was Raquan I was spending time with. I truly feel in my heart he can change, and maybe this drastic move I'm about to make will change our relationship for the better. Maybe he needs to think he's lost me completely to see how much he needs me in his life. God, help me. You're the only one that can guide me in the right direction.

When I walked into my house, I just stood there making sure that nigga wasn't hiding behind any doors, ready to jump out and beat my ass. Everything was clear. I went to the kitchen, got the orange juice out of the refrigerator and took it upstairs with me. As soon as I laid on my bed, I began to pray and talk to myself. No, I'm not crazy, but sometimes we need to speak out loud because then we hear ourselves a lot clearer.

"God, why do I have to be strong all the time? I'm only human and I hurt, bleed and cry like the rest. Why do I have to portray to be this happy, nothing fucks with me, type of female? Deep down I'm killing myself and I'm letting Raquan kill me too. I'm tired of walking around, looking and acting like everything in my life is okay when I know it's not. The only good thing about my life is my kids and my job. When it comes to men, I'm a complete failure. I tend to walk, or shall I say, run away. Why can't he just tell me how he feels? What happened in his childhood? What's so fuckin' hard about saying I love you? God, why doesn't this man love me?" I lay on top of my covers and thought about love, romance, and Raquan until I feel asleep.

~Chapter Fourteen~

"You know what, Damien?"

"What?"

"I haven't heard from Stormie. I wonder if she came home. She stayed out last night and I told her to call me when she got home. its 2 o'clock in the afternoon, I know she's not still in New York."

"Maybe she is, you never know."

"I doubt it. She would never stay that long," Isis said, sounding worried. "I'm going to call her Mom," she said, picking up the phone.

"Hello, Mrs. Luv," Isis said.

"Hello, Isis."

"Have you seen or heard from your daughter?"

"Which one, I have three of them," Ms. Luv said, sarcastically.

"You can get it too," Isis said, jokingly. "I'm talking about Stormie."

"Yeah, she's home sleep. She has a lot on her mind. As a matter of fact, Bianca is doing the same damn thing. The men in their lives, well Bianca had a good man, but she fucked that up. But my baby, Stormie, I told her if she can find the strength to run, she'd better do it."

"I know that's right. Well, I have something like a good man," Isis threw in.

"Yeah, well, they all start out something like a good man."

"Yeah, you're right," Isis agreed. "Well, I'm going to enjoy it while I can. Anyway, I guess I'll call her later," she said, preparing to hang up.

"So, when am I going to meet this 'something like a good man' you have?" Ms. Luv asked.

"In due time. I gotta make sure he's worthy of meeting you," Isis said, laughing.

"Okay, and I'll tell Stormie you called."

"What do you mean something like a good man?" Damien asked, looking at Isis up and down, once she hung up the phone.

"Please, don't you know its bad luck to start out saying you have a good man. You should never say you have something good for at least a year."

"So, I guess I have something like a good woman, huh?"

"Yup," Isis answered looking him dead in the eye, serious as ever.

"A'ight, remember you said that shit," Damien said, slightly pissed off.

"Please, I know you're not upset over that comment. I'm about to go cause I think I've worn out my welcome," she said, beginning to pack up all her shit.

Isis was crazy like that; one false move and she would cut your ass loose. Delete a brother number like it wasn't shit. But she was making a wrong move with this brother; I think he really cared about her.

"Okay, then I'll see you later," Damien said, walking out the bedroom to go to the basement where his studio was. He slammed the basement door behind him and doubled locked it.

What is this, get mad at your mate day? Isis didn't care; at least she pretended she didn't care anyway. She got in her truck and sped off. Her cell phone rung, it was Damien.

She smiled and answered, "What?"

"Don't answer the phone like that again, or I swear to God I'll never dial your number again. I told you I don't have room in my life or my heart for games. I really like you, but if you ever jump up and walk out like that again, there will be no next time."

"What is that, a threat?"

"Nah, I'd never threaten you. That, my dear, is a promise. I take that as a sign of disrespect. I don't know what type of brothers you've dealt with in the past, but I'm not them. You know what I mean. Turn your truck around so we can continue this conversation face to face." The sound of the dial tone caused her to look at her phone.

"No, this nigga didn't." Isis had just been played and she knew it. But she took her played the fuck out ass back to his house.

"I was only playing with you, Damien. You're the one who got all serious," Isis said, after returning to his house.

"Whatever, just don't do that white girl shit again! "Well, I'm leaving!" Damien said mocking Isis, throwing his make believe hair around his face and running out the door.

"I bet you called this 'white girl' back, didn't you?" Isis retaliated, after Damien came back into the house.

"I bet it didn't take long for the little white girl to come back," he said, with one eyebrow in the air and a smirk on his face.

"Whatever," Isis said, turning on the television.

"Whatever my ass. Now go cook us some food before I give you some of this good loving," Damien said, grabbing his private area.

"Please, you better swallow your spit and pretend its soup. Or better yet, swallow my juice and pretend its lobster," Isis said, spreading her legs apart.

"Taste like chicken," Damien said sounding like Chris Rock, jumping on top of her, and kissing her all over.

When I woke up, it was after 7 o'clock. I called my Mother. "Ma, can the kids stay with you tonight, I don't feel like driving?"

"I guess. Are you alright?"

"Yeah, I just woke up. I have a headache and I doubt if I'll go to work in the morning." I had vowed to never let a man get me upset to where I couldn't go to work. Yet Raquan had gotten me so upset, that I didn't even know what I was thinking anymore.

"Well, if you don't go to work tomorrow, come take your kids to school."

"A'ight, I'll call you in the morning." I turned off the ringer and took some medicine so I could go back to sleep. I didn't want to think anymore, all I wanted to do was sleep.

"I knew he was going to find out," Dee Dee said to Chantell, once her brothers went upstairs to bed.

"Well, she had it coming. If you lie, this is what happens; consequences."

"You think he's gonna leave her?"

"Nah, but I think he's gonna cheat on her just to get her back," Chantell said.

"That's so stupid. I hope they can work it out." Dee Dee was scared they might have to move out of their big, beautiful home. "Shoot, I love this house and my room. How could she have been so stupid?"

"I know, right. Let me get a man who moves me out the hood and tells me I don't have to work, I would never cheat on him," Chantell said, laughing. "And he took her, told her to pick any car she wanted on the lot, and she pulled out with a fully loaded Lexus!" Chantell screeched.

"Right, I bet'cha she's thinking hard about that shit now."

"I know I would be. Shh, I think she's coming."

"Hey, Bianca, are you alright?" Dee Dee asked when Bianca walked into the kitchen.

"I'm okay, how about yourself?"

"I'm fine," Dee Dee said audaciously, still looking at her.

"Stop fuckin' staring at me, Dee Dee. I'm not in the mood for your nonsensical ass tonight."

"I was looking at you because I was talking to you."

"Dee Dee, you better go to bed cause tonight I'll beat you like you were a stranger on the street. I'm not in the mood for your smart ass," Bianca said, pushing Dee Dee toward the basement door.

Dee Dee and Bianca have a strange relationship. They fight all the time because Dee Dee doesn't know when to keep her mouth shut. She's a very outspoken girl, and Bianca can't stand that. She always taught her kids to speak their mind, but sometime Dee Dee goes overboard with it.

Dee Dee is very smart; she's not like the average teenager. She sits and writes poems about relationships and how she sees them through her eyes. Some of the things she writes are deep, but it's too bad it's not like that in the real world. Even though she thinks she knows it all, guess what, her time is coming to get hurt by a man. Everybody gets their turn, no one's exempt.

"What?" Bianca stared at Chantell.

"Nothing, I'm just sitting here trying to enjoy this ice cream. So what happened between you and Keith?"

"Nothing," Bianca said, waving her hand. "Look, I don't feel like talking about it."

"Whenever you feel like talking, call me, I'll be in my room. Normally, I'd mind my business, but I feel like you need someone to talk to, or maybe somebody to just listen to you talk. Anyway, I'll be in my room," Chantell said.

Bianca stood in the kitchen staring at her plate. Right now, she was more embarrassed then hurt. She knew she had fucked up, so what was she gonna talk about. She knew nobody felt sorry for her, and she didn't want to hear the "I told you so's."

While she was in the kitchen, she heard the front door open. The first thing she did was look at the clock; it was a little after midnight. She sat down at the table and nibbled on her food. Her stomach was weak, but she tried to eat anyway. Keith walked in the kitchen, looked at her and then walked out. He went in their bedroom and closed the door behind him. He turned on the television and laid across the bed. Keith had went to his homeboy's house, and his homeboy told him to either go home and work it out, or stay there and run and hide like a wanksta.

"Please, I'm no wanksta," Keith replied. "I just can't believe she would do this fucked up shit to our marriage."

"Man, you know what, I'm not going to say what she did was right. My question is, what you were doing to make her go out there in the first place?" his friend said to him. "You've got to provide more than just monetary gifts; it takes more than that, son. You've got to give of your time. Believe me, some women only want the quiet time," his friend preached.

"How can I forgive her, man? Bianca really fucked my head up. I'll never trust her again," Keith said, with a tear in his eye.

"That's to be expected, but you've got to make that decision. I can only give you my advice," his friend said, trying to console him in a manly way.

Keith thought about what his homeboy said, but he couldn't get the nerve to go and talk to his wife. Although she had called him earlier to talk, he couldn't say

146

anything just yet. He turned off the television, took off his clothes and curled up under the covers and went to sleep.

Meanwhile, Bianca continued to sit at the kitchen table until about 2 o'clock in the morning, contemplating on how to approach him. 'He knew I wanted to talk and he took his ass to bed. I guess he wants me to run behind him,' she spoke aloud.

She finally decided that she was going to sleep next to her husband and, if she had to beg for his forgiveness, then she would. As soon as she laid down beside Keith, he jumped. Bianca wrapped her arms around him and held him tight. Keith tried to pull away, but she wouldn't let him go.

"What are you doing?" Keith asked, maliciously.

"I'm holding on to the best thing that's ever happened to me. I'm not going to lose you. I love you more than you can imagine. I fucked up only because I felt your business was more important to you than I was. You never wanted to do anything but work. It wasn't about the sex with him; it was about me being able to just have fun, him putting me before everything. I'm sorry, I'm truly sorry," Bianca was saying, holding onto her husband with tears flowing down her face.

"Listen, Bianca, I'm sorry if I didn't give you all the fun you wanted to have. I was busy trying to make sure we live comfortably, and that your kids get a good education. I didn't mean to neglect you; all you had to do was tell me, 'look I need some of your time' or 'I need some attention,' you didn't have to run into the arms of another nigga!" Keith said, snatching away from her.

"Please forgive me, please! I swear it'll never happen again. I know you love me, and that's the reason why you work so hard. Granted, you give me whatever I want when it comes to material and monetary things, but what about time? When you're home, you're in the bed watching TV. Because of you, I had to go out and find somebody who would give me some of their time! Why should I have to come and tell you something you should already know?" Bianca said, starting to get upset.

"Look, let's finish this in the morning after the kids leave for school," Keith said, cutting her off before she could go on. He didn't like to argue while the kids were in the house.

"How about no!" she yelled. "We're gonna finish this conversation tonight! I know I was wrong; I'm not stupid! But I'll be damned if I lay here and continue begging your ass for forgiveness! Either we're gonna discuss this tonight, or we will never talk about it again," Bianca said, standing up to turn on the light.

Keith looked at her and said, "You're fuckin' nuts! How the fuck is your black ass gonna cheat on me, and then have the nerve to make threats and demand that I talk to you! You're not fit to make a threat, Bianca." Keith was sitting up, damn near in tears. "You fucked around on me! I didn't do anything and I'll say when I want to talk, not you! You played me! You had me out there riding up and down a block that you were never on, looking for a muthafucka that didn't exist! I had my boys looking around, asking questions! And to top it off, you had your daughters, no our daughters, lie for you! You cried so hard that day, I was ready to kill or die for you! Do you see why I'm so upset? Don't stand there with tears in your eyes, cause I didn't do it, you did it to yourself!"

Bianca was crying because she knew he was right "Do you want a divorce? You want me to leave?" Bianca said standing there, wishing he would comfort her.

"I don't know, all I know is I wish you'd turn off the light so I can go back to sleep," Keith said apathetically. He laid back down and pulled the covers over his head.

Bianca turned off the lights, got into bed and turned her back to Keith. She didn't fall asleep right away; she laid there desperately wanting her husband to hold her. When she turned around to look at him, she saw that he wasn't losing any sleep behind any of this. Bianca thought about it and said to herself, Shit, I'm not losing any sleep either.

She turned her back to Keith again, but she still didn't go to sleep until damn near 6 o'clock in the morning. By then, it was time for her to get the kids up, which she couldn't because she had just fallen asleep. Keith got them up, made them breakfast and made sure they were ready for school.

"Is my Mother okay?" Ahmir asked Keith.

"Yeah, she's asleep. Why?" Keith asked.

"Cause yesterday she seemed upset about something. Did you make her mad?" Ahmir asked.

"No, she made herself mad. Now, I'm not going to stand here and let you question me about your Mother. When you come home from school, sit down and talk to her, a'ight," Keith said, looking at Ahmir strangely. "Go get your book bag and your brother and wait for the bus. Ms. Dee Dee, let's go. Chantell, do you have class today?"

"Yup, and I'm ready," Chantell answered, grabbing her coat and books.

Keith took the girls to school and didn't bother to wake Bianca. He decided to talk to her when he returned.

~Chapter Fifteen~

"What the fuck was that boom sound?" Isis thought, jumping up out of the bed. It was Damien; he was shaking and shit, not breathing right.

"Damien, what's wrong?" Isis screamed. She ran to the phone and dialed 911; her hands were shaking. "Hello, operator, something is wrong with my boyfriend! I think he's having a seizure or something! Please get an ambulance to 156 Sheer Avenue!"

She hung up the phone, ran to Damien and put her finger in his mouth so he wouldn't swallow his tongue. Isis didn't know what she was doing, but she was too scared to run downstairs to get a spoon. By the time the ambulance got there, Damien was sitting on the edge of the bed looking delirious. He had hit the side of his face on the nightstand, and he had a small cut on his face.

He told the EMTs that he was having an asthma attack but he refused to go to the hospital. He said he had his asthma medication and that the attack wasn't that serious. Before leaving, the EMTs hooked him up to an oxygen tank so he could breathe easier.

"Why didn't you tell me about this shit?" Isis yelled crying, once the EMTs had left and she knew he was going to be alright.

"Because I normally don't have attacks, but lately I've been under a lot of stress," Damien said, taking a hit of his pump.

"You scared the shit out of me!" Isis was still yelling.

"I'm sorry," he said, walking toward her to give her a hug.

"It's lucky we were at my house, because I don't know your address. I would've had to run all the way outside to get your house number," she said, trying to make a joke out of it.

"I'll be alright as long as you're by my side," Damien said, still hugging Isis. "Let's go back to bed."

"Shit, I can't, it's time for me to get up and get ready to go open up shop," she said.

"I'm going back to sleep," he said, crawling back in the bed.

"Are you gonna be alright while I jump in the shower?" Isis said, pulling on his braids.

"Yeah, I'll be alright," Damien answered, closing his eyes.

Yes, Isis had her man, a man who had asthma and seizures. She thought about what happened, and how seeing him shaking like that on the floor had scared the shit of out her. She asked herself would she be able to handle things if it happened again. She stood looking at her reflection in the mirror; wrapping the finger Damien had bit when she had put her hand in his mouth.

By the time Isis had finished washing up and getting dressed, Damien was asleep. Damn, he looks like a newborn baby, Isis thought.

"Hey," Isis said to Damien, trying to wake him up.

"What?" Damien mumbled.

"I'm leaving now, are you okay? You're going to be fine, right?" she asked, nervously.

"Yeah, I'll be alright," he said, with his eyes closed.

"Shouldn't you go to the doctor to get checked out or something? I mean, I don't want you to get sick and I'm not here to help you."

"Bye, Isis. I'm fine," Damien replied, looking at her through one eye.

"Okay, I'm out. Lock the doors when you leave and please don't ramble through my shit, because if you do, you'll no longer be a guest in my palace," Isis said, giving him a good-bye kiss.

When she got in her car, she realized that she still hadn't heard from Storm. She decided to give her a call to see what was up.

When she called Storm, her voice mail came on, so she left a message. "Where are you and why haven't you called me? Are you okay? Call me as soon as you retrieve this message." She then proceeded to call Storm's cell. "Call me, Storm," Isis said. Where the fuck is she? Isis thought. She decided to go by her house just to make sure she was alright.

Who is this knocking on my door this early, my damn doorbell works! "Who is it?" I yelled.

"It's me, bitch!" Isis yelled back.

"What do you want, Isis?" I asked, while looking through the peephole.

"Open the door, bitch. Do you have company?" she asked, stepping back to see if she saw Raquan's car.

"No, and I don't feel like being bothered," I said, talking through the door.

"Did that muthafucka jump on you? Is your face fucked up like Bianca's shit was?" Isis asked, jokingly.

"Not at all. And yes, I'm okay. I just need some time to myself. And no, I haven't talked to Raquan, he hasn't called me and I'm not calling him. Anymore questions I need to answer or did I answer everything?"

"You answered pretty much everything, even some I didn't ask," Isis said.

"Well, call me later."

"I'll probably call you tomorrow," I said, opening up the door so she could see I was okay.

"You'll be okay, but you gotta finish the 12 steps. Do you need a hug?" she asked, being silly.

"I'm fine, I'll call you," I said, closing the door.

I went into the kitchen and called Mommy to see if she still wanted me to take my kids to school. She said she would take them, thank God. Before going back to bed, I turned my ringer back on and checked my messages. Isis was the only one that had called. I was hoping Raquan would've called. I turned on my cell to see if anyone called that number. Tony had called like three times and Isis had called. I'll call Tony later.

I needed today off to clear my mind, because yesterday I couldn't focus. After getting back in bed, I couldn't fall back to sleep so I got up, started washing clothes and packing up some of the clothes Tania and Ja'Mil couldn't fit anymore. I decided to call Tony in the mist of all that.

"Hey, Tony," I said, waiting for him to curse me out or hang up, but he didn't do neither.

"Hey, how you feel?" Tony asked, concerned.

"I'm doing okay. I needed some time to think about which direction I want to go," I said.

"I understand. Take all the time you need to get your head on straight. Anyway, no work today?" he asked.

"Nah, I'm thinking about taking the whole week off, I really need a vacation. I'm gonna see if my mother will keep my kids for the rest of the week while I go up to the Pocono's and try to relax," I said closing my eyes, envisioning being up in the mountains all alone.

"Word, that sounds like a plan. If you need any company let me know," Tony said, excitedly.

"I was thinking about going alone, only me and a book. I really need time to myself," I said again, because I didn't think he heard me.

"Oh, okay. Let me know if and when you're leaving. I'm heading out, I've got photos to shoot," Tony said, trying not to sound disappointed.

"A'ight. I just wanted you to know I was okay. I'll call you later," I said, before hanging up.

'Damn, I think I just fucked that up. Nice going, Stormie, you should have that kind of attitude toward Raquan. But you don't, that's why he treats you like he does.' I took a blank sheet of paper and began to write down all the things I liked and disliked about Raquan. The dislike won, and I was told if there were more things about a man that you dislike, then you shouldn't be with him.

Later that morning, I was watching this one talk show where homegirl had busted her husband for cheating on her. Not once, but three times with the same bitch and she wanted to know what should she do. "Put his ass out!" I yelled at the television. That bitch was dumber than I was. At least I hadn't caught him cheating on me, not yet anyway. Another sistah got up talking about she just wanted to know why her man always lied and stole her money. She loved him and he could have whatever he wanted from her. "Bitch, he lied and stole from you cause he's on that shit! A blind man could see that!" I said, yelling at my television again.

But the one that really touched me was a female who sat down and asked why her man couldn't express his love for her the way she did. She had been dating him for five years and he had never once said, 'I love you, you're beautiful, nothing.' She was saying that she assumed he cared, but whenever she would ask him, he would just stare at her and call her names. The young lady was in tears, she wanted to leave him but didn't know how.

When they called her boyfriend out, he was laughing. He said if he didn't care he wouldn't be with her. That was the same answer Raquan would give me. A psychologist spoke and told him that sometimes a woman wants to hear that she's beautiful and sexy; she wants to hear her man say I love you.

He told the young lady to find someone else, cause a man like that would never show her the love she deserved. He wasn't taught it, so therefore he didn't know how to express it. The host then asked the man if he were willing to change. His answer was yes. He then turned to his girlfriend, apologized and told her that he did love her and that he wanted to marry her. I got up, and as I went to pick up the phone it rang, scaring the shit out of me.

"Hello," I said, answering the phone.

"What's up?" Raquan asked.

"Nothing," I answered. There was a brief silence between us.

"So, why aren't you at work?" he asked.

"I'm sick. Why did you call me, Raquan?" I asked, upset.

"What, I can't call you anymore? I tried to use my key and it didn't work. Why did you change the lock? You don't want me in your house anymore? I'm outside, can you open the door?" he said, before I could answer his first question.

"I don't know, Raquan, it's too soon. I, no we need to get some shit straight first before I welcome you back into my home," I said, walking to my window to see if he was really outside.

"I agree. So, first and foremost, where you were at on Saturday?" he asked.

"I went and got a room because I needed to think about what's more important to me; my kids and myself or you and me. I'm letting you destroy who I am as a person. I can't continue this relationship not knowing how you feel. Part of me was hoping you'd think the worst and never call me again. Yes, I'd be hurt, but you know what, you would be out of my life." I was mad and rambling, saying all that needed to be said. "You disappear, don't call, won't answer your cell phone, and won't return any of my pages. I can't keep going on like this. Like I said I'm killing myself."

"Are you finished, Storm? I'm sick of you thinking I don't care. If I didn't care, I wouldn't be here."

"Were you deprived of love growing up? Did anyone ever teach you about love, Raquan? 'If I didn't care I wouldn't be here, you always say that stupid shit! I don't trust you, and I'm trying to fall out of love with you," I said, fighting back tears. I didn't want to hear what he had to say, cause I knew I would fall for the bullshit again.

"Storm, listen, open the door. I want to talk to you face to face. I'm really sorry for not expressing my feeling." And guess what my dumb ass did? That's right, I opened the door.

"Raquan, please don't talk to me about promises. I didn't open my door for that shit. I opened my door because I need to know if I'm wasting my time with you. I'm ready to get married, settle down, and I want a man that's not afraid to tell me how he feels. I'm getting too old to play the guessing game. I stayed away because I didn't think you would even notice me not coming home. You don't notice too much of anything about me. Why?" I asked, staring him in the face.

"I don't know, Storm, I never had a girl like you before. I guess I was afraid that you would hurt me, so I wouldn't show or tell you how I felt. I was protecting myself. I knew you were hurting, but I couldn't say the words you wanted to hear. I'm sorry," he said, sounding sincere.

"Raquan," I said stepping back from him, shaking my head, "I can't go on like this; too much shit is flowing through my brains right now. I don't want to hear how you feel because it's too late. You've done just about everything wrong that one man can do. And I know you're cheating on me because I found condoms in your room one night when I was over there and we hadn't used any that night. I knew if I questioned you about it you wouldn't speak to me for a couple of days, so I let it ride. I've never let a man get this close to me before, so you should feel lucky. But your luck has ran the fuck out, Raquan! I can't believe I took this bullshit this fuckin' long! You can't start being one way with me then all of a sudden change! All of a sudden you snapped and started treating me like I'm nothing. You would embarrass me in front of my Isis, and turn your back on me for your so-called female friends. You've been to the Bahamas twice without me!" He went with his Mom. I know cause my stupid ass took them to the airport. I begged him not to go, but he went anyway. "You won't even take vacation the same time as me!" but he tells me he cares. I didn't and wouldn't give Raquan the opportunity to talk. I rambled on until I started getting hoarse. I needed him to hear me.

"Fuck that! You don't do shit for me, you don't participate in anything that might be fun to me. If I don't leave now, I'll be stuck with you forever, forever being miserable! And you need to thank your Step Mom, because she had a lot to do with the decision I'm making," I said.

"My step mom? Why, what does she have to do this?" Raquan asked, puzzled.

I started mocking his Step Mom, 'Baby, let me take you to the Bahamas with me and my boys.' If she were a real woman, she would've asked if I wanted to come too, or see if I was okay with the whole idea. But I can't put all the blame on her; you should've said that you would wait until we could go together. But no, you just went to the Bahamas, not caring how I would feel about you going without me!"

"Oh, I'm stupid cause I didn't wait to take you! Shit, it was a free trip, so I went," Raquan said, shrugging his shoulders.

"Raquan, that's exactly why you're stupid and why this relationship isn't gonna work anymore. You honestly don't know the significance of being in a relationship, and I don't want to tell you who and what's more important. Right now, I really need to see the back of your head heading out of my front door," I said, waving my hand in disgust. When he didn't make a move toward the front door, I said, "Did you even hear anything I said a minute ago? Did you hear me say I'm tired of being mistreated by you?" I asked.

"I heard everything you said, I'm trying to apologize but you won't even give me the chance to talk. I know I haven't been treating you right. As far as those condoms go, I don't know what you're talking about. They've probably been lying there for a while. And those women that I talk to on the phone are all friends. I never have, nor would I ever cheat on you, and I'm sorry if I made it look that way. I don't know what I'd do if you wasn't in my life." Raquan was pleading.

"Well, you're about to find out, cause I can't stand being ignored by you any longer. A man that loves his woman will treat her with respect and he'll do whatever he can to make sure she's happy. Look at how Keith treats Bianca, even Isis has a good man who makes her happy. Raquan, you never went out your way to make sure I was happy. I can't even remember the last time you made me happy. Hell, I don't think you ever made me happy!"

"Lately, I've been trying like crazy to tell you how I feel about you, but you always seem to be going on your little excursions and shit. I can't believe this is happening. I swear to God, I've never done anything to put this relationship in jeopardy. You know sometimes I get in my mood where I just want to be alone. When I don't feel like being bothered I tell you."

"No you don't, you just stop talking to me!" I yelled. "Anyway, lately you never seem to want to be bothered, especially on Fridays and Saturdays, which are the only two days that I really have time to spend with you. If we go out to eat, we don't even talk to each other, we just look around the restaurant like two idiots."

"Raquan, it's not just the lack of attention you show me, it's everything. Please leave. I mean it this time," I said, trying not to cry in front of him. "I love you more than you know, but you fucked that up, not me."

Raquan stood up and walked over towards me. I moved cause I didn't want him to hug me, because my stupid ass would've melted and forgiven him. He stood there and stared at me for a minute, at a loss for words.

"What?" I said, looking away.

"I know you love me, Stormie, but guess what? I love you too." Raquan finally said the words to me, and I think this time he probably meant it.

"It's too late. I don't believe you. I think you're just telling me that so I can forgive you and, as soon as I do, you're going to do the same thing to me again. You make me feel unsexy, ugly and insecure, and I don't like feeling that way. I need a man that automatically knows he should tell me the things that I want to hear," I said not looking at him, walking back toward my kitchen fighting back tears. 'God, you know I love this man, but give me the strength to stay strong,' I silently prayed.

"I can respect that, Storm. I'll see myself out," Raquan said walking out the door, not looking back at me.

As he walked out the door, I wanted to break but I couldn't because I was too mad. I stood there thinking about nothing, my mind was blank. Slowly the tears started coming down my face.

~Chapter Sixteen~

Bianca was still sleeping when Keith returned home from dropping the kids off at school. He stood over her thinking about how much he loved his wife, but he was still fucked up in the head.

"Bianca, wake up," Keith said, shaking her.

"What?" she asked.

"I thought you wanted to talk?" he said, still standing over her.

"Keith, my breath stinks, my head hurts, and my stomach's turning and bubbling. I don't think I can talk just yet," Bianca said, rubbing her eyes. "Let me get myself up and together first. Or do you have somewhere to go?" she asked, while getting up.

Keith just stood there, laughed at Bianca and said, "Nah, I ain't got nowhere to go. I'll be in the kitchen when you're ready to talk."

"Alright, I won't be long."

Bianca had more than enough time to think about the stupid decisions she had made recently. How the fuck could one person make so many wrong decisions? Bianca stood in front of the bathroom mirror staring at herself for a minute before brushing her teeth. She then turned around to take a quick shit because her stomach was feeling fucked up; she was scared and nervous. She honestly didn't know what Keith was going to say to her. When she finished shitting, she jumped in the shower and then went into the bedroom where Keith was waiting.

"Why are you getting dressed, Bianca? Where are you going?" Keith asked edgily, when he saw Bianca looking through her closet for something to wear.

"Nowhere, I just wanted to throw some clothes on, get comfortable. Is that okay with you?" she asked.

She reached in the closet and pulled out a pair of Armani stretch pants and a low cut, fitted dress shirt. By the time she had finished getting dressed, she was smelling like a fruit garden with the Victoria Secret's lotion and body spray she had used. She took her long weave and pinned it up so her long neck would show. She was looking sexy as ever and she knew it.

Bianca made her man forget what he really wanted to say. He sat on the bed pretending like he was watching TV, but he was watching her thinking, damn, my baby looks good!

When she had finished getting dressed, she looked at him and asked, "Well, are you ready to talk?"

Keith looked at her and said, "Bianca, what made you do that stupid shit?"

"I don't know it just happened. I'm sorry. I can't rewind this and change what happened, but what I can do is make sure it never happens again. I can sit here and tell you it happened because you did or didn't do so and so, and the situation would still be the same. My main concern right now is what we are going to do?" she said staring at him, watching his facial expression.

"Well, Bianca, we can fix this, but it's going to take time for me to forgive or even trust you again. So don't start bugging when the questions start. Ya know, the where ya going, where ya at questions. I was thinking maybe you should start working full time in my other office."

"I guess, Keith. So what's next? I mean is this it, or shouldn't you be making me some promises also?" Bianca said.

"Oh yeah. I promise to bust your ass the next time some shit like this happens and then to divorce you. You know the average nigga would leave, cheat or walk around the house without speaking to you, but I'm not that average nigga. I know I had a lot to do with you fuckin' up, so I'll accept the shit this one time, but don't try it again. Bianca, you're my wife, and I took a vow for better or worse. I do promise to start doing things with you and spending more time with you," Keith said, giving Bianca a hug and a kiss. Then he whispered softly into her ear, "I love you."

Bianca returned the words and they did more than kiss, they spent the morning making love. They spent the whole day talking about their future and what they both expected from each other. Bianca promised that if she ever felt she needed some attention from him, she would definitely let it be known and not wait for him to notice. They made love again until it was time to pick up the kids from school. Bianca and Keith decided they would pick them up together. She grabbed her bag and cell phone and got ready. C'mon, Keith, Dee Dee should be outside by now. Was Chantell catching the bus today?" Bianca asked, walking toward the garage.

"Uh, I don't know, she didn't say. I told you to get those girls a cell phone so we could know these things," Keith said.

As soon as they got ready to pull off, Bianca's cell phone rang. "Hello," she said, not recognizing the number.

"Hey, baby, remember me," Hasson said, acting as if they weren't beefing. "I hope you're over your madness. I'm sorry for the problems I caused you. I can respect your feelings, but I was hoping we could still be friends."

Bianca handed Keith the phone while Hasson was still talking. Keith listened for a minute and then said, "Yo, my man, don't call my wife again. You got away with hitting her, but I promise if I ever see you, your ass is mine! I'm going to beat you like you're one of my bitches on the street!"

Hasson was quiet for a moment. Then he went crazy. "Man, fuck you! You don't know me, son! You don't know what I'm capable of doing!" Hasson yelled, into the phone.

"Whenever you want to see me, holla!" Keith said, before hanging up the phone. He then looked at Bianca and said, "You fucked around with a fuckin' crazy muthafucka. It's not going to be easy getting rid of that one, Bianca."

Bianca was thinking, Keith is taking this too calmly. Something ain't right. And Keith was thinking, I can't believe Bianca got me caught up and some shit like this. I'm gonna have to kill that muthafucka.

~Chapter Seventeen~

"Samantha!" Isis yelled, from the ladies room at work. "Samantha, please come here!" she yelled out again.

Samantha was on the phone so she couldn't come right away. When she finally came into the ladies room, Isis was on her knees throwing up.

"What the fuck!" Samantha said, looking at Isis with a smirk on her face.

"Don't just stand there; get me something to clean this shit up with. Go into my office and see if I got a shirt or something in my closet I can put on." Isis had thrown up all over herself and had to come out of her blouse. She sat on the floor next to the toilet waiting to see if she had to vomit again.

"Are you okay?" Samantha asked, handing her a tee shirt.

"Yeah, I'm okay. I ate at Burger King for lunch and that shit came right back up. It smelled funny. I don't know why I continued eating it. I need a mop, is it out front?"

"I'll check, but maybe you should leave, you look a mess," Sam suggested, while looking for the mop.

"Thanks, I kinda look like you today, huh? Isis said sarcastically, laughing to herself.

"Whatever. But seriously, you don't look well."

"I have a meeting today with an advertisement company and I need to be here," Isis retorted.

"Okay, boss lady. But first I hope you run out and buy another shirt because that tee shirt doesn't match your dress pants," Sam said. She turned away to answer the phone.

Looking down, Isis realized she was right. "Samantha, please run across the street to the Gap and buy me a black or white blouse," Isis begged. "I would go but I'm too scared to leave the bathroom right about now."

"Then how and where are you going to have the meeting? In the ladies room, Isis?" Samantha asked, sneering. "Give me the money before you say something else dumb."

"Thanks, girl," she said. "Here take fifty dollars that should be enough."

Samantha and Isis were meant to work together because they acted more like sisters than co-workers. Even though Isis was the boss, Samantha ran the show. She was the receptionist, saleswoman, web designer, she did pretty much the same thing Isis and the two geeky white guys did.

By the time the people came for the meeting, Isis had changed her blouse and was ready. One of the men had on Calvin Klein's 'Crave' cologne, and Isis immediately began to feel queasy again. She showed them her designs and gave them the portfolio to look through. She was trying to hurry up and end this meeting because her stomach was fucked up, and the mixture of the man's cologne and the taste of Burger King on her breath, was not helping.

"Will you gentlemen excuse me for a moment," Isis said, hurrying out of the room. She went to the bathroom down the hall and, as soon as she stepped in the bathroom, she vomited all over the floor and her Gucci shoes.

Samantha came into the bathroom 'cause she had seen Isis go running down the hall a few minutes ago. "Girl, are you alright?" She asked, rubbing Isis' back.

"Yeah, I'm okay. Just go back in there and let them know I'll be right there. Sit in the office with them while I pull myself together, please. Thank you," Isis said, wiping her mouth.

"Girl, you better go and see a doctor today. You might have a stomach virus or food poisoning. My sister was like that a couple of days ago. The doctor had to give her some antibiotics."

"Just go, Sam, damn! Those people are waiting, you can tell me this fuckin' story later!" Isis snapped.

"Rude bitch," Sam mumbled under breath as she closed the bathroom door. "Hello, Isis will be right back. In the meantime, if you have any questions, I'll be more than happy to assist you," Sam said, walking into the room where the men were waiting.

When Isis came back into the room, she took one sniff of that cologne and boom, once again the vomit came up, but this time all over her office floor. The men and Sam had to jump out of the way. Isis was so embarrassed.

"Are you okay?" the man with the cologne on asked.

"What is that you have on, it's making me sick? I'm sorry I can't continue with this meeting because I can't take the smell of your cologne. My assistant will be more than happy to continue on my behalf," Isis said looking directly at the man who had on the cologne, rushing out of her office holding her nose and stomach.

"So, she thinks you stink," another man said, laughing at his friend.

"You're crazy. I have on Crave and it's the hottest cologne out. She must smell something else." The men laughed it off and let Isis design their website.

"Thanks, Sam, I'm glad you were here," Isis said apologetically, after the men had left.

"No problem. Now go home, I'll close up shop tonight."

On the way home, Isis called Stormie. "Girl, I've been vomiting all day. I had a very important meeting with a big advertising company and I almost fucked that up."

"Are you okay now?" I asked.

"Yeah, but one of the men had on some strong ass cologne, and that shit mixed with the Burger King I had brought, almost killed me," Isis said laughing. "Girl, I almost threw up on them, I was sooo embarrassed. I think I'm going to let Sam handle that account. Anyway, how are you?" Isis asked, changing the subject.

"Raquan came over," I said, I knew that was what she wanted to know.

"And?" she asked.

"I told him that I couldn't deal with him and his non-caring ass attitude. Now he wants to tell me he loves me. Of all fuckin' days."

"That's cause his dumb ass knows he's about to lose you. That's what that's all about."

"I know that's right. He needs to see how important I really am to him because he doesn't know."

"Yeah, you never miss your water till the well runs dry," Isis said, sounding like Mommy.

"Well, his well done ran dry," I said, laughing. "Anyway, you said as soon as you smelled that man's cologne you got sick, right?"

"Please, don't make me think of that smell again cause I might get sick just thinking about it," Isis said, frowning.

"This sounds serious. Let me go, I got to pick my kids up from Mommy's house. I'll call you later," I said, hanging up.

Isis was driving and thinking about Damien, hoping he was alright. She hadn't had time to call home to make sure he was okay, and he hadn't bothered to call her and say he was okay either. She decided to give him a call.

"Hey, why haven't I heard from you all day?" Isis snapped as soon as he answered the phone.

"Cause I'm working," Damien snapped back.

"Oh, so work made you forget to call and let me know you were okay?" Isis said.

"Man, don't call me with the bullshit. I was okay before you left this morning, and I'm still okay. Now I've got to go, Isis."

"What, you can't talk, you have company? Is your company the reason why you haven't called me all day?" Isis was talking nasty to him.

"Yup, I have company. I'll talk to you later. Bye, Isis." Damien was getting mad.

"I'm on my way to your fuckin' house!" Isis yelled.

"Yo, don't come over here with the bullshit. What the fuck is your problem, Isis? Why you buggin' the fuck out? What, you think I have female company?" Damien yelled. Isis began to cry. "What's wrong, Isis?" Damien asked agitated.

"Nothing, I'm not coming over there, I'm going home. Call me when you have time to talk!" Isis yelled then hung up on him.

She started to think she was losing her mind. I don't know what's wrong with me. I can't stand Damien, she thought. Fuck him. He can't talk now; well I'm not going to talk to him later. Once she got into her house the phone rang, it was Damien.

"Yo, what's your problem? Let me find out you're weird and shit," Damien said to her.

"What, Damien?" Isis said.

"What do you mean 'what'? You don't want me to call you anymore?" he asked, trying to figure out where her attitude was coming from.

"Baby, I'm sorry. It's just that I'm not feeling good. I've been vomiting all day. I think I've got food poisoning. I've got to go to the bathroom cause I feel like I'm about to vomit again. I'll call you back," Isis said, running toward the bathroom.

"Food poisoning? What did you eat?" he asked.

"Burger King," Isis answered, holding her mouth.

"I'll bring you some ginger ale when I come. In the meantime drink plenty of fluids and keep a bucket by the side of the bed," Damien suggested.

"I'll see you later, Damien," Isis said, hanging up and vomiting once again.

　　　I stopped by Isis house to see if she was feeling better, but when she opened the door she looked a mess and the house smelled like sickness. I fixed her some soup to eat, but she couldn't keep anything on her stomach. I called Damien back and told him to bring the ginger ale as soon as possible. I asked her if she wanted to go to the emergency room, but she said no.

"Damn, bitch, what kind of sandwich did you have?" I asked, jokingly.

"A Whopper with cheese. It didn't smell right, I don't know why I kept eating that shit,' Isis said, shaking her head.

"You'll be alright tomorrow. You just need to rest and drink some ginger ale to settle your stomach," I said, trying to comfort her. "Maybe you also need to think about suing Burger King for selling you a bad sandwich."

When Damien walked into the house without ringing the bell, I thought to myself, *whoa, homeboy has a key*. He walked over and felt Isis' forehead; she didn't have a fever. He then tried to rub her stomach, but his cologne didn't agree with her.

"Baby, my stomach is too weak to handle your cologne. Can you please go take a shower?" Isis said, immediately getting sick again.

"Sure, baby. I'll be right back. Stormie, can you make sure she drinks some of the ginger ale I got for her," he said, handing her the soda and heading upstairs to take a shower.

"How long have you been feeling this way, Isis?" I asked her as soon as Damien walked out of the room.

"It started after I ate lunch today. I'm telling you I was fine till after I ate that sandwich from Burger King. I think I have food poisoning." Isis was in tears by now. "You know how it feels when you don't have anything on your stomach and you still have to throw up."

Isis tried to throw up two more times but couldn't. She finally she fell asleep. I talked to Damien for a couple of hours about Isis and Raquan. He told me that maybe he did care, but just not enough to fall in love with me. He also said that maybe he was with me until something better came along. I told Damien that today Raquan told me he loved me.

Damien was like, "Please, that nigga's just trying to get you back to where you were, which is stupid in love." What he meant by that was, being so in love that you do stupid shit to keep a person. You start doing things you normally wouldn't do, and accepting bullshit you normally wouldn't accept. He told me that he respected my gangsta attitude, but he also knew that sooner or later I was going to take Raquan back. I denied the shit because I'd be a fool if I did.

Damien continued by saying, "Raquan knows you're a good woman, but he's also threatened by you. You're beautiful, smart, independent, hard working, and can pretty much take care of yourself. He doesn't compliment you because of his insecurities. If he were secure with himself, then complimenting you would come naturally to him. He needs a woman that will let him control everything she does and you're not that woman. Anyway, he's not used to having such beauty, Storm. If a person never had anything good, how would they know how to treat a good thing?"

I appreciated Damien's honesty and he gave me something to think about. He told me that it wouldn't be fair to use Tony to get over him.

"If you're gonna hang out with this guy, Tony, then do it, but don't do it only because you're mad at Raquan. And although you're going to get lonely at night, be strong and don't call that nigga. I'm sorry if I sound harsh, but I don't have respect for a man, excuse me, I mean boy who works hard at trying to knock his girl's self-esteem. Don't let him break you, Storm. There's a man out there who would be glad to have you for a girlfriend or wife," Damien said, supporting me. "Muthafucka's like Raquan makes a person feel ugly even though it's them that's fucked up. He's playing a game with you, and he'll win if you take him back. You've got to show that man that hey, life goes on. If at first you don't succeed, try again with someone else," Damien said, laughing.

I didn't want Isis' man to see me cry, but he saw right threw me anyway.

"Listen," Damien said, "Don't cry." But as soon as he said that the tears started coming down my face.

"I wish you could understand my pain, Damien," I said. "I know everything that you're saying is true, but I don't know what to do. He keeps telling me let's take it one day at a time. I don't know if that's what I want to do anymore."

"Fuck him! It's not your lost, it's his!" Damien yelled.

"Thanks for the session, D-Money, I needed that. I wish I could be strong even though I know I'm going to fall victim," I said.

"Well, just be extra mean to his ass, he'll appreciate it. Trust me," Damien suggested.

I left to go pick up my kids, during the drive to get them, my mind started drifting toward Raquan. *Please stop thinking about that nigga,* I said to myself. My cell phone rang, breaking my train of thought. I looked at the number and it was from a blocked number. Whoever it was would have to leave a message. I checked my voice mail and it was Raquan. He said for me to call him because we really needed to talk. Yeah right, not today.

I had called my job this morning and told them that I was gonna be out all week, but fuck that, I'm going in because if I stayed home, I'd do nothing but think about him all day. Once I got to Mommy's house, my kids hugged and kissed me like they hadn't seen me in weeks, even though it had only been two days.

"So, how do you feel?" Mommy asked.

"I'm okay I guess. I just finished talking to Damien, Isis' boyfriend. He was pretty concise with me," I said.

"What did he say?" Mommy asked, sitting at her table getting her ears ready for the word on the street.

I told mommy pretty much everything we talked about, and she agreed with some of the things Damien said to me. Plus she gave me some advice of her own. But, of course, I probably wasn't gonna take either one of their advice; I was going to do what I wanted to do.

While I was sitting there, Bianca called. She and our mom talked about what had happened in her house. Bianca said Hasson called and she gave the phone to Keith. You know I had to pick up the other phone so I could listen in, 'cause if your mom was anything like our mom, she would tell you the gossip all fucked up. Mommy would forget half of what was said and then add some shit that wasn't even mentioned.

We all sat on the phone talking for hours before I realized that it was getting late and that my kids were falling asleep on mommy's living room floor. I decided to stay at her house for the night. I turned my cell off cause Raquan kept calling and I had no intention of answering his calls tonight. Doing him like that felt kinda good, even though I knew it shouldn't because, once upon a time, I was doing the same thing and I didn't like the feeling. But he's a man, so he could take it.

He left a message on my cell phone saying, "I know you're angry, but please think about this drastic decision you're making." This muthafucka didn't understand that I was beyond angry and that I refuse to keep giving my love to someone who can't return the love. Maybe other women will accept it, or they don't mind being last on their man's list, but I'm no longer willing to accept that. I'm strong, beautiful and independent, and I have my own shit. Raquan needs to know that I'm not living for him, I'm living for me and I need to make me happy. I'm going to talk to him, but it's going to be on my terms not his not anymore.

"Isis, I'm calling the ambulance," Damien said, once again cleaning up vomit. "I can't keep cleaning this shit up." She couldn't talk because she wasn't feeling well at all. "You stink. Let me put you in the shower. You smell like garbage," Damien said, trying to joke with her.

"Get the fuck off me, Damien!" Isis snapped. "Muthafucka, I'm sick and you say some shit like that!" she said, with tears in her eyes.

"Girl, you know I'm playing, damn," he said trying to rub her hair, but Isis pushed his hand away. Damien just looked at her and shook his head.

It was after 1 o'clock in the morning, and Isis had only been asleep for about an hour before she was waking up, vomiting again. She vomited all over herself and the bed. Damien had to change the sheets and wash the other ones that she had thrown up on cause she was complaining about the smell.

"This is bullshit!" Damien mumbled. "Isis, you need to go to the doctor. Your ass is lying around here throwing up, and now you have a fever," he said, helping her to the shower.

"I'll go in the morning to my doctor," Isis said, getting into the cool shower.

After getting out of the shower, Damien gave her some more ginger ale, but she didn't like the taste of it. By the time she felt a little better, it was already past 3:30 in the morning. Damien, poor thing, was exhausted from running up and down the steps for Isis, cleaning up vomit and changing sheets. Shit, he had to take his asthma pump before he went to sleep.

I woke up late, called my job and told the receptionist that I would be there by ten. I had been on the phone with Bianca and our mom until after 2 in the morning. I fixed my kids breakfast and got them ready to go to school. Mommy took them to school for me. I turned on my cell and saw that both Raquan and Tony had called me. Tony wanted to know if he could see me this weekend, and Raquan just wanted me to call him when I got a chance.

When I got to work, I had a bunch of shit on my desk. It looked like I hadn't worked in weeks and I had only missed one day. I had about 20 e-mails, jobs that needed to get billed, and payables that needed to get processed and ready for payment. There were also invoices that needed to be faxed, spreadsheets that needed to be created and the payroll had to be done. 'Oh shit, what's today's date?' I asked myself. I've got to get the taxes done.

Before I could get comfortable, I was called in for a morning meeting. "Do I have to be there?" I asked my office manager. "I have too much work on my desk that needs to get done."

She told me I had to be there, and that the other stuff would just have to wait. These fuckin' meetings go on for hours, talking about shit that doesn't concern me. I sat in that meeting thinking about what I was going to say to Raquan when I spoke to him today. Once the meeting was over, I rushed back to my office, shut the door and proceeded to get as much work done as possible. I didn't even take a lunch.

I never had a chance to call Tony or Raquan because I was too busy. I did call Isis to check on her. When Damien answered the phone, he sounded like he'd had a rough night. He told me Isis was still asleep. I told him I might stop by when I got off work.

I was deep into my work until my phone rang. "This is Stormie," I answered.

"Hey," Raquan said.

"Hey, to you," I responded.

"Listen, Storm, I really want to talk. I know you're at work but can I see you?"

"When I get off," I said.

"But I'm right outside your office door," Raquan said walking into my office, looking good for some reason.

"You shouldn't be here. I can't talk to you right now." I stood up, pushing him back out my office door.

"Please, just give me one minute," he begged.

"No! Now please leave. It's too soon, you're not ready. I'll talk to you when I feel you're ready to be honest with me."

"I'm ready to talk, Storm. I love you."

"Please," I said, cutting his sentence short. "I'll call you when I get off work."

Raquan stood there shocked at how I was treating him. He finally turned around and left. He was hurt and it showed on his face. I was hurt for treating him that way, but it needed to be done. Because he had fucked up my train of thought, I had to work late because I needed to get the taxes done.

I called him back while I was working, listening to him beg and plead. He promised to change if I would just give him another chance. He also promised to acknowledge me more and to never make me feel insecure again. I told him I needed time to see if that's where I wanted to be. I also told him that I felt a lot of hatred toward him, but that I also loved him.

He was okay with that and said that he would still call me every day, even if it were just to say hello. By the time I got off work it was after 7 o'clock. I picked up my kids, went home and cooked, cleaned, showered and got ready for bed. I called Tony to confirm our date for the weekend. He asked me where things stood between me and him. I told him we were speaking, but that I honestly didn't know what my next move was going to be.

It's been about month and I still haven't taken him back. I talk to him during the week, but the weekends are Tony's. Raquan says to me every Monday when he's finally able to get in touch with me, 'I guess you were with your little friend.' And I never respond. I love him, that's why I still speak to him, but he still isn't saying what I need to hear.

I've been hanging out with Tony, although I haven't invited him to my house yet. Every weekend we've been to a different hotel all around New York. One weekend we had a honeymoon suite, and that shit came with everything. We went shopping at the Armani store in Manhattan, and then got dressed very elegantly and had dinner in the hotel's restaurant. We were pretending like we were rich folks.

I wore a black, long Armani dress cut low in the back with a diamond strap on the shoulder. Of course, I wore no underwear. My shoes were stilettos with a diamond ankle bracelet. Tony wore a pair of black Armani dress pants with a gray and black stripe Armani button up shirt. His shoes, no doubt, matched his shirt. That's right, they were black with a gray stripe going up the center. They may sound ugly, but if you put them on with the right hook-up, the shit looks good.

After we got back to the room, we made love all night. We even took a midnight dive in the Jacuzzi and worked out in the gym at 6 o'clock each morning.

One day I asked Raquan if he wanted to go away with me one weekend. He said he couldn't, he had to work. I never bothered to ask him again. I told him for a brother that was trying to win a sistah back, he was sure doing a poor ass job. Obviously he didn't want what I wanted, which was to work it out.

~Chapter Eighteen~

Bianca and her husband have been doing fine. She's running the office in East Orange and he's running the one in Newark. He had her cell phone number changed and Bianca is very happy her husband has kept his end of the deal. He takes her out every weekend, and he just finished paying for their trip to the Fiji Islands. They'll be leaving to go there in June for her birthday. I was a little jealous, but I'm happy for her. Tony and I have plans to go to Cancun in June, but I don't know if I'm going. Bianca said I should go, but I don't know.

While Bianca was at the office working, she got a disturbing phone call. Chantell was beaten and taken to the hospital. Bianca screamed because she had a feeling Hasson had something to do with it. She called Keith and told him to meet her at Saint Barnabas. She was alright but had a long cut on the side of her face from her ear to the center of her face. She needed stitches. She tried to question Chantell before Keith got there, but she wasn't able to because he walked in right when she started to question her.

"Who the fuck did this shit, Chantell?" Keith yelled.

"Two girls, I don't know who they were. All I know is one of 'em cut me and I jumped on her, then the other one jumped on me. She started hitting me with a stick or something, but I fucked her friend up real good." Chantell was mad because she had never cursed in front of Bianca before.

Bianca had tears in her eyes; she couldn't believe this shit. She started to cry because she was so upset. Her face was cut and her back was bruised and sore from the girl hitting her. Before she could turn around, her whole family was at the hospital, mad as hell and wanting to know what kind of car they were driving, the color and everything. When Dee Dee got to the hospital and looked at Chantell's face, she started crying. She was mad and ready to murder somebody because that was her road dog.

"Who did this, Chantell? Do they go to your school cause I'll find 'em and fuck 'em up, you know how I roll?" Dee Dee said to Chantell.

"Dee Dee, I never saw those girls before, they came out of nowhere. All I know is I was fighting, then the ambulance was there cause they said I was cut. I was so mad I didn't feel that bitch cut me. But if I ever see them again, I'ma." Her words drifted.

"Do you know what they looked like?" Bianca asked.

"I know what one of 'em looked like. She was short and fat with short hair. If I ever see her again, I'll definitely remember her face," Chantell said.

The doctor came in the room and asked if some of us could go wait in the sitting area. My Mother was upset, she was crying, and Keith was ready to murder somebody. Bianca was nervous; she wanted to tell Keith what she suspected but didn't know how. She knew the female that Chantell had described, cause she'd seen her when she was hanging out with Hasson. She knew exactly where the fat chick hung out and lived. Bianca knew if she told Keith, he'd be there tonight kicking in the doors.

When I saw the look on Bianca's face, I knew she was planning to do some shit on her own, so I whispered to her, "Whenever you're ready let's go. I know Hasson had something to do with this."

"Do you think I should tell Keith?" Bianca asked me.

"Yeah, you should, but I also think we need to fuck those little bitches up ourselves." I know that was the wrong advice but my niece's face was fucked up, and not just from the scar. They had to have hit her a couple of times, cause her shit was all swollen too. They kept Chantell in the hospital because of the swelling.

My brother, Will, was ready to shoot somebody. He hadn't known about Hasson and the whole situation until that night in the hospital. He cussed at Bianca and she cussed his ass right back.

Bianca, Dee Dee and I went to the little fat chick's house. Dee Dee knocked on the door and, as soon as the door was cracked halfway, Bianca kicked that shit in. The first fat person we saw got it. The baby in the house was screaming and crying.

"Where's the bitch that hit my daughter with the stick!" Bianca was yelling.

"I don't know!" screamed the little fat chick.

"Let's go, you're coming with us! I swear to God I'll catch a kidnapping charge tonight if you don't! You don't fuck with my babies! Hasson forgot to tell you little dumb bitches I was a crazy bitch, didn't he!" Bianca was talking and smacking the girl upside her head, while Dee Dee was kicking and pulling her hair at the same time.

"I should take this blade and give you the same scar my sister got, you fat cow!" Dee Dee screamed at the girl.

I took the baby in the other room because I didn't want her to see her Mom getting fucked up. No one else was home. I called the cops and told them what happened earlier. I told Bianca to stop hitting the girl because the cops were on their way. Bianca told her if she told the cops she hit her, she was going to fuck her up some more.

By the time the cops got there, we had cleaned her up. She was crying, and we told the cops she had sliced Chantell's face over some nigga. We told them we knew she did it because Chantell had seen her face. She agreed with the whole story. They took her baby away and took her to jail. We didn't bother to tell the cops about the other chick because we wanted to find her first. The little fat chick had told Bianca where she stayed. She also said Hasson had paid them $500.00 a piece to jump Chantell. Of course, we took what was left of her money.

I called Isis while we were on our way to the other chick's house. I wanted her to come and take Dee Dee home when we were done with this bitch. We had this shit planned out. By the time the cops got there Dee Dee was gone, but not before she beat the shit out of the girl. My niece is tall and skinny, but don't let that fool you.

When we got to the other girl's house, we knocked on her door and, when her Mom came to the door, we had Dee Dee ask for her daughter. Her daughter came to the door only to get greeted by a fist from Dee Dee. She then dragged the girl out of her house, beating the pulp out of her. The girl's Momma came running out and Bianca knocked her fat ass back in the house.

"Your fuckin' dirty ass daughter jumped my baby today! She beat her in the back with a stick! She's gonna get fucked up before she goes to jail!" Bianca was yelling. The girl told the cops that we had somebody jump her. I told the cops it was just the two of us, and that when we got here she was already fighting. We also told the cops about the arrest earlier of her partner. The cops verified our story then took the little bitch away.

The girl's Momma was yelling, "No, that lady hit me! I came to my door and she hit me!"

"Shit, she came out swinging! I was only defending myself!" Bianca was yelling back, so the cops could hear her.

We told the cops what hospital Chantell was in so they could go and talk to her. Chantell pressed charges against both of the girls.

We all met up at Mommy's house. Isis was already there with Dee Dee and my brother, Will. Keith was also there, mad as hell, waiting on Bianca because he knew she had went and did something crazy.

When he asked, she was like, "Well, I took care of the two little bitches that were involved, that's for sure."

"You know who did this shit, Bianca?" Keith asked.

"Yeah. Hasson paid them $500.00 a piece to jump Chantell," Bianca told Keith. "I know where he hangs out, Keith. I want to go there myself, but I'll let you handle him."

"Where the fuck does he hangs out, Bianca?" Keith asked, while calling his boys. "I'm going to take this nut out!"

It was like a family reunion at mommy's house. Bianca told them about how we ran up in the fat bitch's house and how Dee Dee dragged the other bitch outside. We told them that they had both been arrested, and that one of them had her baby taken away from her. She told Keith to be careful and to not do anything stupid, to just get Hasson arrested. Keith heard her, but he was furious right about now.

He said to Bianca, "All of this because you wanted to cheat, was it worth it, Bianca?" Keith was livid and it showed on his face. "Your fuckin' daughter is in the hospital behind this stupid shit!" he said, while getting in his truck. "Think about that, Bianca!" he yelled, as he drove off.

Bianca hated Keith for saying that, even though she knew he was right. She called Chantell crying, telling her how sorry she was for getting her hurt. Chantell told her that it wasn't her fault and that she would be all right. The doctors told her that the scar on her face would heal, but that her pinky was broken. Chantell told Bianca that at the time she had been too mad to feel anything, but she was feeling it now. They had given her some pain medicine, which was making her drowsy and she was getting ready to go to sleep. Bianca told her that she would be there to see her later and that she loved her.

Keith and his boys went to the bar where Hasson hung out. Bianca had described Hasson to Keith, so they had an idea who they were looking for. First Will walked in, then Keith, then about three other jokers. They didn't come in together they came in separately.

Once Keith spotted Hasson it was on. He was at the bar drinking a Heineken and talking to some chick. Will walked by and bumped him, pretending like he was drunk. Hasson just looked at him and Will looked back with a smile that said, "I'm about to fuck you up.' Keith and his other three boys came walking over to Hasson, surrounding him. Of all nights Hasson was alone, his homeboys wasn't around. Will told the girl to get lost.

She gave Will a look like, 'What?' "Bitch, I said get the fuck lost!" Will demanded.

"Yo, do I know you?" Hasson asked scared, but trying not to show it.

"Nah, and my niece didn't know those two bitches you paid to jump her either."

Before Hasson could answer, Will picked up a beer bottle and bust him upside the head. They then drugged Hasson's ass outside and beat the shit out of him. Keith never said anything he was just hitting and kicking Hasson.

When Keith pulled out a gun, Will said, "Man, he's not worth losing everything!

I want to shoot his ass too, but the beating we just gave this muthafucka gets our point across." Will took the gun away from Keith and put it in his pocket. When they finished beating Hasson, he was bleeding from the eyes, nose and ears.

The guy who broke Hasson's pinky said, "Now you know how shorty felt."

When they heard the cops coming, they all ran, jumped in their trucks and sped off. My brother was mad, he wanted to shoot that Hasson, but knew he wasn't worth going to jail over.

Hasson was so fucked up that by the time the cops got there he wasn't moving; he was unconscious. When the cops started asking questions, nigga's pretended like they hadn't seen anything. They didn't feel sorry for Hasson because they had heard Will talking about how Hasson had jumped on his sister then his niece. The ambulance had to rush him to the hospital.

Mommy called to see if Bianca was still there, which she was.

Bianca said, "Keith, I don't appreciate you talking to me like that in front of your friends. Next time, pull me to the side; don't be embarrassing me like that!" Bianca was yelling.

"You embarrassed yourself, Bianca. This whole chaos is because of you. Two young ladies are now behind bars and two people are lying in the hospital courtesy of Bianca the," he started saying, before Bianca interrupted him.

"The what?" Bianca asked. "Say it, Keith, be a man speak your peace. What, were you going to call me a bitch? I'll be that bitch tonight but remember this."

"Bianca, you fucked up, not me! And right now since I'm not in the mood for your voice, stay at your Mom's house tonight, alright." Keith said, cutting her off and hanging up on her.

Bianca called back but he wouldn't answer the phone. "Fuck him!" she yelled out loud. Everything was falling apart for her. She stayed at Mommy's house for the rest of the month. She didn't call Keith and he didn't call her.

Hasson didn't come around Bianca again, which was good. Bianca did find out that Keith and his boys had beat Hasson so bad that day, that by the time he had gotten to the hospital, he had an edema on his head and was bleeding on the inside. He regained conscious, but was in the hospital for a couple of days.

Chantell was out of the hospital and doing better. She had a little scar on her face and her pinky was healing, even though she still couldn't move it. Bianca went to the office everyday and if Keith came in for something, they didn't say one word to each other. They both were acting real immature. I told Bianca she was wrong and that she should apologize first. All she said was, "Shiiit!!" and kept it moving.

She finally went home on Thanksgiving; she wanted to cook dinner for her family. Keith knew she was coming home because they had talked on the phone the day before. Of course, he apologized first because he couldn't hold out any longer. Once again, he had let Bianca win.

I decided to spend Thanksgiving with Mommy. My kids and I sang on the karaoke machine and ate until our bellies were poking out. Ja'Mil ate himself into an asthma attack. Raquan wanted me to come to his house but I told him I didn't feel like driving in the snow. While I was at Mommy's we talked and agreed to try and to make things work between us. I told him for Christmas I would cook for him and his boys. Tony called my cell phone and left a message on my voice mail, which I didn't appreciate, so I didn't call him back.

I think our weekend excursions are over because the message that muthafucka left on my voice mail said, 'I know you're with that nigga who treats you like shit today. Anyway, you could've called me to say have a nice Thanksgiving or something, Storm. I'm getting real tired of your games. If you can't spend at least one holiday with me, then I can't be bothered with you. I've put my life on hold waiting on you. Do you know how many women would love to have me? You know you only wish that faggot ass, half of a man that you have could be me, but he isn't and never will be! Listen, I'm a little upset, call me when you get a chance.

~Chapter Nineteen~

"Girl, I'm taking you to the doctor today!" Damien yelled to Isis. She had been sick on and off for the past couple of months, and she refused to go to the doctor. "I'm alright. Just go get me some soup and ginger ale, please," Isis begged, while curled up on Damien's bed.

Damien had to flip his mattress and change the sheets because she had vomited in his bed last night. This morning Damien had put a bucket beside the bed but she missed it and threw up on the floor.

"Isis, fuck this, I'm calling the doctor. You're throwing up too much!" Damien was furious at Isis. She didn't want to go to the doctor and he knew he couldn't force her to go either. "Shit, I have to get this man's demo together, I can't keep babysitting you. Something is wrong with your stomach and you shouldn't play around with that," Damien was saying to her, trying to console her after he had just yelled at her. "Let me take you to the doctor, please."

Isis agreed because she couldn't take the way she was feeling anymore. One day she's up working and joking and then the next day she can't hold her head up.

Once they arrived at the doctor, Isis was still feeling nauseous. The doctor examining her asked when the date of her last period was, she couldn't remember. He then suggested she go see a gynecologist. He didn't prescribe anything for her because he wanted her to take a pregnancy test first. That fucked Isis' head up and she didn't tell Damien what the doctor said, she just told him that the doctor wanted her to go see a gynecologist. Sometimes men can be so naïve, he just said okay, he didn't even ask why.

"Can you go see a gynecologist today, Isis?" Damien asked once they were in his car, because he couldn't go another day like this with her.

"I guess," Isis answered, looking out the window.

Isis wanted kids and she didn't. Her mind was gone, she was thinking the "what if" thoughts. What if I'm pregnant, what if Damien leaves me, what if he doesn't want any kids? Isis was quiet all the way to the gynecologist. Once they arrived, he did all of the talking.

"Look, she's been vomiting all day and night for the past two or three months, I think maybe longer. I took her to her primary doctor and he told us to come see a gynecologist," Damien explained to the nurse.

"Is she pregnant?" the nurse asked.

"I don't think so," Damien answered, confused. Now his mind went to the "*what if*" thoughts.

"Here, give her this cup so she can pee in it." The nurse handed him a cup.

He took the cup to Isis and asked her if she thought she was pregnant. Isis didn't answer him. She just took the cup and went to the ladies room. When Isis' name was called, they both stood up.

"Where are you going?" Isis snapped.

"I'm going to find out if you're pregnant," Damien said, walking toward the nurse that called her. "Let's go."

"I really can't stand you, Damien. Please wait for me out front," Isis said, trying to whisper.

"No, I'm coming in the back. Shit, I'm up all day and night with you, I have a right to know what's going on with your body."

The doctor examined Isis thoroughly. He took blood, piss, and he did the two-finger examination. Damien couldn't take it when the doctor stuck his fingers in her vagina, so he stood outside the door. He called Damien back into the room as Isis was getting dressed.

"Well, I just want to let you both know that you're pregnant. The baby's due date is June 19th," the doctor was saying, shaking Damien's hand. Damien looked at Isis, and she looked the other way.

"What's the matter?" Damien asked.

"Nothing," she said, quickly.

"You don't want to keep the baby?" he asked, looking at her face.

"What do you think?" Isis snapped.

"I don't know that's why I'm asking. I mean, whatever you choose I'll support you. But I hope you're going to keep the baby."

"I am keeping my baby," Isis said.

"Our baby," Damien said rubbing her small belly, reminding her that he had helped make her baby.

"No wonder when we went to the mall I couldn't fit shit. Stormie and Bianca were teasing me, telling me that I must be in love and that was why I was gaining all that weight. Do I look like I gained a lot of weight?" she asked, hoping for an honest answer.

Damien looked at Isis, turned her around so he could see her little butt then responded, "If you've gained any weight, baby, you've gained it in all the right places."

Isis had never had any ass, now all of a sudden she has a little poking out of her jeans. Her face was fatter and always shining, her hands were light, and her skin was clearer. Yeah, she was pregnant.

Now that she knew for sure she was pregnant, she made Damien get rid of all his cologne. She also got rid of all her perfume. They were only allowed to wear baby oil, because that was the only smell that didn't bother her.

"Girl, what are you going to do about the white house? I mean with a baby and all you're not going to be able to keep everything white," I said to Isis, one day.

"I'm only three months, I have plenty of time to think about that," Isis said, rubbing her belly.

"What did your Mom have to say about you being pregnant?"

"She's happy for me. I'm going to send for her my last month so she can be here with me when the baby is born," she said, fixing herself a sandwich. "What's the deal with you and Raquan, are you two a couple again?" she asked, with her nose turned up.

"Something like that. Did I show you the ring I got from him on Christmas? Mind you he's Muslim and doesn't celebrate Christmas," I said holding my hand out, showing her my ring.

"Damn, bitch, that shit is beautiful. I know he spent some money on that ring.

What is that, White Gold or Platinum?"

"It's a White Gold, Sapphire stone, 3 carat diamond," I said, proudly.

"I don't know jewelry at all, but I know that shit is hot," Isis said, admiring my ring. "You don't even bitch about Raquan as much. He must be doing a lot better."

"He is," I said, thinking about the way he made love to me on Christmas.

On Christmas, I cooked and he and his boys came over. I was shocked he even gave me a gift. I didn't have anything for him. After we finished eating dinner and playing with his kids' toys, we went upstairs to my bedroom. I went to take a hot shower because I was sweaty and sticky, and Raquan joined me. I pretended to be mad at first. I was like, 'what are you doing?' You know, looking him up and down with a frown on my face. I wouldn't let him touch me; I washed my body and left him in the shower alone. His dick was hard as hell too. I almost gave in, but I was like, 'I think I can, I think I can,' repeatedly to myself.

When Raquan came out of the shower, he was butt ass naked. I was lying across my bed watching Barber Shop, pretending like I didn't see his dick pointing at me. He slowly walked over to me, got on his knees and started playing with 'Lolita.' He was finger fucking me, eating, licking, and rubbing my spot. It felt so good that I spread my legs further apart. I told him to stop, but he didn't listen and I really didn't want him to stop. He ate my pussy for at least 30 minutes, and no lie, I must've came at least seven times. Raquan had never eaten my pussy that long before.

While he was eating me, he was humping my bed. His shit was extra hard. Raquan didn't speak the whole time, and when he was ready to insert his penis into my vagina, I tried to stop him but he kept holding onto me, kissing me and rubbing my 'Lolita.' I was so wet and horny that I finally let him insert his erect penis in me and, as soon as he put it in I cried.

I love Raquan so much and I feel bad for cheating on him, but shit, he was the reason I did it. If only he would've gave me the attention that I so desperately needed. Raquan cried and he said that he was sorry and that he loves me with all his heart. We only had sex once that night, but that's okay because that was all we needed.

Isis broke my thoughts when I heard her say something about marrying Damien.

"What?" I asked, looking at her. I didn't hear one word she was saying.

"Damn, bitch, you didn't hear me talking to you. I said I wish we could be married before the baby is born. I always wanted to be married first before I had a child."

"Join the club. What are y'all doing for the New Year?" I asked.

"We might rent some movies and drink apple cider," she said smiling, acting like a teenager.

"Uggghhh!" I said, doing her like she used to do me when I would tell her what Raquan and I was doing or going to do.

"Don't hate," she said. "What are you and Mr. Big Head doing?"

"I don't know. We hadn't planned on doing anything. Me and the kids will probably go over Raquan's to spend the night and watch the ball drop on television."

"Have you heard from Tony?"

"Yeah, he calls every now and again, but I don't have too much to say to him. I told him not call my house again. I blocked his number anyway, but I miss him. He was fun, spontaneous, and very handsome. And giirrrl, talk about a freak in the bed," I said, thinking about those nights in the hotel.

"I can't believe you left him to stay with Raquan. I bet Tony would've brought the New Year in with you at some expensive ass hotel drinking Moet or some ole expensive ass wine. Don't come telling me how Raquan went to sleep on your ass at 11:58, like he's done for the last two New Years," Isis said, laughing.

"Trust me I won't. I'm not going to complain anymore about what he does to me, I'll deal with it myself. Anyway, Damien's only good right now, see me in another year or so. I'll let you get your complain on for a minute," I said, giving her something to think about.

"You're right, but for now I'm going to enjoy what I have," Isis said.

"That's exactly what I'm gonna do. Anyway, I'm on my way to Raquan's house for the night, I'll call you later," I said, putting on the fur coat I bought from Debbie Peiser Furs in New York.

"Girl, that's a bad ass fur. What is that, rabbit?" Isis asked, rubbing the fur.

"Nah, it's Chinchilla," I said. "Have you ever seen a baby blue rabbit? Stop being dumb."

"Hey, they make everything in all colors now," she said, admiring my shit. "If I wasn't pregnant I would have me one too, girl."

I'm glad she's pregnant because I can't stand to see a bitch with the same shit I've got, especially my friends. That shit pisses me the fuck off.

Keith had gotten Bianca a Chinchilla for Christmas, but hers was white. She had gotten him one too. They had decided to go away after Christmas and wouldn't be returning until after the New Year. They haven't had any problem with that Hasson character, so everything was back to normal for her.

~Chapter Twenty~

"Keith, where are those edible undies I put in the suitcase?" Bianca asked.

"Man, I took them out the bag. I'm not putting on those things."

"Stupid, they're not for you to put on, you're supposed to eat your way to the pussy," Bianca said, rubbing her husband's penis. "I came here to fuck every night until the New Year."

"Yeah, okay, but you ain't about to wear me out," Keith said jumping on the bed, grabbing the remote.

"Keith, don't start the bullshit. You could've stayed home if you wanted to watch T.V.," Bianca said, with her face frowned up.

"Whatever. I just drove two hours straight and my legs hurt."

"You act like you just drove to Florida or something. We're only in Wildwood, New Jersey so don't give me that shit. Lazy bastard," she said pissed the fuck off.

"All I know is I'm going to sleep. Just let me sleep for about an hour. C'mon, lie down beside me."

"Fuck that, I'm going to the bar. I'll be back," Bianca said, snatching up her purse and coat.

"Damn, we just got here, what's your rush? Anyway, why are you going to the bar, you don't drink? Baby, we're here for five days, we got time to fuck, eat, sleep, whatever," he said, sitting straight up in the bed.

"I'm going to the bar to see what the atmosphere is like. Then I'm going go and try to find some more edible undies. I want you to be my Pac-Man tonight, chomp chomp," Bianca said, making a face like she was biting something.

"Bring me back something to eat while you're out. I want some shrimp parm," Keith said to Bianca, as she was walking out the door.

"I'ma bring you back something to eat alright, me and some edible undies," she said, slamming the hotel door behind her.

On my way to Raquan's house, I thought about what Isis had said. She was right. He always waited right until 11:58 to fall asleep, but not this year.

"Raquan, do you have to work on New Year's Eve?"

"Uh, I don't know. I'll find out when I go to work, why?"

"I just wanted to know. So what are we doing New Year's Eve?" I asked, hoping he'd say something exciting.

"It's just another day to me. What do we normally do, Storm?" he asked.

"See, that's the problem. I don't want to do what we normally do on New Year's Eve, Raquan!" I began to yell.

"Ma, what do you want to do, go out or something? You can go, I don't give a fuck," Raquan said, nonchalantly.

"You don't care? I wanted us to get a room, have a drink, maybe even a New Year's kiss. I knew I shouldn't have taken your ass back," I said, standing over him.

"Storm, you know what I meant, so don't even try to take it there."

"No, I don't know what you meant, Raquan," I said, looking at him with red eyes and my hands on her hips. Then I got my shit and kids and left his house.

On my way home, I felt like I was the biggest ass in the world. Once again, the nigga had tricked me. Raquan called me on my cell and, like a dummy, I answered.

"What, Raquan!" I yelled, into the phone.

"I didn't mean I don't care about you," he said.

"I know what the fuck you meant, Raquan. I'm not stupid! You meant exactly what you said. Listen, if you can't take me where I want to go for New Year's Eve, then forget about everything. Raquan, it's not about you anymore, it's about me and what I want! There's a man out there right now who's waiting to make me happy and I'm putting him on the back burner for you! So if this is how you're gonna treat me, fuck that and fuck you!" I yelled. "Oh, so you have a friend waiting for me to fuck up?" Raquan questioned.

"You damn right I do," I said. "Raquan, that's what you do best, fuck up. Think about what I said and call me back with a plan," I said hanging up, not knowing if he was going to ever call me again.

I was so mad at myself and I couldn't call Isis cause she didn't want to hear the shit anymore, and Mommy felt the same way. Bianca and her husband were in Wildwood, so I couldn't call her. Oh well, I guess I'll call Tony. "Old faithful" is what I called him.

"Hey, Tony," I said, as soon as he answered.

"Well, look who decided to call. What, your man made you mad or something?" he said, sarcastically.

"No, actually I was calling just to see how you were doing," I said, lying my ass off. I hated him for a hot second for saying that, even though it was true.

"I'm fine. What do you have planned for New Year's Eve?" he asked.

"I don't have any plans at all. I'll probably just hang out with my kids and watch some movies," I said, too embarrassed to tell him the truth.

"Your man isn't taking you anywhere?" he asked, chuckling a little.

"No, he doesn't celebrate holidays. It's just another day to him."

"Sounds like you're going to have a blasting good ole time," Tony said, laughing. "Listen, if you want to hang out with me, just let me know. We can go somewhere loud and dark or quiet and dark, whatever you want."

Damn, why can't Raquan talk that way, I thought. "I don't know just yet, let me think about it, okay."

"Call me on Monday to let me know. Don't have me waiting around like an asshole, Storm," Tony said, a little agitated.

"I won't, I'll call you." I hung up, pulled into my driveway, and thought about it. I hope Raquan had a plan or I was out. I took a hot shower and stayed in the bathroom a long time, contemplating on my so-called relationship with Raquan. Why do I put up with his boring ass? I thought. But Tony was a good man and I needed to give him a chance.

By the time, I stepped out of the shower and walked into my bedroom, Raquan was laying across my bed with some printouts of different hotels he had found online. I just rolled my eyes, happy as hell to see him though.

"So, where do you want to stay?" Raquan asked, pulling me down on the bed with him.

"I don't know, anywhere but your house or mine," I said.

"C'mon, pick a place, Storm. Let me spoil you. I'm sorry for blacking out like that earlier."

"I know it's going to take some time to change, but as long as I see you trying, I'll never leave."

I picked a spot up at the Pocono's. We went online and made reservations for that Sunday, returning New Year's Day. We also made love that night. I can't front, lately this nigga has been putting it down.

"Who the fuck is calling me at 4 o'clock in the morning?' I mumbled to myself. Raquan looked at me, then reached out and answered the phone.

"Hello!" he yelled.

"Raquan, let me talk to Storm!" Isis yelled, into the phone.

"She's asleep!" Raquan yelled back. "Do you realize what time it is?"

"I know what fuckin' time it is, but it's important! Please wake her and give her the phone."

"Storm, here, it Coldness," Raquan said, handing me the phone.

"What's the matter, Isis?" I whispered, still half asleep.

"Girl, I haven't heard from Damien all day. He hasn't called or came over. I went over to both of his houses and he wasn't at either one. Storm, I think he's cheating on me, and he told me he would never cheat on me!" Isis said, crying.

I wanted to curse her stupid ass out for calling me at this time of the morning to talk about her man. But since she was pregnant and sensitive, I didn't say a word.

"Are you there, Storm?"

"Yeah, I'm listening to you. What do you want me to say?"

"Anything, damn! Do you think he's cheating on me?"

I got out of bed and went downstairs into the kitchen so I could talk to her cause Raquan was all in my grill. "Listen, why are you worrying yourself? You're pregnant and shouldn't be worrying. He's alright, maybe he fell asleep somewhere," I don't know why I said that.

"Fell asleep somewhere? Where is it that he could have gone and not called me? I went to his house at 3 o'clock in the morning and he wasn't there. I left a note on his door. Obviously he went to sleep over some bitch's house. I'm dumping his ass as soon as I hear from him."

"Isis, why isn't your ass sleep at 3 o'clock in the morning? If you keep on worrying yourself, you're going to lose that baby."

"Fuck that!" Isis said, with fury in her eyes. "You wait until I see his ass," she continued, biting her bottom lip. "Storm, this isn't the first time this muthafucka's disappeared on me, I just didn't tell you about it."

So, truth be told, Isis' man wasn't perfect. "Well, what are you going to do? I told you men ain't shit. They always start out good but that doesn't last, and you can either deal with it or let it go. I can't tell you what to do, especially with my situation."

"Well, I told you I have something like a good man," Isis said, trying to make a joke out of the situation, but you could hear in her voice that she was hurt. "I don't know what I'm going to do, Storm. I know we've only been dating for a few months, but I'm pregnant and I do have feelings for Damien. He showed me the attention I wasn't getting from other men. And ever since I've been dealing with Damien, I haven't accepted any of Jared's phone calls."

"Please, just forget about Jared, he ain't shit. Maybe Damien really is taking care of business. What excuse did he give you before when he disappeared?"

"He didn't cause I didn't ask. He doesn't even know that I've been to his house looking for him. I didn't want to hear any lies, but I bet'cha he finds out about it today."

Raquan came walking downstairs into the kitchen, listening to my conversation. I waved my hand for him not to say anything. Of course he didn't listen.

"What, is her man cheating on her? Shit, I would too if I was dating somebody fucked up like her," Raquan said, loud enough for Isis to hear. I gave Raquan a hard look, walked out of the kitchen and back upstairs, hoping she hadn't heard what he said, but she did.

"What did that muthafucka say? You tell him that's why you cheated on him!"

"Isis, what do I look like repeating that? I don't know why you even listen to Raquan's stupid ass! You know he's just fucking with you." Raquan came into the bedroom laughing. "That shit isn't funny, Raquan! She's fucking pregnant, she doesn't need to hear that dumb shit from you!" I said, walking out the room and going back downstairs.

I'm getting tired of walking up and down these stairs, I thought. It's fucking 5 o'clock in the morning I should be asleep. Isis was quiet for a minute, so I knew she was mad because she always gets quiet when she's mad.

"Isis, are you alright?" I asked her.

"Yeah. Listen, I'll call you back. Or call me when Frankenstein leaves," she said, hanging up the phone.

I went into the bedroom and told Raquan that what he said to Isis was fucked up. "What I tell you about getting mad at me because of Isis. That's your friend, not mine. She's always saying fucked up shit about people. I can imagine what she had to say about me when I was out of your life," He started mocking Isis, "Girl, leave him and don't take his ass back!" "I know she said those things to you, didn't she?"

"No, she wanted me to get back with you," I said, lying. Isis hated Raquan and she hated the fact that I was back with him, but he didn't need to know that. "Raquan, I'm going back to sleep. When I wake up I want to go to the mall and get some stuff to take to the Pocono's."

"A'ight," Raquan said hugging me, going back to sleep.

Isis finally went to sleep at 6 o'clock. She didn't bother to call Damien anymore because he wasn't answering his cell or Chirp. You know what time it is when your man doesn't answer his cell. If he was with his nigga, he would answer.

Damien came to Isis' house around 9 o'clock in the morning. She was still sleeping and he didn't try to wake her. He had a gift for her, a platinum bracelet, which he put on the nightstand so once she woke up she would see it. In the meantime, he took a shower and went downstairs to fix breakfast for the both of them.

Isis awoke to the smell of blueberry pancakes and bacon. She went downstairs, looked at Damien and started to turn around, but she decided against it. He had told her before to stop acting like a white girl, always running away, so today she decided she would stand up to him.

"Have you been home yet, Damien?" Isis asked, trying not to show her anger.

"Where do you think I'm coming from?"

"I don't know, but it sure ain't home. Listen, I can raise this baby by myself, I don't need you. And you can have this cheap ass bracelet you bought me," Isis said, throwing the bracelet on the kitchen table. "I don't need gifts from you, they won't make me overlook your cheating habits." Isis was very serene. She knew that if she got upset it might put her pregnancy in jeopardy, and she had no intention of losing her baby.

"What fuckin' cheating habits?" he retorted.

"Please, Damien. If you were home, then why haven't you mentioned what I left on your front door? You couldn't miss that big ass note I left there. You know what, this isn't my first time coming to your house in the middle of the night to check on you either. Those days when you forgot to call me, I took my ass over there only to find out that your truck was gone. Before you lie, I checked the other house too. But it's alright, I'm a big girl and I've got my own shit going on. My baby and me baby will be okay. Now, please leave, Damien!" Isis yelled. "I don't want to hear any of your fuckin' excuses!"

"For your information, I fell asleep at my man's house. You know I'm trying to get this CD done for him and I didn't have my cell phone on me."

"Damien, since when don't you carry your cell phone? You're a businessman, right? And since when don't you call me from your man's house? Damien, leave and leave my fuckin' keys too." Isis said, done with him.

"I'm not going anywhere.'

"Oh, you're getting the fuck outta here. You just lied and said you came from home, and then turned right around and said you stayed at your man's house. Which one is it? Go get your story right then call me. Better yet, I don't want to break up with you, but don't call me until you tell the other bitch you can't see her again."

"Whatever."

"Then call her from here, Damien. Call and tell her you don't want to see her again right in front of me. If you leave without calling her, don't ever call me again!" Isis yelled, handing him the phone.

Damien just stood there looking dumb like all men do when they've been busted. He dialed a number and when the female answered the phone, he didn't know what to say.

"Hello, hello," the female on the phone said.

Isis began yelling, "Say something, Damien! Tell the bitch it's over!"

"Listen, Tara, I can't see you anymore," Damien sounded like a little bitch. He knew Isis was a good women and he was willing to make an ass out of himself to keep her close.

"Who the fuck is that yelling in the background?" Tara yelled. "And what do you mean you can't see me anymore? What, are you married?" She was upset. She didn't understand what he was saying because he had just stayed with her last night.

Isis snatched the phone from Damien and said, "He can't see your dumb ass anymore cause he's got a baby on the way and is seriously involved with me!"

"And who the fuck is you? And if he's that seriously involved with you, then why is he fucking me? Who's the dumb one now, huh? I don't give a fuck about you bitch or that baby you're carrying!"

Isis wasn't a fighter so she pretty much let home girl make an ass out of her. She talks and acts tough, but she's a crybaby. She listened to the girl rant and rave about how Damien ate her pussy and took her shopping, but what really fucked up her head was when the bitch mentioned the platinum bracelet.

"You bought this bitch the same bracelet that you bought for me!" Isis yelled to Damien.

"Hell no, she bought that shit herself. She was with me when I bought yours." Damien took the phone away from Isis and began to cuss Tara out. "You fucking, lying ass bitch, don't you ever call me again! You sitting on this phone telling lies to my girl!"

Damien was mad because he had gotten busted. You know a muthafucka gets extra mad when the other bitch starts telling the truth. Sure he cussed Tara out in front of Isis, but that was just a front to get the heat off his ass.

Once they got off the phone, Isis was too upset to eat. She stayed in bed all day crying until she had no more tears. She finally got up and ate the blueberry pancakes and bacon that Damien had cooked earlier. He apologized, claiming that she kept getting on his nerves, fussing all the time so he went out and found him a friend. He said at the time he didn't know she was pregnant and that was the reason for her buggin' out. That still wasn't a good enough excuse. But hey, he's in the music business and pussy is around him all day long. I told Isis before that she needed to show her face more. Let those bitches know he's hers. Not that a bitch would care, but at least they would know she existed.

I called my kids and Mommy at 12 midnight, and then I called Isis. She and Damien were still up, eating popcorn and drinking apple cider.

"Did your man stay up?" Isis asked, being funny.

"Yeah, he did and he also had a drink of bubbly too. Girl, I even got a midnight kiss. I waited two years for that kiss and I finally got it," I said, laughing on the phone.

"Girl, you sound shot the fuck out, let me find out. Anyway, why are you talking to me, did he finally go to sleep?"

"Yeah, he fell asleep a little after 12 midnight, but that's okay as long as he stayed up till 12. This room is beautiful, Isis. There's a big ass Jacuzzi in the center of the room in the shape of a heart. This is my first time staying here."

"Where ya'll at?"

"At the Mt. Airy Lodge. It is really nice. Anyway, I'll see you tomorrow. Happy New Year!"

"Happy New Year, baby," Keith said to Bianca, kissing her all over and nibbling on her edible undies. He ate his way to pussyville, doing exactly what Bianca wanted him to do. What a way to bring in the New Year, huh!

~Chapter Twenty One~

We returned home at 3 o'clock in the afternoon on New Year's Day. We stopped by Mommy's house to pick up the kids. Believe it or not, she had kept both Raquan and my kids. She told us that they hadn't been any trouble and that he should start bringing his boys around more often because they were practically part of the family. But that's just Raquan, he doesn't bring his kids around me much either. I used to complain, but not anymore.

We went back to his house to drop his boys off, and he told them, "Vacation's over, I want y'all to wash clothes, do homework, bathe, eat and get ready for bed."

I personally think he gives his boys way too much responsibility; they're only 13 years old. But I respect that, that's why they didn't give Mommy a hard time.

Once we got to my house I checked the voice mail on my cell and saw that Tony had called. Oops, I had forgotten to call him, and I couldn't listen to his message right now because he was on my ass.

"Raquan, there's one more holiday we've got to celebrate," I said, putting my cell back into my purse.

"What, your birthday? Please, I just spent well over $2000.00 on your ass, I need to make that money back."

"Okay, I understand. Just have me a gift; we don't have to go anywhere."

"What do you want for your birthday so I can go put it on layaway cause you don't know simple too well. Nothing less than the best is your motto Storm."

"It almost sounds like you're complaining. Are you complaining, Raquan? Why don't you just go back to your old self and say, 'we'll see' and then don't buy me anything. Better yet, just get mad at me two days before my birthday."

"I'm out, Storm, you're starting to bug out. I just wanted to know what you wanted for your birthday. I didn't need for you to go through all that. First you ask me to change, and now that I'm changing, you still throw shit in the game. I don't need you to remind me of the way I was, Storm. Cause I can change back with the snap of a finger. I'll call you later." Raquan got his coat and keys and left without giving me a kiss good-bye.

I hated starting that argument, but I needed for him to leave so I could call Tony. I dialed his number and heard three beeps, which meant that his phone was either off or his number had been changed. Unfortunately for me, the number had been changed. I dialed his cell and it was the same thing. I can't believe that I had let Mr. Fine Ass Chocolate Brother go. I guess he got tired of me and my shit. I decided to listen to the message he left on my cell.

"Yo, I told you to call me on Monday, Storm. All you had to do was dial my number and tell me you had other plans. I'm a grown ass man, and I don't have time for your stupid ass childish games! I'm sick of you and that baggage you have. I will no longer ring your phone and please don't ring mine. I hope you and that nigga have a fucked up New Year! Just so you to know, I really loved you and I would've never done anything to make you cry the way that so-called man of yours always makes you cry. But we all have to find out the hard way, don't we."

After I had finished listening to Tony's message, I noticed that he had left me another one. I thought, Maybe he called back to apologize for being so rough on his last message.

"Oh yeah, don't try to call me because I had all my numbers changed. I don't ever want to hear from you again. I won't let you pull me into that fucked up circle you're involved in. It was fun while it lasted. One!"

I don't know why, but I saved both of his messages. I stood in my living room looking like a damn fool. How long did I expect him to stick around? If Raquan fucks up again, who am I going to call? I can't believe this shit. Isis is going to bug out on me. She's going to think this is the funniest because I really thought I had shit on lockdown. Guess I was wrong.

I decided to go to his website and send him an e-mail. I went upstairs, turned on my computer, went to Tony's website and guess what, it was under construction. I knew what that meant. He's changing his web page. This negro was serious about forgetting about me. He had been so fuckin' good to me, how could I have been so dumb and naïve?

I lay across my bed and started to shed some tears. My phone rang and I wiped my face hoping it was Tony. I swear, if it's him, I'm gonna dump Raquan right now just to make it right between us. But when I answered the phone it was him.

"What's up?" Raquan asked.

"I have a headache. Are you coming back over here tonight?" I asked him.

"I don't think so, why what's up?"

"Nothing, I just wanted to know. Let me call you back."

I didn't have a headache, more like a Tonyache. I decided to go to his house this weekend so that we can talk. Maybe we could start over. I called Bianca for some advice, telling her the whole story.

"Girl, as bad as I hate to say this, you should stick with Raquan. Is he really trying to change?" Bianca asked.

"Yeah, but I think Tony could make me happier."

"If you think Tony is different, then go ahead and break up with him. And who says that you won't go through the same shit again. You and Raquan have already weathered the storm, why start over? Sure couples have their ups and downs, but with the power of love you can overcome it. I don't like his ass, but I don't think you'll find a man any different because they all fuck up."

"Not Keith," I said.

"Please, Keith cheated on me when we first started dating, I just didn't tell anybody. He probably hasn't cheated since we've been married, but I know for a fact that he cheated on me once."

"What happened and how did you find you that he cheated on you?"

"I saw him and the chick leaving his house, but I didn't trip. I just rode by and blew my horn so he would see me and kept it moving. After that, Keith ran behind me for months, because I wouldn't call him, go out with him or anything. Every time he called, I'd talk to him for a minute then I'd tell him I was gonna call him back and I'd turn my ringer off. This muthafucka would ride by my house to see if I was home or not. When I decided to take him back it was on my terms. I knew Keith was a good man, and he still is, but he's no different than Raquan. I honestly think Raquan has changed. If it's meant to be for you and Tony, then you'll see him again but don't go running behind him. Anyway how was your New Year's Eve?"

"It was wonderful. Raquan took me to the Pocono's and we stayed at the Mt. Airy Lodge, which is a very nice hotel. Bianca, he actually stayed awake until 12 midnight, can you believe that?" I said, sounding like a fool.

"See, didn't I tell you that he could change? Sometimes you have to make them miss what they have before they'll change. Then when or if they get a second chance, they'll cherish it better."

"Are you cherishing what you have?" I asked.

"You better believe it," Bianca said, laughing.

"How did you bring in your New Year?" I asked.

"Well, I was lying on my back with my eyes shut."

"What, you were sleep or something?"

"No, more like relaxed."

"Anyway, what was Keith doing?"

"Oh girl, he was on his knees acting like Pac-Man!" Bianca busted out laughing.

"Just know, I stayed on the kitchen table with my legs spread more than the food did," she said, laughing even harder. I must admit it was funny.

"You nasty ho, I don't want to hear your war stories. Anyway, you do know Isis is pregnant, right?"

"Yeah, you know news travel fast. She didn't bother to call me, so I didn't call her. Shit, I feel like since she's the one that's pregnant, she could've called me. I figured she was from the way she was eating that day in the mall, and the bitch couldn't fit shit, stomach looking like jello. Who she pregnant by, that dude she won't let nobody meet?"

"I met him. He's always at Isis' house."

"Mommy told me that she said she had something like a good man. I told Mom to tell her that I got a good man. Isis kills me thinking her man isn't fucking around on her."

"Oh, so you haven't heard the latest, huh?" I asked, devilishly.

"What?"

"Her man's been creeping on her with some chick. She told me she made Damien call the bitch and she cussed her out. Then she made him tell the bitch it was over. She said the girl was crying on the phone, begging Damien not to leave her. He called the girl all kinds of bitches, and told the girl that he was just using her. And get this, she said he brought her the same platinum bracelet that he got for Isis. Damien said that she brought her own bracelet."

"Who did the girl buy the bracelet for?" Bianca asked, surprisingly.

"Girl, I don't know."

"Bullshit, he probably got her that bracelet. For Isis' sake, he tried to make it sound like he was using the girl. Shit, she was probably using his dumb ass, you never know," Bianca said.

"I know that's right," I said. "Anyway, thanks for the advice. I'm about to go see Raquan after I put my kids to bed. I'll talk to you later," I said, hanging up the phone. I went and took a shower, then called Raquan.

"Are you sleeping?" I asked when he picked up the phone.

"Something like that, why?" he answered dryly.

"I was coming over, but since you're sleeping, I guess I'll wait till the weekend," I said, a little disappointed.

"That's cool cause I'm drain anyway."

"I don't know why, you slept the whole day yesterday. You only got up to eat, shit, fuck and watch the ball drop, then back off to sleep you went."

Raquan just laughed because he knew it was true. "Shit, it was cold as hell up there. I think the wine we drank had something to do with the way I'm feeling now."

"Whatever, Raquan," I said, laughing at him.

I thought about what Bianca said, maybe he had changed. I'm so confused, because when I talk to him, I realize that I do love him, but I still have feelings for Tony. I'm sad that Tony changed all his numbers, but I'm thinking, maybe it's a good thing he did.

~Chapter Twenty Two~

"Keith, how about you go to Pathmark and buy a case of Pepsi since you always like to drink the last can," Bianca said, holding up an empty Pepsi case.

"Man, I ain't going anywhere right now. I'm watching the game and I got money on this fuckin' game," Keith said bouncing his head up and down, rubbing his hands together like he was trying to start a fire.

Keith, Ahmir, Malcolm and two of his friends were sitting in their movie room, as they called it. They had nothing but chairs and a big ass 72-inch plasma TV with surround sound in that room. When the television is turned up it sounds like a movie theatre, that's why they called it the movie room.

"Go ahead, Bianca. I told your ass I'm not going anywhere right now, so stop playing!"

Bianca wouldn't move. "You shouldn't have drunk all of my soda! You know I don't drink that other shit you have. At halftime you better go and get me some more Pepsi!" she said turning and walking out the room, slamming the door behind her.

"Yo, she gets retarded if she doesn't have her Pepsi. It's like a fuckin' drug for her," Keith said to his homeboys, laughing. As soon as the game was over, he went to find his wife. "Yo, I'm going to send you to rehab. You be buggin' when you can't get a Pepsi, it's destroying our marriage."

"Sounds like a title for a talk show," Dee Dee said as she came into the room smiling, pretending she was a talk show host holding a make believe microphone. "Today on our show couples that say Pepsi, yes the soda, is destroying their marriages. Tell me, how is Pepsi destroying your marriage?" She held the pretend mic under Keith's mouth.

"Well, Dee Dee, if my wife comes home and there's no Pepsi in the refrigerator, she flips. She won't have sex with me. She wakes the kids up yelling and screaming, "Who drunk all the Pepsi?" The kids are afraid of her when she gets that way." Keith was acting like he was afraid.

"All I know is somebody will be on the couch tonight if I don't get a Pepsi soon.

Shit, I can't eat dinner without my soda."

Keith looked at the fake audience and said, "See, Pepsi is destroying my marriage." He grabbed his car keys and told the boys to ride with him. "I'll be back with a case of Pepsi for the man of the house," he said, laughing as he walked out the door.

"You laugh, but you know it's true," Dee Dee commented while walking toward the basement. She knew Bianca was going to send her ass there anyway.

"That's right, you already know what time it is, and tell Chantell to come here." Bianca had gotten extra close with Chantell since all that shit had jumped off. She was always asking her if she was okay. I think she still feels like it was her fault that those fat bitches jumped on her.

"What were you doing?" Bianca asked Chantell when she came into the room.

"My homework. Why?" Chantell answered looking down at the floor, not giving her Mom eye contact.

"You know you have to go to court on Monday."

"I know, I haven't forgotten. I already got my clothes ready. I'm supposed to be there at nine o'clock."

"Well, we're going to get there at eight o'clock."

"Why so early, they said nine o'clock. I know I'm not going to be ready to leave before eight. Anyway, I thought you had something to do."

"Yes, you will be ready by eight, and what, you don't want me to be there? You want me to stay home or something?" Bianca said, looking a Chantell strangely. "Anyway, you have to meet the lawyer at eight."

"Whatever Bianca, I just want all this to be over with. My face is all scared up behind this mess. My pinky is broke!" Chantell begin to cry.

Keith walked in and saw Chantell crying. Keith hates to see Chantell crying, "What's the matter?" He asked looking at Bianca.

"I'm just overwhelmed." Chantell said wiping the tears from her eyes.

"What happen Bianca?"

"I don't know, I was asking her about court on Monday. Then she started crying." Still sitting at the table eating

"No, I didn't just start crying cause we was talking about the courts it's everything! I have this long ass scar from my ear to my cheek bone. Every day I look in the mirror I'm reminded of what my mother did! Now she wants to come to court with me, for what! So she can cause more damage!"

Keith gave her a hug, and then replied "I don't think that's the reason, Chantell I'm sure if your mother would've known that crazy muthafucka was going to send some chicks after you she would've been there every day watching your back. It is not her fault that that man took it to another level.

"He should've never been in her life, y'all can move on, not looking in the mirror being reminded, you have no scars!

"I have no visible scars Chantell, but I do have them. But hey you have to be strong and you need your mom to help you be and stay strong." Keith looked at Bianca waiting for her to jump in, but she didn't. "Listen, we will overcome this. This is a problem that can be solved."

"Look at her," Chantell said looking at her mom through burning red eyes filled with anger. "She don't even care, she don't care about nobody but herself. No I don't want her in court with me, if you can't come with me Keith then I'll go by myself or call my grandmother."

"I'll be there no doubt and so will your mother, she got to be there not only to support you, but because she has to point the girls out and Hasson."

"Well I'm not riding in the car with her."

"Well we will take two separate cars then, that's no problem." Bianca stood up poured a glass of soda sat back at the table and begin to eat. She never said anything. She was going to support her daughter whether she wanted her to or not. Chantell went back to her room satisfied with talking to Keith. Keith turned to talk to Bianca. "Yo, why."

"Right now Keith Chantell is mad," Bianca interrupted. "If I would've said anything to make her change the way she feels she would've been madder."

"She was getting mad because you didn't express yourself." Keith said pulling a chair out.

"She needed to vent, she has the right to be upset with me. Look at her face! It's because of me, all of this is because of me," Bianca finally broke down and cried.

~Chapter Twenty Three~

It was 4 o'clock in the morning and Damien had fallen on the floor; he was having another seizure. This one scared Isis so bad that she immediately called 911.

"Oh my God, oh my God! Damien, are you alright?" Isis screamed, grabbing her telephone. "Please get an ambulance over to 156 Sheer Avenue, my boyfriend is having a seizure!" she yelled into the phone. "Please God, let him be alright!" Isis prayed.

After she called 911, she called Stormie. "Raquan, please put Stormie on the phone! My boyfriend is having a seizure and I'm scared to death!" Isis said, as soon as Raquan picked up the phone.

"Stormie, wake up, get the phone!" Raquan yelled to Stormie. "Is he alright, Isis?" Raquan asked.

"No, he won't wake up. I'm waiting on the ambulance now!" Isis said, nervously.

"What hospital are you going to?"

"Beth Israel. Raquan, he won't open his eyes, I can't wake him up! Okay, I hear the ambulance coming now," she said, running downstairs to open the door. "Please, my boyfriend is upstairs on the floor shaking. I've tried to wake him, but he won't wake up. Please help him!" she said to the EMT.

"Storm, wake up! Isis' boyfriend is sick or something. She says she can't wake him up!"

"What? Where is she at?" I said jumping out of bed, getting an instant headache.

"She's on the phone. They're taking him to Beth Israel," he said. "Hold on Isis, here's Storm," he said, handing the phone to Stormie.

"Isis, I'm getting dressed right now. I'll meet you at the hospital!" I said, quickly.

I threw on some sweat pants and ran outside to start my car for a minute. I came back in, brushed my teeth, and told Raquan to take my kids with him if he left. When I got to the hospital, Isis was in the waiting room crying, holding her stomach.

"Hey girl, you got to stay strong for that baby," I said, giving her a hug. "Where's he at?"

"He's in the back. I walked out here cause I didn't want him to see me crying."

"Did he finally wake up?" I asked.

"Yeah, he was having a seizure in his sleep, that's why I couldn't wake him. Girl, this is the second seizure he's had since we've been together, and this one was the worst."

"Is he going to be alright?" I asked rubbing her back, trying to console her.

"I really don't know. The doctor is with him now. They're gonna take him upstairs to run some tests and get an x-ray of his brain. I walked out here cause I didn't want to hear anything bad. I think his seizures are worse then what he tells me and he won't take his medicine like he's supposed to."

"Fuck that, Isis, you need to ask. You're carrying his baby, you need to know whether this shit is hereditary," I said, getting upset.

"Let's go back in there and you ask him for me, okay?" Isis said, hesitantly.

"Hell no, that's your man, I can't ask him a question like that. You don't have a bit of sense sometimes, Isis," I said, laughing at her. "Hey boy, how do you feel?" I asked Damien, once we walked into his room.

"I guess I could be doing better. Lately, I've been overworking myself on my man's CD and I think it's killing me slowly," Damien said lying in the hospital bed, looking weak.

"You think," Isis said, sarcastically.

"Listen, don't start, Isis. This isn't the time or the place. Shit, I can't help it if I'm sick. I have Epilepsy, always had it and will probably die because of it."

"You have what?" she asked, stunned.

"Epilepsy, you do know what that is?" Damien retorted.

"Yes I do, I'm not fuckin' stupid! Remember, I do have a degree."

"Listen y'all, please don't fight in the emergency room. At least wait until they give him a room." I said, refereeing.

"Man, I'm not staying here. I've got somewhere to be," Damien said, trying to get out of the bed.

"Yeah, right here in the hospital until your ass is better. You better start thinking about this baby and stop being so damn selfish, Damien!"

"Damien, is your condition very serious?" I asked.

"I need an operation, but there's a possibility that I'll experience temporary or permanent limitations with my speech, or movement of certain body parts, or changes in my behavior. I was told that I probably wouldn't make it through the surgery because of the type of surgery I need. And, if I don't have the surgery, there's a possibility I won't make it. I could have a seizure and never wake up. I also have chronic asthma, not to mention the fact that I have a weak heart. It's the size of a 90 year-old man, so if I were to have any type of surgery it might be too much of a strain on my heart. So, what are my options; live until I can't live anymore?"

"What are you saying? How long have you known you've needed an operation?" Isis asked, with tears crawling down her face. "How long will you live if you don't have the surgery?" She really didn't want to know, but she had to ask.

"I don't know a couple of months to a couple of years. Last year my doctor told me that I might need surgery and the consequences. The reason I'm having so many seizures now is because I need the operation, which I told my doctor I'm not having. What's the point if I'm going to die either way? The chances of me surviving surgery are zero to none," Damien said holding her hand, trying to comfort her.

"What!" Isis yelled, snatching her hand away. "This isn't happening to me, to us," she said, holding her stomach. "You said that if you survive the surgery, you might have a little limitation problem, but you have me. I'll be there for you when and if you need me, Damien."

"Isis, I'm not having the surgery, my mind is made up. How will you be able to take care of the baby and me? I have no intention of living the rest of my life as a vegetable. If I'm here when my baby is born, I want to be able to hold him, teach him football or basketball. If it's a girl, I want to teach her how to jump rope. I won't be able to do any of that if I have that surgery."

"Why are you telling me this now, why didn't you tell me sooner?" Her eyes were swollen from crying, and her heart was aching from the news. She couldn't believe this was happening.

"I tried to tell you. I told you I didn't have time to play games."

"That's not telling me shit, Damien! I can't believe this!"

"Baby, don't worry yourself, I'll be fine. I've lived this long, I'm sure I got a few more years left in me."

The doctor came in and explained to Damien that he needed to make a follow-up visit with his primary doctor as soon as possible and then he discharged him. Isis was furious that Damien refused care.

"Isis, I know what's wrong with me, so I'm not gonna sit in this emergency room listening to these doctors tell me what I already know. I'll go see my doctor on Monday and you can come and ask him all the questions you want. There's nothing I can do, the medicine isn't working anymore." Damien was rambling on and on, trying to convince her he was okay.

Isis wasn't listening to him. She had tuned his ass out. She was thinking about her baby and how was she going to handle this if and when the tragic day came. While she was thinking about it she started crying again.

"Damien, please stop talking. Stormie, are you ready to take us home?"

"I'm waiting on you guys," I said. I really didn't know what to say, I was astounded by the whole situation. I was thinking, Damn, if it ain't one thing it's something else. Why couldn't Isis just be happy?

I couldn't imagine how she was feeling, finding out that the man she loves and the father of her child won't be around to see their child grow up. I mean we all die, but to know for a fact that your man will only live for maybe six months to year, had to be overwhelming for her.

"Damien, maybe you should stay with me from now on. I know I'll worry myself into a miscarriage if you're not with me every night. You also need to see if you can get somebody else to help your man with his CD. And please start taking your medicine the way you're supposed to, if not for yourself then do it for the baby. I want you to be around at least to see our baby born, his first step, birthday and-" Isis couldn't finish the sentence.

Damien just held her, crying and telling her he was sorry. I had to step off before I started to cry. I went to get my truck and prayed for them, especially for Isis because she needed a good prayer. Only God knows when he's going to bring Damien home, the doctor can't predict that. Isis and Damien came out of the hospital and sat in the back seat of my truck. I knew Damien felt bad because it showed on his face.

"Listen, Isis, I'm sorry about all of this. I never thought about the possibility of you becoming pregnant, I was having too much fun. Hell, I almost forgot I was sick. But I'm going to make sure that if anything happens to me, you and the baby will be straight. My baby will want for nothing. I swear, Isis, I'm going to take it easy, but first I have to go to LA for a week to handle some business and to sell my studio because I only need the one studio here."

Damien was trying to sell his homes and the one studio in LA so Isis and the baby would be straight. He had also changed his beneficiary to Isis on his insurance policy. The studio in Newark he was keeping and he told his man to run it and make sure all monies go into his baby's trust fund. They had signed an agreement so that no shady shit would happen after he was gone.

Isis never responded. She had enough to worry about without having to worry about him going to LA. That was all she needed to hear after everything else. She didn't even look at him, instead she said, "So, when do you plan on leaving?"

"I'm leaving Tuesday. I was gonna leave on Monday, but I'm going to the doctor first," Damien said, hugging Isis.

I pulled up in front of Isis' house. "Do you want me to come inside?" I asked her.

"No, that's alright, I'm going to sleep," she said, climbing out of my truck.

"See you later, Damien," I said thinking, how stupid can he really be? Doesn't he see how hurt Isis is, or does he even care? He's so concerned about his man's CD and the studio in LA, he doesn't see how much he's hurting her.

"A'ight, thanks for being there, Storm," Damien said, shutting the car door.

I drove off thinking, nigga, I was there for my home girl. I know she's going to be distraught for the next couple of days.

As soon as Isis stepped in the house, she snapped on Damien. "What the fuck you mean you're going to LA for a week? Didn't you just hear what I said at the hospital about what if you get sick or something?"

"I said I'm going to the doctor Monday, and if he tells me not to go then I won't go! But I need to be there, Isis, this is important to me."

"What, my feelings aren't that important to you, Damien? You know what, do whatever you like, but I'm coming with you," she demanded.

"No you're not, so don't even think about it! This is business and I don't need you there nagging me, putting me under a lot of fuckin' pressure. I'll call you everyday and night and my cell phone will be on the whole time," he said, walking toward the kitchen.

"But what if you get sick?" she asked, throwing her hands up.

"I'm not gonna get sick! Damn, stop wishing bad luck on me!" he said, preparing to fix pancakes and bacon.

"Do whatever you like, Damien! I'm going to bed!" Isis yelled.

"You want some break."

"No!" she yelled, before he could finish his sentence.

"I'm fixing you something anyway. You need to feed the baby. I'm sure he's hungry."

"Oh, so now you're concerned about the baby? Ain't that some funny shit."

"Fuck you mean by that?" he asked looking confused, like he was the innocent one.

"Nothing at all. Just that if you were so concerned, you wouldn't that trip to

LA."

"This trip is business, it has to take place. If something happens then it just happens. That's why I didn't want to tell you, because I knew you were going to try to make me stop living, sit in one place and wait for death. Shit, that's not me. I'm going to handle my business whether you like it or not. All I want you to do is support my decisions, a'ight."

"Whatever, Damien," Isis said, fixing a plate of pancakes and bacon and going upstairs.

Damien thought about his baby and how he might not be here when he arrived in this world. "Damn God, why me!" he yelled and hit the kitchen table.

He sat downstairs praying to God that he live long enough to see his baby born. The thought of dying before the birth made him cry. Isis walked in the kitchen and saw Damien crying and she started to cry too. She felt sorry for him, she couldn't imagine being sick.

"Let's make the best of whatever time you have left, okay," she said crying, holding him tight in her arms.

Raquan was still in the bed when I got home. His boys and Ja'Mil were playing the PS2, and Tania was still sleeping.

"Y'all want some breakfast?" I asked the boys.

"No thanks, we ate already," one of them answered.

"What did y'all eat?"

"I made some oatmeal," Tahir answered.

I went in the bedroom, stared at Raquan while he was sleeping, and thought I would die if something like that were to happen to him. I laid on top of him and started kissing him.

"How's Isis' boyfriend?" Raquan asked, waking up and returning my kisses.

"He's okay I guess. He has Epilepsy and a whole heap of other shit wrong with him. He needs an operation. But the thing of it is, if he has the operation he might die, and if he doesn't, he might die or live the rest of his life immobile."

"Damn, his options are fucked up. How's Isis dealing with this?"

"She's been crying all morning. I would probably be doing the same thing," I said closing my eyes, imagining that being me. "I hate to think about shit like that," I mumbled.

"I don't care too much for your friend, but I wouldn't wish this on her. I really am sorry to hear that, but there's nothing we can do except support her through this."

I almost fell out the bed listening to Raquan talk about supporting Isis. Let me find out my man really does have a heart. I called Mommy and told her what happened. She was shocked to hear it. I told her not to tell Isis that I told her, but I know Mommy, she's going to call Isis to see if she's okay.

"Damien's leaving for LA on Tuesday and Isis is livid. She doesn't want him to go."

"Shit, I don't blame her, what if he gets sick," my Mother said, walking around her house. I knew she was walking cause I could hear her slippers scrapping the floor.

"Well, Mom, I'm going back to bed. I'll call you later."

Raquan and I stayed in the bed all day. His boys made lunch for everyone and I told them I was going to order out for dinner.

~Chapter Twenty Four~

Bianca was still in the bed when Chantell came into her room. "What?" Bianca asked, thinking it was Dee Dee.

"I wanted to talk to you," Chantell said.

"I thought you were Dee Dee. What do you want to talk about?" Bianca asked, sitting up in the bed. Keith woke up and asked was everything all right.

"I want to talk to my Mother," Chantell said.

"I guess you want me to get out, huh?" he said, trying to pull himself out of bed.

"That's the plan. I want to talk to her alone," she said, sitting on the bed next to her Mom.

"Then I'll go in the guest room. Bianca, when you're finished, can you make some Sunday breakfast?" Keith said, walking out of the room.

"Alright. So what is it you want to talk to me about, Chantell?" she asked, once they were alone.

"I'm sorry for saying all those things the other day, but I was upset."

"I know. That's why I didn't intervene. You have the right to be upset with me, Chantell. It's my fault but, like I told Keith, I can't rewind this and change what happened. What I can do is make sure from this day forth everything in our life goes the way it should."

"I want you in court with me tomorrow. I'll be glad when this is over and behind me. I also wanted to say thanks for making sure those two girls got a beat down before they went to jail," she said smiling, and finally giving Bianca a hug. "I love you, Bianca."

Bianca hugged Chantell back and returned the words. Then they went into the kitchen and started cooking breakfast. Dee Dee came walking her dramatic ass in there and started hugging Bianca and Chantell.

"What the hell is wrong with you, Dee Dee?" Bianca asked, puzzled.

"I didn't mean to pry, but I heard y'all conversation. It was so touching I almost started to cry," Dee Dee said smiling, showing her deep dimples. "So, what are we making for breakfast?"

"I'm making some pancakes, sausages, eggs and grits," Bianca said, stirring the pancake batter.

"I was thinking maybe we should do a girls day out today. We'll cook breakfast for the boys and then go to the mall," Dee Dee said, helping with the breakfast.

"You know Dee Dee that sounds like a plan to me," Bianca said. "I haven't been shopping in a minute, so let's get this on and poppin'."

Chantell and Dee Dee both stopped and looked at each other, laughing at their Mother's last remark.

"On and poppin' huh?" Dee Dee said, frying the sausage, while Chantell fixed the grits and prepared the table. When they were finished, they got dressed and went shopping.

It's Monday and Chantell has to go to court, Isis and Damien have to go to see his doctor, and I don't know whom to support. I guess I'll go to the doctor with Isis; she needs the most support. I called my office manager and told her that I had to be in court with my niece. She understood and told me to use one of my personal days.

I then called Isis to see if she was ready. "Hey, Isis, are you ready to take Damien to the doctor?"

"Girl, he ain't going to the doctor. He left to go to LA sometime this morning while I was sleeping. He left a note saying that what he needed to do in LA was more important and that I should trust him. He promised to call me as soon as he landed."

She sounded hurt, but there was nothing she could do.

"I'm still coming over, do you need anything?" I asked, speechless.

"Nah, I'm okay. I need to call Sam and let her know that I'll be coming in late. I have a presentation to give later."

"Well, do you want me to come over or what?"

"It's up to you, Storm. I think I'm going to distance myself from Damien. Because the day God decides to take him away, I don't want to be hurt and in a lot of pain. I mean, I'm gonna hurt, but I don't want to be traumatized. You know what I mean?"

"Yeah, I think so. Isis, just try to support him and stay by his side. Maybe he's got a plan, you never know with a man. Or maybe he's too embarrassed; I don't know. Just support him," I said to her, hoping she understood that right now he needed her and she needed him.

"Why would he leave like that? He didn't even wake me up, he just left a fuckin' note! What if something happens to him on the plane or when he lands? I just want to get away from him before I get myself in too deep and he's not going to be around. I've got to think about my baby and myself. Shit, that muthafucka obviously doesn't care!" Isis was upset and talking crazy.

"Isis, you're just upset. Don't say something you might regret in the end."

"Storm, you don't understand what I'm going through! This man knew he was sick and dying, so why would he let me get pregnant and fall in love with him, why? He doesn't care about my feelings, he's only thinking about his stupid studio! I'm in love with a man who only has a few months to live, and I have to prepare myself for single parenthood. I need him out of my life, cause if and when he dies, I don't want to be around!" She was crying, and I was praying to God she was only talking out of anger.

"Isis, stop talking like that. If something happened to Damien right now you would have a nervous breakdown. I honestly believe he loves you, he just needs to straighten some shit out in his life."

"When he calls I'm going to tell him that I don't want to see him anymore. Then I'm going to get all my numbers changed."

"I hope you don't, that's definitely a wrong move. You know I'll support you, no matter what you decide to do, but I hope you think before you make any rash decisions."

"I have thought about it. My heart can't take another heartbreak."

"For once can you stop thinking about yourself, Isis. The fuckin' man is dying! You don't think he's going through some shit right now? I think both of y'all are being selfish. Anyway, I might as well go to work. I'll talk to you later."

I was upset at Isis and the way she wanted to go about their relationship. I called Raquan just to tell him that I loved him and he returned the words. All day at work, I couldn't stop thinking about Isis and the shit she was going through. I decided to call Bianca to see how everything went with Chantell in court.

"Hey girl. How did things go in court today?" I asked her.

"Everything went okay. The two girls that jumped on Chantell got a fine and probation since this was their first offense, plus they were minors. I was hoping the girls got a more excruciating punishment, but they didn't. Hasson was there and charges were brought up against him for paying the girls to jump Chantell. I forget what the charges were, but we have to go back to court in a couple of months. I can't wait till this shit is over," Bianca explained.

"So, how is Chantell?"

"She's okay. When the judge asked her why the girls had jumped her, she said she didn't know. I thought she was gonna say, 'cause Mommy was messing around with Hasson,' but she didn't. But when he asked the girls why Hasson had paid them to jump Chantell, they said he just told them that she had hit him with a brick in the back of his head cause he was dating her Mom, and she wanted him to stop messing around with her because she was happily married. The judge asked them how much did Hasson pay them, and they said they were paid $500.00 apiece. You know Mommy did all the crying, hell, she ended up making me cry."

"What about Keith?"

"He was very supportive, but he kept giving Hasson the, I'm gonna get you sucka look. They didn't call me to the stand. The lawyer said that when we go back to court, I might be called to the stand. Hasson has to stay in jail until his court date. I'm tired and hungry and I have a headache. I just hope we can get through this ordeal," Bianca said, rambling on and on.

"Not trying to change the subject, but you know Damien was supposed to go to the doctor this morning, but he bounced. He went to LA and left Isis a note."

"That's fucked up," Bianca said, pissed the fuck off. "Maybe he doesn't want

Isis to know how long he has left."

"Well, she said she's going to break up with him cause she's not prepared to face what lies ahead. She would rather let him go then go through the pain of losing him."

"That's fucked up too. She's a heartless ass person anyway.

"Listen, I've gotta go, I'm taking the kids out to dinner and I need to take care of a few things at the office before I pick them up. I'll talk to you later," I said, hanging up the phone.

I finished up at work, went and picked my kids up from Mommy's house and we went out to eat. My birthday was coming up and I was hoping Raquan would get me something nice. Things have been going great between us. I just hope it stays that way, even though I still have my doubts. Like this weekend training shit he has to go to for his job, I hope he's being honest about it. I want to believe that he's changed and that I could trust him.

I took my kids to the Old Country Buffet on Route 22. They ran around the buffet eating everything and, you know what, so did I. Raquan called me while we were eating, asking about Isis. I told him what happened earlier.

"That's fucked up if Isis' leaves that man now," he said.

"I feel the same way, but I can't change her mind. I haven't spoken with her since this morning; maybe she's changed her mind by now."

I was feeling a little overwhelmed and I didn't know why. My body was feeling heavy, maybe my period was coming on, or maybe it was Isis, I didn't know. I was trying to be a good friend, but I didn't know how to tell her that what she was planning on doing was fucked up. After I hung up with Raquan, Isis called me.

"What's up, Storm?" she said.

"I'm at Old Country Buffet with my kids," I answered.

"So," she paused for a minute, "I told Damien that when he comes back, I think it would be best if we didn't see each other again. I don't want to be mean or come off like I'm leaving him. I can't handle the pressure, but I have to think about my baby. Mommy told me that I was doing the right thing."

I didn't respond, I just listened, because I'm sure that's all she needed me to do.

"He's coming home tomorrow. He said he had only needed to be in LA for one day to sign some very important papers. He didn't argue with me, he just said he'll see me later then hung up." Isis was starting to cry again and I didn't want to hear her cry, so I told her I would talk to her later.

Isis hung up the phone, sat on her living room couch and cried like a baby. "Why God?" she asked. "Why? What did I do? I finally met someone who loves me and gave me a child and you want to take him away! Why?" she yelled out. She walked to the kitchen, sat at the table and thought about her childhood.

She thought about how her Mom would put her boyfriends before her and her siblings, and how she would do stupid shit just to get her mom's attention. One day she cut her sister's hair and dyed it bright red. She knew she was going to get murdered for it, but she didn't care, she just wanted some attention. When her Mom came home and saw her baby's hair, she was speechless.

Her sister was so excited about the new look, she ran to her Mom and yelled with exhilaration, "Mommy, look at my new hairdo! Isis and I were playing hair salon, isn't it beautiful?" Isis had cut her hair in layers and severely damaged it with the color. Her sister's hair had been very long and beautiful, now it was short, hideous and red. Her mother almost passed out.

"Isis!" her mom yelled. Veins were popping out of her neck. "What the fuck were you thinking! I'm going to bust your muthafuckin' ass!"

Isis ran into her room, locked the door and started crying. She knew her Mom was going to make her pay for this, but she couldn't imagine what the punishment would be. When her Mom had finished unscrewing every screw from her bedroom door, she kicked it in, grabbed Isis by her hair and started cutting the shit out of it.

She screamed, "No mommy, please don't cut my hair! I'm sorry, I'm really sorry!"

Her Father was in and out of her life. He had left when she was really young. He left because her mom was having an affair with a married man who lived only a block away. One day when she and her Mom went to the store, her Mom's lover jumped on her, beating her up in front of the store. Isis didn't know what to do, so she ran for help and left her mom lying there bleeding. The lover went to prison and her father left, that's why Isis was so upset when Hasson jumped on Bianca.

After that, her Mom dated any man that showed her some attention. The men would mistreat her and wouldn't take care of her or her kids. They would beat on her and Isis hated that. She always thought her Mom was too pretty to be putting up with that shit. She vowed to never be like her, so she worked and went to college only to meet someone who persuaded her to move to another state. That's when everything in her life started going downhill for real.

When she met Stormie, she instantly felt their friendship was promising. Everything seemed to be going well in her life. She had started her own web design company, bought her first home and truck, and was living the life of a star, or so she thought. Then she met Jared the Jamaican, another bad decision on her part. See, Isis' problem was she expected to be perfect at all times, not realizing she was living the same life as her Mom.

Now, she had Damien, someone who loved her and whom she loved. She's carrying their first child and was getting ready to plan their wedding when disappointment came knocking on the door again. Isis only knows how to run from difficult situations, she doesn't know how to stick around and fix them. She's always been that way.

As she sat at the table thinking and wishing her life was different, the baby kicked for the first time and it scared her, she didn't know what it was. She sat still and waited for the feeling again, and this time the baby kicked harder. She laughed out loud, felt her stomach and wished Damien was there to feel the baby kicking. She started crying when she thought about how he wasn't going to be around. When the baby kicked her vagina she screamed out because she was scared and it hurt. She called her doctor and he told her that was normal and to come in tomorrow so he could examine her. Then she called me, her mom, father and grandmother and told us that the baby had kicked for the first time, she sounded very excited. She also told us that she was going to concentrate only on her business and baby, cause she had been slacking ever since she found out Damien was sick since she found out she was pregnant.

While listening to Mariah Carey, Isis started packing up all of Damien's belongings. Damien called and left her a message to call him back but she didn't. She started cleaning out her guest room because that was going to be the baby's room. Damien called again and she finally answered.

"What?" Isis said, aggravated.

"Don't answer the phone like that please. I'm on my way home and that shit you was talking earlier, I'd like for you to tell me to my face. Don't break up with me over the phone."

"Well, you shouldn't have written me a fuckin' 'Dear John' letter, letting me know that you were going out of town. You should've woke me up. Listen, I don't want to get into this right now. I'll tell you to your face when I get off work tomorrow, if that will make you happy."

"Yes, that would make me happy. How's the baby?"

"Fine, she kicked the shit out of me today. I got scared and called the doctor."

"Why?"

"Because I didn't know what that feeling was. She did it three times, the last time she kicked me in the vagina, and that shit made me scream," Isis said, laughing. Damien laughed also.

"I wish I was there to feel her kick. Hell, I wish I could've seen your face when she kicked your vagina." He continued laughing. "Listen, Isis, I'm sorry and I understand if you don't want me around. Just call me when things like this happen. I still want to be involved until, you know," he said, not wanting to say the words.

"Damien, I don't want to talk about your situation anymore! I don't even want to think about it. I just have room in my heart for my baby and that's all, nothing else. You lied to me and I can't forgive you. No, I'm not gonna call you when she kicks, move, or when I go into labor. I no longer want you to be a part of my life! At the end of this, I will be the only one hurt, not you. I had plans for us, plans that were to last for an eternity, or at least 30 or 50 years, not a couple fuckin' months."

"So, because I might pass away in a few months, you want to leave me. Is that what you're saying? I thought you loved me, Isis. I thought our shit was deep. You're the selfish one. I'm getting sicker every day, and I went to LA to sell my studio so I could make sure you and the baby will be alright. I signed everything I own over to you, and you tell me that you can't stick around because I'm dying. That's fucked up Isis. Now I know why they call you Isis. But that's alright, I'm still leaving everything to you because you're carrying my baby and you're going to need the help. I do hope you'll come to my funeral." Damien hung up before she could say another word.

Damien sat in the airport thinking about Isis and what she had just said to him on the phone, and he wanted to cry but it was too many people in the airport. He put his head down and stared at his feet. While he was bent over he passed out. People in the airport ran over to help, but he was out of it. He was having another seizure.

A young lady that was sitting next to him screamed out for help and dialed 911. She stayed with him and went along in the ambulance to the hospital. On the way to the hospital, she hit talk on his cell phone so she could call the last person he had been talking to but she got no answer.

Isis turned her ringer off and tried to forget about Damien. She mumbled, 'No, nigga, I will not be at your funeral.' She saw the red light blinking on her phone, but she wouldn't answer it because she knew it was Damien calling. 'Please, nigga, you just hung up on me, I wish I would talk to you.' She turned her music up and continued cleaning her guest room. For the rest of the evening she left her ringer off and refused to check her messages.

~Chapter Twenty-Five~

It was 12:30 in the morning when I felt someone climb into my bed and hold me. I jumped, turned around and saw that it was Raquan.

"Boy, you scared the shit out of me!" I said, hitting Raquan across the head. He just laughed.

"I wanted to sleep next to you, so I decided to get out of my bed and come over here where I could sleep next to you," he whispered in my ear. Then he gently kissed me on my neck and back.

"Whatever." I blushed. "Where are your boys?"

"Home, my Aunt is there with them. She needed somewhere to stay so I told her she could stay with me for a while."

Raquan was kissing me all over then he started caressing my inner thighs. His penis was erect and ready to enter. He crawled under the covers and started kissing Lolita, sticking his tongue in and out of it, eating like it was his last meal. He sucked and licked Lolita until I came in his mouth. After I came he proceeded to gently insert his long, stiff dick into my pussy. That night, we made love in all positions. He flipped me from one side to the other, and he hit it from the front and back. I got on top and rode his dick until he exploded and screamed out like a little bitch. We both were sweating profusely and the room had the smell of sex. I didn't even bother to take a shower because Raquan had worn my ass out. We fell asleep in each other's arms.

The next morning, Raquan got up, took a shower, got dressed and woke me up. "You know I'm going to Connecticut this weekend for training, so if you want to go out you can. But you can only go out either Friday or Saturday, not both," he said, jokingly.

"Please, I'm not planning on going out either night. But let me ask something, why did you make love to me like that last night?" I said, playing in his hair.

"I was dreaming about having sex with you like that, so last night I decided to make my dream come true. And, baby, it was better than the dream could ever be," he said, kissing me on the cheek. "I would kiss you on the lips, but you haven't brushed your teeth yet and your breath is kicking. I'll call you later," he said, laughing and heading out.

"Nigga, your breath stinks also," I said, blowing into my hand to see if it was really stinking. Please, that was his shit.

After Raquan left, I looked at the clock. It was only 5:30 so I turned over and went back to sleep. My phone rang at 7 o'clock and scared the shit out of me.

"Get your ass up!" Raquan yelled playfully, into the phone. "I knew your ass was going back to sleep, that's why I called you."

"Yeah right. Thanks for waking me, baby. Let me get up and get dressed, I'll call you later," I said, dragging myself out of bed.

'Man, I can't have good sex and then get up and go to work cause my ass is going to be dragging all day. I have no energy after sex like that,' I said to myself, as I was getting ready for work.

I took a hot shower, yelled out for my kids to get dressed, and then called my job and lied. I told them my son was having an asthma attack and that I would be in as soon as he got off the machine. I knew I shouldn't have told a lie like that but that was the only thing that came to mind. I was an hour late getting to work; I didn't get there until 9 o'clock.

During the morning, it seemed like time was moving slow. Isis called and told me about her and Damien's conversation and that he had called her back about ten times after he hung up on her.

"He left messages on my phone but I haven't checked them yet. I feel a little bad Storm, but I just don't know what else to do."

"Why don't you be a grown up and handle your responsibilities," I told her.

"What do you mean my responsibilities? Fuck you mean by that! Hell, he's not my responsibility, my health is."

"I know your health is important. I mean don't run from Damien because he's sick, now's the time he needs you the most. You need to sympathize with him, put yourself in his shoes. Would you want him to leave you at a time like this? Your responsibility to him is to stand by his side, Isis. How can you be so impassive, you can't possibly be that mean?" I said, not believing she was being so unsympathetic.

"I'm not impassive; I'm just trying to protect my feelings. Listen, I've gotta go, I'll call you later." Isis hung up, mad because of what I said, but I didn't agree with the way she was handling the situation.

I was exhausted by the end of my workday. I picked my kids up, went home, cooked, took a shower and went to sleep. I didn't feel like talking to anybody, not even Raquan. He called me at about 8:30.

"Why didn't you call me when you got home?" he said, once I picked up the phone.

"I was tired so I cooked and went to bed. You wore me out last night. We can't have sex like that on a work night," I said, laughing. "Are you packed and ready to go?"

"Yeah, I'm not taking much, just the necessities. I'll be back that Sunday evening."

"I'm going to miss you, Raquan."

"Please, I'm only going to be gone for two days."

We talked for about three hours about everything, about Bianca and her drama, and the hottest topic of them all, 'Isis the disdained sistah.'

"I told you she was a fucked up individual," Raquan said.

When Damien woke up, he didn't remember anything. He had no idea that he was in the hospital. He looked over and saw a young lady asleep in the lounge chair next to his bed. He looked under the covers and saw that he had on nothing but a hospital gown. Damien rung the bell for the nurse, he wanted to get out of there.

"Yes," said the thin white nurse, walking toward his bed.

"Where am I and how long have I been here?" Damien asked, confused.

"You're at LA Memorial Hospital, and you've been here for two days. You had what we call a Gran Mal seizure, and you've been in a coma. Have you had seizures like this before?" the nurse asked, looking over his chart.

"Yes, I've been diagnosed with Epilepsy since I've been born. I got to go, I want to discharge myself."

"I'm sorry, but the doctor ordered us to keep you until he arrived today. Once he checks you out, then he'll determine from that point on. Do you need anything else?"

"Who is that lady sleeping on my lounge chair?" Damien asked, not recognizing the woman in the chair.

"She brought you in, she said she was your girlfriend. You don't know her?"

"No, I've never seen her a day in my life."

"Excuse me, miss," the nurse said, waking up the girl.

"Yes," the girl answered sitting up in the chair, wiping her face with her hand, looking straight at Damien. "Oh, you woke up, I'm so happy!" she yelled, looking back and forth between the nurse and Damien, not realizing her cover was blown.

"Who the fuck are you?" Damien asked, in a confused voice.

"Stop playing, boy. You must've bumped your head and developed amnesia or something. I'm your girlfriend, Tatyana."

"No, I think you bumped your head and developed amnesia. I don't know you, Tatyana. I don't have a girlfriend and ain't looking for one."

"Tatyana, I'm sorry but you're going to have to leave. Only family is allowed in here," the nurse said, helping her out of the lounge chair.

"Okay, I'm not his girlfriend. But I'm the person who called 911 and stuck around to make sure he was alright," she said to the nurse. Then she turned to Damien and said, "I called the last number you dialed on your cell, trying to get in touch with someone, but the phone just rang. I left a message for her to call you but she never called back. I called several other numbers and left messages, but your phone went dead so I decided to stick around until you woke up. I didn't mean any harm, and I'm sorry for whatever I've done to offend you," she said, gathering her things. "You know I missed my flight for you."

"I'm sorry, and thank you for sticking around." Damien realized that, not only was she nice enough to stick around to watch over him, but she was fine as hell. Tall and slim, with dimples that showed even when she wasn't smiling. Her complexion was deep cocoa; she looked mixed. She had long, soft straight hair that hung to the center of her back, and a Jennifer Lopez ass.

"That's okay, I want her to stay," Damien told the nurse. He turned to Tatyana and said, "So, where are you from?"

"I'm from here, but I was on my way to Brazil. I had a shoot to do there yesterday," she said, smiling. "I called my agent and told him about my little adventure."

"You're a model?"

"Yes I am. I'm not a very well known model, but I'm making my way up the chart."

"How old are you, if you don't mind me asking?"

"Twenty-five, why?"

"Because you look like a baby. I thought you were about seventeen or something."

"Thanks for the compliment. Hey, the female that I called for you, is that your girlfriend?"

"No, she's just a friend. Actually, she broke up with me over the phone before I had my seizure. I think that phone conversation caused me to have a seizure."

"If you don't mind me asking, why did she break up with you?"

"Personal reasons, reasons I'd rather not discuss. Anyway, can you please hand me my cell phone?"

Sure, I turned it off so your battery could recharge," Tatyana said, getting his phone out of his bag.

"Thanks," Damien said. He checked his voice mail and saw that he had a lot of messages, none of which were from Isis. He called his man back to let him know what hospital he was in. "Let everybody know that hopefully I'll be home tomorrow. Shit, I know people probably think I'm dead," he said, laughing a little.

228

"Hello," I said, answering my cell phone, not recognizing the number.

"Hey, Storm. It's me, Damien."

"Call me on my house phone, do you have the number?"

"Nah, give it to me."

After giving him the number, he called me right back. "Where are you?" I immediately asked when I picked up the phone.

"I'm still in LA."

"Why? You and Isis need to stop the bullshit."

"Storm, I'm in LA Memorial Hospital thanks to your girlfriend breaking up with me over the phone. I fucked around and had a seizure and I've been in a coma since Monday. I'm just waking up today."

"What? Get the fuck outta here! Does Isis know?" I asked, reaching for a chair so I could take a seat.

"Only if she checks her voice mail, cause a young lady that was in the airport called everybody on my cell and left messages. She even stayed with me until I woke up."

"Where is she now?"

"She went downstairs to get us something to eat."

"That was nice of her. So when are they discharging you? Do you need anything?" I asked, still stunned by his news.

"Nah, I don't need anything. I'm waiting for my doctor to get here so he can discharge me. Listen; don't tell Isis I called you. Storm, I came down here to sell my studio so she and the baby will be straight after I'm gone. I have six months or less to live, and I'm trying to take care of shit so I can rest in peace. She told me not to ever get in touch with her again. She pretty much said because I'm dying she doesn't want to be around me."

"Damien, I don't think she means that, she's just pregnant and scared. She's been through a lot and I think she's running because she's afraid of getting hurt again. So, in her mind she thinks if she gets away from you now, when your time comes she won't be as hurt. But I think if she's not by your side when that

229

ungrateful time comes she's going to be more impaired then she can imagine."

"I agree with that, Storm. Listen, just let her know that I do love her, but I can't help my situation. I wish I could turn back the hands of time because I would've changed a lot of things in my life. One thing is for sure, I would've had the surgery a long time ago, but it's too late for me now. I'm dying, Storm, and I'm all alone." Damien began to cry on the phone.

"Damien, you're not alone. I'll be by your side and so will Isis." I felt a tear drop. While I was talking to him my phone beeped, it was Raquan. I let my voice mail take it. Raquan then called my cell. I told Damien to hold on while I answered my phone. I told Raquan that I was talking to Damien and that I would call him back.

Once I got back on the phone, Damien said, "I have no family, only my unborn child and I'm not even allowed to come around to see it grow inside of Isis. I keep trying to talk to her, but she gets upset at me when I tell her things about my sickness. I can't believe she hasn't even checked her voice mail or tried to call to see if I made it back home okay."

"I spoke to Isis on Tuesday and I haven't spoken with her since. I'ma call her tonight and tell her where you're at."

"No, don't tell her, let her listen to her voice mail. Let me call you back, the doctor just came in the door," he said, getting ready to hang up.

"Okay, don't forget because I want to know when you're being discharged. If you need a ride just call me."

"Thanks, I've got a ride. I'll stay in touch."

I called Isis' stupid ass immediately after hanging up with Damien. "You know you're one fucked up person, Isis," I said, as soon as she picked up her phone.

"What are you talking about?"

"Please tell me you checked your voice mail?"

"I sure haven't. I didn't want to hear Damien's half-ass apology."

"You're so fuckin' stupid, Isis. You need to check your voice mail then call me back," I said, hanging up.

I called everybody that I could think of and told them how fucked up Isis was, she gave the word bitch a new meaning. I hope she knows that she'll never be blessed if she doesn't change her ways.

"I keep telling you Isis is one fucked up person," Bianca said.

"Ever since she started her own business she thinks it's all about her. How the fuck can she get mad at the man because he's dying? She will never be blessed," I said to Mommy.

"Um um," Mommy hummed. "I can't believe Isis is acting that way. I feel sorry for Damien. You let him know that if he needs anything he's welcome to it. I hope Isis eventually comes to her senses."

"Please, she doesn't have any sense, that's the problem. Hold on, Mom, my phone is beeping."

"Storm, can you please take me to the airport? My flight leaves at 9:30. I called Damien and told him I was sorry and that I was coming to get him," Isis said, all in one breath and crying when I clicked over.

Damn, I felt sorry for the bitch, so I took her to the airport. But on the way, I told her she'd better change her ways and enjoy each day to the fullest with Damien while he was here and not think about what was to come. Isis cried from the time I picked her up all the way to the airport.

I told her, "That baby is going to be a crybaby." I didn't know what else to say. Isis' stomach was huge, it looked like she'd grown twice in size since the last time I saw her. She went to work maybe twice a week and stayed in the house the other days, eating everything in sight.

I walked her to the gate. She didn't have any luggage, just her carry on bag with her toothbrush and some underwear in it. I stayed and watched the plane take off, then I started crying. My heart really went out to the both of them. They had finally found that right mate and a catastrophe had to step in. My cell phone rang; it was Raquan.

"Yo, why did you leave these kids in the house alone?" Raquan asked, as soon as I answered my phone.

"I just ran out to take Isis to the airport. I'm on my way home now. Where are you?"

"I'm at your house, bring me something to eat. Did your kids eat?"

"No, I'm bringing something for everybody. I'll see you when I get there," I said, hanging up.

My cell rang again. "Hello," I said.

"Storm, its Damien, thanks for calling her."

"No problem. I just watched her plane take off, so she's on her way. When are they letting you go?"

"Friday I hope cause I'm ready to get the hell up outta here!" Damien said, laughing. "Anyway, I just wanted to say thanks."

"Again, not a problem. I'll see you when you return home," I said. I felt a little better hearing Damien laughing instead of crying, thinking he was alone. I wondered where the female was, but I didn't bother to ask him.

"So, I guess I'll be on my way," Tatyana said, standing over Damien.

"Don't leave yet. I want to exchange numbers. Maybe I can take you out to dinner one night to show my appreciation," Damien said holding her soft hands, thinking nasty thoughts.

"It's getting late and you need your rest."

"How can I thank you, Tatyana?"

She just smiled a very seductive smile, kissed him on the lips and whispered, "Maybe one day when you have enough energy, I'll show you how you can really thank me."

"I have more than enough energy now. Don't let the hospital bed fool you. I'll buzz the nurse and tell them not to disturb me."

"Do that, then we'll see what happens next," she said, caressing his penis gently.

He buzzed the burse while holding her breasts and squeezing them. Tatyana threw her head back and moaned softly. She continued caressing his penis.

Tatyana hid in the closet so the nurse wouldn't suspect anything. When the nurse came into the room, he politely asked her not to disturb him for the next couple of hours because he was going to get some much-needed rest. After the nurse left, Tatyana put a chair in front of the door to ensure that no one would be able to just barge in on them.

She then went into the bathroom and returned with a basin full of warm water. She proceeded to gently wash his already erect penis. She started kissing him from his mouth all the way down to his dick. When she licked all around his dick and sucked on balls, Damien was in heaven. He went to caress her, but she wouldn't let him.

"Just lay there and let me take control," she whispered. So he did just that.

She took her clothes off piece by piece. Then she began playing with her pussy while sucking on his dick. Damien couldn't take it; this girl was really freaking him out. She sucked his dick until he came all in her mouth. He screamed out a little, but she wasn't finished. She continued caressing his body and sucking on his balls until he became erect again. She reached into her purse and pulled out a condom. She put it on him and rode his dick until he was ready to come again, but she stopped before he came.

"I want you to put it in my ass," she told Damien, handing him some ky-jelly that she pulled out of her bag.

Damien stood up, bent her over the bed and rubbed the jelly on her ass before gently inserting his dick into her ass. She moaned out loud and his eyes rolled to the back of his head. Tatyana was still in control even though he had his dick in her ass.

"Fuck me harder, I'm getting ready to cum!" she screamed out.

Damien reached around her and put his hand over her mouth because she was really getting loud and he didn't want anyone to come running to his room, thinking something was wrong.

"Shit, you have to be quiet before we get busted," he said, still pumping in and out of her ass. "Don't move, I'm cumming!"

After they had both came, he pulled his dick out of her and went into the bathroom to wash. While he was in the bathroom, she came in and jumped into the shower. When she came out of the bathroom, Damien was back in the bed.

"I have a confession to make," she said. "I've never done anything like this before. But I figured since the chances of me ever seeing you again were slim, I would just go for it. I'm not going to lie, I bought the condoms and jelly when I went to get something to eat. I kinda planned this, I hope you don't mind," she said, smiling.

"Nah, I don't mind. I've never done this before either, but hey, it's done and over with and we both enjoyed it so don't sweat it." Damien's room phone rang. "Hello."

"It's me, I'm at the airport. Are you okay?" Isis asked.

"I'm fine, just bring me some KFC. There's one in the airport."

"Alright, I'll see you when I get there."

."Listen, that was my girl, she's on her way here. You can stay if you like but she's pregnant and moody as hell," he said, after hanging up the phone.

"That's okay, I'm leaving. I have a plane to catch,' Tatyana said, picking up her bag.

"Listen, thank you again for everything. I hope to see you in another life," he said, giving her a hug and a kiss on the cheek.

"I wish you the best, Damien. Maybe we will meet again in another life," she said, leaving the room and taking the bag with the used condom in it with her.

Damien fell asleep. He was tired after their sexual bout. By the time Isis got there, she had to wake him up, and as soon as he looked at her, she started that crying shit again.

"Come on, baby, please don't start crying again. I'm going to make you leave," Damien said, hugging her.

"Here's your food," she said, handing him the bag of food. She stood there and stared at him for a minute.

"What?" he asked, nonchalantly.

"Where's the woman that stayed with you?" she said, looking around the room.

"She left, she had a flight to catch. I asked her to stay so you could meet her but she had to leave."

"Too bad. I wanted to thank her. Baby, I'm sorry for being such a bitch. I should've known better then to not answer my phone, especially knowing you're sick. I would've died if something terrible happened to you."

"Stop thinking about it, Isis. Let's just enjoy the time we have left together. Come here, let me say hello to my baby," he said, patting the bed. "Hey baby, daddy's here and I'm okay," he said, kissing and rubbing Isis' stomach. "Girl, you're huge, look how big your damn stomach has gotten!" While he was talking, kissing and rubbing her belly, the baby kicked the shit out of his mouth. "Oh shit, did you see that?" Damien yelled.

"No, but I felt it," Isis said, grabbing her stomach. "Ouch!" she screamed out. "She kick me in the vagina again!"

"Come here, let me feel it kick again." Damien plucked her stomach and the baby kicked. He did it about three more times before the baby stop kicking. Isis, on the other hand, was in pain, she screamed out every time the baby kicked.

Damien laid there staring at Isis, thinking about Tatyana and how he had just finished fucking her on top of the hospital bed. He was wondering how he could have done something like that? He justified it by telling himself, "I love Isis, but since I know I'm gonna be dead in six months or less, why should I pass up free pussy?'

"So, are we a couple or what?" Damien asked biting into his chicken, trying not to get upset.

"I guess," Isis said, kissing him. Damn, he thought, I ain't shit.

"Maybe we should just be friends, Isis," Damien said looking at the floor, not able to look her in the eyes. "I don't want you to hurt no more then you have to. If being around me makes you hurt, then maybe we shouldn't rekindle this relationship."

"I only hurt when I'm not around you, and I'm gonna stick by you until I can't no more. I want to stop talking about death, not being together, and all the other negative things that can put weight on my shoulders, okay," she said, kissing him again.

"I love you, Isis," he whispered. He stared at her feeling guilty as hell, but he knew he couldn't take back what had happened between him and Tatyana.

One of the nurses brought in a pull out bed for Isis and some fruit and juice. Isis ate the fruit before she fell asleep. Damien couldn't sleep because he had Tatyana on his brain. She hadn't given him her numbers and she wouldn't take his, she just told him to remember her.

The nurse came in the room about 3 o'clock in the morning and asked, "Do you need anything, Damien? Would you like something to help you sleep?"

"Nah, I'm a'ight, just thinking. You know I have a baby on the way?' he said excitingly, trying not to show that he was scared.

"Oh really?" the nurse answered.

"Yeah. Too bad I won't be around to see him or her born. I'm tired of being strong, I'm ready to break, but I know I can't. I've got to stay strong for my girl and my unborn seed."

"You've got to stay strong for your health, too."

"What health? My health is deteriorating every day, every minute. I just wish I could change the things I did in my past."

"Ask God to forgive you for all your sins and He will. Our God is truly a forgiving God; all you've got to do is believe and pray. Once you pray, leave it with Him and soon you'll see the changes in your life."

She was a short, chunky nurse with short hair and a patch of gray in the front. You could tell by the tone in her voice she was a churchgoer, a mother and a grandmother, she had the big momma look.

"When I go to church on Sunday, I'm gonna have my church pray for you and your family. And Damien, it's okay to cry, it's okay to break, God didn't make us unbreakable."

She stood over him, waiting for him to respond but he didn't, he just reached up, hugged her and started crying. She hugged him back and began to pray with him. Isis woke up to the sounds of crying and prayer. She jumped up, ran toward

Damien and told him that she would always be there for him. The nurse left the room so they could be alone.

~Chapter Twenty-Six~

"Where are you going this time of the night, Keith?" Bianca asked.

"I'll be back, I've got some business to take care of."

"This time of the night? Then I'm coming with you," Bianca said, jumping out of bed.

"No the fuck you're not! What the fuck is wrong with you?" he snapped.

"What the fuck is wrong with me?" she said. "I should be asking you that question all of a sudden you're leaving at all times of night and staying out late. Keith, are you cheating on me?"

"Please, let's not forget you're the cheater not me. I'm out here working."

"Oh, so you're working. What's this your new hours?" she asked, furious as hell.

"Yes I am working. I'm looking for someone who owes me money. Me and my man is staking out his house, and the last thing I need right now is you in my way," he said.

"Please, Keith, do you think I'm fuckin' stupid! Ever since we went to court your ass has been distant. You even act like you really don't want to have sex with me."

"Please, I don't have time to talk about this right now. Listen, I'll call you later," he said, getting ready to leave.

"So, I guess you'll be out for the rest of the night," she said, stepping in front of the bedroom door.

"Didn't I just say I'd call you? Now move Bianca, Sean's waiting for me," he said, giving her a look that let her know he was serious and that she needed to get out of his way.

Bianca stepped to the side, hoping Keith was telling her the truth. He gave her a kiss, told her he'd call her later and left out. Bianca went back to bed, contemplating about their marriage. When he had found out I was cheating on him, his ass was too calm. I wonder if he's getting me back. Lately, every other night he seems to have somewhere to go and he usually doesn't come home till the next morning. I know damn well he isn't staking out someone's house every night, Bianca thought to herself.

About two hours after Keith had left; Bianca couldn't get to sleep, so she decided to call him. She dialed his cell and when his voice mail immediately came on, she didn't leave a message. She became mad because, if he wasn't cheating, then why the fuck was his phone going straight to voice mail? Bianca dialed his cell again and when his voice mail came on again, she left a message informing him to call her right back. She hung up and paged him.

"Where the fuck is this bastard?" she said out loud. 'I know he's out there fuckin' some bitch just to pay me back for cheating on him. Bianca got up, put on some clothes and decided to ride around to see if she could catch his ass out there doing wrong. As she was getting dressed the phone rang. She looked at the caller ID and saw that it was Keith calling.

"Keith, where the fuck are you?" Bianca yelled, as soon as she answered the phone.

"Where did I tell you I was going?" he yelled back at her. "Why the fuck are you calling and paging me like you're crazy?"

"Because I'm not fuckin' stupid. I know you're fuckin' around on me!"

"Don't start, Bianca," Keith said, trying to whisper.

"Why the fuck are you whispering? Whose house are you at?" she yelled, hoping the person would hear her voice.

"I'm not whispering. Listen, I'm on my way, I'll see you when I get home," he said.

"Don't hang up this fuckin' phone! You talk to me until you get in front of the house!" she yelled, pacing the floor.

Keith started the car, put it in drive and headed home. The female's house he was over came running to the window only to see Keith leaving. She ran out the house to stop him but he kept driving. you're buggin' out over nothing."

"No nigga, you're buggin' out! You ain't dealing with a dummy, I know you're fuckin' around on me."

Just then Keith's phone beeped. "Hold on, Bianca."

"No! don't click over. Let the bitch leave a message."

"Please, that's Sean. He probably wants to know why I just left like that."

"what's his number, I'll call him on the three way," she suggested

"Please, you ain't embarrassing me. You've already done enough." While he was talking his phone beeped again.

"Don't answer that phone. Its fuckin' 3 o'clock in the morning and you're allegedly staking out someone's house. You should be home not out spending the night with someone else. You better end this shit soon Keith."

"Man, I don't know what you're talking about. There's nothing for me to end. Your ass is just being paranoid."

"Where are you now, Keith?" she asked.

"I'm almost home. Why?"

"On what street was the house you were allegedly staking out?"

"Dover Street. Why?"

"Just curious." There was silence on the phone until Keith's phone beeped again.

"Hold on, Bianca. Let me tell this boy I had to leave cause your ass is buggin' and for him to stay there."

"No! Call him when you get home or let me call him on the three-way!"

"Forget it, Bianca. I'm pulling into the garage, open the door," he said, trying to hang up.

"Keith, don't fuckin' hang up until I open the door! I think you're lying, you're trying to call that bitch back." Bianca talked to him until she opened the door that goes to their garage. When she opened the door, she threw one of her pointy ass shoes at his head. "You must think I'm fuckin' stupid! Who the fuck do you think you're married to, some dumb bitch! I used to play these games you're trying to play! Hell, I helped pioneer this shit! Stake out my ass, you ain't no fuckin' cop!" she was yelling, pointing her finger in his face.

"Yo, why the fuck are you throwing shit at me! Girl, if you would've hit me!

"What! What! You would've done what! Nothing you faggot ass bitch!!"

"Yo, I'm outta here. Crazy muthafucka calls me home for this shit! He said, turning around to go back to his car.

"You ain't going nowhere!" Bianca yelled grabbing Keith, trying to make him stay.

"You hit me or throw something else at me I'm leaving. You need to chill with all the bullshit."

Keith's phone rang again and Bianca yelled, "Answer it!"

"I'm not answering my phone so people can hear our business. I keep my personal business at home," he said, turning off his phone.

Bianca just looked at him and shook her head. "You don't even know how to lie. You need to give it up." She turned and walked in the house. "If you want to go back to her Keith go. Don't stick around only to get back at me and try to stress me the fuck out. Because the difference between us is I don't stress, I just get over it."

Keith shut the garage door and walked in behind her. He was stressing; he'd met him a nice young lady with no kids and he wanted to give it a try. Her name was Dana, she was thirty-three, and worked as a Registered Nurse at Beth Israel. He had met her at The Arena, a bar in Newark about two months ago. He just recently decided to take their friendship to another level. He didn't tell her he was married and that he owned two bail bond businesses. As far as she knew, he worked for Fed Ex as an operational manager. He went and took a shower and thought about the lie he was going to tell her tomorrow.

Bianca was pissed the fuck off, she knew exactly what Keith was doing even though he was denying it. When he got into bed, he tried to hug Bianca only because he was feeling guilty. She quickly pushed his arms off her and turned her back to him.

The next morning when Keith tried to talk to Bianca, she kept walking like he hadn't said one word. The last couple of days, she had been online putting her resume out there and she had a job interview with Verizon at 9 o'clock and she wasn't going to be late. She got dressed, combed out her doobie wrap weave, put on some lip gloss and grabbed her briefcase with her resume and references in it.

She yelled out to her kids to let's go so she could drop them off at school. She looked at Keith as if she was going to say something but changed her mind and kept it moving.

Bianca knew Keith was lying and has been lying for some time. That's why she started putting her resume out there. She figured he was trying to get back at her, so she was going to find a job, an apartment and leave him to play his games by himself. She knew she was getting too old to play these games, and they were either going to forgive each other and move on or stay stuck. She chose not to stay stuck even if it meant walking away from him.

"Where are you going?" Keith asked, mad because she was ignoring his ass.

"I'll be back," Bianca said, nonchalantly.

"Are you coming into the office today?"

"Nah, you're gonna have to handle your own business today, Keith. I have some running around to do."

"So, are you quitting?" he asked standing in the middle of floor, looking every bit of dumb.

She ignored his question, and instead said, "Shouldn't you be at your stakeout, or do you stakeout only at night? Listen, I'm sorry for making you come home last night, it won't happen again. You can stay out as much as you like." She called out to her kids, "Let's go y'all!" Then she turned and walked out the door. Keith stood at the garage door looking dumbfounded. He didn't know what to think, he stood there staring at Bianca while she backed her Lexus out of the garage.

"Why is Keith standing there looking dumb?" Dee Dee asked, staring at Keith.

"I don't know," was all Bianca said as she drove down the driveway, never looking back. Her kids knew she was mad about something so they just sat in the car quiet all the way to school. She dropped her boys off first and advised them to wait for her after school. "Dee Dee, you wait for me, and Chantell, catch the bus to your Grandma's house or either call her to come pick you up. I'll see y'all later." Bianca told her kids as she dropped them off.

Keith went inside, picked up the phone and called Bianca. She wouldn't answer her cell, so he left her a message saying, "Whatever it is you think I was doing last night, you're wrong. Call me when you get this message."

Bianca was thinking to herself, He must think I'm blind or something. I'll stay with Mommy until I get on my feet, I don't need no man taking care of me. Shit, I can take care of myself. Once she listened to his message, she said out loud, 'He's feeling guilty, that's why he left that dumb ass message. Let me concentrate on this interview and pray I get the job.'

After dropping the kids off, Bianca had enough time to stop by Dunkin' Donuts to grab a glazed donut and orange juice. She sat in her car and contemplated on how she was going to leave Keith, get out on her own and live the way she wanted. Not that Keith tried to make her be a certain way, she just felt like he wanted revenge and she wasn't going to stick around and watch him disrespect her and play kiddy games.

Later that morning, Keith was finally able to check his voice mail. "What's going on Keith, why did you leave like that?" said the confused voice. "Call me tomorrow before you go to work."

He thought about calling his friend back but was too embarrassed. He didn't know what type of lie to tell or even if he should tell a lie. Maybe I should just tell her the truth, why hurt her, Keith thought. He dialed her number.

"Hey, baby," he said, as soon as she answered.

"Hey, baby," she said. "What happened? Why did you leave like that?"

"I had to rush home. My alarm kept going off and the fire department and cops were at my house. I'm sorry I didn't run inside to tell you, but I didn't want you to start asking a lot of questions, holding me up. This is the second time somebody tried to break into my house," Keith said, very forthright.

"Oh, I was worried. Shit, I started thinking all kinds of shit. That maybe your wife had called or something."

"My wife, ha! That's funny. Baby, I told you I'm not married," he said, feeling guilty for lying to her.

"I know you did, I was just checking to see if I could catch you in a lie," she laughed. "You know, maybe I can start staying at your house."

"Yeah, I was thinking the same thing," he said, lying. "But for now how about I stay at your cozy house with that big ass Sealy Posturepedic? All I have at my house is a raggedy ass, full size, no name brand mattress that I've been sleeping on since 1997," he said, laughing.

"How about we go shopping for a new mattress for you this weekend?" she suggested.

"Not this weekend cause I'm not going to have the money to spare."

"I'll buy it for you, so I don't want to hear no. We're going and that's that. Now I've got to get back to work, I'll see you tonight."

"Alright, see you then." Keith smiled to himself thinking about his new friend.

After he had finished talking to Dana, he called Bianca and got her voice mail again. This time he didn't leave a message. He got dressed and left for the office.

After Bianca's interview, she felt very confident about how everything went. The man that interviewed her told her that if she were being considered for the position, this afternoon someone would be calling her to set up a date for her to take a test. She prayed all the way to her car. She called Mommy to make sure she was home before she went over there. Since she wasn't home, she decided to go get Dee Dee and Chantell out of school early.

"I want y'all to help me pack up some clothes to take to Grandma's house for a couple of days," she told them once she picked them up from school.

"Are we moving out again?" asked Dee Dee.

"Yup, but this time it's for good. We're going to stay with Grandma until I get on my feet. Hopefully, I'll get this job at Verizon. I should know by this afternoon. If not, then I'm gonna keep looking until I get something." Chantell just looked out the window, never saying a word.

When they got to the house, she told them to pack up the boys some decent clothes and that she would get her things together. She got a suitcase to put most of her things in it. She got a box to put some of her important shoes in. The girls

only had a week's worth of clothes and stood there looking at their Mother pack damn near all her shit.

"Should we be doing the same?" Chantell asked, looking confused.

"No, because I'm going to have Grandma bring y'all back to get some more of y'all stuff. I'm taking what I need. Let's go," Bianca said, out of breath.

"Did we miss something?" Dee Dee asked, mad as hell.

"No," Bianca answered.

Chantell and Dee Dee looked at each other and proceeded to put their things in the car. No one said another word, they all had their own thoughts running through their heads. While Bianca was driving to Mommy's house, Verizon called her. She mumbled, 'Thank you, God,' before answering her phone.

Once she had finished speaking with them, she hung up the phone and yelled out, "Yes, I got the job! We're going to be alright." She then called me at work screaming, "I got the job at Verizon! Girl, I'm gonna be making almost $60,000.00 a year. I went in for one position and came out with another. Stormie, I'm leaving that muthafucka as we speak. We'll be staying at Mommy's house until I can find us something."

"Slow down! Too much incoming information and you ain't making any sense," I said. "Why are you leaving Keith?"

"Cause I don't have time for games. He's found himself another lover, and I'm going to let her have him, whoever she is!"

Chantell and Dee Dee looked at Bianca in shock.

"He thinks I don't know, but I know everything and I ain't as forgiving. I'm going to see a lawyer tomorrow so I can file for divorce and keep my house and car. That's all I want, he can keep the rest."

"Are you serious?"

"Dead ass! I'm not saying another word to him. That nigga has become see through to me. If he knew he couldn't forgive me, he should've let me go. Not keep me here only to torture or mistreat me. Fuck him!"

"Girl, I can't believe you're leaving him just like that. At least talk to the man before you make any final decisions."

"No, I'm gonna let my lawyer do the talking for me. I'm serious, Storm, I'm not going back. I am 38 years old; I have no room for games. Absolutely none! Granted, I know I started it but he said he forgave me and that we were going to work things out and make our marriage stronger. Now he's chosen to leave out every night and not come back until the next morning. Now that I'm gone he can come and go as he pleases."

"Damn, I really don't know what to say. Listen, I gotta go. I'm going to come by Mommy's house later. I'll see you then."

Bianca pulled intoMommy's driveway and started unloading her car. Mommy was home by then and stood in the doorway with her mouth damn near touching the floor.

"What happened?" Mommy asked, dumfounded.

"We're moving back home," Bianca said, bringing their things in.

"What happened?" she asked again.

"Keith decided to cheat and I decided to leave, simple as that. I know I cheated first, but instead of going back and forth with the cheating game I decided to leave."

"Well, what did Keith have to say about you leaving?"

"Nothing. Anyway, I got a job at Verizon as an Office Manager. I have to go and take an administrative test tomorrow so they can see how much knowledge I have on being an Office Manager. I start training on Monday. So I do have some good news to go along with this news," she said, hugging Mommy. Mommy hugged Bianca back and told her that she was going to support her with her decision.

Keith was at the office hoping that Bianca would call him, but she didn't. It was getting late, so he called the house and when no one answered, he called her cell but he only got her voice mail again. He then called Dana. She was working a double and wouldn't be getting home until after midnight. He told her to call him when she got off and he would meet her at her house. He then went and picked up some dinner from a soul food restaurant near his house and went home.

When he pulled into the garage, he noticed Bianca's car was gone. She's probably riding around looking for me, he thought. He walked in the house, which was dark and cold, he shouted out for the kids and no one answered. He then went into their bedroom and, when he cut on the lights, he immediately saw that all of Bianca's stuff was gone. He sat on the bed and let out a long sigh, thinking, 'I guess she moved out again.' He stood up, went into the kids' rooms and noticed that some of their things were gone too. He decided to call his mother-in-law's house to see if she knew where Bianca was.

"Hello, Ms. Luv, sorry to bother you this late, but is my wife there?"

"Yes she is," she answered.

"Well, can I speak to her?"

"Listen, Keith, I don't know what's going on between you and Bianca, but she doesn't want to talk to you. Besides, she's asleep."

"What did she say to you? I don't know what I've done."

"She didn't say anything to me. She just said she was gonna be staying at my house until she gets on her feet, and she's more than welcome to stay here. Like I said, I don't know what happened between y'all, but my daughter and her kids will not be sleeping anywhere where they're not wanted."

"I've never made her or her kids feel unwanted. This is her home; she didn't have to leave Mrs. Luv. I don't know what's going on, but would you please tell her that I called."

"I will," she said, hanging up.

Keith laid down across the bed, staring at the television, trying to figure out what the fuck happened. What is it that Bianca knows, or does she even know anything? He was thinking about when she cheated on him, how he stayed with her, bought her a new car and never turned his back on her. How the fuck can she just walk away like that? She can't possibly be that heartless, but then again, I guess I don't know my wife like I thought I did.

Keith was so busy thinking about Bianca that he forgot to eat his food and that he had told Dana to call him when she got off work. Anyway, his cell phone was downstairs in the kitchen and he wouldn't hear it ringing. He finally dozed off and went to sleep around 2 o'clock.

~Chapter Twenty-Seven~

"On Friday before Raquan left for Connecticut, he came by the house for a quickie. "I got my man downstairs waiting for me, Storm. I'm going to call you when I get settled in," he said, while getting dressed.

"Alright, I should be home. Tomorrow night I might go out with Rhonda, but call me on my cell if you can't reach me at home."

"Well, I'm going to call you tonight. It takes about 3 to 4 hours to get to Connecticut," he said, kissing me good-bye.

When we came downstairs, his friend was playing the game with Ja'Mil.

"You ready?" Raquan asked.

"Man, I've been ready. Shit, I thought you forgot I was down here," he said, laughing.

"Nah, I had to spend some time with my baby before I left. I'm ready now."

"Call me as soon as you get settled, Raquan," I said.

"A'ight," he said, hugging and kissing me again.

Later that night, I called Raquan's cell phone, but he didn't answer. 'Where the fuck is he, and why isn't he answering his phone?' I couldn't sleep; I was worried something might have happened to them on the way to Connecticut. He didn't tell me the name of the hotel he was staying at, so I couldn't call to see if they had arrived. I toss and turned all night, I even got that fucked up feeling in my stomach. I thought, is my man cheating, and did he really go away with his job? I left him a message on his cell phone for the last time around 2 o'clock in the morning and then I fell asleep.

When I got up on Saturday morning, I called his cell phone and it just rang. I decided to go on line because I knew he had taken his laptop with him. Guess who the fuck was on line? I sent him an instant message, but he didn't reply and then he got off line. What the fuck is going on? Is this nigga playing games again? I went and took a shower, put on a pair of sweatpants and a sweatshirt and starting cleaning my house. I started packing his shit. I'm not asking any questions when he comes back, from this day forth I'm single. My phone rang; it was Bianca.

"How's work?" I asked, as soon as I picked up the phone.

"Work is great. It's only been two weeks, so you know I can't complain. The hardest part is getting out of bed. I've gotten lazy being married to Keith." I really didn't have much to say since I had Raquan on my mind. "Where's Raquan?" she asked.

"In Connecticut?"

"Why is he there?"

"Work, he claims. But I've been calling this nigga all night and early this morning and he won't answer his phone. I even sent him an instant message and he signed off as soon as he got the message." Bianca bust out laughing.

"What the fuck is so funny?"

"I'm not laughing at you; it's just that niggas are funny. Don't get mad; just don't give a fuck. Keith has been calling and leaving all kinds of messages with Mom and my kids, but I'm not returning shit. I know he got the divorce notice. It said, 'I'm leaving your dumb ass!' Nah, it didn't really say that but it was close."

"Did he sign them yet?"

"Not yet, I'm still waiting."

"Damn, I can't believe you're leaving him. He's a good man, you need to give him another chance, he gave you one."

"That was his choice. I didn't twist his arm and make him give me another chance."

"You mean to tell me you no longer love him?"

"I still love the shit out of him, but I just don't have time for games."

"Have you spoken to him?"

"Not since I left."

"Damn, Bianca, that's some cold shit. Why haven't you spoken to him yet?"

"Cause I don't have shit to say to him. I know he's cheating, and I'm not willing to forgive him."

"Have you caught him with another woman?"

"No, but…"

"Bianca, no buts. How can you say he's cheating when you haven't caught him?" I said, cutting her off.

"I don't want to talk about Keith anymore. How's Isis doing?" she said, wanting to change the subject.

"She's doing fine. She and Damien are getting along so good. He's buying her a Hummer next week, and he's been shopping for the baby like crazy. She found out that she's having a boy, and she's going to give him Damien's full name. I'm so happy for her."

"How's he doing?"

"Every now and then he gets a little weak, but he's been taking his meds so I guess for now he's doing okay. I gotta go, Bianca, I need to finish cleaning my house."

"Okay, I'll talk to you later."

It was 10:30 and Raquan still hadn't called me and I was pissed the fuck off. I knew he wasn't working cause the last time he went away with his job, he called and gave me the name of the hotel and the room number. If he doesn't call me soon, it's over. If Bianca can walk away from a good man like Keith then damn it, I can walk away from Raquan. When I left this time it was going to be for good, no going back.

I guess he felt like he was being too good, and that he needed me to be in stupid again. But I'm not going back to being like that, not again. I felt a teardrop roll down my cheek. I knew what he was doing, I could

feel it in my guts because normally he calls me like crazy, regardless of who he's with. I'm too embarrassed to tell anybody that I haven't heard from him because he was doing so good. I decided to turn off my cell and my house phone ringer because I didn't want to talk to no one. I was just going to watch movies with my kids.

~Chapter Twenty Eight~

"Boom! Isis!" Damien yelled.

"Damien! Oh God! Damien, Damien!"

Isis picked up the phone and dialed 911. When an operator picked up, she yelled into the phone, "Help me please, my boyfriend is having a really bad seizure, please hurry!" Isis turned back to Damien and said, "Damien, please talk to me! God, don't take him away from me! Please, he's my life! Damien, talk to me baby! I love you, Damien! Please God, not now, I'm not ready! God, he's not ready! Talk to me, Damien!" Isis screamed out.

The EMTs pulled up and could hear Isis screaming. They began to bang on the door. "EMT, did someone call an ambulance? Open the door!" She wouldn't leave Damien's side.

"Please God, don't take him from me now!"

"Please open the door!!" they kept yelling out. Finally one of the EMT worker kicked in the door. "Ma'am, where are you?" they yelled out, once they were in her house.

"I'm upstairs! He's not breathing; please bring him back to me! He's not ready to go, we're having a baby! The doctors gave him six months to live, and it's only been four months!" Isis was completely hysterical by now.

The EMT workers tried reviving Damien. They did mouth to mouth until they got a pulse, and then they strapped him on the stretcher, hooked him up to an IV and quickly transported him to the hospital. Isis just cried and cried and told Damien how much she loved him and thanked God. Isis called my house but my ringer was off, so she called Mommy and Bianca. They met her at the hospital.

"Is he breathing?" Bianca asked Isis, when they got to the hospital.

"He is now, but he only has a slight pulse."

"Isis, you have to calm down. I know it's hard, but you don't want to lose your baby tonight," Mommy said to her. "I'm here to help you try to be strong. I'll be right back; I'm going to talk to the doctors."

"How is Damien Cox doing, ma'am?" Mommy asked one of the nurses.

"He's breathing with the help of the machine. His pulse and blood pressure are low, and he has a very weak heart. He also hit his head while having a seizure and, at the same time, he had an asthma attack. That might be the reason he stopped breathing. Once the doctor examines him, he'll have more details for you," the nurse told her.

"Did anyone get in touch with Stormie?" Bianca asked.

"No, I've been calling her since I got here," Isis said.

"I'm going to go to her house and get her," Bianca said.

"Alright, I'll stay with Isis," Mommy said.

"Mrs. Luv, he stopped breathing. How could God want to take away the only man I will ever love? Why would He do that to me?" Isis cried.

"I don't know, Isis," she said, hugging her tight.

"Stormie!" Bianca yelled, from the front of my house. She scared the shit out of me. "Stormie!" she yelled again.

"What!" I yelled out the window.

"Come open the door!"

"Wait a minute." I wondered what this nigga did to make her come to my house this time of the night. "Why are you over here, Bianca?" I asked, opening my front door.

"It's Isis, she's at the hospital with Damien."

"Is he alright?"

"They had to bring him back, Storm. Isis said he was gone for about 30 minutes."

"Oh, my God!" Tears started flowing down my cheek. "How is she doing?

"How would you be doing if you were pregnant and your man is breathing through a machine?" Bianca said walking towards my kitchen

"Oh, my God," was all I could say. How selfish of me I started thinking about Raquan "I can't go to the hospital. My kids are here alone and I don't know if I can take seeing Isis like that."

"Go to the hospital, Storm, she needs you. I'll stay with your kids. She paused for a quick minute then asked. "Why wasn't you answering your phone?"

"I turned my ringer off so I could get some sleep without being disturbed."

"See what happens when you do that." She said making a shame on you face at me.

"Call your husband and tell him you love him, Bianca. Treasure your loved ones while they're still here on earth to treasure."

"You call him, look, stay out of my business please. Go support your friend; she needs you a lot more than I do. And you need to leave Raquan alone so you can find a good man and be able to sleep with the ringer on. You deserve it, Storm."

I hugged my sister because this was a weird situation. We both wanted to tell each other something, we just didn't know how. I think I got my point across and I know she got hers across.

I prayed for Damien all the way to the hospital. By the time I got there, they had put him in a room. He was unconscious and had all kinds of IVs and tubes in him. I hugged Isis and we both cried. It's funny how love works. I wish I could explain it but I can't. I feel only a selective few get to enjoy love, the rest of us only get to taste it. This experience with love was going to leave a bad taste in Isis' mouth. We all sat there quiet for a moment, staring at Damien.

"You know he called out to me before he died. I heard him yell 'Isis'. I sat straight up in the bed and I felt in my heart God was taking him. The doctor said he had six months. Has it been six months already? I'm not ready to be alone, I love this man." Isis stood up, walked to the edge of Damien's bed and began talking to him. "Baby, I'm sorry for being mad at you when I found out you were sick. I'm sorry for hanging up the phone on you, cursing you out, calling you names, and for saying I hate you when I know deep down I love you so much. I'm sorry for every evil thought I had towards you. I'm so sorry, Damien. I'm going to be strong for our baby, and I'm gonna make sure your son knows everything about you. He's going to love you even if he never has a chance to see you. I'm going home now, and if need be, you can go home too. I will love you forever." She gave him a long kiss on the lips, while the tears flowed down her eyes. I cried, Mommy cried and the nurse that was in the room cried too.

"See you later, Damien." I said, kissing him on the cheek.

It was a quiet ride back to Isis' house. "Do you want me to stay with you, Isis?"

"No, I'll be fine. I need to be alone. Just make sure your ringer is on, okay. I need to rest because this baby is kicking the shit out of me. I have a spare key, come in the house and get it," she said, getting out of the car hugging my mother and saying thanks and good night to her.

"Okay." I said following

"They had to kick in my door to get in, so it's damaged a little. Stormie, has it been six months already?" she asked her again.

"I'm not sure, Isis," I said, feeling bad for her.

"I was two months pregnant when I found out he was sick. I'm seven months now, so it's been about five months."

"Yeah, about that much." Isis seemed to be okay.

"They weren't supposed to revive him. He's what they call a DNR case; do not resuscitate. I didn't tell the EMT workers because I'm not ready for him to go. The doctors haven't said it, but I know he's a vegetable, Storm. I guess tomorrow they'll confirm it and want to unplug him from the machine. I can't be there when they do that. I guess I should call his friends, huh? He had to know, because on Thursday he went and bought the suit he wants to be buried in. He paid $1,500.00 for that suit. It's a soft yellow suit." She laughed a little before continuing. "He tried it on and it looked good on him. Do you really think he knew?" Isis said, rambling.

Before I could answer her, she answered her own question.

"He knew. He told me he loved me before he went to sleep and I told him to move over because I was hot." She laughed a little again. "I was too hot to say I love you back. If I would've known, I would've held him all night and told him I loved him over and over again. I thank God for letting me experience true love with a wonderful man." "Please stop talking like he's dead, Isis. It might not be too late," I said, hugging my friend.

"You're right, let us pray for him. Here, take the key. I'll call you if I need you," Isis said, giving me the spare key that she kept in her kitchen drawer. "Thanks for being there for me, girl."

I dropped Mommy off at home and starting thinking about Raquan. I knew he was doing something with somebody. I knew, but then again, I was oblivious to the obvious. It's definitely time for me to move on.

I called Raquan about 9:30 Sunday morning. He answered the phone in a whisper. "Hello," he said, softly.

"Why are you whispering?" I asked, suspiciously.

"I'm not whispering. What's up?"

"You."

"Me?" he asked, confused.

"Can I get this?" a female voice said, in the background.

"Who was that, Raquan?"

"I don't know who that is. I'm in the store," he said, still whispering.

"Whatever, she's probably with you."

Raquan didn't answer, all I heard was a cash register in the background.

"Is that it, do we need anything else?" the familiar voice said again. Raquan didn't answer.

"Aren't you gonna answer her, Raquan?"

"Let me call you back," he said, hanging up before I could say anything else.

I knew he was with somebody, I knew it! He couldn't answer the bitch while he was on the phone with me.

"Is that it?" Alicia asked Raquan again, after he had hung up the phone.

"Yeah, that's all we need. I'm only making one piss stop on the way back, so don't drink a lot of water."

"I'm not. I'm tired and ready to get in the bed. Thank you, I had a wonderful time," she said, before giving Raquan a kiss. He returned the kiss, but he was thinking about Storm and the lie he would tell her when he got home.

I didn't bother to call Raquan back because I figured he had probably turned off his cell phone anyway. I was hurt but I didn't cry, crying was over for me. I had done enough of that shit. I got up and got dressed so I could go to the hospital with Isis. I had to stay focused for her. She needed me more than anybody right now. I took my kids to Mommy's house, then went to Isis' house to get her.

"Hey," Isis said, looking like she'd just taken a bath in Vaseline.

"Why you shining like that?" I asked her.

"I don't know, it must be the baby."

"Must be. Are you ready?"

"Not really. I called the hospital and his condition has changed severely. His heart is no good, and there's nothing they can do for him. Right now he's still breathing with the help of the machine, but they're talking about taking him off of it today. The doctor said he would wait for me to come up there so that we could discuss things. I've been on the phone all morning with his friends. They're coming up to the hospital too. I'm going to wait for all of them before I let the doctor unplug him."

"I'm so sorry, Isis," I said, giving her a big hug. "I'm truly sorry."

"I know, I'm sorry too, Storm. But God brought him to me for a reason." Isis was big; her stomach was sitting very low. She looked stressed, her hair was all over her head, it was a mess. She was pacing the floor, looking for nothing at all.

"Isis, are you okay? I mean how's the baby?"

"My stomach has been hurting a lot, but I know it's from stress. When I come from the hospital I'm going to rest. I'm going to need for you to handle all of Damien's arrangements. He's already picked out his casket, suit and the funeral parlor. I'm just going to need for you to do the rest, okay."

"No problem. Do you know your stomach has dropped a lot, Isis? Are you sure you aren't in labor?"

"I don't know , I don't know what labor feels like."

"It hurts like hell."

"Then I'm not in labor, because I'm not in any pain. I'll be right back; I'm going to throw on some sweats." She put on a pair of Damien's sweat pants and one of his throwback jerseys. The clothes she put on was the last outfit that Damien had worn. She smelled the cologne in his jersey and started to reminisce about the day she met him and laughed to herself.

As I sat downstairs waiting for her, there was a weird silence in the house. Isis' white house didn't look the same for some reason. Her phone rang and the ringing scared me.

"Hey T," Isis said, answering her phone. She walked down the stairs looking like a big boy. She had even put on one of Damien's fitted baseball caps.

"I'm on my way up there now. No, I have a ride. My cousin, Stormie, is taking me. Thanks anyway," she said, hanging up the phone. "I'm ready, let's go." She had a slight smile, trying to look strong but I saw right through that.

Once we got to the hospital, it was like a nightclub up in there. Everybody was standing around crying, praying, and hugging each other. Once they noticed Isis, they all tried to be strong so she wouldn't get upset. She gave everybody a hug and a crooked smile. She was saying I'm okay to every other person. A Minister from the hospital came to say a prayer for Damien. Isis took a deep breath, closed her eyes and prayed with the Minister. No tears came down. After the prayer, the doctor came in and asked that all persons that wasn't family to please leave. No one moved.

"We're all his family," a voice said.

Isis never took her eyes off Damien. It was like she was talking to him with her mind. "Please proceed," she said, in a very serene voice.

"Okay," replied the doctor. The doctor unhooked Damien from all the machines. Damien opened his eyes, looked up at Isis and said, "I love you, Isis."

"I love you too," she replied, then gave him a kiss.

"Beeeeeeeeeeeeeeeeep!" the machine said. The room was quiet for a moment, and then one by one people started leaving the room crying. Isis stood there staring, wishing he would say those beautiful words to her again. Finally the tears came. T, Damien's best friend, held her.

"Don't worry, Isis, I'm going to be around whenever you need me," he said. Isis

258

couldn't hear T because her mind was on Damien.

I had to get out of there, I couldn't stop crying and I couldn't stand to see Isis fall apart. T brought her out of the room, she was crying and holding her belly. They had to get a wheelchair for her because she couldn't walk. Her pressure was going up and she needed to relax but she couldn't. They took her to the ER because she was putting the baby in danger. They couldn't give her anything to calm her down, so they just put her in a room where they could monitor her and the baby. Isis was in labor, she was seven centimeters and the doctor said they were gonna have to perform an emergency c-section.

"Wait, I can't have this baby today. I've got to be with Damien," Isis mumbled.

"Sorry, Ms. Williams, but your baby isn't going to wait." The doctors immediately got her prepared for a c-section.

~Chapter Twenty Nine~

The birth of Isis' baby was successful, and T and I stayed with her the whole day. The baby was born at 7:30 pm and, even though she was only seven months pregnant, he weighed in at 6 pounds. As the nurses were cleaning him, I noticed that he looked exactly like Damien.

I called Mommy and told her that the doctors had taken Damien off the machine at 10:30 that morning, and that his son was born at 7:30 that night.

"Damn, she'll never forget the day Damien passed away. Tell her I'll be up there later on today or tomorrow morning," Mommy said.

"I have to get his arrangements together. His best friend, T, is going to help me. I don't know if I can do this," I said, crying into the phone.

"You've got to be strong for her, Storm. She can't do it and you're all she has right now."

"I'ma try to arrange everything around the day she comes home. I don't want Damien's body to sit out too long, ya know."

"Yeah, I understand. You know Bianca and I are here to help you."

"Thanks Mom. Tell Bianca that I may need her to pick up Isis' Mom and sister from the airport."

"What time are they coming in?"

"I don't know. I'm waiting for her Mom to call me back with their flight information. As soon as she does, I'll let you know. Mom, she cried the whole time I was on the phone with her. I can't take all of these tears."

"I know, but just keep praying for God to give you the strength to get through this."

"I'll call you back, I'm going to go check on Isis."

"Okay, call me if you need me," Mommy said.

"Hey T, thanks for staying up here with me," I said, after hanging up with Mommy.

"No problem. I had to nah'mean that was my boy in there."

"Just help me get through this, okay. Does Damien have any family around?"

"Nah, he grew up in foster homes. He had no knowledge of his history, none that he ever mentioned to me anyway."

"That's a shame, but at least he had you."

"You know, this is going to be difficult for Isis ya know, especially with their baby being born today. How are you gonna handle this?"

"I don't know, one day at a time I guess. I think I'm going to take at least two weeks off to help her, and plus her Mom and sister are preparing to come up here as we speak."

"Yeah, that's was' sup, she's gonna need them. I'm going downstairs to make a few phone calls, I'll be back," T said, walking toward the elevator.

I went in the room to check up on Isis. She was sleeping and tears were still flowing down her face. I wiped the tears off her face and said a silent prayer for her.

"Yo, if you need a ride to your house, I don't mind giving you a lift. My car is right outside and, besides, you're in no condition to be driving," T offered as soon as he entered Isis's room

"Thanks, T," I said gathering my things.

"No problem, Ma, that's why I'm here." T wasn't an attractive guy, he kinda reminded me of a black Ben Affleck with dimples. He was 6'4 and about 220 pounds, give or take.

The ride to my house was quiet, even the radio was turned off.

"Hey, Storm, do you have a man?" he asked looking at me out the corner of his eye, with an admiring grin.

"Not now, T. Your boy just passed away and my girl just had their baby on the same day."

"I was just asking, trying to make some conversation, ya know." The car was quiet again. "Well, do you, Storm?"

"No T, I'm single, and I'm not looking."

"Okay, I just wanted to know."

"Well, now you know." I'm thinking, How the fuck can this guy flirt with me at

261

a time like this?

"Ya know Damien wanted to hook us up, but he could never find the right time. He told me a lot about you."

"Then you must know about the man I was involved with."

"Nah, he never mentioned him. He just said that you were cool peoples. I know my man wouldn't mind me try'na to holla at you now. I'm not disrespecting him in any kind of way."

"I just don't think now is the time, T. Maybe we can talk on a later day, okay." I blushed and said a silent thank you to Damien in my head. I looked at T and thought he wasn't a bad looking brotha after all. Plus, I needed a change cause I was done with Raquan's ass.

As we approached my house, I didn't notice Raquan's car parked across from my house. I was too busy thinking about Isis and Damien.

"Come on in, T. I need to grab a few things," I said, getting out of his truck.

"A'ight," he said, following me into my house.

"You have to excuse my house; I haven't had a chance to clean it." When I opened the door, I saw Raquan standing in the doorway of my kitchen on the phone. I stopped and stood there for a minute before calmly saying to him, "Can you please leave?"

"What? Yo, who the fuck is this?" he asked pointing at T, but looking at me.

"Don't go there, Raquan. Today is not the day, please just let yourself out." I don't know why I didn't tell him what happened.

"Who you?" he snapped at T.

"A friend. Why, wha'sup?" T wasn't in the mood for any bullshit. He was ready to knock a nigga out.

"Oh, is this your new friend?" Raquan said, walking towards me. "I go away for a couple of days and you get a new friend," he said, shrugging his shoulders as if T was nothing.

"Get the fuck out, Raquan! I'm tryna be nice in front of company! I'm not going to ask you again. Oh and leave my keys too!"

"Fuck you!" he said, throwing the keys at me.

"Fuck you too, nigga!" I said, ducking the keys. "You think I didn't hear that bitch in the background! You think I'm fuckin' stupid!"

"Please, whatever. I didn't even know that lady, she was standing in line."

"Get out, Raquan! I'm not in the right state of mind to talk to you today, tomorrow, or any other day, just go!" I said walking up the stairs to my bedroom.

T was tired of me telling Raquan to go so he stepped in. "Yo, my man, she done asked you to leave like five times already, just leave."

"Yo, this does not concern you. I don't even know you, man," he said, looking at T like he was gonna kick his ass.

"You ain't got to know me. I'm telling you to get the fuck out before I put you out! Faggot ass nigga!"

"What?"

Boom! T hit Raquan with one punch and he was on the floor. T then started stomping him.

I jumped down all the stairs yelling "Stop T! Stop!" I said yelling, trying to make him stop.

T grabbed Raquan by his shirt and threw his skinny ass out of the house. Raquan isn't a fighter, so I felt sorry for him.

"Get the fuck off me!" Raquan swung his skinny arms at T, but missed.

T kicked him off the porch and yelled at me to go back in the house. "Nigga, I will hurt you! She asked you to leave over and over again, now leave muthafucka!" he said, ready to take all the emotions he was feeling out on Raquan.

Raquan left saying, "I'll be back for your ass, son!"

"I want you to come back! You wanna know where I'll be?"

I ran and called Mommy because I was nervous. I didn't know T. Hell he could've been a killer for all I knew.

"Calm down, Stormie! What's going on?" Mommy said.

T came back in the house and asked, "Are you okay? Sorry, but he was getting on my nerves. Was that your man?"

"Mom, let me call you back." After getting off the phone, I turned to T and said, "Are you crazy or something? You just kicked my boyfriend out of my house."

"I know, but I'm under a lot of stress. I don't like that clown ass nigga, tryna look tough," T said, still pissed off.

"It doesn't matter if he's a punk, clown, or whatever; you had no right to kick him out of my house."

"You're right. I'm sorry, you forgive me?" He asked with a small smirk on his face.

"Let me get my things so we can go." I didn't bother to answer him.

"He said he was coming back. Do you wanna wait?" he said, sarcastically.

"No, T, I don't wanna wait," I said, going upstairs.

While I was upstairs, T got on his cell and called his boy, Luck. "Yo, why I just kick this muthafucka outta Storm's house.

Who?" Luck asked surprised.

"Her so-called boyfriend, she's too good for that nigga. Yo, Damien told me how he treats her and the muthafucka comes up in her disrespecting her right in front of me. I threw him out on his fuckin' head," he said, laughing and sounding proud of what he had just done.

"Yo, you buggin' right now, man," Luck said, also laughing. "It's the wrong time to be tryna push up on her, T."

"I know, but this is what D wanted and I'ma make it happen."

"Good luck, but you're starting out all wrong, man," he commented.

"No I'm not. She needed me to do that. Listen, here she comes, I'll see you later."

"Come on, T." I was hot with this nigga. "Take me by my Mom's house so I can drop this stuff off to her," I said, not looking at him. As soon as I got in his car, I checked my voice mail. Raquan had called, cussing me out.

"Look, I'm sorry, Storm, but that nigga was rude," T said, trying to smooth

264

things over.

"Please, T, its okay."

"You sure?"

"Yeah, it's okay," I said, lying. I was mad as hell and I just wanted to get out of his truck. Then again I was laughing because Raquan needed to see another man defending me. I looked at T while he was driving and thought, just maybe.

"What's up?" he asked, once he caught me looking at him with a smile on my face.

"Nothing," I said, quickly turning to look out the window.

~Chapter Thirty~

Isis didn't wake up until the next day after her baby was born. The doctor had to sedate her because she was under a lot of pressure and they wanted her to rest. When she woke up, I was the first face she saw.

"Hey," I said, smiling. T had just left to pick her Mom and sister up from the airport. She had no clue that I paid for them to come up. I wanted to surprise her.

"Hey," she replied. "Where's my baby?"

"He's in the nursery." I said rubbing her forehead. "He has a head full of hair."

She smiled. "Really, I want to see him."

"You will, but you gotta get your strength first." We were quiet for what seemed like forever. She felt her stomach.

"Oh, my God! They cut the shit outta me, huh? Did you see this?" she asked, shocked.

"No, and I don't wanna see it either."

"I'm never gonna be able to wear another two piece," she said, looking at her stomach.

"Are you hungry?" I asked her, trying to get her mind off her stomach.

"Yeah, I slept through the whole day yesterday."

"I know you did. They had to sedate you so you could get some rest."

"Storm, I don't know what to do with myself. Hell, I had my baby on his daddy's death day. I feel like I'm being punished and I don't know why."

"I don't think it's a punishment, Isis."

"What would you call it then?" she asked looking at me, waiting for an answer.

"I don't know, Isis. It's gotta mean something though."

"Stormie, can you buzz the nurse so she can bring me my son, please."

When the nurse brought in her son, she started smiling from ear to ear. "Oh, my God, Storm, he looks just like Damien," she said, kissing her beautiful son. "I now know why God let me have my baby on the same day that Damien died. He gave him right back to me. Look at him, he's beautiful," she said, kissing her baby's rosy cheeks.

Isis started to cry, believing that God had sent Damien right back to her through their baby.

"Hey," a familiar voice said, entering Isis' room.

"Mommmiee!" she screeched, crying.

"Is that my grandson? He's absolutely gorgeous, Isis."

"He looks just like his dad, Mommy."

"Hey, Mecca," she said to her baby sister. She hugged her and ran her fingers threw her hair and laughed a little, thinking of the time she had cut her sister's hair.

After her Mom finished kissing and hugging her daughter and grandson, she turned to me and said, "You must be Stormie." She gave me a hug and a kiss on my cheek. "Thank you for taking care of my baby."

"You're welcome," I said smiling, holding back tears. "Isis, I'm going to get some breakfast and give you some time with your family," I said, getting ready to leave.

"Okay, bye."

"Come on, T," I said, grabbing my bag.

"Mommy, he looks like my Damien. I hope he stays this way," Isis said again.

"He will, baby, he will," she said, brushing her daughter's hair.

"I can't believe I haven't seen you in all these years. You look good, Isis," her sister said, sitting on the bed.

"Thanks. I wish y'all could've met him. He was everything I ever wanted in a man," Isis said, finally breaking down again. Her Mom had to call for the nurse to come and take the baby until she calmed down.

"So, where do you want to eat?" T asked, starting his car.

"Home, I want to go home. Let Isis spend time with her Mom and sister. They haven't seen each other in a couple of years. The doctor is going to keep her in the hospital a few more days, so that gives us enough time to make the funeral arrangements for Damien."

"Yeah, I'm with you for the next couple of days."

"Thanks."

When we got back to my house, I saw that all of my front windows were busted out. I just shook my head like this wasn't happening. I hadn't set the alarm on my house either.

"I know Raquan didn't fuckin' do this," I said.

"I told you that nigga was a faggot! I should've done him in when I had the chance."

"I think you've done enough, T," I said, unlocking my door.

"Let me go in first." T went inside and nothing was gone, Raquan had just busted out my front windows. I stood in my doorway and took a long, deep breath.

"You want me to call the cops?" he asked.

"No, just get my windows fixed. I'll deal with him later."

"I'm sorry, Storm. He must be one crazy muthafucka. I'll get the windows fixed don't worry about it." He said going to get the broom to sweep up the glass.

I went upstairs and took a long, hot shower and shed a little more tears. This time I was crying because of Raquan. Damn, I thought everything was going good, why did he do that. Maybe I should forgive him, I thought. I was standing in the shower thinking about Raquan, Damien, the baby and, for some reason T was on my brain. All of a sudden I heard moving in my room, then banging on the bathroom door.

"Who is it?" I yelled out.

"It's T, are you alright?"

"Yeah, I'm fine.

"Are you going to ride with me to get the windows?"

"No, go ahead. I better stay here just in case."

"A'ight, I'll be back."

I jumped out of the shower, dried off, then wrapped the towel around me and went into my room. T was still sitting there watching television.

"I thought you were gone," I said, clenching my towel tighter.

"I was waiting for you to get out of the shower before I left," he said, trying not to look at me.

"Okay, well I'm out, so you can go now."

"I'll be back."

I walked him downstairs and locked the door behind him. Then I ran back upstairs and threw on my gray velour J-Lo sweat suit and my gray and black Puma sneakers. I called Raquan, he answered on the first ring, like he was waiting for my phone call.

"Is that how you handle situations now, you bust out windows and shit?"

"What? I didn't do that. You better check with that other nigga," Raquan said.

"Don't need to. See I was with him all night so I know he didn't do it." (Click) Raquan hung up on me. I called his ass right back.

"Stupid ass muthafucka!" I yelled into the phone.

"What, Storm? You got what you wanted, I'm outta your life."

"Good, now you can go be with the bitch you were with last weekend!"

"Maybe I will."

I got quiet. It felt like my stomach had dropped to my feet. He had just admitted to being with another bitch.

"So, you were with someone, huh?" I asked.

"Yup, I sure was," he said, very maliciously.

"I'm glad to hear that, Raquan. The guy that was here, that was Damien's partner."

"Oh, that nigga hooked y'all up. I never liked that muthafucka anyway."

"Nah, he didn't hook us up, you just did."

"Whatever."

"Actually, Damien passed away Sunday, and his friend was bringing me home to get some clothes."

"Yeah right, you fuckin' that nigga."

"Not yet, but I am. It's been real, Raquan," I said, hanging up the phone.

I was hurt; my stomach was turning. You know you always want to know the truth but when you do, you really can't handle it. If his heart wasn't in it why didn't he just tell me? Why did he keep me hanging on for so long? He always knew that we weren't going to be together, he just wanted to see me hurting. For so long I knew it was over, I even felt it was over when he came back, but I was hoping. I can hope ya know. The pain was unbearable, no one should feel this way when they are in love. Love is not suppose to hurt

I lay on my sofa thinking what would make a man so mean? What did he get out of hurting me? He knew he was with someone else, he knew he didn't what to be with me. He even told me that he loved me, but he didn't. T came back and saw me lying across my sofa crying.

"What's up, Storm?" he asked, rubbing my back.

"Nothing, I'm okay."

"That nigga said something to you?" My phone started ringing and T answered it.

"Yeah!" he yelled into the phone.

"Put Stormie on the phone!" Raquan demanded.

"Punk ass nigga, come over and talk to her!"

"I ain't got time for you. I know you ain't her man so stop trying, cause she's not gonna be with you."

"That's a'ight, but neither will you cause I'm not going anywhere. And as long as I'm here I know your punk ass ain't coming around."

"Gimme the phone, T," I said. "What do you want Raquan, you said enough?"

"I just said all of that to get you upset. I thought he was with you."

"No, you meant it. I knew you were with someone cause you didn't call me the whole time you were gone and you always call me. I felt that shit, Raquan." By this time, I was walking upstairs to my room away from T's nosey ass. "Just be honest for once, why do you want to be with me?"

"I don't know, Storm, but I love you."

"No, you don't, you just think you do. It's okay though. Damien showed Isis love from the door, so did Keith with Bianca, but you, you never showed me love. I always had to demand it and the things I had to do to get you to finally fall in love with me were ridiculous. Raquan, your heart was never into this relationship."

"Yes, it was."

"When did you stop loving me?"

"Come on, don't ask me a question like that. I'm coming over later. Is that nigga gonna be there?"

"Yes, he's helping me with the arrangements for Damien's funeral."

"Why he gotta be there though?"

"Cause I need him to be. And I really don't think we have anything to talk about, Raquan. I think we shouldn't be together, we shouldn't even try to make it work."

"If that's what you want, Storm. If you need me..."

"I won't, bye." I hung up before he could finish his sentence.

He just held the phone to his ear for a minute then hung it up. "I can't believe this shit!" he said out loud to himself.

HAVE YOU EVER...?
FIFI CURETON

~Chapter Thirty One~

The day of the funeral, as Isis was getting Lil' D dressed and listening to her music, she started talking to him.

"Well, Lil' D, today is the day you get to see you Dad for the first and last time. I'm okay with it now, because at least he isn't suffering anymore. I don't know how much pain he was in, he never discussed it with me," she was saying to Lil' D. "We're gonna be alright though. God left a part of him with me." She started to sing the Barney song to him. "I love you, you love me, we're a happy family, with a great big hug and a kiss from me to you, (she kissed him), won't you say you love me too!"

"Are you alright in there?" I asked Isis.

"Yes, I'm getting dressed, you can come in. Listen, Storm, thank you," she said giving me a hug, once I came into the room.

"Hey, don't thank me, you my girl. I'm sure you would've done the same."

Isis gave me that please look, but she laughed cause she knew she would've done the same.

"So, what's up with you and T? He's been hanging around you a lot."

"Nothing. He's just supporting me, that's all."

"You know he likes you."

"Not now, Isis."

"Why not? I need something else to talk about anyway. So, do you like him?"

"A little."

Isis grinned. "You know Damien was trying to hook y'all two up. He always talked about you to T. He always said, 'Yo man, you gotta meet her, she's fine and a good woman. You need a good woman in your life'."

"Is that right?" I asked, blushing. "Well, I don't think he's going anywhere. He's pretty much moved in with me."

"What? When?"

"The other day when Raquan busted out my front windows."

"What! Why the fuck did he do that?"

272

"He thought T was my new man, and him and T passed some words then T threw him out of my house."

"That's my boy," Isis said, laughing for the first time in weeks. "He put his big head ass out."

"Nah, he threw him out… Literally," I said, pretending like I was holding a fake person and tossed it.

"Damn, I wish I could've seen that. So, T has been staying there ever since?"

"Yup."

"Did y'all…?"

"No, we haven't," I said, cutting her off.

"You don't even know what I was about to ask."

"Well, that was just in case what you were gonna ask."

"Did you put out Raquan's shit?"

"No, T did."

"Oh, you gotta keep him! You hear that Damien," Isis said, looking up toward the ceiling. "I know he's smiling now. I'm happy for you, Storm."

"Why, he's not my man."

"Not yet, but he will be." Isis paused for a minute, looking at her hands with a little smile on her face. She then walked over to Lil' D. "You hear that, Uncle T and Auntie Storm are going to be a couple." She turned back to me and said, "Girl, you betta make him your man. He have no kids and has never been married."

"I know all of that. He told me while he was cooking me dinner last night."

"He cooks too, he's definitely a keeper. Let me get dressed."

I stood in the mirror and looked at the back of Isis' head as she was walking towards her bathroom. She looked so calm. I picked up Lil' D and took him in the room with T.

"Hey, Lil' D," T said smiling, playing with the baby's small fingers. "How's Isis?" he asked me.

"She's trying to be strong."

"That's good. You want me to keep Lil' D with me while you go and get dressed?"

"Please," I said smiling, flirting a little.

"Anything for you."

"Tell me, T, what does the T stands for?"

"Terrell. Terrell Williams." He answered.

"Hum, that's a nice name."

"Thanks, see you in a few,' he said bouncing Lil' D, putting him to sleep. "Yo, my man, you look just like your Dad. I have so much to teach you. Your Dad left me being your godfather and you know what that means. That means I'ma take care of you forever, just like if you were mine. I think we're going to get along very well, what you think?" T was having a conversation with Lil' D. "Let me see those ears. "Yeah, you're gonna get black. I can't wait to get you in the studio, you got that look, fo'sho."

Once the limos came, we walked out, got in the cars and there was dead silence. Lil' D slept through the whole service. The church was crowded; Damien had a lot of friends that really loved him. Isis sat there looking straight ahead, listening to the preacher, nodding her head a little. T made a speech about Damien and so did some other people. Mommy held Lil' D for Isis, and her Mom held her hand. "Damien's in a better place," her Mom whispered.

"Is he really, Mom?" she asked coldly, moving her hand away from her.

Out of nowhere, what sounded like an angel, started to sing, "The Battle Is Not Yours," by Yolanda Adams, while walking down the aisle of the church looking at Damien's lifeless body in the silver colored casket. She looked at Isis with tears in her eyes. While the choir sang, people were crying, standing, clapping their hands, and shaking their heads no. Some was screaming, WHY!! The older woman was shaking, trembling a little, trying to stay in control while singing to Isis. People were so busy crying they didn't have time to figure out who she was. The words to the song were serious, like they were written especially for Isis.

There is no pain Jesus can't feel, No hurt he can not heal, All things work

274

according to his perfect will, No matter what you're going through, Remember god is using you, For the battle is not yours, It's the Lord's.

Isis, still looking straight ahead at Damien, decided to look at the stranger. Just as she did, the woman started singing again, pointing at the crowd, veins pulsating from her neck, jumping up and down, wanting the crowd to understand the power of God and His purpose.

There's no sadness Jesus can't feel

And there is no sorrow

That he can not heal

For all things work

According to the master's holy will

No matter what you're going through

Remember that god is only using you

For the battle is not yoursIt's the Lord's

She sang the hell outta that song. She had everybody in that church, jumping up and down, shouting, shaking, rocking, going crazy. It was like a concert instead of a funeral. Isis was looking at the woman smiling, crying, reaching out for her and gasping for air. Once the song was over, the woman walked over to Isis, they hugged for a very long time. I was wondering if that was Damien's mother or grandmother. She looked at the baby through watery eyes. The tears were flowing heavy down her cheeks. Isis finally introduced her as the nurse who took care of Damien when he was in the hospital in LA. Damien called her Big Ma. He had called her once a week and told her, "If I miss a week, it's because I went home to my God." They developed a mother/son relationship, and she sang that song from her heart, dedicating it to Isis.

Big Ma then signaled for one of the young ladies to come down from the choir stand. Once the young lady reached us, she was introduced as Tatyana.

"This is the young lady that initially brought Damien to hospital in LA and into my life," Big Ma said.

She and Big Ma had stayed in touch. Big Ma pretty much kept her abreast of his condition. Tatyana explained to Isis that she didn't want to seem disrespectful or sneaky, especially knowing that Isis was pregnant. She stated she was really concerned about him after witnessing him in the airport having that seizure and needed to stay in touch indirectly. Before she left the hospital that day, she had given Big Ma her number.

Tatyana said, "You know it was something he said that really got to me. He said he would see me in another lifetime."

Isis looked at Tatyana with her nose slightly turned up as if something stank, and said, "I'm sure he's smiling, knowing that you showed up."

Tatyana ignored the look, because she already knew how Isis was from her conversations with Damien. So, in her mind, she said, 'Yes, I'm sure he is.'

Everybody standing around looked at Isis, as if to say what was that all about. Bianca said she should've been thanking Tatyana for being at the airport when he was having his seizure. But, we all knew Isis, and she was looking at the beauty in the young lady.

At the burial site, Isis took her rose and held it for a long time before dropping it on top of the casket.

"How could you do this to me!" she yelled. How could you do th-" she began to cry before she could finish. "I loved you, Damien! We have a son!" She fell to her knees crying, shaking her head no, screaming and pulling at the casket. T and some of the other people had to help her up. I was frozen, I couldn't move.

"Get off me! I need to be alone with Damien, please."

Everybody began walking away, back toward their cars.

I waved to T and said to him, "Let's stay close by."

"Okay," he said, holding my hand.

"Mom, take Lil' D back to Isis' house with you." Isis' Mom and sister left with her.

Isis sat on the dirt next to Damien's casket, talking to him. "Damien, did I tell you our son weighed 6 pounds. They let me bring him home because he was so big. He looks so much like you, I don't know how I'm going to be able to look at him every day. I need you, Damien, why did you have to leave me?" She was sniffing back tears and snot. Man, I'm not ready to let you go. You showed me so much attention, which you thought I didn't appreciate, but I did. Mommy and little sister are here. Mommy tried to tell me that you were in a better place, but I don't agree. The better place would be at my house, our house."

The gravedigger came. "Ma'am, I'm really sorry, but I've got to let him go down now."

Isis looked at him with her big watery eyes and said, "But I'm not ready yet. Please give me another five minutes."

"I can't ma'am. I need the machine, I have another funeral."

"Okay, let me just tell him that I love him, please."

"Okay," the man said, backing up a little so she could have a little privacy.

"Well, Damien, this is it. I guess I'll see you in another life. Hopefully it will last longer. I love you Big D." She smiled a little, kissed her hand then touched the casket. She looked at the man to let him know that she was finished.

She began walking away from the casket, looked at me, wiped her tears and said, "I know he fucked her, that's why I said what I did at the funeral home."

I just stood there looking shocked. T ignored the comment with no facial expression, thinking that was his boy and it was probably true. I wanted to go a little deeper into it, but I figured not here, not now. Please believe I'm going to dig a little deeper into it with T.

~Chapter Thirty Two~

"Well, Keith signed the divorce papers today, even though he didn't want to," Bianca told us. For the first time she looked sad. "I can't believe it's over. We go back to court in August to finalize the divorce."

"I can't believe you're letting him go," I said to Bianca. "Especially with so many women wishing they had a good man."

I know, right," Isis added. "Damien's a good man," she added.

It's been three months since Damien's funeral and you can't pay her to talk about it. When she does talk about Damien, she talks like he's still around. No one corrects her; we usually just let her talk.

"Was," Bianca said, unable to continue to let Isis live in the past.

"Was what?" Isis retorted.

"Was a good man, Damien was a good man, Isis," Bianca snapped, jumping up from the kitchen table.

"Was, is, what the fuck is the difference!"

"Do you really need me to explain the difference? He ain't here anymore, that's the difference!" Bianca yelled.

Isis jumped up and knocked the shit outta Bianca. "Don't talk about him again! You fuckin' bitch!"

"You done lost your mind!" Bianca yelled back and they began to fight. I jumped up, trying to separate the two of them.

"Stop fighting!" I yelled. "Let her go, Bianca!"

"Nah, this bitch done hit me in my face," she said, pulling Isis' hair.

"You shouldn't talk about my man," Isis was saying, trying to get Bianca out of her hair.

"Your man is dead, bitch!" Bianca replied.

I don't know where Isis got the strength from but she got loose from Bianca and picked her up and threw her across the kitchen. Bianca fell against the refrigerator and fell to the floor. I grabbed Isis and tried to pull her out of the kitchen. My kids came running downstairs to see what was going on.

"Go back!" I yelled to them, pulling on Isis.

"Let me go! I'm sick of her talking about me! Isis, I'ma fuck you up!"

Bianca came running out of the kitchen just as T was coming through the door.

"Get her, T!" I yelled.

"Who?"

"Bianca!" I was pulling Isis' ass up the stairs cause I knew Bianca wasn't gonna stop until she got her back.

"Hol' up, B," T said, grabbing her. "What's going on?"

"I'ma fuck her up, that's what's goin' on! Let me go, T!"

"Nah, Storm said not to," he said holding tight, damn near picking her up.

"Take her outside, T!" I yelled from upstairs.

"Come on, B, you need some air," he said pulling her out the house, onto the porch.

"I'ma get you later, Isis! You betta believe that, bitch!"

"Why y'all fighting?" T asked, closing the door behind him.

"Cause she's a bitch! Let me get my shit so I can go home."

"Nah, I'll get it, you wait right here. Yo, Tania?"

"Yes."

"Grab your Auntie bag out of the kitchen so she can be out."

"Okay." Tania was more than glad to do that because she wanted to see what was going on anyway.

"Here you go, Auntie," Tania said, looking at the blood on her face. "What happened to your face?" she asked.

"I hit it on the refrigerator door. Tell your mom I'll call her later."

"Okay," Tania said, looking at her leave.

"What happened?" T asked Tania.

"I don't know. I just heard her screaming and when we ran downstairs, mommy told us to go back upstairs."

"Damn!" T said, walking back into the house.

I guess you know by now that T has a key to my house. He took

HAVE YOU EVER...?
FIFI CURETON

Raquan's key the day of the funeral and has had it ever since. He doesn't live with me; he's just been staying here every night since the funeral.

The night of the funeral, we left Isis' house about 2:30 in the morning after I put Isis and Lil' D to sleep. When we got back to my house, I took a long, hot shower and went to bed. T was downstairs in the living room watching television. Sometime in the middle of the night he came upstairs and took a shower in my bathroom. Afterwards, he got into bed with me and started hugging me. I ain't gonna front, I was kinda hoping he would do that. When I felt his hand around my waist, I grabbed his hand in mine.

"T," I called out.

"Yes," he whispered.

"What are we doing?"

"Starting a life together," he replied, kissing my ear. "Do you want to?"

"I do but-"

"No buts, Storm. I'm here and I want to make you happy. Can I?"

"Only if your heart is in it," I said, holding his hand tighter...

To Be Continued...

Robbery Report

By Glorious
The First Of A Trilogy

Synopsis

Welcome to the city of New Brunswick, New Jersey or rather New Gunswick, a place where Gerrod Mason aka G Millions, Frank Wilson aka Famous and their home-girl Lisa Mathews aka Lady Pink all contributed to and repped their town's street monarch to the fullest.

Both G Millions and Famous inherited the hustle and gangsterism they displayed in the streets, from making it to taking it. They formed a bond based on loyalty & respect and made a pact long ago that they would get it by any means... And that's exactly what they did state to state, from up north, to the mid- west down to the dirty south.

The charismatic G*Millions and the flamboyant trend setter Famous took a piece of the game from every kind of street savvy individual that crossed their parents threshold, and put their own flavor and spice to it.

Life for the duo was all good but it got even better when Lady Pink, who was a female version of G* Millions, joined the crew. She was the main ingredient to the masterpiece put together. Being sexy, intelligent, loyal and most importantly deadly, she was every man's dream and worse nightmare all rolled up in one.

Together, G*Millions, Famous, Lady Pink and their band of young thugs become the criminal version of the "Dream Team", boosting the crime rate where ever they traveled.

However, like all other crime families, greed and lust emerged, leaving two fatal questions? Will they be able to stay loyal and reconcile their differences in order to continue to break bread together for as long as they so choose? Or will they fall victim to the saying, "There is no honor amongst thieves?"

HAVE YOU EVER…?
FIFI CURETON

283

"THE DUTTY WAY"

BY J.M. BENJAMIN

PROLOGUE

"Arright rude boy, respect," Dutty chimed into the phone in his native language of patwa before hanging up.

He then hopped up and hurried out of his girlfriend's king size bed after receiving the heads up call from his main man Puff. He knew this day would come, he just didn't know when. Not that it had mattered to him one way or another though because he had made preparations ahead of time, with the help of his childhood friend. Now the envelope had been pushed and it was time for him to put his plan in effect.

"Dee-Dee get 'dup," yelled Dutty slipping on his linen pants. "Dee-Dee yuh 'ere me!" he repeated this time shaking his bedside partner.

"What?" a sleepy Dee-Dee sighed as she opened her eyes.

"It's time."

Dee-Dee instantly jumped up hearing Dutty's words. She knew exactly what "its time" meant. Her and Dutty had been together for seven years now and he had prepared and schooled her on everything he needed her to know and what to do in event that his past came back to haunt him. She knew what type of man she had fallen in love with when she was just the young and tender age of seventeen, which was two years Dutty's junior, but his life style did not bother her in the least bit. She had heard many of stories about how vicious of a man her lover was and had been warned about dealing with someone of his caliber who was known in Jamaica as what they called a "Shota". Despite how he was viewed by their peers, Dee-Dee knew the real Dutty and loved him unconditionally.

"Mi want to go wid you," said Dee-Dee with tear-filled eyes.

"Wheh you mean? What mi and you talk bout before, heh? Yuh know yuh can't go wid mi right now Dee. Mi need fe yuh to stay 'ere," he told her. "Trust me, when me git to Foreign and git situated mi a send fe yuh, yuh 'ere," he assured his lady. He knew there was no way he could take her to America with him right now. Not when he didn't even know what was en-stored for him once he reached the un-familiar place.

"You betta," she smiled through sniffles.

"Arright, hurry up and git dressed," he said wiping away the remainder of the tears that hadn't stained her face.

Dee-Dee climbed out of bed in the nude. Dutty took one last look at his beautiful woman, not knowing how long it would be before he'd set eyes on her again. He watched as she slid on her black laced thong over her caramel hips, covering her neatly trimmed sex and became aroused. Even as she slipped on the Bob Marley T-shirt, he could still see the nipples of her breasts penetrating through. Her burgundy micro braids were still intact even after the wild escapade they shared

284

together last night. He was tempted to bed her one last time before he left but after hearing about the police looking for him and raiding his stash house he knew it was just a matter of time before they located Dee-Dee's home. He knew if he was captured it would cost him dearly.

As Dee- Dee jotted to the bathroom, Dutty couldn't help but admire the way her muscular ass cheeks performed a dance of their own as they bounced up and down. Pure heaven thought Dutty as he smiled and made his way to the bedroom's closet. He then pushed Dee-Dee's clothes on the rack to one side, revealing a wall safe. After opening it, he began taking stacks of the American money out of the safe. Each stack contained a hundred Ben Franklins.

The safe held ten stacks. This had been the money Dutty had accumulated over the years from hustling the selling drugs, extortion, doing robberies and sometimes being a gun for hire. Dutty took seven of the stacks out and left the rest for Dee-Dee.

He expected to have more then he had whenever the time came for him to take flight but things had caught up to him at an unpredictable time. With the seventy gees he intended to smuggle into America though he had big plans once he touched down and linked up with one of his country men who had also fled to the states and got a piece of the American pie.

Once he threw the money into the small suitcase, he then grabbed his chrome Taurus from out of the safe and tossed it in his luggage as well.

He had just shoved his P-89 into his shoulder holster when Dee-Dee came out the bathroom.

"Mi lef some money in da safe fe yuh."

"Arright," replied Dee-Dee.

Dutty could detect the sadness in her tone. He knew it was not going to be easy for her when the time came for them to part. He had been grooming and prepping her both mentally and emotionally for this day ever since he allowed her into his circle and heart. Outside of his mother and best friend Puff who was like a brother to him, she was the only other person who he loved and trusted with his life, which is why it was just as difficult for him to leave her as it was for her to watch him leave, but they both knew that this was the only way for him and maybe even her, to stay alive.

"Come 'ere baby gurl," he commanded holding out his arms

Dee stepped into his embrace. They shared an intimate hug along with a passionate kiss.

"Yuh know mi a love yuh like cook food, right."

"Me too," Dee-Dee confessed.

"Yo mi hafi leave yuh now, just gwan keep di pussy tight."

"Everyting curry," Dee-Dee assured him with a smile. She knew how jealous Dutty could be. No man in the entire Jamaica dared to even look at her since the two had been together.

Dutty snatched Dee-Dee up one last time. "Don't make mi hafi come back and kill up di bomba clot," he returned her smile. He then bent his head down to meet Dee Dee's and kissed her on the lips. "Mi soon come back for yuh," he said and then he was out the door...

Puff leaned up against his Platinum color S-type 4.0 Jaguar in the parking lot of the Norman Manly International Airport impatiently waiting for Dutty to arrive. He glanced at his iced-out Jacob watch and sighed. He had called Dutty nearly forty-five minutes ago and knew it only took twenty minutes to get from Dee-Dee's house to the airport. While waiting, the heat began to take its toll on Puff as perspiration started to stain his Gucci Shirt.

"Jah know star! Bumba clot, wheredi man de so long!" Puff complains, frustrated by his friend's tardiness.

Aggravated from the extremely high but normal temperature, Puff stuck his head in the Jag and retrieved the Guinness he had been sipping on just minutes ago. Just as he finished taking a swig, he noticed Dutty's money green M-3 BMW cruising through the parking lot.

Dutty spotted Puff up ahead and pulled up along side of him.

"Star wheh di bumba clot you de so long?" Puff asked as soon as Dutty stepped out of his Beamer. His anger was now showing. But he was not angry at Dutty rather the situation.

"Yo man you know the traffic star, plus you know mi hafi set wifey straight," replied Dutty extending his hand.

"True," Puff agreed as the two long time friends shook hands and embraced.

"Yo ya late you know, just look in my glove compartment and grab the envelope, ya passport and plane ticket are inside. Listen, when you get to Grand Bahamas mi friend name Shawn dem come pick yuh up from the airport. I already described you to dem," Puff told Dutty.

"Yo Dutty, dem youth some rich youth. Dem a go take care of yuh until yuh reach Foreign," he added.

"Yo dawg respect. Love dat. When mi touch down mi a call yuh," was Dutty's parting words...

As Dutty sat in the First Class section awaiting the planes departure the flight attendant approached him.

"Sir can I get you anything?"

"Nah baby mi cool," was the answer Dutty gave the flight attendant. Both his accent and words caused her to blush.

"This flight is about to depart to the Grand Bahamas. A ninety minute non-stop flight, all passengers please fasten your seat belt and prepare for take off."

After another female flight attendant ended her speech and the plane began to move forward, Dutty leaned over and stared out the window. This would be the first time in his life that he had ever left his home land of Jamaica. As the plane lifted off into the air, the reality of the matter began to set in. Although Dutty knew it was necessary he leave his country he had no idea when he would be able to return. With that in mind, he began to travel back in time and reminisce on how life had treated him in his homeland.

Growing up in Riverton City, one of the grittiest and grimiest neighborhoods of West Kingston forced Dutty to grow up faster than the average kid his age. At the age of five, he lost his father to political violence. His father was a PNP (People National Party) activist who fought against the opposite party JLP (Jamaican Labor Party), ultimately causing Dutty to breed hatred towards them.

Seven years later, Dutty sought revenge for the death of his father by retaliating on a member of the JLP. It had spread through the land how the man was found with his head chopped off. Although he was never questioned are charged everyone knew Dutty was behind the gruesome murder. Had it not been for his father's people, Dutty would have been killed himself at a young age.

His mother was highly respected in the community because of Dutty's father, but her biggest fear was that Dutty grew up to be like him. Unbeknownst to her though, it was already too late, because Dutty was a bonafide "Rude boy."

Once he started hanging out with some stickmen (pick pocketers).

And made a name for himself, he began running with his childhood friend who was a known young notorious robber named Puff. Puff was from Seaview Gardens, a neighborhood just as gritty and grimy as Riverton. Dutty was impressed by the way Puff carried himself at such a young age. Dutty would always refer to him as a "Pretty boy" because he sported the latest fashion, and he was also light skinned with a baldhead. All the girls loved Puff and tolerated Dutty because he was his friend.

Back then, Dutty didn't care what females thought of him though. He was dark skinned, gapped tooth, with long dreads, like the rest of the kids in Riverton. Puff was four years his senior and he looked up to him, though he was much bigger than he was.

After awhile they became in separable and together they grind and terrorized neighborhoods throughout all of Kingston for separate reasons.

287

Puff did it because he enjoyed it and it was a rush for him. Dutty on the other hand did it as a means to help take care of his mother, who was struggling. But in the end, the two of them wind up striving for the same thing, Riches. Only Dutty went to more extreme measures to get it, and now because of his action and methods he had to leave Jamaica.

"Ladies and Gentlemen we are now arriving at the Grand Bahamas." The words over the PA brought Dutty back to the present as he prepared for landing...

Coming Summer 2010...